THE SECOND DEADLY SIN

THE SECOND

DEADLY SIN

Lawrence Sanders

G. P. PUTNAM'S SONS,
NEW YORK

THE SECOND DEADLY SIN

1

The studio was an aquarium of light; the woman and the girl blinked in the glare. Victor Maitland slammed the door behind them, locked it, put on the chain. The woman turned slowly to watch, unafraid.

"You didn't tell me your name, Mama," Maitland said.

"You din' tell me yours," she said, smiling, showing a gold tooth.

He stared at her a moment, then laughed.

"Right," he said. "What the fuck difference does it make?"

"You talk dirty, beeg boy," she said, still smiling.

"And think dirty and live dirty," he added.

She looked at him speculatively.

"You wanna draw me?" she asked archly. "Okay, I pose for you. I show you all I got. Everyteeng. Ten dahlair."

"Ten dollars? For how long?"

She shrugged. "All night."

He looked at the olive-tinted lard.

"No, thanks, Mama," he said. He jerked a thumb at the girl. "It's her I want. How old are you, honey?"

"Feefteen," the woman said.

"Don't you go to school?" he asked the girl.

"She don' go," Mama said.

"Let her talk," he said angrily.

The woman looked about cautiously, lowered her voice.

"Dolores ees—" She pointed a finger at her temple, made little circles. "A good girl, but not so smart. She don' go to school. Don' got job. How much you pay?"

"Good body?" he asked.

The woman got excited. She kissed the tips of her fingers.

"Beautiful!" she cried passionately. "Dolores ees beautiful!"

"Take off your clothes," he said to the girl. "I'll see if I can use you."

He strode to the front of the studio. He kicked the posing dais into place beneath the skylight. Warm April sunshine came splaying down. He jerked a crate around and poked through the litter on the floor until he found an 11x14-inch sketchpad and a box of charcoal sticks. When he looked up, the girl was still standing there; she hadn't moved.

"What the hell are you waiting for?" he yelled angrily. "Go on, get undressed. Take your clothes off."

The woman moved closer to the girl, rattled off a mutter of Spanish.

"Where?" she called to Maitland.

"Where?" he shouted. "Right here. Throw her shit on the bed. Tell her she can keep her shoes on; the floor is damp."

The woman spoke to the young girl again. The girl went over to the cot, began undressing. She took off her clothes placidly, looking about vacantly. She dropped her coat and dress in a pile on the cot. She was wearing soiled, greyish cotton underwear. The straps were held up with safety pins. She unhitched the pins. She pulled her pants down. She stood naked.

"All right," Maitland called. "Come over here and stand on this platform."

Mama led the girl by the hand and helped her up on the dais. Then she stepped away, leaving the girl alone. Dolores was still looking off somewhere into space. She hadn't looked at Maitland since coming into the studio. She just stood there, arms straight down at her sides.

He walked around her. He walked around her twice.

"Jesus Christ," he said.

"I tol' you," the woman said proudly. "Beautiful, no?"

He didn't answer. He jerked the crate forward a few feet, propped the big sketchpad on a can of turpentine. He stood staring at the naked girl through squinched eyes.

"You got something to dreenk, beeg boy?" Mama asked.

"Beer in the icebox," he said. "She coppish English?"

"Some."

Maitland went close to the girl.

"Look, Dolores," he said loudly, "stand like this. Bend over, put your hands on your knees. No, no, bend from the hips. Look at me. Like this . . . Now stick out your ass. That's good. Now arch your back. Put your head up. Come on . . . like this. Put it up. Farther. Keep your legs stiff. That's it. Now try to stick your tits out."

"Wheeskey?" Mama asked.

"In the cupboard under the sink. Tits, Dolores! Here. Stick them out. Now you've got it. Don't move."

Maitland rushed back behind the crate and sketchpad. He picked up a stick of charcoal and attacked the white paper. He looked up at Dolores, looked down, and sketched rapidly—slash, slash, slash. He ripped off the sheet of paper, let it fall to the floor. Then he struck at the new sheet, swinging his arm from the shoulder.

He tore off that sheet, let it drop, began a fresh one. Halfway through the third sketch the charcoal stick broke. Maitland whirled and flung the remainder at the brick wall. He laughed delightedly. He strode to the naked girl, grabbed a buttock in one hand, shook it savagely.

"Gold!" he howled. "Pure gold!"

He went to the rear of the studio. Mama was sitting on the cot, bottle of whiskey in one hand, a smeared, half-filled glass in the other. Maitland grabbed the bottle from her, put it to his mouth. He took two heavy swallows and belched.

"Okay, Mama," he said. "She'll do. Five bucks an hour. Maybe two or three hours a day."

"No mahnkey beesness," the woman said severely.

"What?"

"No mahnkey beesness weeth Dolores."

Maitland roared with raucous laughter. "No monkey business," he agreed, spluttering. "Shit, I won't touch her."

"Mahnkey beesness costs more than five dahlair," the woman smiled a ghastly smile.

He let her finish her drink, and then got them out of there. The woman promised to bring Dolores around at eleven o'clock on Monday morning. Maitland locked and chained the door behind them. He went back to the crate, whiskey bottle in his fist. He drank while he looked at the drawings on the floor, nudging them with his toe. He squinted at the sketches, remembering how the girl looked, beginning to plan the first painting.

There was a knock at the studio door. Angry at the interruption, he yelled, "Who?"

A familiar voice answered, and Maitland scowled. He set the whiskey bottle on the crate. He went to the door, unlocked it, took off the chain. He pulled the door open, turned his back, walked away.

"You again!" he said.

The first knife thrust went into his back. High up. Alongside the spine. The blow was strong enough to drive him forward, face breaking, hands thrown up in a comical gesture of dismay. But he did not go down.

The blade was withdrawn and stuck again. And again. And again. Even after Victor Maitland was face down on the wide floor boards, life leaking, the blade was plunged. Fingers scrabbled weakly. Then were still.

2

His stepdaughters were bright, scornful girls, and ex-Chief of Detectives Edward X. Delaney enjoyed their company at lunch. He cherished them. He loved them. But my God, their young energy was wearing! And they shrieked; their laughter pierced his ears.

So when he kissed them a fond farewell at the entrance to their private school on East 72nd Street, Manhattan, it was with mingled tenderness and relief that he watched them scamper up the steps and into the safety of the school. He turned away, reflecting wryly that he had come to an age when he wanted everything *nice*. In his lexicon, "nice" meant quiet, cleanliness, order. Perhaps Barbara, his first wife, had been right. She said he had become a cop because he saw beauty in order, and wanted to maintain order in the world. Well . . . he had tried.

He walked over to Fifth Avenue and turned south, the shrill voices of the children still ringing in his ears. What he wanted at that precise moment, he decided, was an old-fashioned Irish bar, dim and hushed, all mahogany and Tiffany lampshades, all frosted glass and the smell of a century of beer. There were still such places in New York—fewer every year, but they did exist. Not, unfortunately, on upper Fifth Avenue. But there was a place nearby of quiet, cleanliness, order. A nice place . . .

The courtyard of the Frick Collection was an oasis, a center of tranquility in the raucous, brawling city. Sitting on a gleaming stone bench amongst that strong greenery was like existing in a giant terrarium set down in a hurricane. You knew the ugliness and violence raged outside; inside was calm and a renewing sense of the essence of things.

He sat there a long time, shifting occasionally on the hard bench, wondering once again if he had done the right thing to retire. He had held a position of prominence, power, and responsibility: Chief of Detectives, New York Police Department. Three thousand men under his command. An enormous budget that was never enough. A job to do that, considered in the context of the times and the mores, could never be more than a holding operation. Battles could be won, the war never. The important thing was not to surrender.

In a way, of course, he *had* surrendered. But it was his personal surrender, not the capitulation of the Department. He had resigned his prestigious post for a single reason: he could no longer endure the political bullshit that went along with his high-ranking job.

He knew, of course, the role politics played in the upper echelons of the Department before he accepted the position. Nothing unusual about that. Or even contemptible. The City was a social organization; it was realistic to expect a clash of wills, stupidity, strong ambitions, idealism, cynicism, devious plots, treachery, and corruption. Politics existed in the functioning of every social organization larger than two people.

It became unbearable to Chief Edward X. Delaney when it began to intrude on the way he did his job, on who he assigned where, how he moved his forces from neighborhood to neighborhood, his priorities, statements he made to the press, his relations with other city departments, and with State and Federal law-enforcement agencies.

So he had filed for retirement, after long discussions with Monica, his second wife. They had agreed, finally, that his peace of mind was more important than the salary and perquisites of his office. The Department had, he thought ruefully, borne up extremely well under the news of his leaving. (He had "rocked the boat," it was whispered. He was "not a team player.") He had been given the usual banquet, handed a set of matched luggage and a pair of gold cufflinks, and sent on his way with encomiums from the Commissioner and Mayor attesting to his efficiency, loyalty, trustworthiness, and wholehearted cooperation. Bullshit to the last.

So there he was, the age of sixty looming, and behind him a lifetime as a cop: patrolman, detective third-grade, second, first, detective sergeant, lieutenant, precinct captain in the Patrol Division, and then back to the Detective Division as Chief. Not a bad professional career. Second in the history of the Department for total number of citations earned. Physical scars to prove his bravery. And a few changes in method and procedure that wouldn't mean much to civilians but were now a part of police training. It was he, for instance, who had fought for and won the adoption of new regulations specifying that a suspect's hands were to be handcuffed *behind* him. Not on a par with the discovery of gravity or atomic energy, of course, but important enough. To cops.

He would not admit to himself that he was bored. How could a man as rigidly disciplined and self-sufficient as he be bored? He and Monica traveled, a little, and he carefully avoided inflicting his company on the police of Ft. Lauderdale, Florida, and La Jolla, California, knowing what a trial visiting cops (especially retired cops!) can be to a harried department, no matter how large the city.

At home, in their brownstone next to the 251st Precinct house (it had been *his* precinct), he took care not to get in Monica's way, not to follow her about like a lorn puppy as he had seen so many other retired men dog their wives' footsteps. He read a great deal, he visited museums, he wrote letters to Eddie, Jr., and Liza, his children by his first wife. He treated Monica to dinner and the theatre, he treated his stepdaughters to lunch, he treated old Department friends to drinks, listened to their complaints and problems, offering advice only if asked. They called him after he retired. At first, many. Later, few.

And he walked a great deal, all over Manhattan, visiting neighborhoods he hadn't seen since he was a street cop, marveling every day how the city had changed, was changing—a constant flux that dazzled with its speed: a middle-class Jewish neighborhood had become Puerto Rican, a rundown tenement street had been refurbished by young married couples into smart converted brownstones, skyscrapers had become parking lots, factories had become parks, some streets had disappeared completely, one street that had been solidly fur wholesalers was now wall-to-wall art galleries.

But still . . . you could write so many letters, read so many books, walk so many city blocks. And then . . . ?

Get a job, Monica had suggested. In the security department of a store. Or start your own security company. Something like that. Could you be a private detective? A private eye? Like on TV?

No, he had laughed, kissing her. He couldn't be a private eye. Like on TV.

Finally, the afternoon drawing on, the elegant courtyard of the Frick Collection darkening, he rose and walked toward the entrance without visiting any of the galleries. He knew the paintings. El Greco's *St. Jerome* was one of his favorites, and there was a portrait in the long gallery that looked like Don Ameche. He liked that one, too. He walked out past the magnificent pipe organ on the stairway landing.

He had read or heard somewhere a story about old man Frick, the robber baron who had built this palace. It was said that after a stint of crushing labor unions and ruining competitors, Frick would return to this incredible home, put up his feet, and listen dreamily as his private organist played, "When you come to the end of a perfect day . . ."

Smiling at the image, Edward X. Delaney stopped at the cloakroom and surrendered his check.

He gave a quarter to the attendant who brought his hard, black homburg.

The man palmed the coin and said, "Thank you, Chief."

Delaney looked at him, surprised and pleased, but said nothing. He left the building, thinking, They *do* remember! He had walked almost a block before he acknowledged the man might have intended "chief" as "pal" or "fella." "Thank you, buddy." It might have been as meaningless as that. Still . . .

He walked south on Fifth Avenue, enjoying the waning May afternoon. Say what you would—at the right time, the right place, it was a fucking *beautiful* city. At this moment the sun lowering over Central Park, there was a golden glow on the towers, a verdant perfume from the park. The sidewalks of Fifth Avenue were clean. The pedestrians were well dressed and laughing. The squalling traffic was part of it. All growing. It had been there before he was born, and would be there when he was under. He found comfort in that, and thought it odd.

He walked down to 55th Street, lumbering his way through increasing crowds as he moved south. Shoppers. Tourists. Messengers. A chanting Hare Krishna group. A young girl playing a zither. Peddlers. Mendicants. Strollers. He spotted a few hookers, a few bad lads on the prowl. But mostly an innocent, good-natured crowd. Sidewalk artists (butterflies on black velvet), political and religious orators with American flags, one line of pickets with a precinct cop nearby, lazily swinging a daytime stick. Delaney was part of them all. His family, he was tempted to think. But that, he admitted, was fanciful and ridiculous.

He was a heavy, brooding man. Somewhat round-shouldered, almost brutish in appearance. Handsome in a thick, worn way, with grey hair cut *en brosse*. A solemn mien; he had a taste for melancholy, and it showed. His hands were fists. He had the trundling walk of an old street cop on patrol.

He wore a dark suit of dense flannel. A vest festooned with a clumpy gold chain that had been his grandfather's. At one end of the chain, a hunting case in a waistcoat pocket. It had belonged to his father and had stopped fifty years ago. Twenty minutes to noon. Or midnight. At the other end of the chain was a jeweled miniature of his detective's badge, given to him by his wife on his retirement.

Squarely atop his head was his black homburg, looking as if it had been cast in iron. He wore a white shirt with a starched collar. A maroon tie of silk rep. A white handkerchief in the breast pocket of his jacket, and another in his left trouser pocket. Both fresh. And ironed. His shoes were polished to a dull gloss, ankle-high, of black kangaroo leather. The soles were thick. When he was tired, he thumped as he walked.

He suddenly knew where he wanted to go. He crossed 55th Street and turned east.

"Chief!" a voice called.

He looked. There was no mistaking the car illegally parked at the curb: a dusty blue Plymouth. A white man was climbing out, grinning. A black, also smiling, sat behind the wheel, bending over to look up at Delaney.

"Haryah, Chief," the first man said, holding out his hand. "You're looking real good."

Delaney shook the proffered hand, trying to remember.

"Shakespeare," he said suddenly, "William Shakespeare. Who could forget that?"

"Right on," the detective laughed. "We were with you on Operation Lombard."

"And Sam Lauder," Delaney said. He leaned down to shake the hand of the black inside the car. "You two still married?"

"You'd think so the way we fight," Lauder laughed. "How you been, Chief?"

"Can't complain," Delaney said cheerfully. "Well, I can—but who's to listen? How are you doing?"

"Made first," Shakespeare said proudly. "Sam, too. On your recommendation."

Delaney made a gesture.

"You had it coming," he said. He waved at Fifth Avenue, the elegant Hotel Knickerbocker, the last hotel in New York to have a billiard room. "What are you doing around here—slumming?"

"Nah," Shakespeare said. "It's a half-ass stakeout. Sam and me are on temporary assignment to the East Side hotel squad for the summer. Ever hear of a wrong guy named Al Kingston?"

"Al Kingston?" Delaney repeated. He shook his head. "No, I don't think I make him."

"Arthur King? Albert Kingdon? Alfred Ka—"

"Wait a minute, wait a minute," Delaney said. "Arthur King. That rings a bell. Hotel rooms and jewelry shops. Works alone or with a young twist. In and out so slick and so fast, no one could nail him."

"That's the cat," Shakespeare nodded. "Nabbed a dozen times, and it all added up to nit. Anyway, we got a flash from Miami that Al baby had been rousted and was believed heading our way. We picked him up at the airport and have been keeping tabs on him ever since. Loose tail. We just don't have the manpower."

"I know," Delaney said sympathetically.

"Anyway, this is his third visit to the Knickerbocker. We figure he's casing. When he comes out this time we're going to grab him and bounce him a little. Nothing heavy. Just enough to convince him to move on to Chicago or L.A. Anywhere."

"There's a service entrance," Delaney cautioned. "On Fifty-fourth. You got it covered?"

"Front and back," Shakespeare nodded. "Sam and me have been watching the lobby entrance. We won't miss him."

"Sure you will," Delaney said genially. "There's an arcade from the lobby that leads down the block to an outside drugstore. He could slip out through there as easy as Mary, kiss my ass."

"Son of a *bitch!*" William Shakespeare said bitterly, and began running.

Sam Lauder piled out of the car and went pounding after his partner. Delaney watched them go, feeling, he admitted, better than he should have. He was still smiling when he went into the small, secluded Hotel Knickerbocker bar.

It was a dark, paneled box of a room. The mahogany bar was about ten feet long, with six stools padded with black vinyl. There were a dozen small bistro tables placed around, each with two wire chairs, also padded with black vinyl. Behind the bar, covering the entire wall, was a mural from the 1930s, a vaguely Art Decoish montage of skyscrapers, jazz musicians, mustached men in nipped-waist tuxedos and blonde women in shimmery evening gowns—dancing to some maniacal beat. The mural was painted in white, black, and silver, with musical notes in fire-engine red floating across the surface. Along the top, in jerky lettering, was the legend: "Come on along and listen to—the lullaby of Broadway."

Delaney swung onto one of the stools. He was the only patron in the room. The big, paunchy bartender put down his *Daily News* and came over. He was wearing a white shirt with sleeve garters, a small, black leather bowtie clipped to the collar. He had a long white apron tied under his armpits. It covered him from chest to ankles. He smiled at Delaney, set out an ashtray, a wooden bowl of salted peanuts, a paper napkin with the hotel's crest printed on it.

"Good afternoon, sir," he said. "What can I do you for?"

"Good afternoon," Delaney said. "Do you have any ale or dark beer?"

"Dark Löwenbräu," the man said, staring at Delaney.

"That'll be fine."

The man stood there. He began snapping his fingers, still staring at Delaney.

"I seen you," he said. "I *seen* you!"

Delaney said nothing. The man kept staring, snapping his fingers.

"Delaney!" he burst out. "Chief Delaney! Right?"

Delaney smiled. "Right," he said.

"I knew the second you walked in you was somebody," the bartender said. "I knew I seen you in the paper, or on the TV." He wiped his hand carefully on his apron, then stuck it out. "Chief Delaney, it's a pleasure, believe me. I'm Harry Schwartz."

Delaney shook his hand.

"Not Chief anymore, Harry," he said. "I'm retired."

"I read, I read," Schwartz said. "Wear it in good health. But a President, he retires and he's still Mister President. Right? And a governor is

a governor till the day he dies. Likewise a colonel in the army. He retires, but people will call him 'Colonel.' Right?"

"Right," Delaney nodded.

"So you're still Chief," the bartender said. "And me, when I retire,
I'll still be Harry Schwartz."

He took a dark Löwenbräu from a tub of crushed ice, wiped the bottle carefully with a clean towel. He selected a glass from the back rack,
held it up to the light to detect spots. Satisfied, he placed the glass in
front of Delaney on the paper napkin. He uncapped the bottle, filled the
glass halfway, allowing about an inch of white head to build. Then he
set the bottle on a little paper coaster next to Delaney's hand. He waited
expectantly until Delaney took a sip.

"All right?" Harry Schwartz asked anxiously.

"Beautiful," Delaney said, and meant it.

"Good," the bartender said. He leaned across the bar on folded arms.
"So tell me, what have you been doing with yourself?"

It didn't come out like that, of course. It came out, "S' tell me,
watcha bin doon witcha self?" Chief Delaney figured the accent for
Manhattan, probably the Chelsea district.

"This and that," he said vaguely. "Trying to keep busy."

The bartender spread his hands wide.

"What else?" he said. "Just because you're retired don't mean you're
dead. Right?"

"Right," Delaney said obediently.

"I thought all cops when they retire they go to Florida and play
shuffleboard?"

"A lot of them do," Delaney laughed.

"My brother-in-law he was a cop," Harry Schwartz said. "You prolly
wouldn't know him. Out in Queens. A good cop. Never took a nickel.
Well, maybe a *nickel*. So he retires and moves to Arizona because my
sister she's got asthma. Get her to a dry climate, the doc says, or she'll
be dead in a year. So my brother-in-law, Pincus his name was, Louis
Pincus, he retires early, you know, and moves Sadie to Arizona. Buys a
house out there. Got a lawn, the whole schmear. It looked nice the
house from the pictures they sent. A year later, a year mind you, Louie's
out mowing that lawn and he drops." Harry Schwartz snapped his
fingers. "Like that. The ticker. So he goes out there for Sadie's health,
he drops dead, and to this day she's strong as a horse. That's life. Am I
right?"

"Right," Delaney said faintly.

"Ah well," Harry Schwartz sighed, "waddya going to do? That's the way things go. Tell me something, Chief—what about these young cops you see nowadays? I mean with the sideburns, the mustaches, the hair. I mean they don't even *look* like cops to me, you know?"

They didn't look like cops to Edward X. Delaney either, but he'd never tell a civilian that.

"Look," he said, "a hundred years ago practically every cop in New York had a mustache. And most of them were big, bushy walrus things. I mean then you almost had to *have* a mustache to get a job as a cop. Styles change, but the cops themselves don't change. Except maybe they're smarter today."

"Yeah," Harry Schwartz said. "I guess you're right. Ready for another?"

"Please. That one just cut the dust. How about you? Have something with me?"

"Nah," Schwartz said. "Thanks, but not while I'm working. I ain't supposed to."

"Come on."

"Well . . . maybe I'll have a beer. I'll keep it under the counter. Many thanks."

He went through the ceremony again, opening a fresh bottle of imported beer for Delaney. Then he opened a bottle of domestic for himself, poured a glass. He looked around at the empty room cautiously, held up the glass quickly, and said, "To your health, Chief."

"To yours," Delaney replied.

They both sipped, and the bartender hid his glass expertly below the counter.

"If you got your health you got everything—right?" he said.

"Right."

"But it's a miserable job, ain't it? I mean being a cop?"

Edward X. Delaney looked down at his glass. He lifted it off the paper napkin. He set it on the polished bar top and began moving it around in small, slow circles.

"Sometimes," he nodded. "Sometimes it's the most miserable job on earth. Sometimes it's okay."

"That's what I figured," Schwartz said. "I mean you see a lot of shit—right? Then, on the other hand, you are also helping people which is okay."

Delaney nodded.

"I was thinking of becoming a cop," Schwartz reminisced. "I really was. I got out of Korea alive and I come back to New York, and I thought what should I do? And I thought maybe I should be a cop. I mean the pay isn't all that great—at least then it wasn't—but it was steady, you know, and the pension and all. But then I knew I really didn't have the balls to be a cop. I mean it takes balls, don't it?"

"Oh yes," Delaney said, wondering if Schwartz knew what they had called him in the Department—"Iron Balls" Delaney.

"Sure. Well, I figured what the hell, so I didn't. I mean like if someone shot at me, I'd probably piss my pants. I mean that. A hero I ain't. And as for shooting someone, I just couldn't."

"You shot at people in Korea, didn't you?"

"Nah. I was a cook."

"Well," Delaney sighed, "shooting or being shot at is really a very small part of a cop's job. Most people don't realize that, but it's true. Only perhaps one percent or less of a cop's time is spent with a gun in his hand. Most cops put in thirty years on the force, retire, and never fire their guns off the range. The stuff you see in the papers and on TV, the dramatic stuff, happens now and then, sure. But for every shootout there's a thousand cops pounding the beat day after day, settling family squabbles, calling an ambulance for a heart case, getting drunks off the street, rousting junkies or hookers."

"Sure," Harry Schwartz said, "I know all that, and I agree one hundred percent. But still and all, let's face facts, they don't give cops that gun for nothing—right? I mean a cop might go year after year and nothing happens, and that gun could grow right into his holster for all the use it gets. Right? But still and all, the time might come—and bang! There he is and some nut is trying to kill him and he's got to kill that nut first. I mean it happens, don't it?"

"Yes. It happens."

"Still and all," Harry Schwartz said, "I bet you miss it. Right?"

"Right," Edward X. Delaney said.

The garbage had been collected that day and, as usual, the empty cans had been left on the curb. He brought them down in the little areaway below the front stoop and replaced the lids. He could have entered through the basement door, but it meant opening two padlocks and a chain on the outside iron grille, so he went up to the sidewalk again and climbed the eleven steps to the front door.

When he and Barbara had remodeled this old brownstone almost thirty years ago, they had been able to save and refurbish some of the original amenities, including the front door, which had to be, he figured, at least seventy-five years old. Unlocking it now, he admired it anew— polished oak with brass hardware, and set with a diamond-shaped judas of beveled glass.

He entered the lighted hall, double-locked the door, put the chain on.

"I'm home," he yelled.

"In here, dear," his wife called from the kitchen.

He hung his homburg on the hall rack and went down the long corridor, sniffing appreciatively.

"Something smells good," he said, coming into the big kitchen.

Monica turned, smiling. "Meal or cook?" she said.

"Both," he said, kissing her cheek. "What are we having?"

"Your favorite," she said. "Boiled beef with horseradish sauce."

He stopped suddenly, stared at her.

"All right," he said. "What did you buy?"

She turned back to the pots and pans, vexed, a little, but still smiling.

"Stop being a detective," she said. "It wasn't so much. New bedspreads for the girls' room."

"That's not so bad," he said. He took a stalk of celery from a platter of greens and sat heavily at the wooden kitchen table, munching. "How was your day?"

"Hectic. The stores were mobbed. The girls said they had a nice lunch and you drank two highballs."

"The dirty squealers," he said. "They home?"

"Yes. Upstairs. Getting a start on their homework. Edward, they give the kids a lot of homework at that school."

"It won't kill them," he said.

"And Ivar Thorsen called. He wants to see you."

"Oh? Did he say why?"

"No. He wants to come over tonight at nine. He said to call his office if you can't make it. If he doesn't hear from you, he'll figure it's all right to come over."

"All right with me. You? Have anything planned?"

"No. There's a program on Channel Thirteen I want to watch. About breast cancer."

"I'll take Thorsen," he said. "Can I set the table?"

"Done," she said. "We'll eat in fifteen minutes."

"I'll wash up then," he said, rising.

"And chase the kids down," she said, tasting the sauce.

He slid an arm around her soft waist. She came close to him, still holding a big wooden spoon.

"Did I tell you I love you?" he asked her.

"Not today, you haven't."

"Consider it told."

"Oh no you don't, buster," she said. "You don't get off that easy."

"I love you," he said, and kissed her lips. "Umm," he said. "Nothing like a horseradishy kiss. Going to have a beer with dinner?"

"I'll have a sip of yours."

"The hell you will," he said. "Have your own. With boiled beef, I want *all* of mine."

She made a rude gesture with the wooden spoon, and he left, laughing.

She had been Monica Gilbert, the widow of Bernard Gilbert, one of the victims of a psychopathic killer, Daniel Blank. Delaney had been a captain then, in command of a special task force that had taken Blank, and he had met Monica during the investigation of that case. A year after Barbara Delaney had died of proteus infection, the Chief had married Monica. She was twenty years younger than he.

Their evening meal was, as usual, dominated by the lively chatter of the girls. Mary and Sylvia were eleven and thirteen and, of course, knew everything. Most of the discussion involved plans for the summer, whether it would be best for the sisters to attend the same camp or different camps. They spoke learnedly of "sibling rivalry" and "intrafamilial competition." Chief Delaney listened gravely, asked serious questions, and only Monica was aware of his amusement.

Afterwards, Delaney helped clear the table, but left the rest to his wife and stepdaughters. He went upstairs to take off jacket and vest and put on a worn cardigan. He also took off his high shoes, massaged his feet, and slid them into old carpet slippers. He came down to the living room, stopping off in the kitchen to fill a hammered silver ice bucket. The dishwasher was grinding away, and Monica was just finishing tidying up. The girls had gone up to their room again.

"Can we afford it?" she asked anxiously. "Camp, I mean? It's expensive, Edward."

"You tell me," he said. "You're the financial expert in this family."

"Well . . . maybe," she said, frowning. "If you and I don't go anywhere."

"So? We'll stay home. Lock up, pull down the shades, turn on the air conditioner and make love all summer."

"*Knocker,*" she scoffed. "Your back couldn't take it."

"Sure it could," he said equably. "As long as your pearls don't break."

She burst out laughing. He looked at her wryly.

It had happened the first time they went to bed together, about two months before they were married. He had taken her to dinner and the theatre. After, she had readily agreed to stop at his home for a nightcap before returning to her home in the same neighborhood, to her children, a baby-sitter.

She was a big-bodied woman, strong, with a good waist between heavy bosom and wide hips. Not yet matronly. Still young, still juicy. A look of limpid, almost ingenuous sensuality. All of her warm and waiting.

That night she wore a thin black dress. Not clinging, but when she moved, it touched her. About her neck, a choker of oversize pearls. When he kissed her, she pressed to him, clove to him, breast to breast, belly to belly, thigh to thigh. They stumbled, panting, up to his bedroom, where high drama became low farce.

She was lying on the bed crossways, naked except for those damned pearls. Spread out, pink and anxious. He stood at the bedside, crouched and swollen, and lifted her hips. She writhed up to embrace him. The string of pearls broke, spilling down onto the parquet floor. But they were both nutty with their lust and . . .

"You broke my pearls," wailed she.

"Fuck the pearls," roared he.

"No, me!" screamed she. "*Me!*"

But the beads were under his floundering feet, rolling, hurting, and he began skidding about, doing a mad schottische, a wild gavotte, an insane kadzotsky, until laughter defeated them both. So they had to change positions and start all over again, which wasn't all that bad.

Smiling at the memory, they went into the living room, where he mixed them each a rye highball. They sat contentedly, both slumped with legs extended.

Deputy Commissioner Ivar Thorsen arrived promptly at nine. Monica remained in the living room to watch her TV program. The two men went into the study and closed the door. Delaney emerged a moment later to fetch the bucket of ice. His wife was seated on the edge of her chair, leaning forward, arms on her knees, eyes on the screen. Delaney smiled and touched her hair before he went back into the study.

"What, Ivar?" he asked. "Rye? Scotch? Anything?"

"A little Scotch would be fine, Edward. Just straight. No ice, please."

They sat facing in old club chairs, the original leather dry and cracked. They raised their glasses to each other, sipped.

In the Department, Thorsen was called "Admiral," and looked it: fine, silvered hair, cutting blue eyes, a posture so erect he was almost rigid. He was slender, small-boned, fastidiously well groomed.

He had been Edward Delaney's mentor in the Department, his "rabbi," and a good one, for he had a talent for political infighting, an instinct for picking the winner in the ferocious conflicts that periodically racked city government. More, he *enjoyed* that world where government of law crashed against government of men. He stepped his way daintily through the debris, and was never soiled.

"How are things going?" Delaney asked.

Thorsen flipped a palm back and forth.

"The usual," he said. "You know about the budget cuts and layoffs."

"Rates up?"

"No, that's the crazy thing." Thorsen laughed shortly. "Fewer cops, but no great increase in crime. The unions thought there would be. So did I."

"So did I," Delaney nodded. "Glad to hear there isn't. Chief Bernhardt is doing a good job."

Bernhardt was Delaney's successor as Chief of Detectives. A career cop, he had commanded Brooklyn detectives before being brought to headquarters in Manhattan. His wife's father was on the board of a prestigious New York bank that held a vaultful of New York City and State notes and bonds. It didn't hurt.

"Good," Thorsen said, "but not great. But Bernhardt's got his problems, too. The cutbacks have hurt. That's why I'm here."

"Oh?"

"You read about a homicide about a month ago? Victor Maitland? The artist?"

"Sure. Down in Little Italy. I followed it. It fell out of the papers in a hurry."

"There was a lot of other hot news at the time," Thorsen said. "Thank God. Also, we didn't have anything. It's still open."

"Sounded like a B-and-E to me," Delaney said. "A guy with a snootful of shit breaks the door, this Maitland puts up a fight and gets the shiv."

"Could be," Thorsen said. "I don't know all the details, but his place had been ripped off twice before, and he had locks and a chain. They weren't forced. We figured he opened for someone he knew."

"Oh? Anything missing?"

"His wallet. But he never carried much cash. And he still had his credit cards on him. There was an expensive portable radio in the place. It wasn't touched."

"Ah?" Delaney said. "A faked heist? It's been done before. Who inherits?"

"No will. That'll give a lot of lawyers a lot of work. The IRS sealed everything. The guy was loaded. His last painting went for a hundred big ones."

"I've seen his stuff," Delaney said. "I like it."

"I do, too," Thorsen said. "So does Karen. She thinks he was the greatest thing since Rembrandt. But that's neither here nor there. We're dead on the case. No leads. It would be just another open file, but we're getting a lot of flak."

Delaney rose to freshen Thorsen's drink. He also dropped two more ice cubes into his rye-and-water.

"Flak?" he said. "Where from?"

"Ever hear of a guy named J. Barnes Chapin?"

"Sure. A politico. State senator. From upstate somewhere."

"That's right," Thorsen nodded. "His home base is Rockland County. Chapin has been in Albany since the year one. He swings a lot of clout. Right now, there's a bill up for a special State grant to New York City for law enforcement—cops, courts, prisons, the works. Chapin could tip the scale."

"So?"

"Chapin is—or was—Victor Maitland's uncle."

"Oh-ho."

"The funny thing is that Chapin couldn't care less who offed Maitland. From what we've learned, this Maitland was a Grade-A bastard. As the old saying goes, the list of suspects has been narrowed to ten thousand. Everyone hated his guts, including his wife and son. Everyone but his mother. A boy's best friend etcetera. She's a wealthy old dame who lives near Nyack. One daughter, Maitland's sister, lives with her. The mother's been driving Chapin crazy. He's her brother. And he's been driving us crazy. When are we going to find Victor Maitland's killer and get his sister off his back?"

Delaney was silent, staring at Thorsen. He took a slow sip of his drink. The two men locked eyes.

"Why me?" he asked quietly.

Thorsen hunched forward.

"Look, Edward," he said, "you don't have to quote me the numbers. I know the graph: if a homicide isn't solved in the first forty-eight hours, solution probability drops off to nit. It's a cold trail. Granted. And just between you, me, and the lamppost, finding the killer of Victor Maitland comes pretty far down on the Department's anxiety list."

"I understand."

"But we've got to go through the motions. To keep J. Barnes Chapin happy. So he can keep his sister happy. Convince her we're working on it."

"And keep Chapin on the City's side when that new bill comes up for a vote."

"Of course," Thorsen shrugged. "What else?"

"Again," Delaney said, "why me?"

Thorsen sighed, sat back, crossed his knees, sipped his drink.

"Great Scotch, Edward. What is it?"

"Glenlivet."

"Well, for one thing, Chapin asked for you. Yes, he did. In person. He remembers Operation Lombard. Second, we just don't have the manpower to waste on this thing. Edward, it's *cold*. You know it, we know it. It was probably a smash-and-grab like you said, and the cat is probably in Kansas City by now. Who the hell knows? No one's expecting you to break it. For Christ's sake, Edward, there's been a hundred unsolved homicides in the city since Maitland was greased. We can only do so much."

"What do you want from me?" Delaney asked stonily.

"Look into it. Just look into it. Edward, I know you're retired, but don't tell me you're all that busy. I won't buy it. Just look into it. We can cover your expenses. And we'll assign you one man on active duty to drive you around and flash his potsy whenever it's needed. You'll get copies of everything we've got—reports, photos, PM, the works. Edward, we don't *expect* anything. Just take a look at it."

"So you can tell Chapin the murder of his nephew is under active investigation?"

Thorsen smiled wanly.

"That's exactly correct," he said. "It's for the Department, Edward."

Delaney raised his arms and went through an elaborate mime of bowing a violin. Thorsen laughed.

"Iron Balls!" he said. "Well, what the hell, I thought it might interest you, might intrigue you. Get you out of Monica's hair. No?"

Delaney looked down at his glass, turning it in his hands.

"I'll sleep on it," he said. "Talk it over with Monica. All right? I'll call you in the morning, one way or the other."

"Sure," Thorsen said. "That's good enough for me. Fine. Think it over."

He drained his drink and stood up. Delaney started to rise, then suddenly Thorsen flopped back into his chair.

"There's one other thing," he said.

"Had to be," Delaney said sardonically.

"Remember a cop named Sam—Samuel Boone? About fifteen years ago?"

"Sure, I remember him," Delaney said. "He got blown away. I went to his funeral."

"Right. It was in the South Bronx. My precinct at the time. Jewish then. Now it's all Spic and Span. This Sam Boone was the best. I mean, the *best*. They loved him. On his birthday, old Jewish ladies would bring cakes and cookies to the precinct house. I swear it. He was out of Kentucky or Tennessee or West Virginia, or someplace like that. An accent you could cut with a knife, and the Jews on his beat taught him some Yiddish. They'd say, 'Samele, speak me some Yiddish', and he'd say what they had taught him in that corn-pone accent of his, and they'd break up. Anyway, a car pulled into a one-way street, going the wrong way, and piled up against on-coming traffic. Sam was nearby and walked over. The car had Illinois plates or Michigan. Something like that. Knowing Sam, I figure he would have explained to the driver about our one-way streets, get him turned around, and send him on his way with a warning. He leans down to talk to the guy—and pow! pow! pow! Three in the face and chest. The guy had to be an idiot, an *idiot!* What's he going to do? He can't pull ahead; he's bumper to bumper with the on-coming cars. And he can't back up because of the traffic on the avenue. So he piles out of the car.

"Edward, I got there about ten minutes after it happened. The streets were crowded, lots of people on the sidewalks, and they saw Sam go down. I swear we had to *tear* this guy away from them. If someone had had a rope, he'd have been swinging. I've never seen people so infuriated. To this day it scares me to think about it. And of course the clincher is that this guy was facing a GTA back in Michigan, or Illinois, or whatever. Even if Sam had asked for his ID, which, knowing Sam, I doubt he'd have done, the guy faced three-to-five at most, and probably less. But he panicked, and I lost the best street cop in my precinct."

Delaney nodded somberly, rose to pour fresh drinks, add ice cubes to his glass. Then he sat down again opposite Thorsen.

"That's the way it goes," he said. "But what's that got to do with Maitland's murder?"

"Well . . ." Thorsen said. He drew a deep breath. "Sam had a son. Abner Boone. He joined the Department. I kept an eye on him. I figured I owed him. Abner Boone. He's a detective sergeant now. You know him, Edward?"

"Abner Boone?" Delaney said, frowning. "I remember him vaguely. About six-one. One-eighty. Sandy hair. Blue eyes. Long arms and legs. Nice grin. Slightly stooped. Looks like his ankles and wrists are sticking out of his clothes. White scar on the left neck. Wears glasses for reading. That the guy?"

"Remember him vaguely?" Thorsen mimicked. "I should have your memory! That's the guy. Edward, you know when the son of a slain patrolman joins the Force, we've got to keep an eye on him. Maybe the kid did it to get revenge, or to prove he's as good as his daddy was, or to prove he's a *better* man than his daddy was. It can be sticky. Anyway, I kept an eye on Abner Boone, and helped when I could. The kid did just great. Made detective sergeant, finally, and about two years ago they gave him one of those commando homicide squads that are supposed to help out the regular units when the workload piles up or when a big case comes along."

"How are they working out?" Delaney asked. "The special squads?"

"Still being evaluated," Thorsen said. "But I don't think they'll last.

Too much jealousy from the regular units. That's natural. Anyway, this Abner Boone got this squad, and after a year or so, he had a good record. Some important busts and a lot of good assists. Then he started hitting the sauce. Hard. His squad covered for him for a while. Then it couldn't be covered. I did what I could—counseling, doctors, psychiatrists, AA, the lot—but nothing worked. Edward, the kid is trying. I know he is. He's really *trying*. If he falls again, he's out."

"And this is the man you want to assign me on the Maitland case? A lush?"

Thorsen laughed shortly.

"You got it," he said. "I figured we can keep J. Barnes Chapin happy with an on-going investigation, even if it comes to zilch. At the same time, I can get Abner Boone out of the office on detached assignment, and maybe he can straighten himself out. It's worth the gamble. And even if he goes off again, who's to see? Except you."

Delaney looked at him with wonder. Perhaps, he thought, this was the secret of Thorsen's success. You manipulate people, but as you do, you tell them exactly why and how you are doing it. Bemused by the honesty, won by the candor in the ice-blue eyes, they agree to do what you want. It all sounds so reasonable.

"I'll sleep on it," he repeated.

Two hours later, he sat with Monica on the living room couch. The TV screen was dead. They were sipping decaf coffee. He told her exactly what Deputy Commissioner Ivar Thorsen had said. He had almost total recall.

"What do you think?" he finished.

"He's an alcoholic?" she asked.

"Abner Boone? Sounds like it from what Ivar said. Or on his way. But that's not important. If Boone fucks up, they'll give me someone else. The question is, should I do it?"

"Do you want to?"

"I don't know. In a way I do, and in a way I don't. I'd like a chance to stick Maitland's killer. A human being shouldn't be destroyed, and the killer walks away. That's not right. I know that sounds simple, but it's the way I feel. My God, if . . . Well . . . On the other hand, I'm retired, and it's the Department's migraine, not mine. Still . . . What do you think?"

"I think you should," she said.

"Want me out of your hair?" he said, smiling. "Out of the house? Working?"

"Nooo," she said slowly. "You're a pain in the ass at times." He looked up sharply. "But I think this is something you should do. But it's really up to you. It's your decision."

He motioned, and she came over to sit on his lap, a soft weight. He put an arm about her waist. She put an arm around his neck.

"Am I really a pain in the ass?" he asked.

"Sometimes," she nodded. "Sometimes I am too. I know. Everyone is. Sometimes. I really think you should do this thing, Edward. Ivar said he doesn't really expect results, but that was just to convince you to take the job, to challenge you. He really does think you can do it, and so does this Chapin. I don't like that man; he's such a reactionary. Do you think you can find Maitland's killer?"

"I don't know," he sighed. "It's a cold, cold trail."

"If anyone can, you can," she said, and that ended it as far as she was concerned. "Coming to bed?" she asked.

"In a while," he said.

She rose, kissed the top of his head, took their cups and saucers into the kitchen. He heard running water, then the sound of her footsteps going upstairs.

He sat another half-hour by himself, slumped, pondering. It was an injustice to Monica, but he thought of what Barbara, his first wife, would have counseled. He knew. Exactly what Monica urged. He was lucky with his women. It was odd how they felt, their lust for life, their passion for children and plants. They were right of course, he acknowledged. You nurtured it. The spark. You breathed on it to keep it alive. You punished people who destroyed it. The spark . . .

He sighed again, stood up and stretched, began his rounds. First into the basement to test windows and doors. Then, moving upward, checks to make certain chains and locks were in place to keep out the darkness. Mary and Sylvia were sleeping placidly, secure. The whole house was secure. An island.

He undressed as quietly as he could, and slid into bed. But Monica was still awake. She turned to come into his arms. Warm and waiting.

3

The material on the Maitland case was delivered to the Delaney brownstone by an unmarked police car shortly before noon. It came jammed into three battered liquor cartons with a note from Deputy Commissioner Ivar Thorsen: "Sorry it's not in order, Edward—but you're good at that! Boone will call you tomorrow to set up a meet. Luck."

The Chief had the cartons brought into the study and piled on the floor next to his broad desk. He went into the kitchen and made himself two sandwiches: salami and sliced Spanish onion (with mayonnaise) on rye, and ham and cheese (with mustard) on a seeded roll. He took the sandwiches and an open bottle of Heineken back into the study, placed them carefully aside on a small end table, and set to work.

He went through the three cartons slowly and steadily, glancing briefly at each document before adding it to one of four loosely classified piles:

1. Official reports of the investigating officers.
2. Signed statements of those questioned, and photographs.
3. Photos of the victim alive and as a corpse *in situ,* and reports of the Medical Examiner.
4. Miscellaneous bits of paper, most of which were informal reac-

tions of detectives to those they had questioned, or suggestions
for additional lines of inquiry.

Working methodically, stopping occasionally for a bite of sandwich, a
gulp of beer, Delaney had all the records broken down by 3:30 P.M. He
then went through each stack arranging it by date and time, switching a
few documents from one pile to another, but generally adhering to his
original division.

He put on his heavy reading glasses, pulled the green-shaded student
lamp close. He sat down in his swivel chair and began with the photos
and PM, since this was the smallest stack. Finished, he started on the
pile of official reports. He was halfway through when Monica called him
to dinner.

He washed up and joined the family in the dining room. He tried to
eat slowly and join in the conversation. He made a few ponderous jokes.
But he left the table early, declining dessert, and took a mug of black
coffee back into the study with him. He completed the initial reading
shortly after 9:00 P.M. He then began a second reading, slower this
time, with a pad of yellow legal paper nearby on which he occasionally
jotted brief notes and questions.

Monica brought him a thermos of coffee at 11:00 and announced she
would watch TV for an hour and then go to bed. He smiled absently,
kissed her cheek, went back to his reading. He completed the second review by 1:00 A.M. He then filed the material in folders in the bottom
drawer of a metal cabinet equipped with a lock. He dug out his street
map and street guide of Manhattan and located the scene of the killing,
on Mott Street between Prince and Spring.

He knew the section; about twenty years previously, when he was a
dick two, he had been assigned temporarily as a summer replacement
for precinct detectives going on vacation. The neighborhood was practically 100 percent Italian then, part of Little Italy. Delaney remembered
how, later in the year, he had enjoyed the Feast of San Gennaro on
Mulberry Street, one of the city's big ethnic festivals.

He was assigned as partner to Detective first grade Alberto Di Lucca.
Big Al was a jowly, pot-bellied, wine-swilling pasta fiend, and had introduced Delaney to the glories of Italian cooking. He had also taught him
a lot of tricks of the trade.

In July of that year, there was a ripoff of a wholesale warehouse on
Elizabeth Street. Four masked men, armed, forced their way in, tied up
the night watchman, and drove off in a huge semitrailer loaded with im-

ported olive oil. This, to Di Lucca, a man who worshipped spaghetti *al'* *olio,* was sacrilege.

"Now what you got to know," Di Lucca told Delaney, "is that we got a lot of bad boys in this precinct. But generally they go outside the neighborhood for their fun and games. It's like an unwritten law: you don't shit in the living room. Howsomever, in this case I think it was locals."

"How do you figure?" Delaney asked.

"Now take the watchman. Outsiders would have blasted him, coldcocked him, or treated him rough. But no, this old man is asked politely to lie down on a pile of burlap bags, he's tied up, and a piece of tape put gently across his mouth. And before the gonnifs leave, they ask him is he comfortable? Can he breathe okay? They did everything but serve him breakfast in bed. I figure he knew them, and they knew him. Maybe he fingered the job. He's got a lot of relatives, a lot of young, hotblooded nephews. One of them, Anthony Scorese, isn't nice. He runs with three pals: Vito Gervase, Robert Scheinfelt—a Wop, but you'd never know it from that name, right?—and a punk named Giuseppe something. I don't know his last name, but they call him Kid Stick. I think those four desperadoes pulled this job. Let's ask around and see if they're spending."

So Di Lucca and Delaney asked around, and sure enough the Fearsome Four had been spending. Not a lot, but enough to indicate they had come into sudden wealth: good wine and Strega with their meals, blonde broads from uptown, new alligator shoes.

"Now we're going to break them," Di Lucca told Delaney. "They swore undying allegiance to each other. On their mothers' graves. They'll die before they talk. They swore. Now watch this. I'm going to break these stupidos. I'll talk Italian to them, but later I'll tell you what they said."

Di Lucca questioned each of the suspects alone. He'd ask Anthony Scorese, for instance, where he was at the time of the heist. "In bed," Scorese said, then laughed. "I got a witness. This broad, she'll tell you."

"In bed with a broad?" Di Lucca said. He smiled enigmatically. "That ain't what Vito Gervase says."

He let it go at that, and moved to Gervase.

"I was out in Jersey at my uncle's place."

"So?" Di Lucca said softly. "That ain't what Scheinfelt says."

And so forth, over a period of two weeks. He worked on them, asking more questions, playing one against the other. They thought they knew what Di Lucca was doing, but they couldn't be sure. They began staring at each other. Then Di Lucca concentrated on Kid Stick, telling him that because of his youth, he'd probably get nothing more than probation if he cooperated. The Kid began to weaken, but it was Robert Scheinfelt who cracked first and made a deal.

"And that's how you do it," Di Lucca told Delaney. "Honor among thieves? My ass! They'd turn in their twin for a suspended sentence."

Now, staring at the street on the map, the street where Victor Maitland had been knifed to death, Delaney remembered Detective Alberto Di Lucca and wished he was still around with his house-by-house knowledge of the neighborhood. But Big Al had retired a long time ago, had returned to Naples, and had probably suffocated his heart with just one more helping of *costoletta di maiale alla napoletana*.

Delaney sighed, turned out the study lamp, started his security check. He wasn't depressed by what he had read, but he wasn't elated, either. The investigation of Maitland's murder had been a good one, he acknowledged. Thorough. Energetic. Imaginative. A lot of bells had been rung. A lot of pavements pounded. A lot of people questioned. A lot of records had been dug up and reviewed. It all added up to zero, to zip, to zilch. A cipher case.

The body had been discovered by Saul Geltman, owner of Geltman Galleries on Madison Avenue, and Victor Maitland's exclusive agent. Maitland had promised to be at the Galleries at three o'clock Friday afternoon to work with Geltman and an interior designer on plans for a new exhibition of Maitland's work. When he hadn't shown up by four, Geltman had called the Mott Street studio. No answer. He had then called Maitland's home on East 58th Street. He spoke to Alma Maitland, the artist's wife. She didn't know Maitland's whereabouts, but said he had mentioned he was meeting Geltman at the Galleries at three that afternoon.

Neither wife nor agent was particularly concerned about Maitland's absence. It was not the first time he had failed to keep an appointment. Apparently, he was a chronic liar, broke promises carelessly, often disappeared for a day or two at a time. When working in the Mott Street studio, he frequently took the phone off the hook or simply didn't answer calls. He slept there occasionally.

Saul Geltman stated that he continued trying to reach Maitland at his home and the studio all day Saturday, with no success. He also called a few acquaintances of Maitland's. None knew where the artist was. Finally, by noon on Sunday, Geltman was becoming worried. He cabbed down to the studio. The door was closed but unlocked. There were roaches in the blood. Geltman promptly vomited, then called 911, the police emergency number, from the studio phone.

A two-man precinct squad car was first to respond. They put in the call reporting an apparent homicide; police machinery began to grind. Within an hour, the tenement building was roped off. Upstairs, the fifth-floor studio was crowded with officers from the precinct, detectives from the homicide unit covering that area, a doctor from the Medical Examiner's office, lab technicians, photographers, the district attorney's man, and Sergeant Abner Boone and two men from his special commando homicide squad.

The autopsy report stated laconically that Victor Maitland had died of "exsanguination resulting from multiple stab wounds." In other words, the man had bled to death; internal cavities were full, and he was lying in a coagulated pool. The weapon was described as "a knife, a single-edged weapon approximately five or six inches in length, tapering to a fine point." Analysis of stomach contents revealed ingestion of a moderate amount of whiskey just prior to death, which occurred, the ME's surgeons estimated, between 10:00 A.M. and 3:00 P.M. on Friday. They refused to be more precise.

A double investigation was begun. On the assumption that the artist was killed by a thief, a mugger, one team of detectives began searching the files for similar attacks, began questioning neighbors and nearby shopkeepers, copied down license-plate numbers of parked cars in the vicinity, later to question their owners. Catch basins, sewers, garbage cans, and litter baskets in a ten-block area were searched for the weapon. Snitches were queried, police and court records were reviewed for recent releases of knife-wielding smash-and-grab experts.

A second team, working on the assumption that Victor Maitland had opened his locked door to someone he knew and was dirked by that someone, began looking into the painter's private life and personal affairs, questioning anyone they could find who knew Maitland and might, conceivably, have closed him out. Eventually, they concentrated their efforts on seven people.

Before limiting their inquiries to this group, detectives questioned a depressingly long list of artists, models, art dealers, art critics, prostitutes, drinking companions, and a few distant relatives, none of whom seemed particularly distressed by the sudden blanking of Victor Maitland, and made little effort to hide their indifference. Depending on the education and/or social status of the acquaintance questioned, the dead man was described as everything from "an offensive and disagreeable individual" to "a piece of shit."

But after a heavy investigation that lasted almost six weeks, after the expenditure of thousands of man-hours of slogging work, the Department was no closer to the solution of the crime than they had been when Saul Geltman made his call to 911. Everything was gone over three times. New detectives were brought in for a fresh look at the evidence collected. Researchers went back to Maitland's two-year hitch in the army, even to his school days, looking for a possible motive.

Nothing.

One of the homicide dicks summed up the feelings of all of them:

"What the hell," he said wearily. "Why don't we say the son of a bitch stabbed himself in the back, and forget about it?"

Monica Delaney devoted every Thursday to volunteer work at a local hospital. Before leaving the house, she delivered a written list of instructions to Chief Delaney: a timetable detailing when he was to put the roast in the oven, at what temperature, when he was to put the potatoes in the stove-top baker, when he was to take the Sara Lee chocolate cake from the freezer. He inspected the list solemnly, his glasses sliding down his nose.

"And I'll try to get the windows done," he told her.

She laughed, and stuck out her tongue at him.

He went into the study, sat down at his desk. He left the door open. He was alone in the house; he wanted to hear every unfamiliar and unexpected creak and thump.

He took a new manila file folder from a desk drawer. He had intended to write on the tab: "Killing of Victor Maitland." But he paused. Perhaps he should write: "Murder of Victor Maitland." There was a difference, he felt, between a murder and a killing. It went beyond the legal definition of First Degree: "With malice aforethought . . ."

Delaney tried to analyze his feeling, and decided that the difference he saw between the two was in the deliberation of the act. The soldier in war usually killed, he didn't murder. But an assassination was a murder, not a killing. Unless the assassin was hired. A fine line there that involved not only deliberation but passion. Cold passion.

If Victor Maitland had been offed because he resisted a thief, that would be a killing. If he had been stabbed to death by someone known to him, someone who had pondered and planned, for whatever reason, it would be a murder. Delaney shook his head ruefully. This decision was to color his whole approach to the case, he knew. He was hardly into it, and already he was faced with the very basic question that had flummoxed the Department. Finally, taking a deep breath, he wrote on the folder tab: "Murder of Victor Maitland," and let it go at that.

Inside the folder he placed two pages of notes and questions he had jotted down while reviewing the Department's records. Then he drew the legal pad to him and began listing the things he planned to do in his private investigation. He wrote them down in no particular order, just as they occurred to him.

When the list was as complete as he could make it, when he ran out of ideas, he began putting the items in the proper sequence. As important as the ideas themselves. He struggled with it, juggling, trying to construct the most logical order. That completed, he added the final sequence to the manila folder. It pleased him. This was *his* paper. Up to now, the Maitland case had consisted solely of other men's paper. The phone rang while he was preparing additional file folders, labeled VICTIM, AGENT, WIFE, MISTRESS, etc.

"Edward X. Delaney here," he said.

"Chief, this is Detective sergeant Abner Boone."

There was a pause, each waiting for the other to speak again. Finally . . .

"Yes, sergeant," Delaney said. "Thorsen said you'd call. When can we get together?"

"Whenever you say, sir."

The voice was slightly twangy, not quite steady. There was no slur, but the agitation was there, controlled but there.

Delaney's first impulse was to invite the man for dinner. With a standing rib roast and baked potatoes, there'd be plenty of food. But he had second thoughts. It would be wiser if his initial meeting with Boone was one-on-one. Then he could evaluate the man. Before introducing him to the family.

"Would this evening at nine inconvenience you, sergeant?" he asked. "At my home? Do you have anything planned?"

"No, sir. Nothing planned. Nine will be fine. I have your address."

"Good. See you then."

Delaney hung up and went to his file cabinet for the stacks of official reports and signed statements. He began to divide these into his new folders: VICTIM, AGENT, WIFE, MISTRESS . . .

He had a sandwich and a glass of milk at noon, went for a short walk along the streets of Two-five-one Precinct, smoking a cigar. He returned home in the early afternoon and continued his filing chores. This was donkey work, but most police work was. In fact, he found a curious satisfaction in this task of "putting things in order."

That's what a cop's job was all about, wasn't it? To restore and maintain order in a disordered world. Not only in society, but in the individual as well. Even in the cop himself. That was the reason for the multitude of forms, the constantly increasing mass of regulations. That was the reason for the formalistic, and sometimes ridiculous officialese. A cop never nabbed a crook. Not in a filed report or court testimony he didn't. He apprehended a suspect, or took a perpetrator into custody.

"Officer, when did you first encounter the accused?"

"I approached the defendant at nine-fifteen on the morning of April two, of this year, as he was exiting the premises of Boog's Tavern, located on Lexington Avenue and Ninetieth Street, City of New York, Borough of Manhattan. I identified myself as an officer of the law. I thereupon recited to this person his legal rights, as required, and placed him under arrest, charging him with the criminal act specified. I then accompanied the accused to the Two-five-one Precinct house, where he was duly incarcerated."

A touching search for precision in a lunatic world . . .

So Chief Edward X. Delaney worked away at his files, trying to create order from the murder of Victor Maitland.

The dinner was fine, the roast of beef blood-rare, the way Delaney liked it. Monica and the girls took their slices from the well-done ends; he liked his from the dripping middle. They had a California jug burgundy; Mary and Sylvia were each allowed one glass, cut half-and-half with water.

The girls went upstairs to their homework. Delaney helped Monica clear the table, put leftovers away, stack the dishwasher. Then they took second cups of coffee into the living room. He began telling her about the Maitland murder. He had learned a long time ago, when Barbara was alive, that it helped him to verbalize a case to an attentive listener. Even if the listener could offer no constructive suggestions, sometimes the questions—untrained, ingenuous—opened new paths of inquiry, or forced Delaney to re-examine his own thinking.

Monica listened intently, her eyes squinching with pain as he described what had happened to Victor Maitland. Remembering what had happened to her first husband, Bernard Gilbert . . .

"Edward," she said, when he had finished, "it could have been a robber, couldn't it?"

"A burglar."

"A burglar, a mugger . . . whatever."

"Could have been," he acknowledged. "What about the unlocked door? No sign of forced entry."

"Maybe he just forgot to lock the door."

"Maybe. But he had been ripped-off twice before. And he hated interruptions while he was painting. His wife and his agent both say he was paranoiac about it. He *always* locked up."

"Like you," she said.

"Yes," he smiled. "Like me. Also, he was stabbed several times. Someone spent a lot of time on that. A chance mugger might stab him once, or twice, but he probably wouldn't stand over him plunging the knife again and again. Once Maitland was down and obviously incapable of resistance, a thief would go to work stripping the place. All right, maybe the thief killed him so Maitland couldn't identify him later from mug shots. But if Maitland saw him, then he should have been facing him and the wounds would be in the front. Follow? I'm just going by percentages. Maitland's wallet was taken, true, but it could have been an attempt to make it look like a heist. There was an expensive portable radio that wasn't touched, and a box of snappers in plain view on a dresser top."

"What are snappers?"

"Ampules of amyl nitrite. You break them and sniff. Supposed to increase your sexual power. Want me to try them?"

"No, thanks, dear. I don't think I could take it."

"God bless you," he said. "Anyway, snappers—sometimes they're called poppers—are used legitimately to treat heart disorders. By prescription only. But of course they're sold on the street. Maitland had no record of heart trouble, and his doctor never prescribed amyl nitrite for him. The detectives on the case made a half-assed effort to find out where Maitland was buying, but came up with a big, fat naught. It's one of the things I want to go into more thoroughly."

"You think there's a drug angle?"

"Oh no. The PM said no evidence of habituation. No, I don't think drugs had any great importance in this. The snappers are just a loose end. But they might lead to something that leads to something. I don't like loose ends."

"You said the autopsy report said he had been drinking."

"Moderately, that morning. But I think he hit it pretty hard; his liver was enlarged. There was a half-empty bottle of whiskey in the studio, on a crate where he had been sketching. The bottle was dusted, but all they got were Maitland's prints, smudges, and a few partials of someone else. Not enough for a make. Ditto for a glass that was on the sink. It had held whiskey, the same brand that was in the bottle. Which tells us exactly nothing."

"Maybe the killer had a drink after—after he did what he did."

"Maybe," Delaney said dubiously, "but I doubt it. The bottle was at one end of the studio, the sink at the other. If the murderer had had a drink, bottle and glass would probably be close together. You said, '—after he did what he did.' *He.* How about a woman? Female killers frequently use knives. At least, more often than they do guns. Percentages again."

"I don't think a woman would stab him so many times."

"Why not?"

"I don't know . . . It just seems so—so awful."

"Man or woman, it was awful. All those stabs indicate hot blood, fury, or just an absolute need to make certain the man was dead. The strange thing is that whoever did it didn't kill him after all. Not right then. After a dozen stab wounds, he was still alive. He finally bled to death."

"Oh Edward . . ."

"I'm sorry," he said quickly, reaching out to touch her. "It upsets you. I shouldn't have started talking about it. I won't discuss it with you again."

"Oh no," she protested. "I want to hear about it. It's interesting. Fascinating, in a horrible kind of way. No, talk to me about it, Edward. Maybe I can help."

"You can, just by listening."

The doorbell chimed, and she rose to answer it.

"I still don't think it was a woman," she said firmly.

He smiled after her. He didn't think it was a woman either, but not for her reasons. He didn't think so because the PM had mentioned that several of the knife blows had been delivered with such force that the blade had penetrated completely, and the killer's knuckles had bruised the surrounding flesh. That indicated powerful thrusts, masculine power. Still, it might have been an extremely strong woman. Or an extremely enraged woman . . .

Chief Delaney's memory had been accurate: Detective sergeant Abner Boone was a tall, thin, shambling man, with floppy gestures, and a way of tilting his head to one side when he spoke. His hair was more gingery than sandy. His skin was pale and freckled. He was, Delaney guessed, somewhere between thirty and thirty-five; it was difficult to judge. He had the kind of face that would change very little in sixty years. Then, suddenly, he would be an old man.

There was an awkward, farmerish quality in his manner, in the way he bowed slightly over Monica's hand and murmured shyly, "Pleased, ma'am." His grip was firm enough and dry enough when he shook Delaney's hand, but when he was seated in one of the cracked-leather club chairs in the study, he didn't seem to know what to do with his hands—or feet either, for that matter. He kept crossing and recrossing his ankles, and he finally thrust his hands into the pockets of his worn tweed jacket. To hide a tremor, Delaney guessed.

"Would you like something?" the Chief asked. "We have some rare roast beef. How about a sandwich?"

"No, thank you, sir," Boone said faintly. "Nothing to eat. But I'd appreciate coffee. Black, please."

"I'll get a thermos," Delaney said.

When he went into the kitchen, Monica was emptying the dishwasher, putting things away on the shelves.

"What do you think?" he asked her in a low voice.

"I like him," she said promptly. "He seems so innocent."

"Innocent!"

"Well, kind of boyish. Very polite. Is he married?"

He stared at her.

"I'll find out," he said. "If not, you can alert Rebecca. Matchmaker!"

"Why not?" she giggled. "Don't you want the whole world to be as happy as we are?"

"They couldn't endure it," he assured her.

Back in the study, he poured steaming coffee for both of them. Boone

picked up his cup from the tray with both hands. Now the tremor wa
obvious.

"I suppose Deputy Commissioner Thorsen told you what the dea
is?" Delaney started.

"Just that I'll be working under you on a continuing investigation c
the Maitland thing. He said it's okay to use my own car; he'll cover m
on expenses."

"Right," Delaney nodded. "What kind of car?"

"Four-door black Pontiac."

"Good. As long as it isn't one of those little sporty jobs. I lik
to stretch my legs."

"It's not very sporty," Boone smiled wanly. "Six years old. But prett
good condition."

"Fine. Now—" Delaney paused. "What do I call you? Boone? Abner
Ab? What did the men call you?"

"Mostly they called me Daniel."

Delaney laughed.

"Should have known," he said. "Well, I prefer sergeant, if it's a
right with you?"

Boone nodded gratefully.

"I'll try to work regular hours," Delaney said. "But you may have t
put in weekends. Better warn your wife."

"I'm not married," the sergeant said.

"Oh?"

"Divorced."

"Ah. Live alone?"

"Yes."

"Well, I'll want your address and phone number before you leave
How much time did you put in on the Maitland case?"

"My squad was in on it from the start," Boone said. "I got there rig
after the body was found. Then we were in on questioning the famil
friends, acquaintances, and so forth."

"What was your take? Someone he knew?"

"Had to be. He was a big, hefty guy. And mean. He could have p
up a fight. But he turned his back on someone he knew."

"No signs of a struggle?"

"None. The studio was a mess. I mean all cluttered. But the ager
said it was always like that. It was the way Maitland lived. But no sign

of a fight. No chairs knocked over or anything broken. Nothing like that. He turned his back, bought it, and went down. That simple."

"Woman?" Delaney asked.

"Don't think so, sir. But possible."

Delaney thought a moment.

"Your squad check the snappers?"

Boone was confused, twisting his fingers.

"Uh—ah—I really don't know about the snappers, Chief. I got taken off the case. Thorsen tell you? About my trouble?"

"He told me," Delaney said grimly. "He also told me that if you fuck-up once more, you're out."

Boone nodded miserably.

"When did it start?" Delaney asked. "The divorce?"

"No," Boone said. "Before that. The divorce was one of the results, not the cause."

"A lot of cops crawl into a bottle," Delaney said. "Pressures. The filth."

"The pressures I could take," Boone said, raising his head. "I took them for almost ten years. The filth got to me. What people do. To each other. To themselves. I was handling it—the disgust, I mean—then I caught a sex case. Two beautiful little girls. Sisters. Cut. Burned. Everything. It pushed me over the edge. No excuse. Just an explanation. The only choice was to get hard or to get drunk. I had to sleep."

"You're not a religious man?"

"No," Boone said. "I was a Baptist originally, but I don't work at it."

"Well, sergeant," Edward X. Delaney said coldly, "don't expect any sympathy from me. Or advice. You're a grown man; it's your choice. If you can't hack it, I'll have to tell Thorsen to give me someone else."

"I know that, sir."

"As long as you know it. Let's get back to the case . . . I've read the file, but I'll have some questions on your personal reactions as we go along. For instance, what's your take on Maitland?"

"Everyone says he was the greatest painter in the country, but an A-Number-One shit. Some evidence he beat his wife. His son hated him. Still does, I guess. Humiliated his agent in public. Always getting into brawls. I mean breaking up bars and restaurants. A mean drunk. Got beaten up himself several times. Things like insulting a woman who was with a guy bigger than Maitland. Crazy things. Like he *wanted* to be kicked to hell and gone. A hard guy to figure. I guess he had talent to burn, but he was one miserable human being."

"Miserable?" Delaney picked up on that. "You mean he himself was miserable, like sad, or he was a poor excuse for a human being?"

Boone pondered a moment.

"Both ways, I'd guess," he said finally. "A very complex guy. Before I got taken off the case, I bought a book of his paintings and went to see the ones in the Geltman Galleries and in the museums. I figured if I could get a handle on the guy, maybe it would help me find who offed him, and why."

Delaney looked at him with surprised admiration.

"Good idea," he said. "Learn anything?"

"No, sir. Nothing. Maybe it was me. I don't know much about painting."

"You still have that book? Of Maitland's paintings?"

"Sure. It's around somewhere."

"Can I borrow it?"

"Of course."

"Thank you. Tomorrow's Friday. The PM says he was knocked on Friday, between ten and three in the afternoon. Can you pick me up tomorrow morning around nine? I want to go down to that Mott Street studio and look around. And the neighborhood. We'll be there from ten to three, when it happened."

Abner Boone looked at him intently.

"Anything special, Chief?" he asked.

Delaney shook his head.

"Not a whisper," he said. "Just noodling. But we got to start somewhere."

He saw the sergeant brighten and straighten when he said "we."

Both men stood up. Then Boone hesitated.

"Chief, did they send you the inventory of Maitland's personal effects from the ME's office?"

"Yes, I got it."

"Spot anything unusual?"

"Nooo," Delaney said. "Did I miss something?"

"Not something that was on the list," Boone said. "Something that wasn't." Suddenly, unexpectedly, he blushed. His pale face reddened; the freckles disappeared. "The guy wasn't wearing any underwear."

Delaney looked at him, startled.

"You're sure?"

Boone nodded. "I checked it out with the guys who stripped the corpse at the morgue. No underwear."

"Odd. What do you make of it?"

"Nothing," Boone said. "I had a session with a Department shrink—I guess Thorsen told you about that—and just for the hell of it I asked him what about a guy who didn't wear underwear. He gave me the usual bullshit answer: it might be significant, and it might not."

Delaney nodded and said, "That's the trouble. In a case like this, it's a temptation to see all facts as of equal significance. They're not. But crossing off the meaningless stuff takes just as much time as tracking down what's important. Well, we've got plenty of time. The Department really doesn't expect a break on this. See you in the morning, sergeant."

Boone nodded, and they shook hands again. The sergeant seemed a little more cheerful, or a little less beaten. He left his address and phone number. Delaney saw him out, locked and chained the door behind him.

Monica was motionless in bed, but stirred when Delaney began undressing.

"Well?" she asked.

"Divorced," he reported.

"That's nice," she said drowsily. "I'll call Rebecca in the morning."

4

They parked on Houston Street and got out of the car.

"Aren't you going to show an 'Officer on Duty' card?" Delaney asked.

"Don't think I better, Chief," Abner Boone said. "The last time I displayed it, they stole my hubcaps."

Delaney smiled, then looked around slowly. He told Boone of the tour of duty he had served in this precinct twenty years ago.

"It was all Italian then," he said. "But I guess it's changed."

Boone nodded. "Some blacks. Lots of Puerto Ricans. But mostly Chinese moving up across Canal Street. Mulberry Street is still Italian though. Good restaurants."

"I remember," Delaney said. "I could eat those cannoli like there was no tomorrow."

They sauntered over to Mott Street, then turned south. The Chief looked up at the red-brick tenements.

"It hasn't changed all that much," he said. "The first day I was down here I got hit by airmail. You know what that is?"

"Sure," Boone grinned. "Flying garbage. They throw it out the windows into the street."

When he grinned, the boyishness Monica had noted became more evident. He had big, horsey teeth, but they didn't seem out of place in his long, smooth face. His eyes were pale blue, small and watchful. He walked in a kind of springy, loose-limbed lope, all the more youthful in contrast to Delaney's heavy, splay-footed trundle.

It was a warm, hazy May morning, beginning to heat up. But there was a dark cloud bank hovering over New Jersey; the air smelled of rain.

"Do you remember the weather for that Friday?" Delaney asked. "When Maitland died?"

"Clear, bright, but about ten degrees colder than it is now. It rained on Saturday. When we got there on Sunday, it was grey and overcast. Clammy."

Delaney stopped at Prince Street and looked around.

"Lots of traffic," he said. "Lots of activity."

"One of the problems," Boone said. "So busy that no one saw nothing. The precinct had Italian- and Spanish-speaking cops do the door-to-doors. No one offered anything. I don't think they were covering; they honestly didn't see. Probably one guy in and out in five minutes. Who's to notice?"

"No screams? No thumps or crash when Maitland fell?"

"There are ten apartments in his building. Everyone was at work or out shopping except for a deaf old lady on the third floor, a guy who works nights sleeping on the second, and the super and his wife in the basement. None of them heard anything, didn't see anything. They say."

"No lock on the outside door of the house?"

"Supposed to be, but it had been jimmied so many times, the super gave up trying to fix it. Anyone could have walked right up those stairs."

"What's the break-in rate on the street?"

Boone flipped a palm back and forth.

"About average, sir. Not the best, not the worst."

They crossed Prince Street, walking slowly, looking about.

"Why did he have his studio down here?" Delaney wondered. "He could have afforded something better than this, couldn't he? He had money."

"Oh, he had plenty of money," Boone nodded. "No doubt about that. And spent it as fast as he made it, according to his wife. We asked his agent the same thing—why he worked down here. The answers weren't logical, but I guess they make sense considering the kind of man he was. This was where he lived and worked when he first came to New York and was just getting started. This was where he did the first paintings that sold. He was superstitious and thought the place brought him luck. So he kept it as a studio after he got married and moved uptown. Also, it was off the beaten track. The guy was a loner. He hated the usual art-colony bullshit of Greenwich Village. He got sore when the galleries spread to SoHo, and more and more artists began taking lofts across Lafayette south of Houston, and even on the Bowery. He told his agent the shitheads were surrounding him, and if it got any worse, he'd have to find some place the art-fuckers hadn't discovered yet. That's Mait-land's phrase: 'Art-fuckers.' Here, this is the house, Chief."

It was a grimy red-brick building exactly like dozens of others on the street. A stoop of nine grey stone steps leading up to an outer door. The first-floor apartments on either side had rusted iron grilles over their dusty windows.

"I know the layout," Delaney said. "And this wasn't in the file; I've seen hundreds of tenements like this. Two apartments on each floor. Railroad flats running front to back. The super's apartment in the base-ment. He can enter through that door in the areaway under the steps, but he usually keeps it locked and goes in through the hallway and down a flight of backstairs to the basement. In addition to his apart-ment, the cellar's got the boiler, heater, fuse boxes, and so forth. Storage space. And a back door that opens out into a little paved courtyard. Maitland's studio on the fifth floor was one big room—the whole floor. Sink and tub, but toilet in a little closet on the top stairway landing. How's that?"

"You got it, sir," Boone said admiringly. "The door in the basement, the one to the backyard, is kept locked. It's got iron bars with a chain and padlock on it. It wasn't touched. Our guy didn't get out that way. Besides, the super and his wife were in their apartment. They said they'd have heard someone in the basement. They didn't."

"Let's go," Delaney said.

They trudged up the steps. The outer door was not only unlocked but unlatched; it swung open a few inches. Delaney paused to look at the names on the mailboxes.

"Mostly Italians," he noted. "One Spanish. One Chinese. One 'Smith' that could be anything."

The inner door was also unlocked, the handle missing.

"He said he'd replace it," Boone said.

"Maybe he did," Delaney said mildly. "Maybe someone busted the new one."

There were two short flights of stairs between floors. They went up slowly. They were on the third-floor landing when one of the doors jerked open to the length of its chain, and an angry woman poked her face out at them. She had a head of bright red hair wound around beer-can curlers. She was wearing a wrapper of hellish design she kept clutched to her scrawny neck.

"I seen you staring at the house," she accused them. "Watcha want? I'll call the cops."

"We *are* the cops, ma'am," Boone said softly. He showed the woman his ID. "Nothing to fret about. Just taking another look upstairs."

"You catch him yet?" the woman demanded.

"Not yet."

"Shit!" the woman said disgustedly, and slammed her door shut. They heard the sound of locks being turned and bolts being closed. They continued their climb.

"Where was she when we needed her?" Delaney growled.

They paused on the top landing, both of them breathing heavily. Delaney looked into the WC. Nothing but a stained toilet. The tank was up near the ceiling, flushed by pulling a wooden handle attached to a tarnished brass chain. There was one small window of frosted glass, cracked.

"Unheated," Delaney remarked. "In winter, a place like this could make it a pleasure to be constipated."

Boone looked at him, starled by the Chief's levity. They moved over to stand before the door of Victor Maitland's studio. There was a shiny new hasp and padlock. There was also a sign tacked to the door: THESE PREMISES HAVE BEEN SEALED BY THE INTERNAL REVENUE SERVICE, AN AGENCY OF THE U.S. GOVERNMENT. In smaller type, the sign detailed what an interloper might expect in the way of imprisonment, a fine, or both.

"Ah, hell," Boone said. "What's this about?"

"He died intestate," Delaney said. "No will. That means the IRS wants to make sure it gets its share of the goodies. Also, the IRS had a back claim he'd been fighting for years. Well . . . what do we do now?"

Boone glanced around.

"Uh, Chief . . ." he said in a low voice. "Uh, I got a set of picks. Okay?"

Delaney stared at him.

"Sergeant," he said, "you're looking better to me every minute. Sure okay."

Abner Boone took a flat pouch of black suede from his inside jacket pocket. He inspected the heavy padlock, then selected one of the picks— a long, thin sliver of stainless steel with a tiny hook at one end. Boone inserted the hook end into the keyhole of the padlock. He probed delicately, staring up at the ceiling. The pick caught. Boone turned his wrist slowly. The lock popped open.

"Very nice," Delaney said. "And the first time you've done it, too."

Boone smiled and put his picks away. He pushed the door open. They entered, closed the door behind them.

"Stand right here," Delaney commanded. "Take a good look around. See if it's all about the same as it was when the body was found. Anything out of place? Anything missing? Take your time."

He waited patiently while Boone inspected the interior of the studio. Sunshine was flooding through the overhead skylight. One of the panes of glass was broken and had been stuffed with a blue rag. There was a wire mesh over the skylight. But no ventilator. The room smelled musty, spoiled.

Delaney glanced at his watch.

"About ten-thirty," he said. "It must have looked like this six weeks ago. You said it was a bright, clear day, so he wouldn't be using the lamps. The sun is higher now, of course, but it should be just about as it was."

"I don't see anything missing or out of place," Boone said. "I have the feeling that glass on the drainboard was closer to the sink than it is now. They moved it after dusting. And the mattress on the cot was flipped. Old semen stains on the top side. Nothing fresh. Otherwise, it looks exactly the same to me."

"Were the windows open?"

"No, sir. Shut, like they are now."

"Radio on?"

"No. Switched off. That stuff at the far end, all his paints and brushes and rolls of canvas, all that mess, that's not in the original position because we went through it. But as far as I know, nothing was taken. We left it all right here."

"No paintings?"

"No. The agent said he had just finished a series and brought the last to the Geltman Galleries. There's a couple of rough sketches on the floor. The agent wanted to take them, but we wouldn't let him. He said they might have been Maitland's last work and belonged to the estate."

Delaney walked over to the chalked outline on the floor and stared down. The wood around it was stained a dark brown, almost black in patches.

"The outline about right?" he asked Boone.

"About. The right arm, here, wasn't exactly straight. More bent at the elbow. And the knees were bent a little. But he went down flat on his face and spread out."

Delaney knelt by the rude outline of the dead painter, staring at it through half-closed eyes.

"Was his face right down on the floor?"

"Turned a little to the left maybe, but mostly straight down."

"Do you know where he carried his wallet?"

"We figured right hip pocket. He had a comb in his left hip. His wife and agent confirmed."

The Chief stood up, dusting his knees.

"Smell?" he asked.

"Plenty," Boone said. "That was a warm, clammy weekend."

"No, no," Delaney said. "I mean, did anyone get down on him to smell him?"

Abner Boone was bewildered.

"No one I saw, Chief," he said. "What for?"

"Oh . . ." Delaney said vaguely. "You never know . . ."

He went over to the sink, inspecting the stained basin and the drainboard.

"The drain searched?"

"Sure. And the tub drain. And the toilet and the tank."

The old-fashioned bathtub, on claw feet, had a white enameled metal lid. Delaney lifted it to peer underneath, then crouched to look under the tub.

"Roaches," he reported.

"Plenty of those," Boone nodded. "All over. He wasn't exactly what you'd call Mister Clean."

Delaney walked slowly toward the front of the studio. He paused at the platform under the skylight.

"What's this thing?" he asked.

"The agent said it's a posing dais. The model got up there when Maitland was making drawings or paintings."

Delaney moved around the clutter on the floor, stopped, looked down.

"I can figure what most of this stuff is," he said. "But why the saw, nails, hammer? And that thing—that claw—what's that?"

"Geltman said Maitland stretched his own canvas. Bought it in rolls. Made a wood frame, then stretched the canvas over it and tacked it down. The claw helped him pull the canvas taut. Those little wooden wedges went into the inside corners of the frame to help keep the canvas tight."

"What's this black stuff near the wall? Black crumbs?"

"Pieces of a charcoal stick. The agent helped us identify all this shit. It seems Maitland used charcoal sticks for sketching. Most artists use pencils."

"Why all the little pieces?"

"It breaks easily. But there's a mark on the wall, up there, to your right. Looks like Maitland threw the stick at the wall. Geltman says he'd do something like that."

"Why?"

"He didn't know, unless Maitland's work wasn't going good and he got sore."

Delaney picked up the two sketches from the floor, handling them with his fingernails at the corners, and brought them closer to the front windows to examine them.

"There's a third drawing on the pad on the crate," Boone said. "Half-finished. And there's half a charcoal stick alongside it. The agent said it looked to him like Maitland was doing the third sketch, the charcoal stick broke in two, and Maitland threw the piece he was holding at the wall."

Delaney didn't reply. He was staring at the drawings, awed. Maitland had been putting a three-dimensional torso on two-dimensional paper, working with hard, bold strokes of his charcoal. There was no conventional shading; the line itself suggested the modeling of the flesh. But in two places he had made fast smudges with thumb or finger to suggest hollow and shadow.

The body was that of a young girl, juicy, bursting. You could almost feel the heat. She stood bent over in a distorted pose that bunched muscles, jutted breasts. Maitland had caught swoop of back, flare of hips, sweet curve of shoulder and arm. The face, in profile, was barely suggested; something vaguely Oriental about it. But the body, to the knees, leapt from the white paper. The black lines seemed alive, seemed to writhe. There was no doubt that a heart pumped, breath flowed, blood coursed.

"Jesus," Delaney said in a low voice. "I don't care what the guy was, he shouldn't be dead." Then, in a louder voice, he asked: "Did the agent know when these were done?"

"No, sir. Could have been that morning. Could have been a week before. He had never seen them before."

"Did he know the model?"

"Said not. Said the sketches looked to him like preliminary work, the kind of throwaway stuff Maitland might try with a new model. To see if he could catch what he wanted."

"Throwaway stuff? Not these. I'm going to take them. I'll return them to the estate. Eventually. Where's the third?"

"Here. Still on the crate."

Chief Delaney inspected the still life atop the rough crate: sketchpad propped on a can of turpentine, half a charcoal stick, bottle of whiskey. He looked from the whiskey to the studio entrance and back again. Then he tore the third drawing from the pad and flipped through the remaining pages to make certain there was nothing more. There wasn't. He carefully rolled the three sketches into a tight tube. Then he looked around.

"Can't think of anything else," he said. "Can you?"

"No, Chief. There was no address book. No books at all. A few old newspapers under the sink, some catalogues from art-supply stores. There're a few numbers written on the wall near the telephone. We checked them out. A neighborhood liquor store that delivers. Ditto for a delicatessen over on Lafayette. The number for an artist friend named Jake Dukker. He's in the file. That's all there was. No letters, no bills, nothing. A few pieces of old clothes in the chest of drawers. Most of his personal stuff he kept uptown in his apartment. Not that that was of any more help."

They put the padlock back on the door and trudged downstairs. The red-haired woman stuck her face out again.

"Well?" she demanded.

"Good day, madam," Edward X. Delaney said politely, lifting his homburg.

Out on the street Abner Boone said, "If the IRS comes around asking questions, she can make us."

"Conjecture," Delaney said, shrugging. "She didn't actually see us *in* the place. Don't worry; if necessary, Thorsen will scam it."

They strolled back to Houston Street in silence. Boone walked around his car, inspecting it. It hadn't been touched. They got in, and Delaney lighted a cigar. Boone found him a rubber band in the cluttered glove compartment to put around his roll of drawings. The sergeant had also brought the book of Maitland's paintings, in an old manila envelope. Delaney held it on his lap. He didn't open it.

They sat awhile in silence, their comfort with each other growing. Boone lighted a cigarette. His fingers were stained yellow.

"I'm trying to cut down," he told Delaney.

"Any luck?"

"No. Since I've been off the sauce, it's worse."

The Chief nodded, put his head back against the seat rest. He stared through the windshield at a noontime game of stickball being played in the middle of traffic on Houston Street.

"Let's play games, too," he said dreamily, not looking at Boone. "Try this on for size . . . Maitland picks up a young twist. On the street, in a bar, anywhere. Maybe he figures she really would make a good model—that body in the drawings is something—or maybe it's just his con to get a slab on the mat. Anyway, she shows up at the studio Friday morning. She strips. He does the sketches of her. I don't know what *he* thought of them; I think they're great. The charcoal stick breaks on the third drawing. Maitland throws the piece in his hand against the wall. Maybe he's sore it broke, maybe he's just feeling frisky. Who knows? He gives the bimbo a drink. Near the sink and cot. Those are her partials on the glass. Maybe they talk money. He boffs her or he doesn't boff her. She leaves. He locks the door, goes back to the crate with the bottle of whiskey, looks at his sketches. Knock-knock at the door. Who is it? Someone answers, a voice he recognizes. He puts the bottle on the crate, goes to the door, unlocks it. The door opens. The guy comes in. Maitland turns his back and walks away. *Fini.* How does it grab you?"

"Motive?"

"Jesus Christ, sergeant, I haven't even *begun* to think about that. I don't know enough. I'm just trying to figure what happened that Friday morning. The action. How does it listen?"

"Possible," Boone said. "It covers all the bases. They might have screwed around for an hour or two. The killing was some time between ten and three."

"Right."

"But there's no hard evidence to show her presence. Those sketches could have been done a week before Maitland was snuffed. There's no face powder, no bobby pins, no lipstick smears on the glass. Just that one safety pin."

Delaney jerked erect. Whirled. Stared at Boone.

"That what?" he said furiously.

"The safety pin, sir. On the floor near the cot. Wasn't it in the file?"

"No, goddamn it, it wasn't in the file."

"Should have been, Chief," Boone said softly. "One safety pin. Open. The lab boys took it to check it out. No different from zillions of others. Sold in a million stores."

"How long was it?"

Boone held thumb and forefinger apart.

"Like so. About an inch. No fibers or hairs on it. Nothing to indicate if Maitland used it or if it belonged to a broad."

"Shiny?"

"Oh yes. It had been used recently."

"Definitely a woman's," Delaney said. "What's Maitland going to do with it—hold up the underwear he wasn't wearing? No, a young piece was there that morning."

They were both silent on the long, slow ride uptown. Around Fourteenth Street, Delaney said, "Sergeant, I'm sorry I barked at you about that safety pin not being in the reports. I know it wasn't your fault."

Boone turned briefly to give him that boyish grin.

"Bark all you like, Chief," he said. "I've taken worse than that."

"Haven't we all," Delaney said. "Look, I've been thinking . . . I've been in this business a long time, and I know, I *know* there are a lot of things that don't go into the reports. An investigating officer can't put *everything* down in writing, or he'd spend his life behind a typewriter and have no time for investigating. Just the act of making out a report is a process of selection. The officer picks out what he thinks is meaningful, what's significant. He doesn't include in the record that the guy he was tailing was chewing gum, or the woman he questioned was wearing Chanel Five perfume. He leaves out all the innocuous crap. Or what he *thinks* is innocuous. You understand? He reports only what he thinks is important. Or really what he thinks his superior will think is important. Agree so far?"

"To a point," Boone said cautiously. "Sometimes an officer might include something that doesn't mean much to him, but it's so unusual, so odd or different that he figures the higher-ups should know about it."

"Then he's a good cop, because that's exactly what he should do. Even if nothing comes of it. And if it turns out to be hot, then he's off the hook, because he filed it. Right?"

"Right, sir. I agree with you there."

"But still," Delaney persisted, "a lot of stuff never gets put down. Little-bitty things. Most of it's nothing and never should be reported. But sometimes, very occasionally, if it had been reported, it would have helped break a case a lot sooner. I worked a homicide up in the Two-oh. A strangling in this big apartment house. Ten apartments on the floor. Naturally, the neighbors were questioned. No one heard a thing; the hallway had a thick carpet. One old dame mentioned that the only thing she heard was a dog sniffing under her door and making little whining sounds. But it doesn't mean anything, she tells the dick, because four people on that floor have dogs, and they're always taking them for walks. And the moron takes her word for it and doesn't put it in his report. Two weeks later we're at a standstill and start all over again. The old lady tells about the dog sniffing under her door again. This time it's in a report, and the lieutenant has me check all the people on that floor who own dogs. None of them took their dog for a walk at that time. But the guy who got strangled, he had a rough boyfriend, and *he* had a dog. Never went out without him. So one thing led to another, and we nailed him. If that miserable sniffing dog had been mentioned in an early report, we'd have saved a month of migraine. Now a lot of men were working on the Maitland thing, and I know there was stuff that's not in those records. I'm not blaming the men. I know their workload. But it's possible that some things they sluffed in the scramble to break this case would be a big help to you and me, now that we've got all the time in the world to look into every little thing with no one breathing down our necks."

Boone picked up on it at once.

"What do you want me to do, Chief?"

"You know most of the men who worked on the case—at least the heavies—and you can talk to them better than I could. Whenever we're not working together, I want you to go see these guys, or call them, and ask them if there was anything they remember that wasn't reported. I mean *anything!* Tell them they won't get their ass in a sling. You won't even tell me their names. That's the truth. I don't want to know their names. But see if you can get them to dredge their memories and come up with something they didn't report. Someone must have seen something or heard something. It doesn't have to be big. In fact, if it was big, it would probably be in the file. What I'm looking for are odds and ends, little inconsequential things. You understand, sergeant?"

"Sure," Abner Boone said. "When do you want me to get started?"

"This afternoon. Will you drop me at home, please? I have enough to keep me busy for the rest of the day. You can start looking up the men who worked on the Maitland case. And while you're at it, drop by the labs, or call them, and find out why that safety pin wasn't mentioned in their analysis of physical evidence. Maybe it was, and I missed it. But I don't think so. I think it was a foul-up, and it scares me, because maybe it happened more than once and there are things I won't know about by reading the file. That's why I'm happy you're working with me."

Sergeant Boone was happy, too, and showed it.

"One more thing," Delaney said. "I intend to write up a report of this morning's visit to Maitland's studio. What I saw, what I found, what I took. I'll write a daily report of my investigation, just as if I was on active duty. I want you to write daily reports, too. You'll find they'll be a big help to keep things straight."

"All right, sir," Boone said doubtfully. "If you say so."

He let Delaney out in front of his brownstone. The Chief came around the car and leaned down to Boone's open window.

"Did Deputy Commissioner Thorsen tell you to keep him privately informed on the progress of my investigation?" he asked.

Boone lowered his head, blushed again, the freckles lost.

"I'm sorry, Chief," he mumbled. "I had no choice."

Delaney put a hand on the man's arm.

"Report to him," he told Boone. "Do just as he ordered. It's all right."

He turned and marched up the steps into the house. Boone watched the door close behind him.

Delaney hung his homburg on the hall rack, carried his drawings and book directly into the study, put them on his desk, and then came back into the hallway.

"Monica?" he called.

"Upstairs, dear," she called back. She came to the head of the stairway. "Did you have lunch?"

"No, but I'm not hungry. I think I'll skip. Maybe I'll just have a beer."

"If you want a sandwich, there's ham and cheese. But don't touch the beef; that's for tonight."

He went into the kitchen and opened the refrigerator door. He took out a can of beer, peeled off the flip-top. The bulk of the rib roast, the leftovers wrapped in aluminum foil, caught his eye. He stared at it, then resolutely shut the door. He went toward the study, hesitated, stopped. Out into the hallway. Peered up. No Monica. Back to the kitchen. Sharp carving knife. Swiftly took the beef out, peeled away the foil. There, pinned to the meat with a toothpick, a little note: "Only one sandwich. M." He laughed and made his one sandwich, taking it with the beer into the study.

He unrolled the sketches on his desk and weighted the corners so the paper would lose its curl. Then he took Sergeant Boone's book of the paintings of Victor Maitland from the envelope. He settled down in his swivel chair and put on his reading glasses. He flipped through the book quickly.

It was practically all black-and-white and full-color reproductions of Maitland's paintings on slick paper. The limited text consisted of a short introduction, a biography of the artist, a listing of his complete *oeuvre,* and an essay by an art critic analyzing Maitland's work. Chief Delaney was not familiar with the critic's name, but his professional record, stated in the introduction, was impressive. Delaney began to read.

He learned little from the biography that had not been included in the copies of the Department's records sent over by Deputy Commissioner Thorsen. The essay by the art critic, although attempting to be moderate and judicial in tone, added up to a paean. According to the writer, Victor Maitland had breathed fresh life into the techniques of the great Italian masters, had turned his back on the transient fads and fashions of contemporary art and, going his own way, had imbued the traditional, representational style of painting with a fervor, a passion that had not been seen for centuries.

There was much more of a technical nature that Edward X. Delaney could not completely comprehend. But it was not difficult to understand the critic's admiration, his *awe* at what Maitland had done. "Awe" was the word used in the text. Delaney responded to it because it was exactly what he had felt on first looking at those rough sketches in Maitland's studio. Not only awe at the man's talent, but wonder and a kind of dread in seeing beauty he had never known existed.

"At last," the critic concluded, "America has a painter of the first magnitude who devotes his art to the celebration of life."

But not for long, Delaney thought morosely. Then, standing, the better to view the illustrations in the oversized book, he began slowly to turn the pages engraved with the paintings of Victor Maitland.

He went through them twice, turned back a third time to a few that had particularly moved him. Then he closed the book softly, moved away from the desk. He saw his sandwich and beer, untouched. He took them to one of the club chairs, sat down, began to eat and drink slowly. The beer was warmish and flat by now, but he didn't care.

He was an untrained amateur when it came to the appreciation of art. He acknowledged this. But he loved painting and sculpture. And the cool, ordered ambience of museums, the richness of gilt frames, the elegance of marble pedestals. He had tried to educate himself by reading books of art history and art criticism. But he found the language so recondite that he wondered if it was not deliberately designed to obfuscate and confuse the uninitiated. But, he admitted, the fault might be his: an inability to grasp art theory, to follow the turgid logic of cubists, dadaists, abstractionists, and all the other art "schools" that followed one after another in such rapid and bewildering succession.

Finally, he was forced back to his own eye, his own taste: that much scorned cliché "I know what I like when I see it," sensing dimly that it served for the butcher who liked sunsets painted on black velvet as well as for the most ideological of art experts who wrote knowingly of asymmetrical tensions, ovular torpidity, and exogenous calcification.

Edward X. Delaney liked paintings that were recognizable. A nude was a nude, an apple an apple, a house a house. He found technique interesting and enjoyable; the folds of satin in the paintings of Ingres were a delight. But technique was never enough. To be truly satisfying, a painting had to *move* him, to cause a flopover inside him when he looked upon life revealed. A painting did not have to be beautiful; it had to be true. Then it was beautiful.

Munching his cold roast beef, sipping his tepid beer, he reflected that most of Victor Maitland's paintings were true. Delaney not only saw it, he felt it. There were a few still lifes, one or two portraits, several cityscapes. But Maitland had painted mostly the female nude. Young women and old women, girls and harridans. Many of the subjects were certainly not beautiful, but all of the paintings were bursting with that "celebration of life" the critic had noted.

But that was not what impressed Chief Delaney most about Maitland's work. It was the purpose of the artist, the use he made of his talent. There was something frantic there, something almost deranged. It was, Delaney thought, a superhuman striving to be aware of life and capture it with cold paint on rough canvas. It was a manic greed to know it all, own it all, and to display the plunder.

5

"I'm having lunch with Rebecca," Monica said.

"That's nice," Chief Delaney said, flapping a "commuter fold" into his copy of *The New York Times*.

"Then we might go shopping," Monica said.

"I'm listening, dear," he said, reading of the aborted plan of a Central American politico to sell 10,000 submachine guns to the Mafia.

"Then we'll probably come back here," Monica said. "For a cup of coffee. At three o'clock."

He put down his paper, stared at her.

"Do you know what you're doing?" he asked. "The man's a heavy drinker, a *very* heavy drinker."

"You said he's off it."

"*He* said he's off it. Do you really want to mate your best friend with an alcoholic?"

"Well, it surely wouldn't do any harm if they just met. By accident. It doesn't mean they have to get married tomorrow."

"I wash my hands of the entire affair," he said sternly.

"Then you'll bring him back here around three?" she asked.

He groaned.

Sergeant Abner Boone was parked in front of the Delaney home, reading the *Daily News*. When the Chief got into the car, Boone tossed the newspaper onto the back seat.

"Morning, Chief," he said.

"Morning," Delaney said. He gestured at the newspaper. "What's new?"

"Nothing much. They fished a car out of the East River. They opened the trunk, and lo and behold, there was old Sam Zuckerman, sent to his reward with an ice pick."

"Zuckerman? I don't make him."

"He owned a string of massage parlors on the West Side. I guess someone wanted to buy in, and Sam said no. We've been playing pitty-pat with him for years. We'd jail him and leave the door open because Sam would be out on the street in an hour. He must have spent a fortune on lawyers. But of course he had a fortune. Now Sam's gone to the great massage parlor in the sky."

"How did you make out?" Delaney asked.

Boone took out a small, black leather notebook and flipped the pages.

"About the safety pin . . ." he said. "The way I get it, the guy in the lab was making out the physical-evidence list. In the middle, he gets a call from the lieutenant of the homicide unit asking about the pin. The lab guy tells him it's an ordinary pin, no way to trace it, no fibers caught in it, no hair, nothing. They talk about the pin for a couple of minutes and hang up. Then the lab guy was interrupted. His words, and I quote: 'Then I was interrupted,' unquote. He didn't say whether he went to lunch, got a call from his wife, or went to the can, and I didn't push it. After the interruption, whatever it was, he continues typing out the list. But because the conversation with the lieutenant is fresh in his mind, he thought he had already included the safety pin. So, naturally, it got left out."

Delaney was silent. Boone looked sideways at him.

"It was just a human error, Chief."

"Is there any other kind?" Delaney asked sourly. "All right, we'll forget about it. Did you make any calls to the men who worked on the Maitland case?"

Boone sat quietly a moment, tapping his notebook on his knee, staring straight ahead.

"Chief," he said finally, "maybe I'm not the right guy for this job. I called three men who worked the case. I've known them for years. They were friendly, but cool. They all know the trouble I'm in, and they didn't want to be too buddy-buddy. You understand? Like I had a contagious disease, and they might catch it."

"I understand," Delaney said. "A natural reaction. I've seen it before."

"That's one thing," Boone said. "The other is that they all know I'm working with you on the Maitland thing. I don't think they'll be too happy to see us break it. They put in long hours, a lot of hard work, and came up with a horse collar. Then we come along—and bingo? It doesn't set so good. It would make them look like bums. So they're not too anxious to cooperate."

Delaney sighed.

"Well . . ." he said. "That, too, is a normal reaction. I guess. I should have anticipated. So you got nothing?"

"I called three. Nothing from two of them. In fact, they got a little sore. They said I was hinting their records weren't complete, that they had left something out. I tried to explain that it wasn't like that at all, that we just wanted the little useless junk that every cop runs across in an investigation. But they said there was nothing that wasn't in their reports. The third guy was more sympathetic. He understood what we were after, but he said he had nothing."

"So that's that," Delaney said resignedly.

"No, no," Boone protested. "There's more. That third guy called me back about an hour later. He said he had been thinking about what I said, and he remembered one thing he saw that he didn't put in his report. He was one of the guys who questioned Jake Dukker, Maitland's artist friend. This Dukker is a rich, fancy guy with a studio on Central Park South. He's even got a secretary. This dick goes up to question Dukker, and the secretary shows him into the studio and says Dukker will be with him in a few minutes. So while the guy is waiting, he looks around. The walls of Dukker's studio are covered with drawings and paintings, apparently all of them by friends of Dukker. And this dick sees a signed drawing by Victor Maitland in a frame with glass over it. But what he remembered was that the drawing had been torn. It had been torn down the middle, and then the two pieces had been torn across. But the four pieces had been put back together again with Scotch tape, and then framed. This cop I talked to didn't know what that meant, if anything. I don't either."

"I don't either," Chief Delaney said. "Not now. But it's exactly the kind of thing I was hoping to learn. Keep at it, sergeant; maybe we'll pick up some more bits and pieces."

"Will do."

"I called the widow and Saul Geltman, and set up appointments to see them today. Mrs. Maitland is first at ten this morning. It's on East Fifty-eighth. You know the address?"

"Sure. Chief, how come you called them first? Wouldn't it make more sense to walk in on them unexpectedly, so they have no time to set up a con?"

"Ordinarily it would," Delaney agreed. "But everyone involved in this case has been questioned a dozen times already. They've got their stories down pat. True or false. Let's get started."

Boone drove over to Second Avenue and turned south. Morning traffic was heavy; they seemed to hit a red light every block or so. But Delaney made no comment. He was engrossed in his own little black notebook, flipping pages.

"How did you handle the questioning?" he asked Boone.

"By the book. We sent three or four different guys for the first three or four sessions with each subject. Then those guys would get together with the lieutenant and compare notes. Then they'd figure which guy got the most, which guy had established the best relationship with the subject. That guy would go back for a final session, or more if needed."

"Who did you handle?"

"Me personally? I had one session with Mrs. Maitland, one with Geltman, and two with Belle Sarazen, the woman Maitland was screwing. Then I got taken off the case."

Chief Delaney didn't ask for Boone's reactions to these witnesses, and the sergeant didn't volunteer any.

The Maitland apartment was a duplex occupying the top two floors of what had originally been a private townhouse on East 58th Street between First Avenue and Sutton Place. It was an elegant building, with a uniformed doorman and tight security. Boone gave their names and showed his ID. They waited while the doorman announced their arrival over an intercom. When he got approval, he directed them to the single elevator at the side of the small lobby.

"Fourth floor rear, gents," he told them, but Delaney didn't move.

The doorman was big, fleshy, red-faced. His uniform might have fit him once, a few years ago. Now the jacket was straining at its brass buttons.

"We're investigating the Maitland murder," Delaney said.

"Still?" the man said.

"You knew him?" Delaney asked.

"Sure, I knew him," the doorman said. "Listen, I told this to a dozen cops. I answered a hundert questions."

"Tell *me*," Delaney said. "What kind of a guy was he?"

"Like I told the others, an okay guy. A heavy tipper. Very heavy."

"Ever see him drunk?"

"Does a goat smell? Sure, I seen him drunk. Lots of times. He'd have a load on, and I'd help him out of the cab, into the elevator, up to his door. Then I'd ring the bell for him. The next day he'd always give me a little something."

"They have many friends, the Maitlands?" Delaney asked. "Guests? Did they entertain a lot?"

"Not so much," the doorman said. "Mrs. Maitland, she has lady friends. Once or twice a year maybe they'd have a party. Not like Jacobson on two. That guy never stops."

"Maitland ever bring a woman home with him?"

The doorman's jaw clamped, his beefy face grew redder.

"Come on," Delaney urged.

"Onct," the doorman whispered. "Just onct. The wife raised holy hell. A real bimbo he brought home. She came flying down out of here about five minutes after she came."

"When was this?"

"About a year ago. The only time since I been dooring here. Seven years come July."

"The son ever bring a girl home?"

"I never seen one. Maybe a couple would come in with him. Not a single girl."

"You smoke cigars?" Delaney asked.

"What?" the doorman said, startled. "Sure, I smoke cigars."

Delaney reached into his inside pocket, brought out a pigskin case, a Christmas gift from Monica. He took off the top, held the filled case out to the doorman.

"Have a cigar," he said.

The doorman took one daintily, with the tips of his fingers.

"Thanks," he said gratefully. "Would you believe it, it's the first time in my whole life a cop gave me something."

"I believe it," Delaney said.

Alma Maitland was waiting for them outside the door of her fourth-floor apartment.

"I was afraid you got lost," she said. Cold smile.

"The elevator was busy," Delaney said, taking off his homburg. "Mrs. Maitland? I am Chief Edward X. Delaney. This gentleman is Detective sergeant Abner Boone."

She offered a cool hand to each of them.

"I've already met Sergeant Boone," she said.

"Yes," Delaney said. His manner was weighty, almost pompous. His voice was orotund. "It is indeed good of you to see us on such short notice. We deeply appreciate it. May we come in?"

"Of course," she said, impressed by his solemnity. She led the way into the apartment, closing the door. "I thought we'd talk in the family room. It's cozier there."

If Mrs. Maitland considered her family room cozy, Delaney hated to think of what the rest of the apartment was like. The austere chamber into which Mrs. Maitland led them looked like a model room in a department store. It was so coldly designed, so precisely arranged, so bereft of any signs of human use that a cigarette ash or a fart seemed a blasphemy.

They sat in undeniably expensive and uncomfortable blonde wood armchairs. They placed their hats on a cocktail table that seemed to be a sheet of plate glass floating in space. There was a slight odor of lemon deodorant in the air. The room had all the warm charm of an operating theatre. Delaney had expected blazing Maitland paintings on the walls. He saw a series of steel etchings depicting London street cries.

"Mrs. Maitland," he said formally, "may I first express my sincere sympathy and condolences on the tragic death of your husband."

"Thank you," she murmured. "You're very kind."

"He was a great artist."

"The greatest," she said loudly, raising her head to look directly at him. "The obituary in the *Times* called him the greatest American painter of his generation."

She was, Delaney saw, a handsome woman, big-boned, with a straight spine and the posture of a drill sergeant. She sat in the middle of a couch upholstered in beige wool, sitting toward the edge, not relaxing against the back. Her hands were folded demurely in her lap. Her ankles were crossed, lady-like, both knees bent slightly to one side.

She wore a high-necked, long-sleeved dress of nubby black silk. Her stockings, or pantyhose, had a black tint. Black shoes. No jewelry. Little makeup. The only color that saved her from chiaroscuro was a great mass of burnished coppery hair, braided into a gleaming plait, wound around and around into a crown atop her head. With her erect carriage, the effect was queenly.

Her features seemed to Delaney to be beautiful without being attractive. Too crisp. Too precise. Too perfect in their sculpted smoothness. On a face like that, a pimple would be a godsend. But her complexion was an unflawed porcelain glaze. Big eyes like licked stones. An expression so serene it was blank. Beneath the black dress was a hint of generous bosom, bountiful hips. But the face, the posture, the demeanor, all denied humor. She would never leave a note to her husband toothpicked to a roast of beef.

"Mrs. Maitland," Chief Delaney began, "I regret the necessity of intruding further on your grief. But the investigation into your husband's death continues, and I am certain you will endure any inconvenience if it aids in bringing to justice the person or persons responsible for this vicious crime."

He had, quite deliberately, adopted the manner and language to which he thought she might respond. His instinct was correct.

"Anything," she said, lifting her chin. "Anything I can do."

"Mrs. Maitland, I have read your statements to the investigating officers who questioned you. Please let me review briefly what you told them, and when I have finished, you can tell me if it is accurate. On the Friday he was murdered, your husband left this apartment at approximately nine in the morning. He told you he was going to his studio, then had an appointment at the Geltman Galleries at three that afternoon, and should be home about six or seven that evening. You yourself left this apartment at approximately ten o'clock. You spent the morning shopping. You met a friend for lunch at one-thirty at Le Provençal on East Sixty-second Street. After lunch you cabbed back here. At about four that afternoon, Saul Geltman called to ask if you knew your husband's whereabouts. Do I have it right?"

"You do, Chief Delano," she said. "I pre—"

"Delaney," he said. "Edward X. Delaney."

"Pardon me," she said. Her voice was low-timbred, husky, but curiously dry. "Chief Delaney, I presume you have checked my story?"

"We have," he nodded gravely. "The doorman on duty confirmed your time of leaving. Your friend affirmed she had lunch with you at the time and place specified. The records of the restaurant bear this out. Unfortunately, we have not been able to find witnesses to your shopping from ten to one-thirty."

"I went to Saks, Bonwits, Bergdorfs, and Gucci," she said. "But I didn't buy anything. I don't suppose anyone would remember me; the stores were crowded."

"No one did," he said. There was a short pause while he leaned toward her earnestly. "But, Mrs. Maitland, that could be entirely normal and understandable. You purchased nothing, tried on no clothing, made no special inquiries; it's quite natural that no one would have any special recollection of your presence in those stores. You didn't try on any clothing, did you?"

"No, I did not. I saw nothing I liked."

"Of course. Meet anyone you knew at any time between ten and one-thirty? A salesperson, an acquaintance, a friend?"

"No. No one."

"Make any telephone calls during that period?"

"No."

"Mail any letters?"

"No."

"Speak to anyone at all? Have any personal contact whatsoever?"

"No."

"I see. Please understand, Mrs. Maitland, all we're trying to do is clear up loose ends. It appears to me you acted in a perfectly normal manner. I trust you are not offended by the tone of these questions?"

"Not at all, Chief Delaney."

"Was your husband cheating on you?" he asked harshly.

If he had slapped her, the effect would not have been any more dramatic. She jerked back, her face reddened, her hands flew up.

"Believe me, Mrs. Maitland," he continued, once again in his smooth, almost unctuous voice, "it grieves me to pry into your personal life, your private relations with your husband. But surely you must see the necessity for it."

"My husband was the dearest, sweetest man who ever lived," she said stiffly, her lips white. "I assure you he was completely faithful. He loved me, and I loved him. He expressed his love frequently. By telling me and in—in other ways. Ours was a very happy marriage. A perfect marriage. Victor Maitland was a very great artist, and it was an honor to be his wife. Oh, I know the filthy gossip that has been circulated about him, but I assure you that he was as fine a husband and father as he was a painter. I assure you."

"And your son shares your feelings, Mrs. Maitland?"

"My son is young, Chief Delaney. He is presently going through an identity crisis. When he is older, and more experienced, he will realize what a giant his father was."

"Yes, yes. A giant. How true, Mrs. Maitland. Well put. And by the way, where is your son? I was hoping to meet him."

"Now? He's at school."

"Studying to be an artist, is he?"

"In a way," she said shortly. "Graphic design."

"But your husband *was* an artist, Mrs. Maitland. Specializing in the female nude. He was alone in his studio with naked models for long periods of time. Did that not disturb you?"

"Oh my!" she laughed, a tinny sound that clanged through the deodorized air. "You have some very middle-class ideas about the life style of artists, Chief Delaney. I assure you that to most artists, the naked female body is about as exciting as a bowl of fruit or an arrangement of flowers."

"Of course, of course."

"The body is just a subject, an object to them. Let me show you something. Don't get up. I'll bring it to you."

She jerked to her feet, rushed from the room. Sergeant Boone looked at Delaney with wonder.

"Wow," he said. "You're something else again, Chief. First the velvet glove, then the knuckle sandwich. You sure shook her."

"She needs shaking," Delaney growled. "She's playing a role. Did you catch it? While he was alive, she played the Betrayed Wife. Now that he's dead, she's playing the Bereaved Widow. Have you ever heard such shit in your life? Shh. She's coming."

She came striding into the room, thumbing through the pages of an oversized book. Delaney admired the way she moved: energetically, healthily, power in her thighs and shoulders. She found the page she wanted, reversed the book, held it out to Delaney. Boone rose and moved behind him to look over the Chief's shoulder.

It was a copy of the book of Maitland's paintings the sergeant had loaned to Delaney. It was open to a full-color plate. A nude lay on her side on a rough wood plank, her back to the viewer. The curve of raised shoulder, narrow waist, swell of hip, diminishing rhythm of leg flowed

like water. It was not one of Delaney's favorite paintings in the book.
The model was in repose. The best of Maitland's nudes were charged
with vigor, caught in movement, captured in postures that surged, bursting. But now, looking at this particular reproduction that Mrs. Alma
Maitland had thrust into his hands, Chief Delaney saw only the flame of
coppery hair spilling down from the model's head, across the rough
wood plank, to the painting's border.

"Me!" Mrs. Maitland said proudly, raising her chin again. "I posed
for that. Years ago. And many others. I was Victor's first model. So I
assure you, Chief Delaney, when I tell you of artists and models, I know
whereof I speak. I posed for many artists. Many. My body was considered classic. Classic!"

"Beautiful," Chief Delaney murmured. "Very beautiful indeed," and
wondered why it was the only nude in the book in which the face was
not shown.

He closed the book and put it aside. He took up his homburg and
rose to his feet.

"Mrs. Maitland," he said, "I thank you for your valuable assistance,
and only hope I have not caused you undue anguish."

"Not at all," she said, obviously glad to see him going.

"And I hope, as our investigation progresses, you will be kind enough
to grant me additional time. Things do come up, you know, and we like
to clear them up if we can. And as the one person closest to this great
artist, we are depending on you for information no one else can
furnish."

"I will be happy and eager to do anything I can to help you find the
man who robbed the world of such a talent," she said solemnly.

Sergeant Abner Boone looked at the two of them in amazement. A
couple of loonies.

Delaney started toward the door, then stopped.

"By the way, Mrs. Maitland, how did your husband get from here to
his studio?"

"He usually took a cab. Sometimes he went by subway."

"Subway? Did he ride the subway frequently?"

"Occasionally. He said he liked to look at the faces."

"The doorman confirms that your husband left the building at approximately nine o'clock that Friday morning. But he did not ask the
doorman to call a cab; he just walked westward. And we've been unable
to find a cabdriver who dropped a fare at your husband's address on

Mott Street. So perhaps he took the subway that morning. Did he tell you how he intended to spend the day?"

"No. I presumed he would be working."

"Mentioned no particular painting or model?"

"No."

"Did he call during the day?"

"The maid says he did not. Of course I wasn't here."

"Of course, of course."

Delaney paused, pondered a moment, staring at the brown carpeting. "One more thing, Mrs. Maitland . . . What's your personal opinion of Saul Geltman?"

He looked up. Her face had tightened. Delaney fancied those slick stone eyes dried as he watched.

"I would rather not express an opinion of Mr. Geltman at the present time," Alma Maitland said coldly. "Suffice to say that I am currently consulting an attorney in an effort to get a complete and truthful accounting from Geltman Galleries as to monies paid and owed to me. I mean to my husband's estate."

"I see," Delaney said softly. "Thank you again, Mrs. Maitland."

When they left the apartment house, the doorman was standing outside, his hands clasped behind him. He nodded to the two men.

"Find the dear lady?" he asked.

"We found her," Delaney said. "Tell me something . . . You said that Maitland left that Friday morning about nine o'clock. What time did he usually leave in the morning?"

The doorman stared at him, then slowly, deliberately winked.

"As soon as he could," he said. "As soon as he could."

In the car, Sergeant Boone said, "Well?"

"She knew he was cheating," Delaney said. "Everyone knew he screwed anything that moved. But she's busy creating the giant, the Great Man, of spotless character and immaculate integrity. She's making a statue out of the guy."

"Did you believe what she said about artists and models?"

"Come on," Delaney said. "If you were an artist and had a naked piece of tush alone in a studio, would you consider it an object?"

"Yeah," Boone laughed. "A sex object. Chief, I followed most of your line except for the last question about Geltman. What was the reason for that?"

Delaney told him the story of old Detective Alberto Di Lucca down in Little Italy, and how he had broken the warehouse heist by pitting one suspect against another.

"I've used variations of that technique ever since," he told Boone. "With good results. I could have pushed it farther with Mrs. Maitland, but she gave us enough for starters. Now I'll ask Geltman what he thinks of her. Eventually we'll get them all biting each other, and maybe we'll learn something. What did you think of that painting Maitland did of her?"

"Nice ass," Abner Boone said.

"Yes," Chief Delaney said, "but he didn't show her face. Why didn't he show her face?"

"I don't know, Chief. She's a beautiful woman."

"Mmm."

"And strong."

"Oh, you caught that, too? Yes, a big, strong woman. Think she could be a killer?"

"Who couldn't?" Sergeant Boone said.

They had lunch at Moriarty's on Third Avenue, sitting in the front room. Boone looked around at the Tiffany lamps, the long mahogany bar.

"Nice place, Chief," he said.

"Nothing fancy," Delaney said. "Solid food, honest drinks. Order what you like; it's on the Department."

They both ordered steak sandwiches with home fries, Delaney had a Labatt's ale, Boone had an iced tea.

"She's the only one with a loose alibi," the sergeant said casually, scrubbing his face with his palms.

"Where were you last night?" Delaney asked.

"What?"

"Where were you last night?" Delaney repeated patiently.

"Why?"

"Just answer the question."

"I was home, sir."

"Alone?"

"Sure."

"What did you do?"

"Wrote some checks, watched some TV, read some magazines."

"Can you prove it?"

Sergeant Boone smiled crookedly.

"All right, Chief," he said. "You made your point."

"Alibis are about as much use as fingerprints," Chief Delaney said. "If they exist and can be checked out thoroughly, all well and good. But most of the time you get partials; they don't say yes, they don't say no. Maybe Alma really did go shopping. Except women usually meet, go shopping together, and then have lunch. Or they meet for lunch, and then go shopping together. She says she went shopping alone, met her friend for lunch, and then went home. It bothers me. I have the friend's name and address in the file. Will you check her out? Just ask why she didn't go shopping that Friday with Mrs. Maitland."

"Will do. Ah, here's our food . . ."

They had a leisurely lunch, trading Department gossip and occasionally exchanging stories of cases they had worked.

"Who collects in this Maitland thing, sir?" the sergeant asked.

"Good question. He didn't leave a will. I'll have to get an opinion on it from the Department's legal eagles. I think the widow takes all, after taxes. I know she's definitely entitled to half. I want to know if the son's entitled, too."

"You know we got copies of Maitland's bank accounts," Boone said, "and he didn't leave all that much. No safe-deposit boxes we could find. And apparently his only unsold paintings are up in the Geltman Galleries."

"Which reminds me," Delaney said, "we better get going. We can walk over; it isn't far."

The Geltman Galleries occupied the ground floor of a modern professional building on Madison Avenue. Enormous plate-glass windows, set back from the sidewalk, fronted one long room high enough to accommodate a half-balcony reached by a spiral iron staircase. Paintings and sculpture were customarily displayed on the main level, prints and drawings on the balcony. Offices and storage rooms were at the rear of the ground floor. Entrance to the Galleries was directly from the street.

When Chief Delaney and Sergeant Boone walked over after lunch, they found the high plate-glass windows covered from the inside with drapes of oyster-white burlap. A sign stated that the Geltman Galleries, temporarily closed, were being prepared for a memorial exhibit of the last works of Victor Maitland, paintings that had never been shown before. The sign urged visitors to return after June 10th, when "we will be proud to present the final creations of this premier American artist."

The street door was locked. A smaller notice, handwritten, stated that those with deliveries to make should enter through the building lobby and ring the bell on the Galleries' interior door. Delaney and Boone went into the lobby, to discover the side door open, workmen passing in and out, carrying plasterboard, lighting fixtures, boxes of eighteen-inch tiles of white and black vinyl. They followed the workmen inside, looked around at the bustling confusion: shouts, men hammering, a lad with a foulard kerchief knotted about his neck rushing about with a roll of blueprints under his arm. They stood irresolutely a moment, then a slat-thin young girl hurried up to them.

"We're closed," she said breathlessly. "The show doesn't open until—"

"I have an appointment with Mr. Geltman," Chief Delaney said. "My name is—"

"Please, no more interviews," she frowned. "No photos. Absolutely none. A press conference and reception will be held the evening of—"

"—Edward X. Delaney," he finished in heavy voice. "Chief, New York Police Department. I have an appointment at one o'clock with Saul Geltman."

"Oh," she said. "Oh. Wait right here, please."

She disappeared into the jumble. They waited stolidly, inspecting. The walls were being repainted from a delft blue to a flat white. The white and black tiles were being laid in a diagonal diamond pattern. Temporary partitions were being erected to break up the room into several compartments of varying widths. Lighting fixtures of a brushed-steel teardrop design were being attached to the walls.

"Must be costing a fortune," Boone said.

Delaney nodded.

The girl was back in a few minutes.

"This way, please," she said nervously. "Mr. Geltman is expecting you. Watch where you step; everything is in such a mess."

She led them toward the rear. They watched where they stepped and arrived at the back office without misadventure. She stayed outside, motioned them in, closed the door behind them. The man behind the desk, talking on the telephone, smiled at them and lifted a hand to beckon them forward. He continued speaking on the phone as he waved them to armless chairs arranged in front of his desk. The chairs, in black leather on chrome frames, looked like jet-plane ejection seats. But they were comfortable enough.

"Yes, darling," Saul Geltman was saying. "You better if you know what's good for you . . . Yes . . . Put it down in your little mauve book . . . June ninth from eight o'clock on . . . Of course . . . Darling, but everyone! . . . I can expect you then? Marvelous!" He made kissing sounds into the telephone.

The two detectives looked about the office. A square room painted dove grey. The most startling fixture was a window behind Geltman's desk. Through the window they saw waves breaking on a rocky coast. It took a second or two for their minds to adjust. It was a marvel of *trompe l'oeil*. An actual wooden window frame had been fixed to the wall. The panes were glass. There were curtains of white nylon ninon. The seacoast was a large phototransparency, lighted from behind. The effect was incredibly realistic. The icing on the cake was that the bottom half of the window had been slightly raised, and a concealed fan billowed the curtains.

Both men smiled; a whimsical trick, but a good one. There was nothing else on the office walls, no paintings, drawings, etchings. The furnishings were all white and black leather and vinyl on chrome and stainless-steel frames. The desk appeared to be pewter (over wood?) supported on a cast-iron base. The desk fittings—rocker blotter, pen set, letter opener, etc.—were antique mother-of-pearl. In one corner of the room was an ancient safe, at least a hundred years old, on big casters. It was painted black, delicately striped, the front decorated with an ornate American eagle, wings outspread. There were two tumblers and two polished brass handles.

"Black-and-white," Geltman said on the phone. "White walls . . . But you know Maitland's colors, darling; you just can't compete . . . Correct . . . Darling, leave it to Halston; he'll know what to do . . . Yes, *dear!* . . . See you then. Byeee."

He hung up and made a face at the two officers.

"Rich, lonely widows," he said ruefully. "The story of my life."

He bounded to his feet, hurried around the desk to them, hand outthrust. Then they saw how small he was.

"Don't get up, don't get up," he said rapidly, motioning them back. "Take you five minutes to fight your way out of those chairs. Sergeant Boone, nice to see you again. You must be Chief Delaney."

"Yes. Thank you for seeing us on such short notice. It's obvious you're very busy."

"Listen, Chief," Geltman said, rushing back behind his desk again,

"I'll see you every day in the week and twice on Sunday, if you say so. Just as long as the cops haven't forgotten Victor Maitland."

"We haven't forgotten," Delaney said.

"Glad to hear it." Geltman pressed his forefingers together, tapped them against his lips a moment, then straightened up, sighing. "The poor guy."

"What kind of a man was he?" Delaney asked.

"What kind of a man?" Geltman repeated. He spoke quickly; occasionally spraying a mist of spittle. "As a human being, a terrible, frightening, mean, contemptible, cruel, heartless son of a bitch. As an artist, a giant, a saint, a god, the one real genius I've seen in this schlocky business in the last twenty years. A century from now you gentlemen and I will be nothing. Dust. But Victor Maitland will be something. His paintings in museums. Books on him. Immortal. Like David and Rubens. I really mean that."

"So you put up with his miserable personality because of his talent?" Delaney asked.

"No," Geltman smiled. "I put up with his miserable personality because of the money he made me. Fifteen years ago I had a hole-in-the-wall gallery on Macdougal Street in the Village. I sold a few crappy originals for bupkiss, but mostly I sold cheap reproductions. Van Gogh's sunflowers and Monet's water lilies. Then Victor Maitland entered my life, and today I'm in hock for almost a quarter of a million, I have three lawsuits pending against me, and my ex-wife is threatening to sue for non-support. Success—no?"

They laughed with him; it was hard not to.

He was a small man, made somehow larger by his vigor. He was in constant motion: slumping, straightening, twisting, gesturing, drumming his fingers on the desk top, crossing his knees to scratch his ankle, pulling an ear lobe, smoothing the brown-grey hair combed sideways across a broad skull.

He wore a beautifully tailored Norfolk suit of brown covert with a white turtleneck sweater of some sheeny knit. His little feet were shod in Gucci loafers, and Chief Delaney noted a bracelet of heavy gold links hanging loosely from one thin wrist.

His head seemed disproportionately large for his body, and his features seemed small for the head. Big face, but small eyes, nose, and mouth, like a pumpkin jackknifed with tiny openings. But the voice that came booming from this pleasantly ugly little man was warm, confiding, bubbling with good humor and laughter at himself.

"Not entirely correct," he told them, speaking so quickly he sometimes stuttered. "About putting up with Maitland's nastiness because of the money he made me. Half-correct, but not *all* correct. The bulk of my income came from him; I don't deny it. But I represent other artists. I do okay. If Maitland had left me, I wouldn't have starved. He got killed, but I'm still in business. The money I liked, I admit it. But something else . . . When I was a kid, I wanted to be a violinist." He held up a hand, palm out. "God's truth. Another Yehudi Menuhin I wanted to be. So I studied, I practiced; I practiced, I studied, and one day I was playing a Bach concerto, and I suddenly stopped, put the fiddle away, and I haven't touched it since. I don't mean I was bad, but I just didn't have it. At least I had sense enough to know; no one had to tell me. Studying isn't enough, and practicing isn't enough. If you haven't got it in the genes, you'll always be a second-rater, no matter how good you force yourself to be. Maitland had it in his genes. Not just talent—genius. Hey, genius and genes! Is that where the word comes from? I got to look it up. But Maitland had it, and it's too rare to let go of just because the guy insults you in public and treats you like dirt. I represent a lot of other artists. Good artists. But Maitland was the only genius I had, and probably ever will have. Well . . . you don't want to listen to me dribble on and on. What do you want to know?"

"No, no, Mr. Geltman," Delaney said. "Just keep talking. It may be a help. Tell us about your financial arrangements with Maitland. How did that work?"

"Money," Geltman said. He smoothed his hair again, leaned back in his chair. "You want to know about the money. First, let me tell you something about the art business. Like any other business, you buy low and you sell high. That's basic. But art—now I'm talking about original paintings, drawings, sculpture, and so forth—is different from other business. Why? Because Kellogg's makes umpteen million boxes of Corn Flakes every year, and all those boxes are identical and make a lot of money. Closer to home, a writer writes a book, and a million copies of that book are sold, if he's lucky. And a singer or even a violinist makes a recording and maybe a million copies are sold. But a painter? One. That's all. One. Oh, maybe guys like Norman Rockwell and Andy Wyeth can make deals to sell reproductions, and drawings and etchings and lithographs can be reproduced in limited numbers. But now we're talking about oil paintings. Originals. One of a kind. Maybe the artist worked a year on it, maybe more. He wants to get paid for his work, his time, his talent. That's natural. Normal. But how many people in this country, in the world, buy original works of art? Original oil paintings and sculptures? Especially from artists who haven't made a reputation yet? Guess how many?"

"I couldn't guess," Delaney said. "Not many, I'd say."

"You'd say right," Saul Geltman said, clasping his hands behind his head. "Three thousand. Four thousand maybe. In the whole world. Who'll pay a good price for original art. That's where an agent comes in. A good agent. He knows those three or four thousand people. Not all of them, of course, but enough of them. You follow? The agent builds a reputation, too. The rich people who collect art, they trust him. Damned few of them trust their own taste, so they trust an agent. Maybe they want to buy art just for an investment—a lot of them do; I could tell you stories of profits you wouldn't *believe!*—or they want art to match their drapes, or maybe, just a few of them, like art the way I do. I mean they just *like* it. They want it in their homes. They want to see it every day. They want to *live* with it. A good agent knows all these kinds of art nuts. That's how he makes a living. That's the service he supplies to the artists he represents. Thirty percent. That's what I got on Victor Maitland." Geltman grinned cheerfully. "The bullshit buildup was so you wouldn't think it so much. I took thirty percent of the selling price. From a new artist I'd take on, it would be maybe fifty percent. Up or down, depending on the type of thing the guy does, what the critics say, how much work he turns out, and so forth."

"Thirty to fifty percent," Delaney repeated. "Is that normal for most galleries?"

Geltman flipped his hands up in the air.

"Maybe a little more, maybe a little less. With the rents we got on Madison Avenue, I'd say thirty to fifty is about right."

"And what determines the selling price of a painting?" Chief Delaney asked.

"Oh-ho," Saul Geltman said, jerking forward suddenly. "Now you've opened a whole new can of worms. Is the guy known? Has he had any good reviews from the critics? Is he turning out the stuff like sausages or does he really sweat them out? Have any museums bought him? Has he got something to say? Has he got a new way of saying it? Has someone important bought him? Has he got a good gallery behind him? Has he got a following who'll buy anything he does? And on and on and on. It's not one thing; it's a lot of things. I charge what I think the traffic will bear, after considering all those factors."

"I read Maitland sold for a hundred thousand," Delaney said. "What made him so special? I happen to like his work, but what made it worth that much?"

"Yes, I sold *Study in Blue* for a hundred," Geltman said. "He brought it in, I made one phone call, sold it sight unseen. So I made thirty G's on one phone call. But it took me twenty years to learn who to call . . ."

He spun in his swivel chair until he was facing the fake seacoast. He stared at the unmoving waves. The breeze ruffled his hair.

"To answer your question," he said, speaking to the wall. "What made him worth big money . . . Victor was a throwback. A dinosaur. He knew what was going on in painting in this country in the Fifties and Sixties. Abstract Expressionism, Pop-Art, Minimal, Op-Art, Less-is-More, Flat, all the avant-garde idiocies. But Maitland paid no attention to it. He went his way. Traditional. Representational. If he painted a tit, it was a *tit*. And you'd be surprised how many people want paintings they can recognize, paintings that tell a story, *beautiful* paintings. And Maitland could paint beautiful. A marvelous colorist. A marvelous draftsman. A marvelous anatomist."

"But it can't be wholly a matter of technique," Delaney said. "It was something more."

"Oh, yes," Geltman nodded. "Much, much more. Without trying to intellectualize what Maitland did, I think it's obvious that he, in a way, spiritualized sensuousness. Or maybe a better way of putting it would be to say that he conceptualized physical passion. So you can look at his nudes and feel no more lust than you would on viewing the *Venus de Milo*."

"Can *I*?" Delaney said dryly.

Geltman laughed shortly.

"Well, let's say *I* can," he said. "To me, there's nothing carnal in Maitland's work. I see his paintings as essentially sexless. They're more the idea of sex, the visual representation of a conception. But I admit, that's my personal reaction. You might see something entirely different."

"I do," Delaney assured him.

"That's one of Maitland's greatest gifts," Geltman nodded. "He's everything to everyone. He gives you back what you bring to his art and confirms your secret dreams."

He swiveled to face them, his eyes wet.

"What can I tell you?" he said, his voice clogged. "I was so ambivalent about him. I hated his guts. But if I had the money, I'd buy everything he did, buy it for myself, line my apartment walls with it, lock the door, and just sit there and stare."

Chief Delaney flipped through his notebook. The tears didn't impress him one way or the other. He remembered an accused ax murderer who had literally banged his head against the wall in horror and despair of being charged with such a disgusting crime. Which he had committed, of course.

"Mr. Geltman," he said, "I know you've been questioned several times before. I just want to review briefly your movements from Friday, the day Maitland was killed, until you discovered the body on Sunday. All right?"

"Sure," Geltman said. "Shoot." Then he added hastily, "Except maybe that isn't the right thing to say to a cop!"

Delaney ignored the weak joke.

"According to our records, you said you had an appointment with Maitland on Friday. He was to meet you and an interior designer here at three o'clock to go over plans for the installation of a new exhibition."

"Correct. Now it's a memorial show. The interior designer is that fag running around out there dressed like a cowboy."

"Let me finish, please. Then we can go back and pick up any additions or changes you'd like to make."

"Sorry."

"Let's start with that Friday. You arrived here at the Galleries about nine, maybe a little before. Talked to your staff, sent out for coffee-and, did a little business on the phone. Went through the morning mail. At about ten, you walked around the corner to your attorney's office, Simon and Brewster. Your lawyer is J. Julian Simon. You had an appointment with him at ten. You were with him till about one-thirty. You didn't go out for lunch; the two of you sent out for sandwiches around twelve-thirty. Roast beef on whole wheat."

"With sugar-free Dr. Peppers," Geltman said solemnly. Delaney paid no heed.

"You and Simon discussed personal matters—taxes, the lawsuits pending against you, and so forth. Until one-thirty. Approximately. You returned directly here. Busy with mail, phone calls, business in general. The interior designer showed up at three, on schedule, but no Maitland. You didn't worry; he was usually late."

"Invariably."

"But by four o'clock, you were concerned. The interior designer had another appointment, couldn't wait. You called Maitland's Mott Street studio. No answer. You called his home. His wife didn't know where he was. You made five more calls on Friday, and, you estimate, at least a dozen on Saturday. Now you were also calling Maitland's friends and acquaintances. No one knew where he was. No one had heard from him. On Sunday morning you called his home again. They hadn't heard from him. You called his studio again. No answer. So you cabbed down and found him. At about one-twenty Sunday afternoon. Any additions, corrections, comments?"

"No," Geltman said shortly, his face pale. "That's about it."

"*About* it?"

"No, no. That *is* it. How it happened. Jesus, just remembering . . . Of course, you've checked it out?"

"Of course. Your staff saw you here Friday morning between nine and ten. Your lawyer says he was with you from ten to one-thirty. Your staff and customers saw you here from one-thirty to six that evening. The people you say you called said you did call. We even found the hackie who took you down to Mott Street on Sunday. Yes, we checked it out. I just hoped you might have something to add."

"No," Saul Geltman shook his head. "I have nothing to add."

"All right . . . Now let's get back to your financial dealings with Maitland," Chief Delaney said. "I'm trying to get a picture of how it worked. Suppose Maitland finished a new painting in his Mott Street studio. Would you send for it, or would he bring it up here?"

"Usually he brought it up here in a cab. Then we'd talk about it."

"You gave him your opinion of it?"

"Oh, God, no!" Geltman said, coming alive again. "I wouldn't dare! With Maitland, I had a standard comment for his stuff: I'd say, 'Victor, it's the best thing you've ever done.' Then maybe we'd discuss how it should be framed if it was going into a show, or if we should leave it unframed, on the stretcher."

"Stretcher?"

"That's the interior frame, made of wood, over which the canvas is stretched and tacked down. Maitland made his own stretchers."

"Then what would happen, after you discussed the framing?"

"I'd enter the painting in the book. I keep a ledger for every artist I represent. I keep telling them they should keep a journal themselves: a list of their paintings, when started and when completed, title, size, brief description, and so forth. A great help if there's ever any question about the provenance or a forgery. But most artists are lousy businessmen and don't keep complete records. Maitland didn't. So when he'd bring in a new painting, I'd have a color Polaroid taken of it. I'd paste that in his ledger, with the date it was delivered, the title, the size in centimeters, and so on. When it was sold, I'd enter date of sale, name and address of buyer, amount received, and the number and date of the check I mailed to Maitland. Here, let me show you . . ."

Geltman bounced to his feet, strode to his antique safe, worked the combination on both dials, swung open the heavy door. There was another locked door within, this one sheet steel opened with a key. The agent took out a large buckram ledger with red leather corners. He carried it back to his desk. Chief Delaney and Sergeant Boone fought their way out of their deep chairs and stood on either side of Geltman, dwarfing the diminutive agent.

"Here's one we called *Red Poppies*. Delivered March third, nineteen seventy-one. The Polaroid shot. The size. Date of sale. Amount. Check. Go ahead, take a look. That's how I handle all my merchandise."

"Who set the selling price?"

"I did. But with Maitland, I always checked with him first before making the deal."

"Did he ever object? Want more?"

"That happened a few times. I never argued with him. Once he wanted to hold out for more, and we did get more. The other times he settled for what I recommended."

Delaney flipped through the book, one painting per page, glancing mostly at the selling prices.

"He did all right," he noted. "A gradual increase. He starts out at one hundred bucks and ends up with a hundred big ones."

"Yes, but look at these," Geltman said, turning to the back of the book. "His new work that'll be in the show. Unsold. Look at this one. Magnificent! I'll get two hundred for that, I know. At least."

"And after these are gone?" Delaney asked. "No more Maitlands?"

"Well, that I can't say for sure," Geltman said cautiously. "You know, most artists are nuts. They're *nuts!* They do paintings and squirrel them away. For a rainy day. In case they get sick and can't work. Or maybe just something to leave the wife and kiddies. Their inheritance."

"You think Maitland did that?"

"I don't know," Geltman said, troubled. "He never said. Once I came right out and asked him, but he just laughed. So I don't really know."

"I'm surprised Mrs. Maitland is letting you have this show," Delaney said. "Letting you sell his last work."

"Surprised?" Geltman said. "Why should you be surprised?"

"She told us she was suing you," Delaney said, looking at him.

Geltman laughed, went behind his desk to flop into his swivel chair.

"She'll have to get in line," he said cheerfully. "Wives and widows of artists—the curse of my profession. If you can call it a profession. They all think we're screwing their poor, impractical husbands. Well, there's the ledger. I told Alma she's welcome to bring her lawyer in and examine it any time she wants. I have all the canceled checks I gave Maitland. What she is afraid of finding, of course, and what she *will* find, is that he was doing paintings he wasn't telling her about. The checks were given to him in person or mailed to his Mott Street studio. She didn't know anything about it—but she suspected. He was spending that money himself."

"On what?" Delaney asked.

"Wine, women, and song. But very easy on the song."

Delaney and Boone lowered themselves cautiously into their reclining chairs again.

"Mr. Geltman," Delaney asked, "what's your personal opinion of Mrs. Maitland?"

"Dear Alma? I knew her in the Village, you know. Twenty years ago. She tried her hand at painting for a while, but gave it up. She was terrible. Just terrible. Much worse than me on my violin. So she decided to make her contribution to art by modeling. I admit she had an incredible body. Big. Junoesque. Maillol would have loved her. But you know what we called her in the Village then? The Ice Maiden. She wouldn't screw. She-would-not-screw. I often wondered if she was a closet lez. So Maitland married her, that being the only way he could make her without her filing a rape charge."

"She told us she was his first model."

"Bullshit!" Saul Geltman said explosively. "He had plenty of models before she came along. And he layed them all: young, old, fat, thin, beautiful, ugly—he didn't care. The man was a stallion. And after he married Alma, he told everyone she was the worst lay of the lot."

"Hardly a gentleman."

"No one ever accused Victor Maitland of *that!*"

"Why did they stay married?"

"Why not? He had someone to cook his meals and mix his paints, to run down to the store for a jug, and nurse him through his hangovers. Also, he had a free model. She had the type of body he liked. It was a good deal for him."

"What about her?" Delaney asked. "What did she get out of it?"

Geltman leaned back, clasped his hands behind his head, stared at the ceiling.

"You've got to remember that the Ice Maiden was a very beautiful woman. Very. A lot of men were in love with her. Or thought they were. I might have thought so myself. Once. She loved that. Loved having men wildly in love with her. The center of attraction at any party. The professional virgin. I think it gave her a sense of power: all of us sniffing around with hard-ons. She didn't believe there was any man who didn't love her. She just took it for granted."

"Did Maitland love her?"

"Come on, Chief; you know better than that. He probably told her he did. He'd tell a woman *anything* to get in her pants. And he was beginning to sell, so I guess she figured he was a good catch. So of course he made her miserable. He made everyone miserable. She just couldn't believe he didn't come home nights because he was out drinking or shafting someone older and uglier than she was. She wanted all of him. I mean *all* of him. But I'll tell you something funny. Well . . . maybe not so funny. If he had been a good husband and didn't cheat and swore off the booze, she still wouldn't have been satisfied. She'd have wanted more of him and more and more and more, until she had him all. Then, I think, she would have turned to someone else."

"A barracuda," Sergeant Abner Boone said suddenly, and then blushed when the other two looked at him in surprise.

"Exactly, sergeant," Geltman said gently. "A beautiful barracuda. But Victor wasn't having any. He knew her greed, but he wasn't about to be devoured. At least, that's the way I figure it."

"Interesting," Delaney said noncommittally. He snapped his notebook shut, struggled out of that damned chair again. Sergeant Boone followed suit. "Thank you very much, Mr. Geltman, for giving us so much of your valuable time. I hope you'll be willing to see us again if it's necessary."

"I told you, any time at all. Can I ask a question now?"

"Of course."

"Those three drawings that were in the studio—what happened to them?"

"They're in my possession at the present time," Delaney said. "They'll be returned to Mrs. Maitland eventually."

"What did you think of them?" Geltman asked.

"I thought they were very good."

"More than that," the agent said. "I've seen some of his preliminary work before. I've sold some of it: drawings, studies for paintings. But those are something special. Rough, fast, strong. Something primitive there."

"Have any idea when they were done?"

"No. Recently, I'd guess. Maybe just before he was killed."

"You said you didn't recognize the model."

"No, I didn't. Very young. Looked Spanish to me. Well . . . Puerto Rican or Cuban. Latin."

"Spanish?" Delaney said. "I thought Oriental."

"The body was too full to be Oriental, Chief. I'd say a Latin-type. But maybe Italian or Greek."

"Interesting," Delaney said again. He moved toward the door. "Thank you once more, Mr. Geltman."

"Say!" the agent said, snapping his fingers. "I'm having a big reception here before the opening. A combination press party and just plain party. A kind of wake, I guess. A lot of important people. The beautiful people. Oy! And important customers, of course. How would you and the sergeant like to come? At eight o'clock on June ninth. Bring your wives. Or girlfriends. Plenty to eat and drink. How about it?"

Chief Delaney turned slowly to smile at the agent.

"That's kind of you, Mr. Geltman," he said softly. "I'd like very much to come." He looked at Boone. The sergeant nodded.

"Good, good, good," Saul Geltman said, rubbing his palms together. "I'll make certain you get invitations. And look, wear your uniforms if you like. Maybe then I won't lose so many ashtrays!"

They walked back to Boone's car, parked on Lexington Avenue.

"Reticent little fellow, isn't he?" the sergeant said sardonically.

"Oh I don't know," Delaney said. "It helped. We learned a lot."

"Did we, sir?" Boone said.

In the car, Delaney glanced at his watch.

"My God," he groaned. "Almost three. Where does the time go? Can you get me home?"

"Sure, Chief. Ten minutes."

On the ride uptown, Delaney said, "You're going to check with more of the men who worked on the Maitland case? To see if they remember anything not in the reports?"

"Right," Boone said. "But I'm running out of names of guys I know. Could you give me some more from the file?"

"Of course. Come in with me when we get home. I also want to give you the name and address of Mrs. Maitland's friend. The one she had lunch with. To ask why the two of them didn't go shopping together."

"Will do."

Just before they parked near Delaney's brownstone, the Chief said, "You know, he's not as frail as he looks. I hefted that ledger. It's heavy, but he handled it like a feather. And did you catch the way he swung that safe door open? It must be six inches of steel. He didn't have any trouble."

"Maybe the door was well balanced and well oiled, Chief."

"Not on those old safes," Delaney said. "No way. It took muscle."

They spent a few moments in Delaney's study while Sergeant Boone copied names and addresses in his notebook, and the Chief flipped through *his* notebook, fretting over cryptic jottings he had made during the interviews with Alma Maitland and Saul Geltman.

"More questions than answers," he grumbled. "We'll have to see these people again. But I prefer to see all the principals first, before we start the second round."

Boone looked up.

"What Geltman said about his financial condition," he said. "The money he owed, the lawsuits, and so on . . . Was that legit?"

"Apparently," Delaney said. "It's in the file. But maybe not as bad as he put it. He's got some heavy loans. But those lawsuits are piddling stuff. One guy is suing because he wants to return a painting that his wife didn't like, and Geltman won't give him his money back. He seems to have a good income, but his bank balances don't reflect it. You'd think a man who can make thirty G's by picking up a phone would have *something* tucked away, but it looks like Mr. Geltman is suffering from a bad case of the shorts. I wonder where it goes? The next time we see him, let's try to schedule it in his apartment. I'd like to see how he lives."

"Chief—" Boone started, then stopped.

"What were you going to say?"

"You think he's a flit?"

Delaney looked at him curiously.

"Why do you say that?"

"A lot of little things," Boone frowned. "None of them significant in themselves—but maybe they add up. He's so fucking *neat*. The bracelet. Calling the interior designer a fag. There was no need for that. Except to prove his own masculinity, figuring we'd think that way, too. He's got an ex-wife, he said. The way he touches himself. He said he might have loved Alma Maitland. Then he added, 'Once.' And that fake window. That's flitty."

"You're good," Delaney said. "You really are. Good eye, good memory."

Boone blushed with pleasure.

"But I don't know," Delaney said doubtfully. "As you say, each item is innocent. But maybe they do add up. Then we've got to ask ourselves, 'So what?'"

"Maybe he was in love with Maitland and couldn't stand the thought of the guy alley-catting around."

"Original idea. Another possibility. That's the trouble with this thing: all smoke, nothing solid. We'll see Jake Dukker and Belle Sarazen tomorrow. That leaves only Maitland's son, and his mother and sister up in Nyack. After we talk to all of them, we'll sit down and try to—"

There was a brisk rap-rap on the closed study door. Then it was opened, Monica Delaney stuck her head in . . .

"Hullo, dear," she said to her husband. "Rebecca and I just— Why, Sergeant Boone! How nice to see you again!"

She came swiftly into the room. Abner Boone jerked to his feet, took the proffered hand, almost bowed over it.

"Pleasure, ma'am," he murmured.

Chief Delaney carefully avoided smiling as he watched the effect of his wife's formidable charm on the sergeant. It was strictly no contest.

"Edward," Monica said brightly, turning to him. "Rebecca and I have been shopping, and she came back with me for a cup of coffee. We

stopped at the Eclair and bought some of those petits fours you love.
Why don't you and the sergeant take a minute off and have coffee with
us? Just in the kitchen. Informal."

"Sounds good to me," Delaney said, picking up his cue dutifully.
"You, sergeant?"

"Just fine," Boone nodded.

The poor fish, Delaney thought. He hasn't got a chance.

They sat around the kitchen table on wooden chairs, and laughed at
Monica's droll description of the trials and tribulations of shopping in
crowded department stores.

"And," she concluded, "I know you'll be happy to hear, dear, we
didn't buy a thing. Did we, Becky?"

"Not a thing," Rebecca Hirsch vowed.

She was a shortish, plump, jolly woman, with soft eyes set in a cheru-
bic face. Her complexion seemed so limpid and fine that a finger's touch
might bruise it. She wore her black, glistening hair parted in the middle,
falling unfettered to below her shoulders. Her body was undeniably
chubby, but wrists and ankles were slender, hands and feet delicate. She
moved with robust grace.

She was wearing a tailored suit, but even beneath the heavy material,
bosom and hips were awesome. There was a rosy glow to her, and if not
especially beautiful, there was comfort in her prettiness and no guile in
her manner. Her voice was light, somewhat flutey, but her laugh was
hearty enough. Delaney found much enjoyment in chivying her. Not
maliciously, but only to see those button eyes suddenly flash, the innocent mien change to outraged indignation.

The talk bubbled. Nothing of an artist bleeding to death in a Mott
Street tenement. Just the weather, the latest cosmic pronouncements of
Mary and Sylvia Delaney, Rebecca's continuing feud with the superior
of a private day-care center where she worked four days a week, the
high cost of flounder filets, and the problems of getting tickets to Broadway theatrical hits.

"The problem is," Rebecca Hirsch said seriously, "the problem is
that it's practically impossible to do anything on impulse these days.
You decide in the evening that you'd like to go to a Broadway show or
see a first-run movie. But then you discover you've got to buy tickets
weeks in advance for the show or stand in line for three hours to see the
movie. Don't you agree, Sergeant Boone?"

"Uh," he said.

"Or going somewhere," Monica Delaney said quickly. "A trip or vacation. The *planning!*"

"Yes," Chief Delaney nodded solemnly. "The planning . . ."

His wife looked at him blandly.

"You were going to say, dear?" she asked.

"Just agreeing," he said equably. "Just agreeing."

After a while, the coffee finished, the petits fours demolished, Rebecca Hirsch rose to her feet.

"Gotta go," she sang. "One dog, two cats, three African violets, and a mean-tempered parakeet to feed. Monica, Edward, thank you for the feast."

"Feast!" Monica scoffed. "A nosh."

"The calories!" Rebecca said. "Sergeant Boone, nice to have met you."

"I'm leaving too," he said. "I have a car outside. Can I drop you anywhere?"

They left together. Monica and Edward Delaney waved from the stoop. Inside, the door closed, she turned to him proudly.

"*See?*" she said triumphantly.

That evening, after dinner, alone in his study, Chief Edward X. Delaney carefully wrote out complete reports of his day's activities: the questioning of Mrs. Maitland and Geltman. He wrote slowly, in the beautifully legible Palmer method he had been taught. Twice he rose to mix a rye highball, but most of the time he sat heavily in one position as he doggedly put the interviews down on paper, consulting his notebook occasionally for exact quotes, but generally relying on his memory for the substance, mood and undertone of the meetings.

When he had finished, he read over what he had written, made several minor corrections, and appended lists of additional questions to ask at further interviews. Then he filed the reports away in the proper folders, and pondered the usefulness of asking Sergeant Boone for copies of his reports. He decided not to, for the time being. He went up to bed.

Shortly after midnight, the bedside phone shrilled, and Delaney was instantly awake. He grabbed it off the hook before the second ring was finished, then moved cautiously, trying not to disturb Monica.

"Edward X. Delaney here," he said in a low voice.

"Chief, this is Boone. Sorry to disturb you at this hour. I hope you're still awake. I'd hate to think—"

"What is it?" Delaney asked, wondering if Boone was sober.

"I spoke to four guys who worked the Maitland case. Got nothing from them, but at least they were reasonably friendly. But that's not why I'm calling. I finally got through to Susan Hemley. She's the friend of Mrs. Maitland. The friend who had lunch with her that Friday."

"I know."

"The reason I'm calling so late is that she had a date and just got home. And the reason she didn't go shopping that Friday morning with Alma Maitland is that she couldn't. She's got a job. She's a working girl."

"Simple solution," Delaney sighed. "We should have thought of it."

"Not so simple," Abner Boone said. "Just for the hell of it, I asked her where she worked. Are you ready for this? At Simon and Brewster, attorneys-at-law, on East Sixty-eighth Street. She's the personal secretary of J. Julian Simon, Saul Geltman's lawyer."

There was silence.

"Chief?" Boone said. "Are you there?"

"I'm here. I heard. Any ideas?"

"None. Total confusion. You?"

"Let's talk about it in the morning. Thank you for calling, sergeant."

He hung up and rolled carefully back under the covers. But Monica stirred.

"What is it?" she murmured.

"I don't know," he said.

6

Sergeant Boone apologized for his late call the previous night.

"It could have waited, Chief," he admitted. "It wasn't all that important. But I got excited. It's the first *new* thing we've turned up. It wasn't in the file, was it?"

"No," Delaney said. "No, it wasn't. I looked this morning, in case I had missed it."

They were seated in Boone's car, parked in front of the Chief's brownstone. Both men had their black notebooks open.

"I stayed awake half the night trying to figure it," the sergeant said. "Then I thought, what the hell, the two were just friends, that's all. Why shouldn't Mrs. Maitland be friendly with the secretary of Geltman's lawyer? That's probably how they met. But then I remembered how hostile Mrs. Maitland sounded when you mentioned Geltman's name. So maybe she was using the secretary as a private pipeline, to keep track of what the little guy was up to. What do you think?"

"That could be," Delaney nodded. "Except the two had lunch at Le Provençal on East Sixty-second Street. That's not far from the Geltman Galleries. If Mrs. Maitland was playing footsie with this Susan Hemley, maybe even paying her for information, wouldn't she have picked some place for lunch where there was no danger of running into Geltman?"

"I suppose so," Boone sighed. "Right now, it makes no sense at all, no matter how you figure it."

"One thing's certain," Delaney said grimly. "We're going to have a talk with J. Julian Simon and the Hemley woman."

"Today?"

"If we have time. Belle Sarazen first, at ten o'clock. Then Jake Dukker at two this afternoon. We'll see how it goes. You know where the Sarazen woman lives?"

"Yes, *sir!*" Boone said. Then he grinned. "Wait'll you see her place. A Persian whorehouse."

He pulled out slowly into traffic and headed north to Eighty-fifth Street, to take a traverse across Central Park to the West Side. There was a fine, warm mist in the air, but they had the windows open. The sun glowed dimly behind a grey scrim; it looked like it might burn through by noon.

"The file was skimpy on Belle Sarazen," Delaney remarked. "Seemed to me everyone was walking on eggs. You said you questioned her twice. What was your take?"

"Remember the Canfield case?" Abner Boone asked. "In Virginia? About ten, fifteen years ago?"

"Canfield?" Delaney repeated. "Wasn't he the heir to tobacco money who got his head blown off? His wife said she thought she was blasting an intruder?"

"That's the one. Our Belle was the gal behind the twelve-gauge Buckshot. Spread him all over the bedroom wall. She was Belle Canfield then. Youngish wife, oldish husband. He was an heir all right, but they kept him out of the tobacco business. Heavy drinker and heavy gambler. There had been attempts to break in; no doubt about that. In fact, he had bought her the shotgun for protection and taught her how to use it. Still, she knew he was out with the boys that night and pulled the trigger without even asking, 'Is that you, darling?' The coroner's jury—or whatever they have down there—called it 'a tragic accident,' and she waltzed away with almost two mil."

"And the county prosecutor retired to the French Riviera one year later."

"I don't know about that," Boone laughed, "but the Canfields practically *owned* that county and were kissin' cousins to half the money in Virginia. The Sarazens weren't money, but they were family: one of the oldest in the state. Belle sold the old plantation and the horses and moved to Paris. She cut a wide swath through Europe. French poets, English race drivers, Italian princes, and Spanish bullfighters. And I think there was a Polish weightlifter in there somewhere. The money lasted for five years and three marriages. Then she came back to the States and married a Congressman."

"Now I remember!" Delaney said. "Burroughs of Ohio. The guy who dropped dead while making a speech against socialized medicine."

"Right! But while he was alive, Belle was the most popular hostess in Washington. The scandal mags said John Kennedy, quote, Enjoyed her hospitality, unquote. Anyway, after the Congressman conked, she came up to New York. Still has a lot of political friends."

"Oh-ho," Delaney nodded. "I'm beginning to understand why the file was so cautious. But she doesn't use any of her married names; that's probably why I didn't make her."

"No, now she's just plain Belle Sarazen, a little ole gal from Raccoon Ford, V-A. But she's still flying high, wide, and handsome. One of Saul Geltman's Beautiful People. The Jet Set. Gives lavish parties. In big with the art and museum crowd. Contributes to the Democrats. Models for charity fashion shows and for fashion magazines, and sometimes for artists and photographers."

"She must be pushing forty," Delaney said. "At least."

"At least," Boone agreed. "But she's got the body of an eighteen-year-old. You'll see."

"Where does the money come from?" Delaney asked. "For these lavish parties and political contributions?"

"I think she hustles," Boone said, then laughed when he glanced sideways and saw Delaney's startled expression. "No con, Chief. I asked her directly. I said, 'What is the main source of your income, Miss Sarazen?' And she said, 'Men give me gifts.' So naturally, I said, 'Money gifts?' And she said, 'Is there any other kind?' Maybe she was putting me on, but I doubt it. She just doesn't give a damn."

"Did Maitland give her money?"

"According to her, yes. Plenty. Did they have sex together? Yes. Did she love him? God, no, she said, he was a savage. But she thought he was amusing. Her word: 'amusing.'"

"Yes, I read that in your report. Where did you pick up the other stuff on her? The background stuff?"

"From her scrapbooks. She's got three fat scrapbooks of newspaper clippings about herself. And magazine articles. Photos with famous people. Letters from politicians and royalty. She let me go through them as long as I wanted."

"Anything from Maitland? Or about Maitland?"

"Not a thing, sir. And I looked carefully."

"I'm sure you did, sergeant. It must be that building—the highrise across from Lincoln Center. Listen, I noticed in our interviews with Mrs. Maitland and Geltman that you hardly opened your mouth. Don't be afraid to speak up. If you think of something I haven't covered, ask it."

"I'd rather let you carry the ball, sir. First of all, they're liable to be more intimidated by a chief than a sergeant. And also, I'm studying your interrogation technique."

"My technique?" Delaney said, smiling. "Now *I'm* amused."

The door to the twenty-ninth-floor penthouse was opened by a Filipino manservant wearing livery of an unusual color: a blue-grey with an undertint of red. Not lilac or purple or violet, but something of all three. Looking around at the Persian whorehouse, Delaney saw the identical shade had been used on the painted walls, the curtains and drapes, the upholstered furniture, even the hassocks, pillows, and picture frames. The effect was that of a purpled grotto, a monochromatic cave that tinged skin and even seemed to color the air.

"I tell Miss Sarazen you are here, gentlemens," the butler said, almost lisping "Mith Tharathen," but not quite.

He disappeared into an inner room. They stood uneasily, hats in hand, looking about the stained chamber.

"Is the whole place like this?" Delaney whispered.

"No," Boone whispered back. "Every room a different color. The bedroom is blood-red. I had to use the can; it's dead black. The one I used was. She said that the place has three bathrooms."

"Hustling must be good," Delaney murmured.

The Filipino was back in a moment, to lead them down a hallway with walls covered with framed autographed photos. He ushered them into a bedroom, closed the door behind them. Here, again, was a one-color room: blood-red walls, curtains, drapes, bedspread, carpet, furniture—everything. The only striking exceptions were the white leotard, silvered hair, and chammy skin of the woman exercising near wide French doors. They led to a tiled terrace that provided a view, in the distance, of Central Park and the towers of the East Side.

"Sit down anywhere, darlings," she called to them, not interrupting her slow, steady movements. "There's champagne and orange juice on the cocktail table. Push the intercom button by the bedside table for anything stronger—or weaker."

They sat cautiously in fat armchairs with plump red cushions, facing the French doors. Daylight was behind the woman. There was a nimbus about her, a glow; it was difficult to make out her features.

She was seated on the floor, legs spread wide, flat out. She was bending from the hips, touching right hand to bare left toes, then left hand to bare right toes, the free arm windmilling high in the air. She wore a skin-tight white leotard, cut high to the hipbones, tight over the crotch. A soft mound there. The garment was sleeveless, strapped—a tanktop.

The body was that of a dancer, long-legged, hard, with flat rump, muscled thighs, sinewy arms, small breasts (nipples poking), and a definite break between ribcage and waist. Her exercise was strenuous— both men realized they could not have done it—but she had not huffed or gasped when she spoke, and Delaney saw no sweat stains on the leotard.

The silvery hair was fine, cut short and parted on the left. It was combed and brushed sideways, like a boy's haircut. It lay absolutely flat against her well-shaped skull: no wave, no curl, no loose tips or bounce to it. A helmet of hair, as tight and gleaming as beaten metal.

She ended her toe-touching, folded her legs, bent forward and rose to her feet without using her hands for support. Chief Delaney heard Sergeant Boone's low groan of envy.

"I want to thank you, Miss Sarazen," Delaney said mechanically, "for seeing us on such short notice."

She stood erect, feet about eighteen inches apart, clasped her hands over her head as high as she could reach. She began to bend slowly to each side alternately, hips level, her upper torso coming down almost to the horizontal.

"Call me Belle, sweet," she said. "All my friends call me Belle. Even the Scarecrow calls me Belle. Don't you, Scarecrow?"

Boone turned to Delaney with a sickly smile.

"I'm the Scarecrow," he said. "Yes, Belle," he said to her.

"I hope we're going to be friends," she said, still bending steadily. "I so want to be friends with the famous Edward X. Delaney."

"Not so famous," he said tonelessly.

"Famous enough. I'm a fan of yours, you know. I imagine I know things about you that even you've forgotten."

"Do you?" he asked, uncomfortable, realizing he was losing the initiative.

"Oh yes," she said. "The Durkee case is my favorite."

He was startled. The Durkee case had happened twenty years ago. It had certainly been in the New York papers, but he doubted if anyone in Raccoon Ford, or in all of Virginia for that matter, had read of it.

Ronald Durkee, a Queens auto mechanic, had gone fishing in Long Island Sound early one Saturday morning, despite threatening weather and small-craft warnings. When he had not returned by midnight, his distraught young wife reported his absence to the police. Durkee's boat was found floating overturned a few hundred yards offshore. No sign of Ronald Durkee.

The missing man had twenty thousand in life insurance, was in deep to the loansharks, and was known to be a strong swimmer. When the wife applied almost immediately for the insurance, Delaney figured it for attempted fraud. He broke it by convincing the wife that her missing husband had a girlfriend, even producing a fraudulent photograph to show her.

"This is the woman, Mrs. Durkee. Pretty, isn't she? We think he ran off with her, I'm sorry to say. Apparently he was seeing her on his lunch hour and after work. He did come home late from work occasionally, didn't he? We have statements from her neighbors. They identified your husband. He visited her frequently. I hate to be the one to tell you this, Mrs. Durkee, but we think he's gone off with her. Florida, probably. Too bad, Mrs. Durkee. Well, they say the wife is the last to know."

And so on. After a week of this, she broke, and Delaney picked up Ronald Durkee in a motel near LaGuardia Airport where he had grown a mustache and was patiently waiting for his wife to show up with the insurance money. Delaney wasn't particularly proud of his role in the case, but you worked with what you had.

It had resulted in a lot of newspaper stories, and his name had become known. A year later he was promoted to lieutenant.

"The Durkee case?" he said. He could not bring himself to address her as Belle. "That was long before you came to New York. You must have been checking into my background."

"As you checked into mine, dearie," she said. Her voice was lilting, laughing, with just a hint of soft Virginia drawl. "You did, didn't you?"

"Of course. You seem to make no secret of it."

"Oh, I have no secrets at all," she said. "From anyone."

She began reaching high overhead, then bending deeply from the hips to touch the floor. But not with her fingertips; her palms. He could see then what a slender, whippy body she had. No excess anywhere. He recalled with pleasure a line from an old movie he had enjoyed. Spencer Tracy looking at Katharine Hepburn: "Not much meat on her, but what there is, is cherce."

"Then you know I killed my husband," Belle Sarazen said casually. "My first husband. Four husbands ago. A tragic accident."

"Yes, I know of it."

"Tell me, Edward X. Delaney," she said mockingly, "if you had been investigating that, what would you have done?"

"My usual routine," he said coldly, tiring of her flippancy. "First, I would have checked to see if your husband really was out drinking with the boys that night. Or was he with another woman? Or if not that night, then any other night? Was there another woman in his life, or more than one other woman, that would make you jealous enough to blow away an intruder without yelling, 'Who's there?' or screaming or maybe just firing your shotgun into the ceiling to scare him away?"

"What time is it?" she asked suddenly.

Abner Boone glanced at his watch.

"Almost ten-thirty, Belle," he said.

"Close enough," she said. "That's my daily hour devoted to the carcass."

She stopped exercising. Came toward them. Turned on a floor lamp (with a blood-red shade). Bent forward to shake the Chief's hand.

"Edward X. Delaney," she said. "A pleasure. Scarecrow, good to see you again. I have this pitcher of champagne and orange juice waiting for me. A reward for my labors. Somewhat flat, which is good for little girls in the morning. Anything for you boys? Coffee?"

"That would be appreciated," Delaney said. "You, sergeant?"

Boone nodded. They watched her push a button and speak into a small intercom on the bedside table. No one said anything until the manservant entered bearing a silver tray with coffee pot, sugar bowl and creamer, two cups, saucers, spoons. She poured for them. They both refused sugar and cream. Delaney leaned forward to examine the tray.

"Handsome," he said. "Very old, isn't it?"

"So I understand," she said carelessly. "Daddy said it belonged to Thomas Jefferson—but who knows? Listen to Virginians, and Thomas Jefferson must have owned six thousand silver serving trays."

She folded down onto the floor at their feet. Went down without putting a hand out to aid her. She sat in the Lotus Position, back straight, knees bent and legs crossed so tightly that each foot rested on the opposite thigh, soles turned almost straight up. She sipped from a champagne glass that had not lost a drop during her descent.

"Yoga," she said. "Ever try it?"

"Not me," Delaney said. "You, sergeant?" he asked solemnly.

"No sir."

"Keeps the spine flexible," she said. "Puts pow in the pelvis. Improves performance." She winked at them.

Delaney could see her triangular face clearly now. High cheekbones— Indian blood there?—tight skin, somewhat slanted eyes widely spaced. Open, astonished eyes. Thin lips extended a bit above the skin line with rouge to give the impression of soft fullness. Hard chin. Small ears revealed by the short, flat silvered hair. Thin nose, patrician, with oval nostrils. Not a wrinkle, mark, or imperfection. She felt Delaney's stare.

"I work at it," she said laconically.

"You succeed," he assured her, and meant it.

"You want to know about Victor Maitland," she said, more of a statement than a question. "Again?"

"Not really," Chief Delaney said. "I want to know about Jake Dukker. What's your personal opinion of him?"

He noted, with some satisfaction, her small start of surprise. He had her off-balance.

"Jake Dukker," she repeated. "Well, Jake is an artist."

"We know that."

"Very facile, very competent. You cops are lucky he never decided to become a forger. Jake can copy *anyone's* style. Rembrandt, Picasso, Andy Warhol . . . you name it."

"Could he copy Victor Maitland?"

"Of course he could. If he wanted to. But why should he? Jake does very well indeed doing his own thing."

"Which is?"

"Whatever's selling. Superficial stuff. Very trendy. As soon as something shows signs of making money, Jake gets in on it. Abstracts, Calligraphy, Pop-Art, Op-Art, Photo-Realism—he's been into it all. You know what he's doing now? You'll never guess. Not in a million years. A nude of me painted on aluminum foil. Ask him to show it to you. Fan-tas-tic. It's not finished yet, but it's already sold."

"Who bought it?" Sergeant Boone asked quickly.

"A friend of mine," she said, taking a sip of her drink. "A very important man."

"Do you model frequently?" Delaney asked.

She nodded. "Mostly nudes. I enjoy it. Painters and photographers." She looked down at her body, stroked her small, hard breasts, ribs, waist, hips, her bare thighs. "Not a bad bod for a thirty-five-year-old chippy—right, men? I have this friend who wants to make a plaster cast of my body. The whooole thing. But I'm not sure I want to. I understand it gets hot as hell while that plaster is hardening. Is that right?"

"I wouldn't know," Chief Delaney said. "Did you ever model for Victor Maitland?"

"No," she said. "Never. I wasn't his type. His type of model, I mean. He liked the zoftigs. Big tits, big ass. He said I was the Venus of the Computer Age. That's what Jake Dukker is going to call his aluminum-foil nude of me: *Venus of the Computer Age.*"

"Could Dukker have killed Maitland?" Delaney asked directly.

Again he rocked her. He decided this was the way to do it: keep her off-balance, switch from one topic to another before she could get set. If he followed a logical train of thought, she'd be two questions ahead of him.

"Jake?" she said. "Jake Dukker kill Maitland?"

That was what people did when they wanted time to think: they repeated the question.

"Maybe," she said. "They were friends, but Victor had something Jake will never have. It drove him ape."

"What was that?"

"Integrity," she said. "Old-fashioned word, but I'll bet you just dote on old-fashioned words, Edward X. Delaney. Jake is the better painter. Listen, I know painting, I really do. God knows I've screwed enough artists. Jake is better than Maitland was. Technically, I mean. And as fast. But Victor didn't give one good goddamn what was in fashion, the fads, what was selling. I tell you this, and I know for a fact: if Victor Maitland had never sold a painting in his life, he wouldn't have changed his style, wouldn't have stopped doing what he wanted to do, what he had to do. Jake isn't like that at all, and can never be. He hated Victor's integrity. *Hated* it! At the same time he wanted it, wanted it so bad it drove him right up a wall. I know it. He told me once and started crying. Jake likes to be spanked."

That stopped them. They didn't know if she meant it literally or metaphorically. Delaney decided not to press it.

"Sergeant Boone tells me you admitted you were intimate with Victor Maitland."

" 'Intimate with Victor Maitland,' " she mimicked. "You sound like daddy. I always did have a thing for older men. All my shrinks have told me I'm a father-fucker at heart. Sure, I balled Victor. I wish he had bathed more often, but sometimes that can be fun, too. What a savage!"

"And he paid you?"

"He gave me gifts, yes," she said, unconcerned.

"Money?"

"Mostly. Once a small painting, which I sold for ten thousand."

"You didn't like it?"

"The painting? I loved it. A little still life. A single poppy in a crystal bud vase. But I liked those long, green still lifes even better."

"Did you tell Maitland you had sold his painting?"

"Of course."

"What was his reaction?"

"He thought it was funny as hell. He said I got more for it than Geltman would have."

"Apparently Maitland was a generous man."

"He wasn't cheap," she acknowledged.

Delaney rubbed his chin, squinting through the French doors. The mist was burning away. He could see fuzzy shadows forming on the tiled terrace.

"Did you ever procure women for Maitland?" he asked.

There was a moment of silence, brief, heavy.

"Procure," she said. "I don't like that word. I suggested models for him occasionally. Girls I thought he could use. His type."

"He paid you for this—this service?"

"Of course. Don't worry, Edward X. Delaney; I declared it all on my tax return. I'm clean."

"I'm sure you are," he said blandly. "Let's get on to the Friday he was killed. You said you left here about ten-thirty and went to your yoga class for an hour."

"Yoga and meditation," she said. "For twenty minutes we sit naked on the floor and go, 'Ooom.' "

"After that you went to Jake Dukker's studio on Central Park South. Did you pose for the aluminum-foil nude then?"

"No, Jake was setting up for a photo session. He's a photographer, too, you know, and a good one. Mostly fashion. He's in *Vogue* and *Town & Country* all the time. I sat around kibitzing until they broke for lunch."

"That was at twelve? Or thereabouts?"

"Thereabouts."

"And then?"

"Then Jake and I went upstairs to his apartment. He's got a duplex, you know. Jake made lunch for us. He thinks he's a great gourmet cook. He's lousy. I lived in Paris, and I *know*. He made an herb omelet that was barely edible. But he had a nice chilled Spanish white. I filled up on that."

"And did you have relations?"

She looked at him blankly.

"Sexual relations," he said. "While you were up in his apartment? Before, during, or after lunch?"

"You know," she said, "you're not going to believe this, but I don't remember. I really don't."

"I believe you," he said. "After all, it was six weeks ago."

She laughed her trilling laugh, up and down the scale.

"Oh, Edward X. Delaney," she said. "You're a sly one, you are. All right, I remember that awful herb omelet, but I don't remember if we screwed. Probably not."

"Why 'Probably not'?"

"Because his assistants and the fashion models were waiting for him downstairs. And the models get paid by the hour. Jake is all business."

"Even in his painting?"

"You better believe it, buster. If the Hudson River School ever comes back into style, Jake will be sitting out there on the Palisades, painting the river and trees and clouds and Indians in canoes."

"So then, after lunch, you and Dukker went downstairs to the studio, and he resumed shooting that photography assignment at about one-thirty. Is that correct?"

"That's correct."

"How late did you stay?"

"Oh, for another hour or so. I had an appointment at the hairdresser's."

"How many models were involved in this photography session at Dukker's?"

"I don't remember."

"One?"

"No, two or three, I guess."

"Perhaps four? Or five?"

"There could have been," she said. "Is it important?"

"What were they modeling?"

"Lingerie."

"Why did you attend? Photography shootings are usually boring, aren't they?"

She shrugged. "I just dropped by to kill a few hours. Before my appointment."

"It wasn't to take a look at the models, was it? For your friends? The important men?"

At first he thought he had cracked her. He watched her head jerk back. Thin lips peeled away from wet teeth. He thought he heard a faint hiss. But she held herself together. She smiled bleakly.

"Edward X. Delaney," she said. "Good old Edward X. Delaney. I don't run a call-girl ring, you know."

"I do know that," he said. "You wouldn't be involved in anything as obvious and vulgar as that."

He was conscious of Boone stirring restlessly in the chair alongside him. He turned to him.

"Sergeant?" he said. "Anything?"

"Belle," Abner Boone said, "you said you provided Maitland with models."

"Occasionally," she said tightly. "And I didn't *provide* them; I *suggested* girls to him."

"Ever suggest a very young girl?" Boone pressed on. "Maybe Puerto Rican? Or Italian? A Latin-type?"

She thought a moment, frowning.

"Can't recall anyone like that," she said. "Recently?"

"Say a few weeks before he died. Maybe a month."

"No," she said definitely. "I didn't send Victor a girl for at least six months. Who is she?"

Boone looked at Delaney. The Chief saw no reason not to tell Belle Sarazen why they were interested. He described the three drawings they had found in Maitland's studio. He said it was believed they had been done shortly before Maitland's death. Maybe on the morning he had been killed.

"Where are they now?" she said. "The drawings?"

"I have them," Delaney said.

"Bring them around," she suggested. "I'll take a look. Maybe I can identify her. I know most of the girls Victor used, and a lot more besides."

"I may do that," Delaney said. He rose to his feet, putting his notebook away, and Sergeant Boone did the same. They thanked Belle Sarazen for her cooperation, and asked if they might return if more questions came up.

"Any time," she said. "I'll be right here."

She rang for the Filipino to show them out. They were at the bedroom door when she called Delaney's name. He stopped and turned slowly to face her.

"You don't really think I knew it was my husband when I fired the shotgun, do you?" she asked. Her smile was flirtatious, almost coy.

His smile was just as meaningless.

"We'll never know, will we?" he said.

They sat in Boone's car, comparing notes and blowing more smoke.

"There's nothing in the file about her and drugs," Delaney said. "No record of busts. But a woman like that, living a life like that, has *got* to be on. I'd be willing to bet she's feeding her nose. Maybe she was the source of the poppers they found in Maitland's studio."

"Could be," Boone said. "And maybe dealing a little with her important friends. You were a mite rough on her, Chief. Think we'll get any flak?"

Delaney considered a moment.

"We might," he acknowledged. "She could be humping the entire Board of Estimate, and I wouldn't be a bit surprised. If I get a call from Thorsen tonight, I'll know we made a dent. How do you figure her motive?"

"For wasting Maitland?"

"No, no. For living. The way she does."

"Money hungry," Boone said promptly. "Anything for a buck."

"I don't agree," Delaney said, just as promptly. "That might do for Saul Geltman. By the way, did you catch the way he referred to the art he sells as 'the merchandise'? But I don't think it holds for the Sarazen woman. Money, sure; she needs it. We all need it. But as a means to an end; not money for the sake of piling it up."

"What, then?"

"Here's how I see her: a spunky kid from a good family that's seen better days. Marries a wealthy, older man. Big house, horses, mistress of the manor—the whole enchilada. Now she *is* someone. But he strays, and she's got pride and a temper. So she blows Canfield away, with a lot of publicity, her name and picture in the papers. She likes that. Off she goes to Paris and starts spending, feeling pretty good, a tough, smart twist who got away with murder. But Europe is full of jackals, tougher and smarter, and in five years the money is gone, and who cares about Belle Sarazen from Raccoon Ford, Virginia? If she stays in Europe, she'll be peddling her ass in flea markets. So she comes home and marries Congressman Burroughs. Now she's someone again: the Washington hostess with the mostest. Big parties. Entertaining the President. It doesn't cost Burroughs that much. I know how D.C. works; she'd have no trouble getting lobbyists and PR men to pick up the tab if she could collect the right guests and maybe provide some push-push on a crucial vote. Then Burroughs conks, and she's lost her power base. Washington is full of Congressional widows. So she moves to New York and gets in with the art and museum crowd. Keeps up her old friendships with politicos. Helps them out with high-class girls and maybe some dust when needed. Lends her apartment for their fun and games. Takes gifts for these services, money gifts, and gets high-level protection in return. More important to her—she's on all the society pages: party-thrower, woman-about-town, model for famous artists and fashion photographers; she's still *someone*."

"But *why?*" Boone wanted to know.

"If not fame, then notoriety," Delaney said somberly, almost speaking to himself. "As long as the world knows Belle Sarazen exists. Those scrapbooks are the tip-off. She's got to reassure herself about who she is. Some people are like that. They have such a low opinion of themselves that to endure, they've got to create another image in other people's eyes. She's a mirror woman. Now she can look in the mirror and see a sexy beauty with a face that looks like it hasn't been lived in, and a body that doesn't stop. The scrapbooks tell her who she is. But if it wasn't for the publicity, if it wasn't for the world's reaction to her, she'd look in the mirror and there would be nothing there. That's why she'll do almost anything for those important friends. She's got to hang onto the movers and shakers. To prove *she's* important, too. The poor doxy."

"Chief, you really think she knew it was Canfield when she blasted?"

"Of course. She gave herself away when she said the Durkee case was her favorite. We broke that one by working on a jealous wife, a woman who thought she had been scorned. Belle could identify with that; she had been a scorned woman herself."

"But could she have chopped Maitland?"

"I think so—if he was threatening her self-esteem, her vision of herself. And obviously she has the strength."

"Or for kicks," Boone said wonderingly. "Maybe she did it just for kicks."

"She's capable of that, too," Delaney said stonily. "She got away with it once. After they've done that, they think they can keep kicking God's shins."

"Listen, Chief," the sergeant said hesitantly. "Sounds to me that with the girls and the important friends, she's in a good position for some polite blackmail."

Delaney shook his head.

"Not our Belle," he said. "I told you she's not money hungry. All she wants is to call Senators by their first names."

They had time before their meeting with Jake Dukker, and they talked about lunch.

"Something quick," Delaney said. "And light. You have your big meal at night, don't you?"

"Usually," Boone said. "The doc's got me on a high-protein diet. Mostly I cook at home. Easy stuff like steaks, fish, hamburgers, and so forth."

"How are you doing?" Delaney asked, staring straight ahead.

"On the drinking?" Boone said calmly. "All right, so far. There isn't a minute I don't want it, but I've been able to lay off. Keeping busy on this Maitland thing helps."

"Does it bother you when you're with someone, and the other man orders a drink? Like yesterday, when I had an ale at lunch, and you had iced tea?"

"No, that doesn't bother me," the sergeant said. "What bothers me is when people joke about it. You know, friends and comics on TV who make jokes about how much they drink, and funny stories about drunks, and all. I don't think it's funny anymore. For a while there I was working at getting through the next hour without a drink. Now I work at getting through a whole day without a drink, so I guess that's an improvement."

Delaney nodded. "I know it sounds stupid to say it, but you've got to do it yourself. No one can do it for you, or even help."

"Oh, I don't know, Chief," Abner Boone said slowly. "You've helped."

"I have?" Delaney said, pleased. "Glad to hear it."

He didn't ask how.

The sun was at full blast now, the sky rapidly clearing, a nice breeze coming from the west. They decided to park somewhere near Columbus Circle, buy hotdogs from a street vendor, and maybe some cold soda, and have their lunch on a bench in Central Park. Then they could walk over to Jake Dukker's studio.

They pulled into a No Parking zone near the Circle, and Boone put the OFFICER ON DUTY card behind the windshield, hoping for the best. They found a vendor near the Maine Monument, and each bought two hotdogs, with sauerkraut, pickles, relish, mustard, and onions, and a can of wild-cherry soda. Delaney insisted on paying. They carried their lunch, bundled in paper napkins, into the park and finally discovered an empty bench stuck off on a small hillock covered with scrawny grass.

They ate leaning forward, knees spread, to avoid the drippings. The opened cans of soda were set on the bald ground.

"The way I see it," Sergeant Boone said, mouth full, "Sarazen and Dukker have got a mutual alibi for ninety minutes. We got statements from Dukker's assistants and from the models placing Sarazen and Dukker in the downstairs studio before twelve and after one-thirty. But for ninety minutes the two of them were upstairs, alone together. They say."

"You think one is covering for the other?"

"Or they were both in on it together. Look, Chief, those times are approximate. You know how unreliable witnesses are when it comes to exact time. Maybe they were out of the studio for more than ninety minutes. Maybe as much as two hours."

"Keep talking. It listens."

"They probably didn't take a cab. We checked thousands of trip sheets and followed up on every drop in the vicinity of the Mott Street studio between ten and three that Friday. But suppose they had a private car waiting. I think one of them, or both, could get down to Mott Street from Dukker's place and back in ninety minutes, or maybe a little more."

"That's assuming they didn't have to go through the downstairs studio to get out. Is there a door to the outside from the upstairs floor? The apartment?"

"That I don't know, sir. Something we'll have to check. Assuming there is, they leave the studio at twelve, go upstairs, pop out the door, go downstairs and head for their car. Or even—how's this?—they drive over to Lex and Fifty-ninth, by private car or cab, and take the downtown IRT subway. There's a local stop on Spring Street, less than two blocks from Maitland's studio. By taking the subway, they eliminate the risk of getting stuck in traffic. And I think they could make the round trip in ninety minutes to two hours, allowing five or ten minutes for killing Maitland."

"I don't know," Delaney said doubtfully. "It's cutting it thin."

"Want me to time it, sir?" Boone asked, getting a little excited about his idea. "I'll drive from Dukker's place to Maitland's studio and back, and then I'll try the same trip by subway. And time both trips."

"Good idea," Delaney nodded. "Make both between ten and three on a Friday, when the traffic and subway schedule will be approximately the same as they were then."

"Will do," Boone said happily.

They were silent awhile, working on their dripping hotdogs. When they used up the paper napkins, both used their handkerchiefs to wipe their smeared faces and fingers.

"Well, let's go brace Jake Dukker," Delaney said. "We can walk over . . ."

The building, tall, narrow, sooty, was one of the oldest on Central Park South. It had been designed for artists' studios, for painters, sculptors, musicians, singers. Ceilings were high, rooms spacious, walls thick. Floor-to-ceiling windows provided a steady north light and afforded a fine view of Central Park, an English farm set down in the middle of the steel and concrete city.

Jake Dukker occupied a duplex on the fourth and fifth floors. The lower level had been converted to a reception area, working studio, models' dressing room, a photographic darkroom, prop room and storage area, a lavatory, and a tiny kitchenette with refrigerator, sink, stove and a small machine that did nothing but produce ice cubes, chuckling at intervals as cubes spilled into a storage tray.

The studio was all efficiency: rolls of seamless paper and canvas, a battery of flood and spotlights with high-voltage cables, a stage, posing dais, overhead illumination of a theatrical design, mirrors, sets, stainless-steel and white-cloth reflectors, easels, a working table littered with paints, palettes, mixing pots . . . The walls were covered with framed paintings, prints, etchings, lithographs, drawings. Most of them signed.

The fifth floor, reached by an interior spiral staircase, provided living quarters for the artist: one enormous chamber with enough sofas, chairs, and floor pillows to accommodate an interdenominational orgy. Two bedrooms, two bathrooms, a spacious, well-equipped kitchen—copper-bottomed pans and pots hanging from the walls, a gargantuan spice rack—and a dining area with a glass-topped table long enough to seat twelve.

The living quarters were jangling with color, a surprisingly comfortable and attractive mix of the owner's short-lived enthusiasms: Bauhaus, Swedish Modern, Art Deco, New York Victorian, Art Nouveau, and such soupy examples of modern furnishings as iron tractor seats on pedestals and rough wooden cocktail tables that were originally the reels for telephone cable.

The owner of this hodgepodge was also a jumble of trendy fashions. He wore faded blue jeans cinched with a wide leather belt and tarnished brass buckle inscribed with the Wells Fargo insignia. Negating these symbols of rugged masculinity were the soft, black ballet slippers he wore on his long, slender feet. His overblouse was Indian tissue cotton, cut to the pipik, embroidered across the shoulders with garlands of roses, and boasting loose sleeves full enough to inspire a gypsy to make his violin cry. In the cleavage of this transparent shirt, a sunburst medallion swung from a clunky gold chain.

The man himself was tall and lanky, his slender grace somewhat marred by a well-fed paunch, half a bowling ball that strained the leather belt and threatened to eclipse Wells Fargo. He didn't move so much as strike a quick succession of poses, feet turned so, arms akimbo, head tilted, shoulder thrust, knee bent artfully. He was a stop-motion film, click, click, click, each shutter advance showing a different arrangement of features and limbs. But there was no flow.

The nubile receptionist told the officers to go into the studio. As Jake Dukker came forward to meet them, two cameras hanging from leather thongs about his neck, the first things Chief Delaney saw were the Stalin mustache, a bushy, bristly growth, and the glowering eyes, swimming and seemingly unfocussed. The nose was a sharp beak, the teeth as square and chiseled as small tombstones, faintly stained. The caved cheeks were pitted and shadowed; he had not shaved well. Black hair, cut in Mod style, full, brushed, and sprayed, covered his ears. Like Saul Geltman, he wore a gold bracelet. Unlike Geltman, there was nothing spruce, neat, or particularly clean about his person. But that, Delaney charitably decided, might have been due to the hot studio lights.

After the introductions, Dukker said, "Just finishing up. A few more shots. Take a look around. Don't trip on the cables."

At the center of the raised stage, posed against a roll of seamless purple paper, a young model with a teenager's body stood with her back to the lights and reflectors manned by Dukker's two assistants. She wore the bottom half of a bright red bikini; her upper back was bare. Atop her head was an enormously wide-brimmed white straw hat with a violet ribbon band. She assumed a hip-sprung pose, both arms to one side, hands perched on the handle of a closed pink parasol.

Jake Dukker lifted one of his cameras, a Nikon, and moved into position, crouching . . .

"More ass, honey," he called. "Magnificent. Lean onto the umbrella. Sensational. Profile to me. That's it. Sexy smile. Wonderful. Weight on that leg. More ass. Beautiful. Here we go . . ."

The girl held her pose, and Dukker was up, down, leaning, stretching, moving forward, moving back, clicking, winding. He switched quickly from one camera to another, adjusted his setting, continued his gymnastics with hardly a pause, snap, snap, snap, until finally he straightened up, arched his shoulders back, lifted his chin high to stretch his neck.

"That's it," he called to his assistants. "Kill it."

All the burning lights went off. One of the assistants came forward to take the cameras from Dukker. The model relaxed, took off her hat, shook her blonde hair free. She turned to face forward, showing little breasts with surprisingly large brown aureoles.

"Okay, Jake?" she asked.

"Incredible, honey," he said. "Sexy but pure. Gretchen will have your check."

"Anything coming up?" she asked.

"Me," he said, showing his teeth. "Cover up; it's the cops. Don't call us, sweetie, we'll call you. And stop eating. Five more pounds and you're dead."

He turned to Delaney and Boone, his pitted face glistening with sweat.

"A paperback cover," he explained. "No tits, but it's okay to titillate."

He grabbed up a soiled towel and wiped his face and hands.

"The place is air conditioned," he said, "but you'd never know it when the lights are on."

"You work hard, Mr. Dukker," Delaney said.

"The name of the game," Dukker said. "I do everything; fashion, book covers, record slips, paintings, magazine illustrations, posters, ads. You name it; I do it. A guy called me this morning and wants me to do a pack of playing cards. Can you believe it?"

"Pornographic?" Chief Delaney asked.

Dukker was startled.

"Close," he said, trying to smile. "Mighty close. I turned him down. Want to look around? Before we go upstairs?"

"Just for a minute," Delaney said, moving to inspect the framed art on the walls. "You have some beautiful things here. You know all these artists?"

"All of them," Dukker said. "Lousy friends and rotten enemies. Take a look at that one. The drawing over by the window, the one in the thin gold frame. That should interest you."

Obediently, Delaney and Boone found the sketch and stood before it. It had been torn twice, the four pieces patched with transparent tape and pressed behind glass. In the corner, a scrawled but legible signature: Victor Maitland.

"An original Maitland," Delaney said.

It was a hard, quick sketch of a running woman. In profile. Bulge of naked breast and ass caught in one fast S-stroke, a single charcoal line. A suggestion of high-stepping knees, hair flaming, the whole bursting with life, motion, young charm, vigor, a bright gaiety.

"No, sir," Jake Dukker said. They turned to look at him. "A *signed* Maitland. An original Dukker!" Then when he saw their expressions, he showed his teeth again, a pirate. "Come over here," he commanded. "I'll explain."

They followed him to a corner of the studio, a three-sided enclosure lined with pegboard. Pinned to the walls were photographic prints and contact sheets, sketches, clippings from newspapers and magazines, sheets of type fonts, illustrations of photo distortions, and color samples of paper and fabric. The small room was dominated by a tilt-top drawing table with a long T-square, jars of pens, pencils, chalks, pastels, plastic triangles and French curves, liquid-cement pot, a battered water-color tin, and overflowing ashtrays everywhere.

Behind the drawing table, facing a window, was a sturdy workbench. Clamped to the bench was a curious device, a prism at the end of a jointed chrome arm. It was positioned between a vertical and a horizontal drawing board.

"See that?" Dukker said. "It's called a camera lucida. Commonly known as a 'luci.' A kind of visual pantograph. Suppose you want to do a drawing of a nude. So you photograph a nude, the body and pose you want. Make an eight-by-ten print. Pin the print on the vertical board. Put your drawing paper flat on the horizontal board. Then you look through that prism at the end of the jointed arm. You see the photo image and at the same time you see the flat drawing paper. You can trace the photo with pen, pencil, chalk, charcoal, pastel stick, whatever. Absolute, realistic likeness."

They looked at him, and he laughed.

"Don't knock it," he said. "Takes too much time and work to do it the old-fashioned way, with sittings and all. Even if the artist or illustrator had the talent to do it. And most of them don't. Anyway, one night I was tracing a photo of a family group on my luci when Maitland shows up drunk as a skunk. He starts giving me a hard time about what a mechanic I am. I'm not an artist. I can't draw my way out of a wet paper bag. I'm a disgrace. And so forth and so on. Really laying it on me."

Dukker stopped suddenly, staring at the empty drawing board. His eyes squinched up, as if he was staring at something pinned there. Then he sighed and continued . . .

"Finally I got fed up, and I said, 'You son of a bitch, I've had all the horseshit I'm going to take from you. I'm twice the draftsman you'll ever be, and to prove it, I'm going to do an original Victor Maitland that any art expert in the world will swear is genuine.' He laughed, but I grabbed a pad, a charcoal stick, and I knocked out that sketch you see there, the nude running. Victor was a fast worker, but I'm faster. I'm the best. It took me less than three minutes. Then I showed it to him. He looked at it, and I thought he was going to kill me. I really was scared. His face got pale as hell, and his hands started shaking. I really thought he was going to get physical; it never did take much to set him off. I started looking around for something to hit him with. I'd never go up against that crazy bastard with my bare fists; he'd cream me."

Dukker paused to scratch at the tight denim across his crotch, looking up thoughtfully at the ceiling.

"Then he tore my drawing in four pieces and threw them at me. Then I put some more booze into him, and later that night we patched my drawing together with tape, and he signed it. Then he thought it was a big joke. It really is my drawing, but he admitted he wasn't ashamed to put his name to it. Shit, it's better than a lot of things he did. And I didn't trace a photograph either. I just knocked it off. He wasn't so great. I could have been . . . Everyone thinks . . . Well, let's go upstairs and relax. I got another shooting in an hour or so. Got to keep going. Can't stop."

Before he led them up the spiral staircase, he grabbed up a maroon beret from the littered work table and jammed it rakishly over one eye. They watched him put it on, but said nothing. They were cops; human nuttiness didn't faze them.

Upstairs, he asked if they'd like a drink. When they declined, he insisted on making a fresh pot of coffee for them. He made it in an unusual glass container with a plunger arrangement that shoved a strainer of ground coffee down through hot water.

"You'll love this," he assured them. "Better than drip. And the coffee is my own blend of mocha, Java, and Colombian that I buy in the bean at this marvelous little place on the Lower East Side. I grind it fresh every morning. Full-bodied, with a subtle bouquet."

Chief Delaney thought it was possibly the worst cup of coffee he had ever drunk. And he could tell from Boone's expression that his opinion was shared. But they sipped politely.

They were seated somewhat nervously on a short crimson velvet couch shaped like human lips. Jake Dukker slouched opposite them in a soft leather chair shaped like a baseball mitt.

"So . . ." he said. "What can I do for you?"

They took out their notebooks. Chief Delaney reviewed the record of the artist's activities on the Friday that Victor Maitland had been killed. Dukker's receptionist and assistants had come to work around 9:00 A.M. They had set up for the fashion assignment. The models appeared around 10:00, and shooting commenced about thirty minutes later. Belle Sarazen showed up around 11:30. At noon, she and Jake Dukker had come upstairs for lunch.

"A divine omelet," Dukker interjected.

They had gone back downstairs around 1:30, and Belle Sarazen left the studio about an hour later, maybe a little less. Shooting was completed slightly before 3:00 P.M., and the models departed. Dukker remained in his apartment until seven that evening, when he went to a dinner party with friends in Riverdale, driving up.

"Your own car?" Delaney asked.

Dukker nodded. "A waste of money really. I usually take cabs. Trying to park in midtown Manhattan is murder. Most of the time I keep it garaged. On West Fifty-eighth Street. Want the name and address of the garage?"

"No, thank you, Mr. Dukker," Delaney said. "We have that information. What about Belle Sarazen?"

"What about her?"

"Were you intimate with her?"

Dukker took a long swallow of his coffee and grimaced.

"Oh God, yes," he said. "Like half of New York. Belle distributes her favors regardless of race, creed, color, or national origin."

"She says you hated Victor Maitland," Delaney said tonelessly.

Dukker jerked erect, some of his drink slopping over onto his jeans. "She said *that?*" he said. "I don't believe it."

"Oh yes," Delaney nodded. He looked down at his notebook. "Said you hated him because you envied Maitland's integrity. Her word—'integrity'—not mine."

"The bitch," Dukker said, relaxing back into the baseball mitt. "Envied maybe. Yes, I suppose I did. Hated? I don't think so. Certainly not enough to kill him. I cried when I heard he was dead. I didn't want him dead. You can believe that or not, but I really took it hard."

"Well, that's something different," Delaney said. "You're the first person we've talked to who was close to Maitland who's expressed any kind of sorrow. Except possibly his agent, Saul Geltman."

"His *agent?*" Dukker said. Unexpectedly he laughed. "Is that what you call him?"

"He was Maitland's agent, wasn't he?"

"Well . . . yes, I suppose so," Dukker said, still smiling. "But they don't like to be called 'agents.' 'Art dealer' is the term they prefer."

"We had a long discussion with Geltman about art agents," Delaney said stubbornly. "How much they make, their duties and responsibilities, and so forth. Never once did Geltman object to being called Maitland's agent."

"Maybe he didn't want to rub you the wrong way," Dukker shrugged.

"But I assure you that art *dealer* is what they want to be called. Like a garbage man likes the title of sanitation engineer."

"Do you have an agent, Mr. Dukker?" Sergeant Boone asked. "Or an art dealer?"

"Hell, no," Dukker said promptly. "What for? I sell directly. People come to me; I don't have to look for customers. Why should I pay thirty percent of my gross to some leech who can't do anything for me I can't do myself? Listen, my stuff sells itself. I'm the best."

"So you told us," Delaney murmured. "To get back to Belle Sarazen, can you tell us anything about her relationship with Victor Maitland?"

"Hated him," Dukker said immediately. He put his drink aside, half-finished. He slumped lower in his leather baseball mitt, laced his fingers across his pot belly. "Hated his guts. Vic hated phonies, you see. Hated sham and hypocrisy in any way, shape or form. And Belle is the biggest phony going."

"Is she?" Delaney said.

"You bet your sweet ass," Dukker said enthusiastically, rubbing his bristly jaw. "Listen, Vic Maitland was a rough guy. I mean, if he thought you were talking shit, he'd tell you so. Right out. No matter who was listening. I remember once Belle had a big party at her place. A lot of important people. Maitland showed up late. Maybe he hadn't been invited. Probably not. But he'd hear about parties and come anyway. He didn't care. He knew they really didn't want him there because he got into trouble all the time. I told you, he'd get physical. He'd deck art critics and throw things. Food. Drinks at people he didn't like. Stuff like that. Anyway, Belle was having this fancy party, and Vic showed up. Drunk, as usual. But keeping his mouth shut. Just glaring at all the beautiful people. Then Belle started talking about what a big shot she had been in Washington. You know, entertaining the President and dancing with ambassadors and playing tennis with Senators and teaching yoga to Congressmen's wives. All that crap. Everyone was listening to Belle brag, not wanting to interrupt. After all, she swings a lot of clout. Then Maitland broke in. In a loud voice. Everyone heard him. He called Belle the World's Greatest Blower. He said she had blown off her husband's head, had blown a fortune in Europe, and had ended up blowing the Supreme Court."

Delaney and Boone smiled down at their notebooks.

"He broke up the place," Dukker grinned, remembering. "We

couldn't stop laughing. He was such a foul-mouthed bastard, really dirty, but at the same time he was funny. Outrageous. Sometimes."

"How did Belle Sarazen take this?" Delaney asked.

"Tried to laugh it off," Dukker shrugged. "What else could she do? But she was burning, I could see. Hated him right then. Could have killed him. I knew she'd never forget it."

"Why did Maitland do it? Say those things?"

"Why? I told you why. Because he couldn't stand phonies. Couldn't stand sham and hypocrisy."

"Well . . ." Delaney sighed, "sometimes people use complete honesty as an excuse for sadism."

Jake Dukker looked at him curiously.

"Right on, Chief," he said. "There was that, too. In Maitland's personality. He liked to hurt people. No doubt about it. He called it puncturing their ego-balloons, but there was more to it than that. At least I think there was. He could get vicious. Wouldn't leave anyone a shred of illusion or self-esteem. Like he did to Belle that night. You can hate someone like that, someone who strips all your pretense away and leaves you naked."

The two officers were busy scribbling in their notebooks.

"You said the Sarazen woman swings a lot of clout," Delaney said, not looking up. "What did you mean by that?"

"Well . . . you know," Dukker said. "Political influence. She really does know some important people. Knows where the bodies are buried. Also, she's a powerhouse in the New York art world. She can promote a gallery show for some shlocky little cartoonist. Or get her rich friends to buy some guy's stuff. Great on publicity and promotion. Throws parties. Knows everyone. She can be valuable to artists. To dealers. To collectors."

"You think she knows what's good?" Delaney asked. "I mean, does she have good taste in art?"

Jake Dukker burst out laughing.

"Good taste?" he spluttered. "Belle Sarazen? Come on! She'll find some kid in the Village with a long schlong, and she'll bring his stuff to me and say, 'Isn't he fan-tas-tic? Isn't he great?' And I'll say, 'Belle, the kid just hasn't got it. He's from stinksville.' A month later the kid will have a show in a Madison Avenue gallery, and a month after *that* he'll be dead, gone, and no one will ever hear of him again. Which is all to the good because he didn't have anything in the first place. All Belle's doings. She picked the guy up, gave him a gallery show, and dropped him just as quick. After showing him a few positions even the Kama Sutra doesn't include. Then she's on to someone else, and the original guy is back in the Village, eating Twinkies, and wondering what the hell hit him. Art is just one big game to Belle."

"But you like her?" Delaney asked, staring at Dukker without expression. "You like Belle Sarazen?"

"Belle?" Dukker repeated. "Like her? Well . . . maybe I do. Like goes to like. We're both a couple of phonies. I could have been . . . well, what the hell's the use of talking about it. Belle and me, we know who we are, and what we are."

"But Victor Maitland wasn't a phony?" Abner Boone said softly.

"No," Dukker said defiantly. "He was a lot of rotten things, but he wasn't a phony. The miserable shit. He wasn't too happy, you know. He was driven, too. He was as greedy as all of us. But for different things."

"What things?" Delaney asked.

"Oh . . . I don't know," Dukker said vaguely. "He was a hell of a painter. Not as good as me. Technically, I mean. But he had something I never had. Or maybe I had it and lost it. I'll never know. But he was never as good as he wanted to be. Maybe that's why he worked so hard, so fast. Like someone was driving him."

There was silence a few moments while Delaney and Boone flipped through their notebooks. From downstairs they heard voices and the clatter of props and equipment as Dukker's assistants set up for the next shooting.

"Mr. Dukker," Delaney said, "did you ever provide or suggest models for Maitland?"

"Models? Once or twice. Mostly he found his own. Big, muscular women. Not the type I dig."

"Did you suggest anyone to him recently? A very young girl? Puerto Rican or Latin-type?"

Dukker thought a moment.

"No," he shook his head. "No one like that. No one at all in the last six months or so. Maybe a year. Why?"

Chief Delaney told him of the sketches found in Maitland's studio. Dukker was interested.

"Bring them around," he suggested. "I'd like to see them. Maybe I can identify the girl. I use a lot of models. For photography and illustration. Painting, too, of course. Though I'm doing less and less of that.

The big money's in advertising photography. And I'm beginning to get into film. Commercials. Lots of dinero there."

He lurched suddenly to his feet, the maroon beret jerking to the back of his head.

"Got to get downstairs," he said briskly. "Okay?"

The two cops looked at each other. Delaney nodded slightly. They snapped notebooks shut, stood up.

"Thank you for being so cooperative, Mr. Dukker," Delaney said. "We appreciate that."

"Any time at all," the artist said, waving, expansive. "You know, you've got an interesting face, Chief. Very heavy. I'd like to sketch it some time. Maybe I will—when you come back with those Maitland drawings."

Delaney nodded again, not smiling.

"Can we leave from up here?" Sergeant Boone asked casually. "Or do we have to go downstairs to get out?"

"Oh no," Dukker said, "you can leave from here. That door over there. Leads to the fifth-floor landing and elevator."

"Just one more thing," Chief Delaney said. "Belle Sarazen told us you were doing a painting of her. A nude on aluminum foil."

"Belle talks too much," Dukker said crossly. "It'll get around and everyone will be doing it before I'm finished."

"Could we see it?" Delaney asked. "We won't mention it to anyone."

"Sure. I guess so. Why not? Come on—it's downstairs."

They were waiting for Dukker in the studio—the receptionist with a sheaf of messages, the assistants behind their lights, a model perched on a high stool. She was wearing a sleazy flowered kimono, chewing gum, and flipping the pages of *Harper's Bazaar*. Behind her, on the stage, the assistants had put together a boudoir scene: a brocaded chaise longue, a tall pier glass on a swivel mount, a dresser covered with cosmetics, a brass bedstead with black satin sheets.

"Hi, Jake, honey," she called as Dukker came down the stairs. "Were you serious? Is this really for a deck of playing cards?"

Dukker didn't answer. The officers couldn't see his face. He led them to a stack of paintings leaning against a wall. He flipped through for the one he wanted, slid it out, set it on a nearby easel. They moved close to inspect it.

He had glued aluminum foil to a Masonite panel, and prepared the surface to take tempera. The background was ebony black, which lightened to a deep, deep Chinese red in the center, a red as glossy as old lacquer ware. Belle Sarazen was posed in the center portion, on hands and knees, on what appeared, dimly, to be a draped bench.

She had, Delaney thought, almost the position of a hound on point: back arched and rigid, head up and alert, arms stiff, thighs straining forward. The artist had not used skin tones, but had allowed the aluminum foil, unpainted, to delineate the flesh. Modeling and shadows of the body were suggested with quick slashes of violet, the sharp features of the face implied rather than detailed.

The painting was a startling tour de force. There was no questioning the artist's skill or the effectiveness of his novel technique. But there was something disquieting in the painting, something chill and spiritless. The woman's hard-muscled body hinted of corruption.

That effect, Delaney decided, was deliberately the artist's, achieved by tightly crumpling the foil. Dukker had then smoothed it out before gluing it to the board. But the skin, the unpainted foil, still bore a fine network of tiny wrinkles, hundreds of them, that gave the appearance of crackle, as if the flesh had been bruised by age, punished by use, damaged by too-frequent handling. He could not understand why Belle Sarazen was so proud of a portrait that seemed to show her a moment before she fell apart, splintered into a dusty pile of sharp-edged fragments.

"Very nice," he told Dukker. "Very nice indeed."

He and Boone walked slowly back to their parked car. They stared at the sidewalk, brooding . . .

"The garage checked, Chief?" Boone asked.

"Yes," Delaney said. "The only record they had was when he took his car out at seven that evening. But check them again."

"Will do," the sergeant said. "You know, these people worry me."

"Worry you?"

"Yes, sir," Boone said, frowning. "I'm not used to the type. Most of the stuff I caught up to now involved characters with sheets. Addicts. Double offenders. Professionals. You know? I haven't had an experience dealing with people like this. I mean, they *think*."

"They also sleep," Delaney said stonily. "And they eat, they crap, and one of them killed. What I'm trying to say is that one of them is guilty of a very primitive act, as stupid and unthinking as a muscle job by some punk with a skinful of shit. Don't let the brains worry you. We'll get him. Or her."

"You think the killer fucked-up somewhere along the line?"

"I doubt it," Delaney said. "I'm just hoping for chance. An accident. Something they couldn't possibly foresee and plan for. I know a guy named Evelyn Forrest. He's the Chief in Chilton, New York, a turnaround in the road up near the Military Academy at West Point. Forrest is Chilton's one-man police department. Or was. An old cop gone to beer. I hope he's still alive.

"Anyway, this Forrest told me about a cute one he caught. This retired professor, his second wife, and his stepdaughter bought an old farmhouse with some land near Chilton. The professor is writing a biography of Thoreau, but he's got time to make it with the stepdaughter. So he decides to snuff the wife and make it look like an accident. He's got a perfect situation: On their land they've got this small apple orchard, and the local kids and drifters are always sneaking in to swipe apples. Lots of apples. Not off the ground; right off the trees. So this professor buys a twenty-gauge with birdshot, and every time they see or hear someone swiping their apples, they run out yelling and spray the orchard with their shotgun. Far enough away so no one gets hurt. Just to scare the kids.

"So the professor with the hots for the stepdaughter, he sets up the murder of his wife very carefully. Everything planned. A half-buried rock under one of the apple trees, a rock that anyone could trip over. Takes his wife out there for a stroll late one afternoon. Blows her away when she's at the rock. He's wearing gloves. Puts the shotgun in her hands for prints. Runs back to the house. Hides the gloves. Screams on the phone for help. His wife tripped, the shotgun hit the ground and blew, she's got no chest, and what a horrible, horrible accident it is. This Chief Forrest went out to look around. He thought it smelled, but there was no way he could shake the professor's story. Until a local farmer brought his scared kid around to Forrest to tell his version. The kid had seen the whole thing. He was up in that tree swiping apples. So much for careful planning . . ."

That evening, the girls staying the night with friends for something called a Pillow Party, Monica and Edward X. Delaney had a lonely kitchen dinner. She tried for a while; then, knowing his moods, she gave up trying to make conversation and said nothing when he excused himself to go into the study and close the door.

He felt his age: lumpy and ponderous. And somewhat awkward. His clothes were damp and heavy on his skin. His joints creaked. He seemed to be pressing down into his swivel chair, all of him dull and without lift. He had a sudden vision of a young girl leaning on a pink parasol. The tanned skin of her naked back. He shook his massive head, and doggedly began writing out detailed reports of the interviews with Belle Sarazen and Jake Dukker.

When they were finished, and filed away, he took the three drawings found in Victor Maitland's studio and fixed them to his wall map of the 251st Precinct, mounted on corkboard. He used pushpins to attach them over the map, then tilted his desk lamp so they were illuminated. He sat behind his desk and stared at the sketches.

Youth. Vigor. All juice, all bursting. Caught in the hard, quick lines of a frantic artist who wanted it all. Wanted to own it all, and show it. Maitland was driven, Jake Dukker had said. Delaney could believe that. In all these interviews, from all this talk, these words, he was beginning to see most clearly the man who was dead. The painter, the artist, Victor Maitland. That gifted hand moldering now, but not so long ago eager and grasping. A filthy human being he might have been. Malicious, besotted, maybe sadistic. But there was no law that said only saints could be talented.

The trouble was, Delaney brooded, the trouble was that he was beginning to feel sympathy. Not only for the victim—that was natural enough—but for all the others involved in the murder. One of whom, he was convinced, had plunged the blade. The trouble was that he liked them—liked Mrs. Maitland, Saul Geltman, Belle Sarazen, Jake Dukker. And, he suspected, when he met Maitland's son, and his mother and sister, he'd like them, too. Feel compassion.

"They *think*," Sergeant Boone had said. But it was more than that. They were spunky, bright, *wanting* human beings, touching in their hungers and illusions. There was not one he could hate. Not one he could hope would prove to be the killer and deserving of being boxed and nailed.

His sympathy disturbed him. A cop was not paid to be compassionate. A cop had to see things in black and white. *Had* to. Explanations and justification were the work of doctors, psychiatrists, sociologists, judges, and juries. They were paid to see the shades of grey, to understand and dole out ruth.

But a cop had to go by Yes or No. Because . . . well, because there had to be a rock standard, an iron law. A cop went by that and couldn't allow himself to murmur comfort, pat shoulders, and shake tears from his eyes. This was important, because all those other people—the ruth-givers—they modified the standard, smoothed the rock, melted the law. But if there was no standard at all, if cops surrendered their task, there would be nothing but modifying, smoothing, melting. All sweet reasona-bleness. Then society would dissolve into a kind of warm mush: no rock, no iron, and who could live in a world like that? Anarchy. Jungle.

He drew his yellow legal pad to him, put on his heavy reading glasses, began making notes. Things he must do to find the murderer of Victor Maitland.

It was getting on to midnight when the desk phone rang. The Chief picked it up with his left hand, still scribbling at his notes.

"Edward X. Delaney here," he said.

"Edward, this is Ivar . . ."

Deputy Commissioner Thorsen chatted a few moments, asking after the health of Monica and the girls. Then he inquired casually, "How's Boone making out?"

"All right," Delaney said. "I like him."

"Glad to hear it. Off the booze, is he?"

"As far as I know. He's completely sober when I see him."

"Any signs of hangovers?"

"No. None." Delaney didn't appreciate this role; he wasn't Boone's keeper, and didn't relish reporting on the man's conduct.

"Any progress, Edward?"

"On the case? Nothing definite. I'm just learning what went on, and the people involved. It takes time."

"I'm not leaning on you, Edward," Thorsen said hastily. "Take all the time you want. No rush."

There was a moment of silence then. Delaney knew what would come next, but refused to give the man any help.

"Ah . . . Edward," Thorsen said hesitantly, "you questioned the Sarazen woman today?"

"Yes."

"She a suspect?"

"They're all suspects," Delaney said coldly.

"Well, ah, we have a delicate situation there, Edward."

"Do we?"

"The lady has some important friends. And apparently she feels you were a little rough on her."

Delaney didn't reply.

"Were you rough on her, Edward?"

"She probably thought so."

"Yes, she did. And called a few people to complain. She said . . ." Thorsen's voice trailed away.

"You want me off the case?" Delaney said stonily.

"Oh God, no," Thorsen said quickly. "Nothing like that. I just wanted you to be aware of the situation."

"I'm aware of it."

"And you'll treat her—"

"I'll treat her like everyone else," Delaney interrupted.

"My God, Edward, you're a hard man. I can't budge you. Listen, if that lady is guilty, I'll be delighted to see her hung by the heels and skinned alive. I'm not asking you to cover up. I'm just asking that you use a little discretion."

"I'll do things my own way," Delaney said woodenly. "This is the kind of bullshit that made me retire. I don't have to take it now."

"I know, Edward," Thorsen sighed. "I know. All right . . . do it your own way. I'll handle the flak. Somehow. Anything you need? Co-operation from the Department? Files or background stuff? Maybe another man or two?"

"Not at the moment, Ivar," Delaney said, thawing now, grateful. "But thanks for the offer."

"Well . . . keep at it. Give me a call if anything turns up, or if you need anything. Forget what I said—about handling the Sarazen woman with chopsticks."

"I already have," Delaney said.

"Iron Balls!" Thorsen laughed, and hung up.

Delaney sat a moment, staring at the dead phone in his hand. Then his eyes rose slowly. Almost against his will, his gaze sought those drawings pinned to the wall. The victim's final statement. His last words . . .

Delaney hung up and, on impulse, looked up the phone number of Victor Maitland's Mott Street studio. It was an unlisted number, but had been included in the police reports of the homicide.

Then he dialed the number. It rang and rang. He listened a long time. But of course there was no answer.

7

"Dinner will be at seven sharp," Monica Delaney said firmly. "I expect you and Sergeant Boone to be back by then."

"We're just going out of the county, not out of the country," Chief Delaney said mildly. "We'll be back long before seven. What are you having?"

"London broil and new potatoes."

"What kind of London broil?" he demanded.

"A nice piece of flank steak."

"Good. That's the best flavor. Want me to pick up anything on our way back?"

"No—well, we're low on beer. Or will you have wine?"

"Either. But I'll pick up some beer—just in case."

"He doesn't object if other people drink, does he?"

"I asked him, and he said he didn't."

"All right, dear. Have a good trip. And a *very* light lunch."

"I promise," he said. "I know a good inn near Dobbs Ferry. They serve excellent London broil and new potatoes."

She laughed and poured them their second cups of breakfast coffee.

Sergeant Abner Boone was waiting for him outside. All the car windows were rolled down; Boone was fanning himself with a folded newspaper.

"Going to be a hot one, sir," he said cheerfully. "Seventy-three already."

Delaney nodded, tossed his homburg onto the back seat. Both men took out their notebooks and went through the morning ritual of comparing notes.

"I checked Dukker's garage," Boone said. "No record of him taking his car out before the evening. So then, just for the hell of it, I talked to the doorman of Belle Sarazen's apartment house. She doesn't own a car —or if she does, she doesn't garage it there. I don't think she does; I ran a vehicle check, and she's got no license. The doorman said that sometimes she rents from a chauffeured-limousine service. He remembered the name, and I checked them out. No record of her hiring a car on that Friday. I suppose she could have used another service. Want me to run down the list, Chief?"

"No," Delaney said. "Hold off. It's a long shot."

"Well, they still might have used the subway," Boone said stubbornly. "I'll run a time trial tomorrow."

"You still think they're it?"

"A possible," Boone nodded. "Either one, or both together. Give them two hours, and they could have made it down to Mott Street and back."

"All right," Delaney said. "Keep hacking away at it until you're satisfied. I'm not saying you're wrong. Thorsen called last night. The Sarazen woman beefed to her important friends."

"Was Thorsen sore?"

"Not very. He'll schmaltz it over for us. He's good at that."

"One more thing," Boone said, consulting his notes. "I talked to a few more guys who worked the case. One of them had gone up to Nyack to check out the mother and sister. They said they were both home that Friday from ten to three. They couldn't prove it, and he couldn't disprove it. They've got a housekeeper, but it was her day off. No one saw them there; no one saw them leave."

"They own a car?"

"Yeah. A big, old Mercedes-Benz. Both mother and sister drive. But what this dick remembered, what wasn't in his report, was when he was leaving, the mother grabbed him by the arm and said something like, 'Find the killer of my son. It's very important to me.' This guy thought that was kind of funny. 'Very important to *me*,' she said. It stuck in his mind."

"Yes," Delaney nodded. "An odd way of putting it. Of course, she may have meant it to mean avenging the Maitland family name, or some such shit. Well, let's talk to the lady. How do you figure on going?"

"I thought we'd take the FDR, across the George Washington to Palisades Parkway, and then 9W into Nyack. Okay, sir?"

"Fine with me."

"I'm going to take off my jacket and get comfortable," the sergeant said. "You, Chief?"

"I'm comfortable," Delaney said.

When Boone removed his lightweight plaid sports jacket and leaned over to put it on the back seat, Delaney saw he was carrying a .38 Colt Detective Special in a black short-shank holster high on his hip. The two cops talked guns while Boone was maneuvering through city streets over to the FDR.

As they crossed the George Washington Bridge, traffic thinned, they could relax and enjoy the trip. It was warming up, but a cool river breeze was coming through the open windows and the air was mercifully free of pollution. They could see the new apartment houses on the Jersey side rising sharply into a clear, blue sky. There was some slow barge traffic on the river. A few jetliners droned overhead. Nice day . . .

"Chief, was your father a cop?" Abner Boone asked.

"No," Delaney said, "he was a saloon-keeper. Had a place on Third near Sixty-eighth, then opened another place on Eighty-fourth, also on Third. I used to work behind the stick in the afternoons when I was going to nightschool."

"My father was a cop," Boone said.

"I know," Delaney said. "I went to his funeral."

"You did?" Boone said. He seemed pleased. "I didn't know that."

"I was a sergeant then and brought over a squad from the Two-three."

"I was sure impressed," Boone said. "They even had cops from Boston and Philadelphia. The Mayor was there. He gave my mother a plaque."

"Yes," Delaney said. "Your mother living?"

"No, she's gone. I've got some cousins down in Tennessee, but I haven't seen them for years."

"You and your wife didn't have any children?"

"No," Boone said, "we didn't. I'm glad. Now."

They rode awhile in silence. Then Delaney said, "I want you to do something on this Maitland thing, but I don't want you to get sore."

"I won't get sore," Boone said. "What is it, Chief?"

"Well, first of all I want to question Maitland's son—what's his name? Theodore. They call him Ted. I want to question him myself. Alone."

"Well, sure, Chief," Boone said. He kept his eyes on the road. "That's okay."

But Delaney knew he was hurt.

"The way I figure is this," he explained. "From the files, and from what his mother said, I think the kid is a wise-guy. The kind of snotnose who calls cops 'pigs' or 'fuzz.' I figure if we both go up against him, he'll feel we're leaning on him. Pushing him around. But if I go up against him alone, all sweetness and light, playing the understanding older man, the father he never had, maybe he'll crack a little."

Boone glanced at him briefly, with wonderment.

"Makes sense," he said. "But I wouldn't have thought of it."

"In return," Delaney said, "I want you to brace that Susan Hemley alone. How did she sound on the phone? Young? Old?"

"Youngish," Boone said. "But very sure of herself. Deep voice. Good laugh."

"Well, here's what you do," Delaney said. "I'll meet the Maitland kid tomorrow. Alone. You do the time trials on the subway from Dukker's place to the Mott Street studio. Either before or after, go up to the office of Simon and Brewster and see this Susan Hemley. Your scam is that you dropped by to set up an appointment for you and me to talk to her boss, J. Julian Simon. Any day next week, morning or afternoon, at his convenience."

"I get it," Boone said, feeling better. "You want me to romance her—right?"

"If you can," Delaney nodded. "See what she's like. If she gives a little, ask her to have lunch. I think it's a one-on-one situation, and we'll get more if you go in alone. If you can make lunch, don't push it. You know—just idle talk. Did she know Maitland, and wasn't it awful what happened to him, and so forth. You know the drill. You can listen, can't you?"

"I'm a good listener," Boone said.

"Fine. That's all I want you to do. Don't drag anything out of her. Just make friends."

"What if she asks about the case?"

"Play it cozy. Tell her nothing, but make it sound like something. Tell her Maitland wasn't wearing any underwear. That'll make her think she's getting the inside poop that wasn't in the newspapers. Also, later we'll try to find out if she told Mrs. Maitland about the underwear. That'll be a tip-off on how intimate the two women are, just what that relationship is. But keep it hush-hush with the Hemley woman. Very confidential. You lean to her and say, 'I want you to promise not to breathe a word of this to anyone, but—' She'll get all excited, and maybe she'll start trading you secret for secret. Think you can handle it?"

Boone took a deep breath, blew it out heavily.

"Oh, I can handle it," he said. "But I'll tell you one thing, Chief: if I ever waste someone, I hope you don't catch the squeal."

They stopped in Nyack to ask directions, and shortly after noon they cruised slowly by the Maitland home and grounds, taking a good gander.

The grounds were an impressive size: a wide expanse of lawn leading up from the road, bordered by a thick stand of oaks, maples, a few firs. The driveway from the road was graveled, led under a side portico, and then to the wide doors of a smaller building that looked as if it had been built as a barn, then converted to a garage. An old black Mercedes-Benz was parked under the side portico.

The house itself was a rambling structure, two stories high, with a widow's walk facing the river. The building was sited atop a small hill with good drainage; trees at the rear had been cut away to provide a splendid river view.

The main entrance had four wooden pillars going up the entire height of the house to support a peaked portico. There were dormers, small minarets, plenty of gingerbread around porticos, windows, doors, and a screened-in porch overhanging a bank that sloped steeply to the river. At one side, close to the trees, was a gazebo that looked unused.

"I'd guess seventy-five years old," Delaney said. "Maybe a hundred. It looks like it started with that main house in the center, and the wings were added later. But the barn is original."

"She's supposed to have money," Boone said, "but it sure doesn't look like it. At least she's not spending much on upkeep."

The lawn badly needed mowing, the trees should have been trimmed, and the undergrowth cut away. Several windows of the gazebo were broken. The graveled driveway had bald patches. The flowerbeds close to the house grew in wild, untended profusion, choked with weeds. The house itself, and the barn, were peeling, a weather-beaten grey, almost silver in spots.

"Seedy," Delaney said. "The house looks sound, but it would take a crew a month to get this place in shape. But nothing could spoil that view. Well, let's go . . ."

They drove slowly up the driveway and parked in front of the three-step entrance. Sergeant Boone put on his jacket before they walked up to the front door. The paint was cracked, the brass knocker tarnished. Chief Delaney rapped sharply, twice.

The door was opened immediately. The tall woman who glowered at them was gaunt, almost emaciated. Rawboned and sunburned. A big-featured farm face. There were stained carpet slippers on her feet, the heelbacks bent under so the slippers were actually scuffs. The shiny black dress had soiled ruching at throat and cuffs. The woman was wearing a cameo brooch on her flat bosom and, unexpectedly, a man's gold digital wristwatch.

"Yes?" she said. Her voice was harsh, peremptory.

"Mrs. Maitland?" Chief Delaney asked.

"No," the woman said. "You the po-leece?"

"Yes, ma'am," Delaney said softly, trying to smile. "Mrs. Maitland is expecting us."

"This way," the woman commanded. "They on the poach."

Delaney couldn't place the accent. Possibly tidewater Virginia, he thought.

She held the door open just wide enough for Delaney and Boone to slip through, one at a time. They waited while she locked and bolted the door. Then they followed her as she flap-flapped across the uncarpeted parquet floor, down a long, narrow hallway to the river side of the house. The officers, looking around, caught a quick glance of dark, heavy furniture, dried flowers under glass bells, dusty velvet drapes, antimacassars, ragged footstools, gloomy walls of dull mahogany paneling and stained wallpaper. A fusty smell, with vagrant scents of cats, a heavy perfume, furniture polish.

The hallway debouched into a screened porch overlooking the river. Hinged windows had been opened inward and secured with cheap hooks and eyebolts. The porch, which had the appearance of having been added after the main house was built, was approximately twenty feet long and eight feet deep. It was furnished with a ratty collection of wicker furniture, once white, with faded chintz cushions. There was a frazzled rag rug on the planked floor. A small portable TV set was on one of the chairs, a fat, sleepy calico cat on another.

The two women on the porch had their armchairs drawn up near a sagging wicker table. On it was a black japanned tray with a pitcher of what appeared to be lemonade, surrounded by four tall, gracefully tapered glasses decorated with raised designs of enamel flowers, each glass different. Delaney guessed the lemonade set to be authentic Victoriana.

Neither woman rose to greet the visitors.

"Mrs. Maitland?" Delaney asked pleasantly.

"I," the older woman said, "am Dora Maitland."

She held out her hand in a kiss-my-ring gesture. Delaney came forward to clasp the firm hand briefly.

"Chief Edward X. Delaney, New York Police Department," he said. "A pleasure, ma'am."

"And *this*," Mrs. Maitland said, a lepidopterologist pointing out a rare specimen, "is my daughter, Emily."

The younger woman held out her hand obediently. This time, Delaney found the hand plump, soft, moist.

"Miss Maitland," he said. "My pleasure. May I present my associate, Detective sergeant Abner Boone."

Boone went through the hand-shaking ceremony, murmuring something unintelligible. Then the two officers stood awkwardly.

"Please to pull up chairs, gentlemen," Mrs. Maitland said sonorously. "I suggest those two chairs in the corner. I pray you, do not disturb the cat. I fear she is in heat and somewhat ill-tempered. I have had this pitcher of lemonade prepared. I imagine you are thirsty after your long drive."

"Very welcome, ma'am," Delaney said, as the two cops carried the unexpectedly heavy wicker chairs to the table. "A close day."

"Martha," Mrs. Maitland said imperiously, "will you serve, please."

"I got the sheets to do," the gaunt woman whined. She had been standing in the doorway; now she turned abruptly and flap-flapped away.

"So hard to get good help these days," Mrs. Maitland said imperturbably. He hadn't, Delaney reflected, heard that line in twenty years. "Emily," she commanded her daughter, "pour."

The younger woman heaved immediately to her feet.

"Yes, Mama," she said.

She was wearing a sleeveless caftan with a mandarin collar. But even this paisley-printed tent could not hide the obesity, the billows of breast and hip. Her bare arms belonged on a butcher's block, and three chin rolls bulged above the high collar. Even her fingers were fat; puffy toes swelled through strap sandals.

But she had the flawless skin of many fat women, and if her face at first glance seemed girlish and vacant, it was also pleasant and without malice. As she poured the lemonade, she spilled a few drops and said, "My land!" and colored with almost pretty confusion. Delaney guessed her age at about thirty-two, and wondered what her life might be like, with that balloon body, stuck out here ten miles from nowhere.

When she handed him his glass of lemonade, he looked closely at her brown eyes and saw, he fancied, a shrewd intelligence, which startled him. And for all her excessive weight her movements were sure and graceful. Almost dainty. Her voice too was light, younger than her years, with a warm, flirty undertone. When she handed a glass to Boone, she smiled nicely and said, "There you are, sergeant!" and Delaney noted she contrived to have their fingers briefly touch.

The lemonade had been freshly squeezed, lightly sugared, and well chilled. It was delicious, and Chief Delaney told Mrs. Maitland so. She inclined her head regally.

He then admired the view, watching a cruise boat move slowly upriver from New York to Bear Mountain between wooded shores. "Magnificent," Delaney commented, and Mrs. Maitland said, "Thank you," as if she had designed it.

Then, amenities at an end, she said crisply, "Chief Delaney, what exactly is being done to find the murderer of my son?"

"Ma'am," Delaney said, leaning forward to deliver what he later described to Boone as "the bullshit speech," and looking directly in the woman's eyes, "I assure you the full and complete resources of the New York Police Department are presently engaged in the search for your son's killer. Nothing is being left undone to find the person or persons responsible. Sergeant Boone and I have been relieved of all other duties to concentrate wholly on this case, and the enormous man-power and technical know-how of the Department are available to us. Believe me, speaking for Sergeant Boone and myself, the search for your son's murderer has Number One priority. The case is open and very active indeed."

His eagerness seemed to impress Mrs. Maitland. It took her a few moments to realize Chief Delaney had really said nothing at all.

"But what is being *done?*" she demanded. "Is anyone suspected?"

"We have several promising leads," Delaney said. "Very promising. I wish I could tell you more, Mrs. Maitland, but I cannot without slandering possibly innocent people. But I assure you, we are getting close."

"And you think you will find the killer?"

"I believe we have an excellent chance."

"And when will an arrest be made?"

"Soon," he said softly. "It is a very difficult case, Mrs. Maitland. I cannot recall working on a more difficult or more important case. Can you, sergeant?"

"Never," Boone said promptly. "A very tough case. Very complex."

"Complex," Delaney cried. "Exactly! Which is why we have come up from New York to see you and your daughter, Mrs. Maitland. In hopes that you may provide information that will help resolve those complexities."

"We have already been questioned," she said edgily. "And we signed statements. We told all we knew."

"Of course you did," he soothed. "But that was soon after the death of your son. When you were both, quite understandably, numb with grief and shock and horror. But now, with the passage of time, perhaps you can recollect some important information you didn't recall at that time."

"I don't see what possible—"

"Oh Mama," the daughter said, smiling prettily, showing teeth as shiny and small as white peg corn, "why don't we just answer Chief Delaney's questions and get it over with?"

Her mother whirled on her furiously.

"You shut your mouth!" she said. Then she turned to the officers. "More lemonade, gentlemen? Please help yourselves."

Sergeant Boone rose to do the honors, topping off the ladies' glasses first.

"Thank you, sir," Emily Maitland said pertly.

During this pause, with the sergeant moving about, Delaney had the opportunity to examine Dora Maitland more closely.

It was a face, he decided, that belonged on a cigar box. The skin was dusty ivory, eyes dark and flashing, lips carmine, and hair pouring in curls of jet black to below her shoulders. It *had* to be a wig, and yet it suited her exotic appearance so perfectly that Delaney wondered if it might not be her own hair, darkened, oiled, and fashioned into those glossy ringlets by the hairdresser's art.

He guessed her age at about sixty; face and hair denied it, but the hands were the tip-off. She wore lounging pajamas, not too clean, of bottle-green silk. The blouse was styled like a man's shirt, with an open collar that showed a magnificent, unwrinkled throat and hinted at shoulders just as luscious. She was fleshy enough, but without her daughter's corpulence.

Both men were conscious of her musky scent. Even more conscious of the mature voluptuousness of her ungirdled body. Her feet were bare; toenails painted the same red as fingernails and lips. Just below one corner of her mouth was a small black mole, although it could have been a velvet *mouche*.

She moved infrequently and had the gift of natural repose, not unlike the cat sleeping carelessly on a nearby chair. She exuded a very primitive sensuality, no less impressive because it was partly the product of artifice. Her physical presence was as deliberately mannered as Cleopatra's on her barge, and just as confident. Such a role, essayed by even a younger woman of less talent and smaller natural gifts, might inspire laughter. Neither officer had any desire to laugh at Dora Maitland; they were convinced.

"Very well, Chief Delaney," she said. "What is it you wish to know?"

Her voice was low-pitched, throaty, with a tendency to raspiness. She had not lighted a cigarette since they arrived, but Delaney thought hers the voice of a heavy smoker.

He took out his notebook, and Sergeant Boone followed suit. Delaney slid on his heavy reading glasses.

"Mrs. Maitland," he started, "you have stated that on the day your son was killed, you and your daughter were here, in this house, during the period from ten in the morning until three in the afternoon. Is that correct?"

"Yes."

"And on that Friday, the housekeeper was not present because it was her day off?"

"That's correct."

"The housekeeper is Martha, the lady who let us in?"

"Yes."

"During that time period, did you have any visitors?"

"No."

"Did you make or receive any phone calls?"

"I don't recall. I don't think so. No, I didn't make any calls or receive any. Emily, did you?"

"No, Mama."

"Did you go anywhere in your car?" Delaney asked. "Shopping, perhaps? To visit? Or just for a ride?"

"No, we went nowhere on that Friday. I had a dreadful headache, and I believe I spent most of the day lying down. Isn't that right, Emily?"

"Yes, Mama. I brought lunch to your room."

"Now I would like both of you to listen to my next question carefully," Delaney said solemnly, "and think very carefully before you answer. Do either of you know or suspect anyone who for whatever reason, real or fancied, disliked or hated Victor Maitland enough to murder him?"

The two women looked at each other a moment.

"I'm sure there were people who disliked or even hated my son," Dora Maitland said finally. "He was a very successful artist in a very competitive field, and there are always those who are jealous of talent. I know something of this, you see. I was on the stage before I married Mr. Maitland, and achieved quite some success and was myself the object of very bitter jealousy, cruel gossip, and all sorts of vile rumors. But one learns to expect this in the creative arts. People without talent become so frustrated that their jealousy sometimes drives them to malicious cruelty. I'm certain my son suffered many such attacks."

"But do you know of anyone specifically who was capable of killing him, or who threatened him with physical harm?"

"No, I do not. Emily?"

"I don't know anyone, Mama."

"Your son never mentioned anyone threatening him?"

"No, he did not," Dora Maitland said.

"You saw your son frequently?"

There was the barest of pauses before she said, "Not as frequently as I would have wished."

"And how often did your son visit you, Mrs. Maitland?"

Again a brief pause, then, "As often as he could."

"How often? Once a week? Once a month? Less often or more often?"

"I really don't see what this has to do with finding my son's murderer, Chief Delaney," she said coldly.

He sighed and leaned toward her, the sincere confidant.

"Mrs. Maitland, I am not trying to cause you pain, or to pry into the relationship between you and your son. After all, it was a normal, loving mother-son relationship. Was it not?"

"Of course it was," she said.

"Of course it was," he repeated. "He loved you and you loved him. Isn't that correct?"

"Yes."

"Miss Maitland, would you care to comment?"

"What Mama says is right," the younger woman said.

"Of course," Delaney nodded. "So when I ask how often your son visited you, it is not to doubt that relationship; it is only to establish a pattern of his movements. Who he saw, and when. Where he traveled and how often. Did he come up here once a month, Mrs. Maitland?"

"Less," she said shortly.

"Once a year?"

"Perhaps," she said. "When he could. He was a very busy, successful artist."

"Of course," Delaney said. "Of course." He took off his glasses, gazed out at the murky river flowing slowly to the sea. "A very successful artist," he said musingly. "Did you know that your son had sold a single painting for a hundred thousand dollars?"

"I read of it," she said tonelessly.

"Think of it!" Delaney said. "A hundred thousand for one painting!" Then he turned suddenly to stare at her. "Did he send any of that money to you, Mrs. Maitland?"

"No."

"Did he ever contribute to your support? Ever make any effort to share his financial success with his mother?"

"He never gave us a cent," Emily Maitland burst out, and they all turned to look at her. She colored, giggled, took a sip of lemonade. "My land!" she said. "I got all carried away. But it is true—isn't it, Mama?"

"I never asked him for anything," Mrs. Maitland said. "I am not without my own resources, Chief Delaney. I'm sure that if I had been in need, Victor would have offered help gladly and generously."

"I'm sure he would have," Delaney murmured. "You are well provided for, Mrs. Maitland?"

"Comfortable," she said. "The late Mr. Maitland . . ." She let her voice trail away.

"When did your husband die, Mrs. Maitland?" Sergeant Boone asked quietly.

"Oh . . ." she said. "Quite some time ago."

"Twenty-six years in November," Emily Maitland said.

"From illness?" Boone persisted.

"No," Dora Maitland said.

"My father committed suicide," Emily said. "Mama, don't look at me so. My land, they'll find out anyway. My father hanged himself in the barn."

"Yes," Dora Maitland said. "In the barn. Which is why we never use it. The doors are nailed shut."

Delaney busied himself with his notebook, looking down, saying, "Just a few more questions, ladies, and then we'll be finished. For the time being. Now I am going to mention several names. Please tell me if you know these individuals or ever heard your son speak of them. The first is Jake Dukker. D-u-k-k-e-r. An artist."

"I never heard of him," Dora Maitland said. "Emily?"

"No, Mama."

"Belle Sarazen. S-a-r-a-z-e-n."

Dora Maitland shook her head.

"I never heard Vic speak of her," Emily Maitland said, "but I've read about her. Isn't she that beautiful thin blonde lady who gives all the big parties? She sponsors charity bazaars, and she poses naked for artists and photographers."

"Emily!" Dora Maitland said. "Where did you read such things?"

"Oh Mama, it's in all the newspapers and magazines. And she's been on TV talk shows."

Dora Maitland muttered something that no one could catch.

"Yes, that's the lady," Delaney nodded.

"Lady!" Mrs. Maitland said explosively.

"You never heard your son mention her name?"

"No. Never."

"Nor you, Miss Maitland?"

"No."

"How about Saul Geltman? G-e-l-t-m-a-n. Your son's agent, or art dealer. Do you know him, or of him?"

"Saul? Of course I know him," Dora Maitland said. "A dear, sweet little man. He has been up here to visit us."

"Oh?" Delaney said. "Frequently?"

"No. Not frequently. On occasion."

"How frequently?"

"Perhaps two or three times a year. Maybe more often."

"More often than your son," Delaney said. It was a statement, not a question.

"Oh Mama," Emily said with a light, little laugh. "You'll have the officers thinking Saul Geltman came to visit us." She turned to him, smiling. "He didn't, of course. Saul has friends in Tuxedo Park he visits frequently. He drives up from New York and on his way stops by here to say hello. He never stays long."

"Do you know the names of his friends in Tuxedo Park?" Boone asked casually.

Emily Maitland considered a moment before she answered.

"No, sergeant, I don't believe he ever did mention their names. Just some nice boys, he said, who gave a lot of parties. I remember once I teased him about why he never asked me to the parties. But he said I'd probably be bored. I expect he was right."

Delaney nodded and, watching Dora Maitland, said, "The final name on the list is Alma Maitland, your son's widow. I wondered if you could tell us something about your daughter-in-law, Mrs. Maitland?"

She looked at him with basalt eyes.

"Tell you what?" she asked huskily.

"Well, let's start with your personal relations with her. Are you friendly?"

"Friendly enough. Hardly what you'd call close. She goes her way, and we go ours."

"I gather she did not accompany her husband when he visited you here?"

"You gather correctly." A harsh bark of laughter. "But don't get the wrong idea, Chief Delaney. There is no argument between Alma and me. No open warfare."

"More of an armed truce?" he suggested.

"Yes," she agreed. "Something like that. Hardly an unusual state of affairs between mother-in-law and daughter-in-law."

"That's true," he assented. "Would you mind telling me the cause of your, ah, disagreement?"

"I didn't think much of the way she was raising Ted, and I told her so. The boy needed discipline and wasn't getting it. We have spoken very little since."

"But we always get Christmas cards from her, Mama," Emily said mischievously, and her mother glared.

"One final question, Mrs. Maitland," Chief Delaney said. "When your son visited you here, how did he come up? By train or bus? Or did he drive?"

"He drove," she said.

"Oh?" Delaney said. "I understood he didn't own a car. Well, perhaps he rented one."

"No," she said. "On the few trips he made, he borrowed Saul Geltman's car."

"It's a station wagon, Mama," Emily said.

"Is it?" her mother said. "I know very little about cars."

Delaney stood up slowly, tucked notebook and spectacles away, moved to the doorway. Sergeant Boone joined him.

"Mrs. Maitland," the Chief said with grave courtesy, "Miss Maitland, we thank you both for your hospitality and patience. Your cooperation has been a very great help."

"I don't see how," Dora Maitland said.

Delaney ignored that.

"One final favor . . ." he said. "If we may impose on you a few moments longer, would you object if we looked about your lovely grounds a bit? It's not often we get out of the city, and it's such a pleasure to breathe clean air and see this beautiful, peaceful place. Could we see a little more of it before we go back to the streets?"

He had, unwittingly, ignited her with his reference to "this beautiful, peaceful place." She came alive, insisted on donning webbed sandals and conducting the officers on a tour. They paired off, Mrs. Maitland with Delaney, Emily with Sergeant Boone, and wandered off onto the grounds. The housekeeper was nowhere to be seen, but a radio was blasting country music in one wing of the house.

Dora Maitland showed Chief Delaney the cluttered flower beds of peonies, irises, and lilies; a gnarled oak she claimed to be 150 years old; a broken birdbath half-hidden in the undergrowth; the tangle of wild ground cover on the bank sloping down to the river; a small, sandstone plaque set into the brick foundation of the house on which the legend "T.M. 1898" could be dimly discerned.

"My husband's father, Timothy Maitland, began building this house that year," she explained to Delaney. "He died of TB before it was finished. His wife, my mother-in-law, completed the main building, added the wings, and did much of the landscaping herself. My husband and I added the gazebo, installed the driveway, and made many modern improvements inside. Of course it all needs work, as you can see. I had planned to restore everything to its original beauty, but Victor died, and I'm afraid I lost all my ambition. But I feel my strength and resolve coming back more each day, and I intend to go through with it. It's really a dream, you see. Oh, Chief Delaney, you should have seen this place when I was a young bride carried over the threshold. One of the finest, loveliest homes in this area, with a view that no place in Rockland County could equal. A velvety lawn. Everything spanking clean and neat. The river glittering. The air. The sky. Birds and flowers. Like you, I came from the city streets, and this place seemed paradise to me. I am determined to make it a paradise once again. Oh yes. Everything is here. I have not sold off an acre of land. You would not *believe* the taxes! And the house is structurally sound. I intend to make it just as lovely as it was when I first saw it."

"I'm sure you shall," he murmured.

She clutched him urgently by the sleeve.

"You will find him, won't you?" she whispered, desperation in her voice. "The killer, I mean?"

"I'll do my best," he said. "I promise you that."

They moved around to the front of the house again. Emily and Sergeant Boone were strolling between the garage and the gazebo. She was talking brightly, although Delaney could not hear what was being said. But the sergeant was stooping slightly, head lowered, listening intently.

Dora Maitland and Delaney waited at the entrance for the other two to come up. Mrs. Maitland clasped her hands to her bosom dramatically, raised her eyes to the pellucid sky.

"What a divine day!" she exclaimed rapturously.

Delaney could believe she had once been on the stage.

Finally, bidding goodbye to the ladies, the two officers went through the hand-shaking ceremony again, nodding and smiling. They then drove down the graveled driveway.

"Did you see the doors?" Delaney asked.

"Yes, sir," Boone said. "They're nailed shut all right."

"You were correct about Geltman," Delaney said. "He is a flit."

"And she's a lush," Boone said stolidly.

"You're sure?"

"It takes one to know one," Boone said matter-of-factly.

"What were the tip-offs?"

"That huskiness—from whiskey, not from smoking."

"Her fingers were nicotine-stained," Delaney noted.

"But she didn't dare light up; we'd have seen the tremble. And she didn't move. Like her head was balanced and might roll off. I know the feeling. And she gripped the arms of her chair, again to hide the shakes. Drank two full glasses of lemonade to put out the fire."

"You think she had a few before we came?"

"No," Boone said, "or she'd have been looser. She wanted to be absolutely sober, even if it hurt. She didn't want to risk blabbing."

"She did with me," Delaney said. "At the end."

"When she figured the danger was over," Boone said. "Take my word for it, Chief; she's on the sauce."

"She's what used to be called 'a fine figure of a woman,'" Delaney said.

"Still is, as far as I'm concerned," the sergeant said. "A great pair of lungs. Sir, can we stop for some food?"

"God, yes!" Delaney said. "I'm starved. But leave room for dinner tonight, or my wife will make my life miserable. It's London broil and new potatoes, by the way."

"I'm sold," Boone said. "Want me to pick up Rebecca?"

"No need," Delaney said. "She's coming over early to help Monica."

They stopped at the first luncheonette they hit. It was crowded and noisy, but they had lucked onto a gem; their ham-and-scrambled were good. They strolled out to the car replete, Boone sucking on a mint-flavored toothpick. Delaney got behind the wheel.

The Chief drove cautiously until he got the feel of the car. After they were over the bridge, he relaxed, held it slightly below the legal limit, and stayed in the right-hand lane, letting the speed merchants zip by.

"What did you get from the girl?" he asked Boone. "Although I don't know why I call her 'girl.' About thirty-two, I figure."

"Thirty-five," Boone said. "She volunteered that. Which probably means thirty-eight. Did you catch Mama's reference to more discipline for her grandson? That's the way I see it: plenty of discipline for Victor and Emily. But Victor wouldn't take it, and split. Emily stayed under Mama's thumb."

"I'm not so sure," Delaney said slowly. "The girl's got moxie; she's not beaten. Maybe the drinking is a recent thing, and Mama is losing control. Why did the old man do the Dutch? Did you get that?"

"He owned a lumberyard. Construction material. Stuff like that. Very successful. A big wheel in county politics. But he kept thinking he could draw to an inside straight. Also horses and local crap games. It all went. So he kicked the bucket, literally, and all the lawyers could salvage were the house and grounds, plus enough income from blue-chips to keep the two women going. Nothing from Victor baby. They're not starving, far from it, but they're not rolling either."

"Funny," Delaney said. "Thorsen thought she was a rich old twist."

"Emily said that's what everyone thinks. But they're not. Just getting by."

"With a housekeeper," Delaney reminded him. "Hardly poverty. Dora boasted of never selling off an acre. That land must be worth a mint. But she keeps coming up with the taxes and hanging on."

"For what?" Boone said.

"Her dream," Delaney said. "To restore it all the way it was. A paradise. Birds and flowers. She's got to have it."

"No," Boone said, "that's not what I meant. What is she hanging on *for*? A windfall? Like an inheritance?"

"Ah," Delaney said. "Good question. A shrewd lady. Did you catch that business of how she was a victim of malicious gossip when she was on the stage? I'll bet she was! All that bullshit was just to disarm us if we went digging. Well, it was a profitable morning."

"Was it, sir?" Boone asked. "How?"

"A lot of things we have to do now. We'll have to come up here again. At least one more time. We'll come on a Friday, when the housekeeper is off. We'll get her full name and address from the local postman, or somehow. I want you to check her out."

"Me?"

"How did you make her accent? I figured Virginia."

"Farther south than that, Chief," Boone said. "Maybe Georgia."

"That's why I want you to check her out. You're a good old boy. You've got the accent."

"I do?" Boone said. "I didn't think I had."

"Sure you do," Delaney said genially. "Not much, but it's there. And you can force it without faking."

"You want to know how often Victor Maitland and Saul Geltman visited?" Boone guessed.

"Right," Delaney nodded. "That for starters. And anything else you can glom. Like Dora's drinking and does fat Emily have any larcenous boyfriends."

"What else?"

"I'll handle the bank account. I don't know what it'll take; maybe a court order, or maybe just a letter or call from Thorsen to the locals will do. We've got to walk on eggs here. After all, Dora's brother is J. Barnes Chapin, and the last thing in the world we want is for him to get his balls in an uproar. But I've got to see those banks records."

"Chief, you really think Dora or Emily or both drove that great big old Mercedes down to New York that Friday and nixed the son? For the loot?"

"It's possible. He didn't leave any will, but maybe the mother would share. That's another thing I've got to check out. But even if they didn't do it themselves, a hefty bank withdrawal in, say, the last six months would be a red flag."

Boone pondered a moment.

"She hired someone?"

"Could be," Delaney said. "Happens all the time."

"Jesus Christ, Chief, she's his *mother!*"

"So?" Delaney said coldly. "It used to be that seventy-five percent of all homicides were committed by relatives, friends, or acquaintances of the victim. Things have changed in the past five years; the number of 'stranger-murders' has increased. But family and friends still do about two-thirds of the killing. It's basic. If you catch a homicide, you look at the family first."

Abner Boone sighed. "That's depressing," he said.

Delaney glanced at him sideways.

"Sometimes, sergeant," he said. "I think you may be an idealist. We work with what we've got. We'd be morons to disregard percentages. And I think both Dora and Emily are big enough and strong enough to have done it. At first, I didn't think it was a woman. My wife doesn't think so. But I'm beginning to wonder. How much strength does it take to push in a shiv?"

"More than I've got," Sergeant Boone said.

They were in the city, heading downtown on Columbus Avenue, when Delaney pulled over, double-parking.

"I'll just be a minute," he said, and went into a bodega to buy a cold six-pack of Ballantine ale. When he returned, Boone asked him to wait a minute, and dashed across the street to a florist. He came back with a bunch of small white mums wrapped in green tissue paper.

"For your wife," he said.

"You didn't have to do that," Delaney said, pleased.

They had to park in a restricted area in front of the 251st Precinct house, but Boone's car was known to the local cops by now, and wouldn't be plastered or hauled away. Just to make sure, the sergeant put the "Officer on Duty" card behind his windshield.

The women were in the kitchen, flushed and laughing. Partly due to a pitcher of martinis Monica had prepared. Delaney helped himself to a double over ice, and added a slice of lemon peel. Boone had a small bottle of tonic water poured over ice and a squeezed wedge of lime.

The two men were willing to sit around the kitchen shmoozing, but the ladies chased them out. They went into Delaney's study, slumped into the worn club chairs gratefully, stretched out their legs. They sat awhile in comfortable silence.

"I remember a homicide I worked, oh, maybe twenty years ago," Delaney said finally. "It looked to be an open-and-shut. This young kid, maybe about twenty-five, around there, said he killed his father. The kid had been in Korea and smuggled in a forty-five. The old man was a terror. Always beating on the old lady. A long record of physical assaults. She filed complaints, but never pushed a prosecution. The son took it just so long, he said, then blasted away. Holy Christ, you should have seen that room. They had to replaster the walls. A full magazine had been fired, and the father took most of them. I mean, he was *pieces*. The son waltzed into the precinct house and slammed the pistol down on the desk. The duty sergeant almost fainted. The son admitted everything. But it didn't add up. The kid had been an MP. And no dummy. He knew how to handle that Colt. He wouldn't have sprayed. One pill would have done it."

"The mother," Boone said somberly.

"Sure," Delaney nodded. "The son was covering for her. That's what everyone thought. And who could blame her? After taking all that abuse. And what would she get? No one's going to put an old lady in the slammer for blowing away a husband who talks to her with his fists. What would she get? A slap on the wrist. Probation, probably. Everyone knew it; everyone was satisfied."

Delaney stopped and sipped his martini. Boone looked at him, puzzled. The Chief's expression revealed nothing.

"So?" Boone said. "What's the point, sir?"

"The point?" Delaney said, almost rumbling, his chin down on his chest. "The point is that I couldn't buy it. I went digging. The kid had a chance to buy in on a garage, and the old man wouldn't lend him the dough. He had it, but he wouldn't give his son a chance. 'I worked hard for every penny I got. You go out and dig ditches—whatever.' That kind of shit. Plenty of arguments, hot arguments. So finally the son blew him away in a fury, but not so furious that he didn't make it look like the old lady had done it, knowing she'd get home free. It was the son all along. He figured we'd think he was covering. I told you he was no dummy."

"Son of a bitch," Boone said slowly. "So what happened?"

"I dumped it in the lieutenant's lap," Delaney said. "He could have killed me. He was all set to charge the old lady and see her walk. Now it was his decision on charging the kid. Finally he decided to go with the old lady. He buried my paper and told me he was doing it, and I could have his balls if I wanted them. I didn't. He was a good cop. Well, maybe not so good, but he was human. So he buried my paper on the kid, the old lady got charged, and like everyone expected, she walked. There was some insurance money, and the kid invested in his garage and lived happily ever after. Kept his nose clean; never strayed from the arrow. So where was justice in that case?"

"Just the way it came out," Boone said stoutly. "A no-goodnik gets wasted, a wife gets out of a miserable marriage, and the son gets a start on a clean life."

"Is that how you see it?" Delaney asked, raising his eyes to stare at Abner Boone. "There hasn't been a day since that case twenty years ago that I haven't regretted not pushing it. I should have racked up that kid, and if my lieutenant got in the way, I should have racked him up, too. Sergeant, that kid murdered a human being. No one should do that and get away with it. It's not right. I've made my share of mistakes, and letting that kid off the hook was one of them."

Boone was silent awhile, staring across at the brooding figure slumped wearily in the club chair.

"Are you sure of that, sir?" he said softly.

"Yes," Delaney said. "I'm sure."

Boone sighed, took a deep swallow of his tonic water.

"How did you break it?" he asked. "How did you figure it wasn't the abused wife who blasted the old man?"

"She couldn't have done that," Delaney said. "She loved him."

Then after a moment, the Chief said, "Why did I tell you that story? Oh . . . now I remember. I was wondering if anyone loved Victor Maitland."

Rebecca Hirsch flung open the door, stood posed, a dish towel folded over one arm.

"Gentlemen," she announced, "dinner is served."

They laughed, dragged themselves to their feet, went into the dining room. The table was set for six, with candles yet, and Sergeant Boone's flowers in a tall vase in the center. Chief Delaney sat at one end, Monica at the other, with Mary and Rebecca on one side and Sylvia and Sergeant Boone on the other.

They started with an appetizer of caviar that everyone knew was lumpfish, and didn't care. This with sour cream, chopped onions, capers, and a lemon wedge. A salad of oiled endive and cherry tomatoes. The London broil with new potatoes, plus fresh stringbeans and a bowl of hot spinach leaves with bacon chunks.

Edward X. Delaney stood up to carve, and said, "Who wants the drumstick?" Monica and Rebecca Hirsch writhed with laughter, and the Chief looked at his wife suspiciously.

"Did you tell Rebecca I'd say that?" he accused.

It was a good meal, a good evening. Two, three, even four conversations went on at once. The London broil was pronounced somewhat chewy but flavorsome. Everyone had seconds, which pleased the cook. The salad disappeared, as did a chilled bottle of two-year-old Beaujolais. Potatoes, stringbeans, and spinach were consumed dutifully, and by the time the key-lime pie was brought in, the diners had lost their initial momentum and were beginning to dawdle.

The girls kissed Monica, Rebecca, and their stepfather good night, shook hands solemnly with Sergeant Boone, giggling, and took their wedges of pie and glasses of milk upstairs to their room. Delaney moved around the table, pouring coffee. He paused to lean down and kiss his wife's cheek.

"Wonderful meal, dear," he said.

"Just great, Mrs. Delaney," Boone said enthusiastically. "Can't remember a better one."

"I'm glad you enjoyed it," she smiled happily. "Where did you boys have lunch?"

"A greasy spoon," Boone said.

"You shouldn't eat at places like that," Rebecca said severely. "Instant heartburn. If not ulcers."

Now she and Boone were sitting across from each other. When their eyes met, they looked casually away. She called him "Sergeant," and he avoided addressing her directly by name. Their manner with each other was polite, coolly friendly.

Son of a bitch, Delaney thought suddenly; they've been to bed.

Abner Boone had suffered through cocktails and wine—drinking only water during dinner—and Delaney couldn't see torturing him further by inhaling a snifter of cognac. So he sipped his coffee with every evidence of satisfied benignity, silent as he listened to Boone and the women discuss the best way to roast a goose.

Talk was quiet, almost subdued, although no one felt constraint. But there was no need for chatter. Each hoped the others felt equally content: a good meal, a surcease of wanting. The peace that comes when covetousness vanishes, even temporarily.

"Rebecca," Chief Delaney said, almost lazily, "is your mother living?"

"Oh yes," she said. "In Florida. Thank God."

"Why 'Thank God'?" he asked. "Because she's living or because she's living in Florida?"

She laughed and hung her head, the beautiful long hair falling forward to hide her face. Then she threw back her head suddenly, the hair flinging back into place. Sergeant Boone stirred restlessly in his chair.

"I shouldn't have said that," she confessed, "but she's a bit much. A professional mother. When she lived in New York, she drove me up a wall. Even from Florida, I still get the nudging. What to eat, what to wear, how to act."

"She wants to run your life?" Delaney asked.

"Run it? She wants to *own* it!"

Monica turned to look at him.

"Edward, why the interest in Rebecca's mother?"

He sighed, wondering what he should and should not say. Still, they were women and their insights might be useful. He'd use anyone, and not apoloize for it.

"This thing Sergeant Boone and I are working on . . ." he said. "We ran into an interesting situation today. A mother-and-daughter relationship . . ."

He described, as accurately as he could, Dora and Emily Maitland, their ages, physical appearance, the clothes they wore, the house they lived in, their voices, manner, and behavior.

"Is that an accurate description, would you say, sergeant?" he asked Boone when he finished.

"Yes, sir, I'd say so. Except you seemed to see more—more spirit in the girl than I did. I thought the mother was the heavy."

"Mmm," Delaney said. Then, without telling Monica and Rebecca that the two women under discussion were suspects in a murder investigation (although surely Monica guessed it), he asked them directly, looking back and forth, "How do you see a relationship like that? Specifically, why is the daughter still hanging around? Why didn't she take off? And does mother dominate daughter or vice versa?"

"Take off where?" Monica Delaney demanded. "With what? Mama controls the money, doesn't she? What's the daughter going to do—come to New York and walk Eighth Avenue? The way you describe her, I don't think she'd make out. Is she trained for anything? Can she hold down a job?"

"Then why didn't she leave home fifteen years ago and learn to support herself?" Rebecca asked. "Maybe she likes it there. The nice, safe cocoon."

"That's my point, too," Sergeant Boone said. "Chief, if she had as much chutzpah as you—"

"Hoo-hah!" Rebecca cried. "Chutzpah. Listen to the knacker!"

Boone blushed, smiling.

"Well . . . you know," he said lamely. "If the girl had as much courage as you think, Chief, she'd have split years ago."

"Maybe she's afraid," Monica said.

"Afraid?" Delaney said. "Of what?"

"Of the world," his wife said. "Of life."

"You said she's overweight," Rebecca said. "That could be from loneliness. Believe me, I know! You're miserable, so you eat. Stuck out there in the country with a crazy mother—or am I being redundant?— what else is there to do but eat? She wants something else, something better. The Is-this-all-there-is-to-life syndrome? But like Monica said, she's afraid. Of change. And every year it gets harder to make the break."

"Or maybe she's waiting for Mama to die," Monica said. "That happens sometimes. But also, sometimes it takes so long that by the time it *does* happen, the daughter has become the mother. If you know what I mean."

"I know what you mean," Delaney nodded, "but I'm not sure you're right. This girl isn't dead. I mean, inside she isn't dead. She still feels things. She's got urges, wants, desires. My question is why hasn't she done something about getting what she wants?"

"Maybe she has," Rebecca said. "Maybe she's working on her ambitions right now, and you don't know anything about it."

"That's possible," Delaney acknowledged. "Very possible. Another explanation might be that she's lazy. I know that sounds simple, but sometimes we credit people with more complex motives than they're capable of feeling. Maybe this girl is just bone-lazy, and likes that slow, sluggish life she's living out there."

"Do you believe that, sir?" Boone asked.

"No," Delaney said, "I don't. There's something there. Something. No idiot she. She's not just a lump. Going by the book, I'd have to say the mother is running her. But I can't get rid of the feeling that maybe she's running the mother."

"That would be a switch," Rebecca said.

"But understandable," Delaney said. "How's this: At first the mother was the honcho. The iron fist and strict discipline for her children. Then, as she grows older, the vigor fades. The mother weakens; the daughter senses it. The mother seems to be living in the past, more every year. There's a power vacuum. The daughter moves in. Slowly. A little at a time. Remember, there's no man around the house. As the old lady's energy gets less and less, the daughter gets more and more. The mother is weary of trying to make ends meet, trying to live in style. All she wants are her dreams of the past. She can't cope with today. Like there's an X-quantity of resolve there, and less for the mother means more for the daughter. Like an hourglass. The sand runs from one container to another. The mother loses, the daughter gains. Well . . ." He laughed briefly. "It's fanciful, but that's the way I see it."

"The mother wants her dream," Boone said. "The house restored. The grounds prettied up. Just the way everything was when she was a bride. Okay. Admitted. But what does the daughter want?"

"Escape," Delaney said.

They looked at him with strange expressions.

"Edward," his wife said, "is this the way detectives work? Trying to guess why people do what they do?"

"Not usually," he said. "Usually we work with physical evidence. Hard facts. Percentages, timing, weapons, testimony of witnesses, things you can look at, hold in your hand, or put under a microscope. But sometimes when none of this exists, or not enough to break a case, you've got to turn to people. As you said, why they do what they do. You try to put yourself in their place. What drives them? What do they want? Everyone *wants*. But some people can't control it. Then want becomes need. And need—I mean a real greedy need—the kind that haunts you night and day—that's motive enough for any crime."

His listeners were all silent then, disturbed. Delaney lookd at the sergeant. Boone jerked immediately to his feet.

"Getting late!" he sang cheerily. "Busy day tomorrow. Got to get going."

There was the usual confusion of departure: "More pie?" "Oh no!" "Coffee?" "Not a thing!" Then Rebecca Hirsch and Abner Boone left together. Delaney locked up and came back to help his wife clear the dining-room table, straighten up, load the dishwasher, store away leftovers.

"They're making it, aren't they?" he asked casually.

"Yes," she nodded.

"I hope she doesn't get hurt," he said.

His wife shrugged. "She's a grown woman, Edward. She can take care of herself."

8

It was not the first time Detective sergeant Abner Boone had mused on how similar police work was to theatre. Undercover cops were closest, of course, with their costumes, makeup, accents, and fictitious identities. But detectives were into theatre too, and so were uniformed street cops. You soon learned the value of feigning emotions, of delivering speeches in other men's words, of acting roles best suited for the situation.

"Now, now," a street cop says soothingly, patting the shoulder of a frenzied husband. "I know exactly how you feel. Haven't I been through the same thing m'self? I know, I know. But bashing her head in will do you no good. Just give me the brick like a good lad. I know, I tell you. I know exactly how you feel."

"I know you're not involved," the dick says shamefacedly. "Look, I don't even like the idea of bothering you. A girl of your intelligence and good looks. You're too good for the likes of him; that's easy to see. But I've got to ask these questions, you know. I don't *want* to, but it's my job. Now then . . . was he *really* with you when the shop was ripped off?"

Not always sympathetic, of course. When a heavy is needed, one is supplied . . .

"You're nailed, cheese-brain. Signed, sealed, and delivered. No way out of this. Three-to-five in the slammer, and you'll be a faggot in a week. Locked in with all those horny studs. You'll be gang-banged the first night. That's what it's like, pal. And your wife on the outside, looking around for company. You dig? Your life is over, kiddo. But tell me who else was in on it, and maybe we can work a deal. There are ways . . ."

And so forth. The roles fitted to circumstances. So Abner Boone dressed with extra care that Friday morning. No brassy slacks and screaming jacket, but a conservative suit of tan poplin, with white shirt and black knit tie. Something that wouldn't spook a woman who worked as legal secretary to an attorney. He also shaved carefully and used his best cologne. Zizanie. And he powdered his armpits. There wasn't much he could do with his short, gingery hair, but at least it was clean.

He folded his jacket neatly onto the back seat of his car, then drove downtown to Central Park South and double-parked outside the studio of Jake Dukker. The doorman wandered over, and Boone had to flash his tin. He waited patiently, smoking his third cigarette of the morning, until his watch showed exactly ten o'clock. Then he started up.

He drove east to Park Avenue and turned south. He planned to take it all the way down to what used to be called Fourth Avenue, and was now Park Avenue South. Then he figured to cut over to Broadway on 14th Street, and take that south to Spring Street, then over to Mott and Victor Maitland's studio. There were a dozen other routes, but one was as good, or bad, as another.

He obeyed all traffic regulations, didn't jump any lights, and when he got caught in jams, he didn't press it. It took forty-three minutes to reach the Mott Street studio, and Boone made a careful record in his notebook. He sat in front of Maitland's studio for exactly ten minutes, smoking another cigarette placidly, then started back. He arrived in front of Dukker's place on Central Park South at precisely 11:53. The northbound traffic had been heavy, and he had been caught in a three-minute jam at 42nd Street. Still, he had made the round-trip in one hour and fifty-three minutes, allowing ten minutes for the chopping of Victor Maitland. Jake Dukker or Belle Sarazen, or both, could have done the same on that Friday. At least he had proved it was possible in under two hours. He wondered if Chief Delaney would be pleased or disappointed. Probably neither. Just another fact to add to the file.

Boone then drove east and north, and found a parking space a block away from the offices of Simon & Brewster on East 68th Street. He put on his jacket, locked the car, and popped a chlorophyll tablet into his mouth. He walked over to the lawyer's office, his back held deliberately straight, trying to compose his features into the picture of a pleasant, boyish officer of the law, eager and ingratiating.

She was sitting alone in the outer office, typing with blinding speed on an electric IBM. She kept working a moment after he came in and halted before her big, glass-topped desk. He had time to make her as a tall, skinny blonde with no chest. None at all. Then she stopped typing and looked up.

"Miss Hemley?" he smiled. "Susan Hemley?"

"Yes?" she said, cocking her head to one side, puzzled.

"I spoke to you on the phone the other night," he smiled. "Detective sergeant Abner Boone."

He unfolded his ID and handed it over. She took it and examined it carefully, something people rarely did.

"You've come to arrest me?" she asked archly.

"Sure," he smiled. "For attracting a police officer. Actually, this is just a social visit, Miss Hemley. To thank you for your cooperation. And to try to set up an appointment with Mr. Simon. For my boss, Chief Edward Delaney."

"A chief," she said. "Oh my. Sounds important."

"Not really," he smiled. "Just a few routine questions to get the record straight."

"The Maitland murder?" she asked in a hushed voice.

He nodded, still smiling. "Any morning or afternoon next week at Mr. Simon's convenience."

"Just a minute, sergeant," she said. "Let me check."

She rose and moved to an inner door, knocked once, entered, closed the door behind her. Boone was grateful; his face felt stretched. She was back in a moment. He saw she moved loosely, with a floppy grace. Thin as a pencil, with good, long legs. A smooth, unmarked face. An egg-shaped head. The blonde hair was in short, tight curls. Black, horn-rimmed glasses were, somehow, sexy. He thought she would be a terror in bed. Yelping. Kicking hell out of the sheets.

"How's for Tuesday morning at ten?" she asked.

"Fine," he said, smiling again. "We'll be here."

He began to move away, hesitated, turned back to her.

"One more favor," he smiled. "Where can a hungry cop get a good lunch in this neighborhood?"

Twenty minutes later they were seated opposite each other on the upper level of a Madison Avenue luncheonette.

"I'm afraid they don't serve drinks," she apologized.

"No problem," he assured her. "Order what you like. We'll let the City pay for it. You're a taxpayer, aren't you?"

"Am I ever!" she said, and they both laughed.

He watched his manners, and they got along swimmingly. They talked about the subject of most interest to both of them: her. He hadn't exaggerated when he had told Delaney he knew how to listen; he did, and before the iced tea and sherbet were served, he had her background: Ohio, business college, a special training in legal stenography, eleven years' experience in law offices. Which would make her, he figured, about thirty-seven to thirty-eight, around there. Good salary, good vacation and fringe benefits, a small office, but a relaxed place to work. J. Julian Simon was a pleasure. Her words: "That man is a pleasure." Boone assumed she meant to work for.

"How about you?" she asked finally. "You're working on the Maitland case?"

He nodded, looked down at the table, moved things about.

"I know you can't talk about it," she said.

He looked up at her then.

"I'm not supposed to," he said. "But . . ."

He glanced about carefully, was silent while a waitress cleared a neighboring table.

"We're getting close," he whispered.

"Really?" she whispered back. She hunched her chair forward, put elbows on the table, leaned to him. "The last story I read in the papers said the police had no leads."

"The papers," he scoffed. "We don't tell them everything. You understand?"

"Of course," she said eagerly. "Then there's more?"

He nodded again, looked about carefully again, leaned forward again.

"Did you know him?" he asked. "Victor Maitland? Did you ever meet him?"

"Oh yes," she said. "Several times. At the office. And once at a party in Mr. Geltman's apartment."

"Oh?" Boone said. "At the office? Was Mr. Simon his lawyer too?"

"Not really," she said. "He just came up once or twice with Mr. Geltman. I don't think he had a personal attorney. Once he said to Mr.

Simon, 'The first thing we do, let's kill all the lawyers.' I don't think that was a very nice thing to say."

"No," Boone said, "it wasn't. But I guess Maitland wasn't a very nice guy. No one seems to have liked him."

"I certainly didn't," she said stoutly. "I thought he was rude and nasty."

"I know," he said sympathetically. "That's what everyone says. I guess his wife put up with a lot."

"She certainly did. She's such a lovely woman."

"Isn't she?" he agreed enthusiastically. "I met her, and that's exactly what I thought: a lovely woman. And married to that animal. Did you know—" Here he lowered his voice, leaned even closer. Susan Hemley also leaned to him, until their heads were almost touching. "Did you know—well, this wasn't in the papers. You've got to promise not to breathe a word of it to anyone."

"I promise," she said sincerely. "I won't say a word."

"I trust you," he said. "Well, when they found him, dead, he wasn't wearing any underwear."

She jerked back, eyes widening.

"Nooo," she breathed. "Really?"

He held up a hand, palm out.

"'Struth," he said. "So help me. We don't know what it means yet, but he definitely wasn't wearing any underwear."

She leaned forward again.

"I told you he was nasty," she said. "That proves it."

"Oh yes," he said. "You're right. We know he was very nasty to Mr. Geltman."

"He certainly was," she said. "You should have heard how Maitland talked to Saul. And in public. In front of everyone. He was so nasty."

"And to think Geltman was in your office at the time Maitland was killed," Boone said, shaking his head. "Makes you think. Maybe if Geltman hadn't been there, we'd have suspected him. But he was there all right. Wasn't he?"

"Oh sure," she said, nodding her head so violently that the blonde curls bounced. "I saw him come in. And I spoke to him a minute or two before he went into Mr. Simon's office."

"About ten o'clock that was," Boone said reflectively. "And then you saw him come out around one-thirty in the afternoon. Right?"

"Oh no," she said. "At one-thirty I was at lunch with Alma. Alma Maitland. Don't you remember?"

"Of course," Boone said, snapping his fingers. "How could I forget? Well, anyway, the other people in the office saw him come out. Didn't they?"

"Nooo," she said slowly. "Just Mr. Simon. Mr. Brewster was in court all that day, and the clerk, Lou Broniff, was out with the flu."

"Well," he said, "Mr. Simon told us when he left, and that's good enough."

"It certainly is," she said. "Mr. Simon is a fine man. A pleasure."

"Mr. Geltman spoke very highly of him," Boone lied casually.

"I should think so," she laughed. "They've been friends for years. I mean they're more than lawyer and client. They play handball together. After all, they're both divorced."

"Very buddy-buddy," Boone observed, enjoying this.

"They certainly are. Mr. Geltman is such a nice little man. He really says funny things. I like him."

"I do, too," Boone agreed. "A lot of personality. Too bad he and Mrs. Maitland don't seem to get along."

"Oh, that," Susan Hemley said. "It's really just a little misunderstanding. Maitland was doing some paintings and making Geltman sell them and not telling his wife about them. I told Alma it wasn't Saul's fault. After all, he had to sell what Maitland brought him, didn't he? That was his job, wasn't it? And what Maitland did with the money was none of Saul's business, was it? If Maitland didn't tell his wife how much he was making, she really shouldn't blame Mr. Geltman."

"I agree with you," Boone said. "And you told Alma Maitland that?"

"I certainly did. But she seems to think there was more to it than that."

"More to it than that?" Boone asked. "I don't understand. What did she mean by that?"

"Goodness!" Susan Hemley cried. "Look at the time! I've got to get back to the office. Thank you so very much for the lunch, sergeant. I really enjoyed it. I hope to see you again."

"You will," he smiled once more. "Tuesday morning at ten o'clock. With Chief Delaney."

He returned to Jake Dukker's studio on Central Park South. It was now almost two P.M., not precisely corresponding to the hour of the murder but close enough, he felt, for a time trial by subway.

He found a parking space on the north side of 59th Street, locked his car, checked his watch. He decided to walk to the subway station of Lexington Avenue rather than wait for a cab. He walked rapidly, threading his way through the throngs, occasionally stepping down into the gutter to make better time. Like a man with murder on his mind, he dashed across streets against the lights, not heeding the blasting horns and screamed insults of the hackies.

In the 59th Street IRT station he waited almost four minutes for a downtown express. He changed to a local at 14th Street, took that to Spring, got off and walked quickly over to Maitland's Mott Street studio. He looked at his watch; forty-six minutes since leaving Dukker's place.

He then strolled around the block, using up the ten minutes allotted for the murder of Victor Maitland. Then he started back by the same route. This time he had a long wait for the local, and suffered the vexation of seeing two express trains thunder by on the inside track. Once aboard the local, he decided to stay with it to 59th Street. The train jerked to a halt for almost five minutes, somewhere between 14th and 23rd. It was one of those inexplicable New York subway delays for which no explanation is ever given the sweltering passengers.

He hurried off the train and out of the station at 59th, shouldering his way through the crowds, and dashed westward across town to Dukker's studio. He arrived under the canopy, puffing, his poplin suit sweated through. He looked at his watch. One hour and forty-nine minutes for the round trip. He could hardly believe it. He had made better time by walking and taking the subway than by driving the entire distance. It certainly proved his theory was plausible: Dukker or Sarazen could have made that trip, fixed Maitland and returned without their absence noted by the models and assistants in the downstairs studio. It would mean, of course, the two of them were in on it together.

Satisfied, jacket off, tie and collar jerked open, he drove home to East 85th Street. He lived in a relatively new high-rise apartment house. The rent and underground garage fee kept him constantly on the edge of bankruptcy, but he had lacked the resolve to move after his divorce. He would have *had* to move to a cheaper place if Phyllis had demanded alimony. But fortunately, she was into Women's Lib, took a five-thousand cash settlement, most of the furniture, and they shook hands. It was all civilized. And so awful he could never think of it without wanting to weep.

He collected his mail, bills and junk, and rode alone up to his eighteenth-floor apartment. It was sparsely furnished after Phyllis cleaned it out, but he still had a couch, chair, and cocktail table in the living room. The bedroom was furnished with bed, chest of drawers, and a card table he used for a desk, with a folding bridge chair. Rebecca Hirsch had brought over a little oak bedside table and some bright posters for the living-room walls. They helped. Rebecca kept talking about curtains and drapes, and he supposed he'd get around to them eventually. Right now, the venetian blinds sufficed.

He flipped on the air-conditioner, and stripped down to his shorts. He got a can of sugar-free soda from the fridge and sat down at the bedroom card table to write out a report while the interview with Susan Hemley was fresh in his mind. He typed out the report rapidly on an old Underwood that his ex-wife had left behind.

After he finished with the Hemley meet, he typed up a record of his two time trials, consulting his notebook to get the times exactly right. Then he added everything to his personal file on the Maitland homicide, wondering, not for the first time, if anyone would ever read it, or even consult it. But Delaney had told him to make daily reports, so he made daily reports. He owed the Chief that.

He took a tepid shower, dried in front of the air-conditioner, and felt a lot better. He started on his second pack of cigarettes and thought, fleetingly, of an iced Gibson. He opened another can of diet soda.

He checked his wallet and made a quick calculation of how much he could spend daily until the next payday. And he made a mental list of which creditors he could stiff, which he could stall, and who had to be paid at once. He knew how easy it was for a cop to get a loan, but he didn't want to start stumbling down that path.

Finally, he called Rebecca Hirsch. She sounded happy to hear from him, and said she could offer a tunafish salad if he could stand it. He told her he had been dreaming of a tunafish salad all day and would be right over. After dinner, he said, they could take a drive, or see a movie, or watch TV, or whatever.

She said she would prefer whatever.

9

On the same Friday morning that Detective sergeant Abner Boone began his time trials, Chief Edward X. Delaney was in his study planning the day's activities. He jotted down a list of "Things to do," and folded the note into his jacket pocket. He unpinned the three Maitland sketches from the map board, rolled them up, slid a rubber band around them. Then he called to Monica that he wouldn't be home for lunch, and started out. He carefully double-locked the outside door behind him.

His first stop was at a Second Avenue printing shop that also made photostats. Delaney ordered three 11x14 stats of each Maitland sketch. The clerk examined the nude drawings, then looked up with a wise-ass grin that faded when he saw Delaney's cold stare. He promised to have the photostats ready at noon.

The Chief then began walking slowly downtown to East 58th Street; his appointment with Theodore Maitland was at 11:00. Delaney had been doing so much riding in Boone's car recently, he figured the exercise would do him good. For a while he tried inhaling deeply and slowly for a count of twelve, holding the breath for the same time, then exhaling slowly for another twelve-count. That regimen lasted for two blocks, and he didn't feel any better for it. He resumed his normal breathing and ambled steadily southward, observing the bustling life of the morning city and wondering when he was going to get a handle on the Maitland case: a break, a lead, an approach, anything that would give him direction and purpose.

He knew from experience that the first hours and days of an investigation were hardest to endure. Disparate facts piled up, evidence accumulated, people lied or spoke the truth—but what the hell did it all mean? You had to accept everything, keep your wits and nerve, let the mess grow and grow until you caught a pattern; two pieces fit, then more and more. It was like the traffic jam he saw at Second Avenue and 66th Street. Cars stalled every which way. Horns blaring. Red-faced drivers bellowing and waving. Then a street cop got the key car moving, the jam broke, in a few minutes traffic was flowing in a reasonably orderly pattern. But when was he going to find the key to the Maitland jam? Maybe today. Maybe tomorrow. And maybe, he thought morosely, he already had it and couldn't recognize it.

Mrs. Alma Maitland was nowhere to be seen, for which Delaney was grateful. A Puerto Rican maid ushered him into that cold "family room," where he sat on the edge of the couch, homburg on his knees. He waited for almost five minutes, guessing this was the son's form of hostility, and willing to endure patiently.

He had seen photos of Victor Maitland, of course, and was surprised at the close resemblance when the son finally stalked into the room. The same husky body, burly shoulders. Heavy head thrust forward. Coarse, reddish hair. The glower. Big hands with spatulate fingers. A thumping tread. The young face was marked by thick, dark brows, sculpted lips. Older, it might be a gross face, seamed, the mouth thinned and twisted. But now it had the soft vulnerability of youth. Hurt there, Delaney decided, and anger. And want.

He rose, but Ted Maitland made no effort to greet him or shake hands. Instead, he threw himself into one of the blonde wood armchairs, slumped down, began biting furiously at the hard skin around a thumbnail. He was wearing blue jeans with a red gingham shirt open almost to his waist. The inevitable necklace of Indian beads. Bare feet in moccasins. A bracelet of turquoise chips set in hammered silver.

"I don't know why I'm even talking to you," the boy said petulantly. "Only because Mother asked me. I've gone over this shit a hundred times with a hundred other cops."

Delaney was shocked by the voice: high-pitched, straining. He wondered if the kid was close to breaking. His movements and gestures had the jerky, disconnected look the Chief had seen just before a subject tried to climb barbed wire or began screaming and couldn't stop.

So he sat down slowly, set his hat aside slowly, spoke slowly in a low, quiet, and what he hoped was an intimate tone.

"I know you have, Mr. Maitland," he said. "And I'm sorry to put you through this once again. But reading or even hearing reports is never good enough. It's always best to go right to the source. A one-on-one, man-to-man conversation. Less chance of misinterpretation. Don't you agree?"

"What difference does it make if I do or don't agree?" Theodore Maitland demanded. His eyes were on his bitten thumb, on the rug, the ceiling, the walls, the air. Anywhere but on Delaney. He would not or could not meet his eyes.

"I know what you've been through," the Chief soothed. "I really do. And this shouldn't take long. Just a few questions. A few minutes . . ."

The boy snorted and crossed his knees abruptly. He was, Delaney thought, a handsome lad in a bruised, masculine way—his father's son—and he wondered if the kid had a girlfriend. He hoped so.

"Mr. Maitland—" he started, then stopped. "Would you object if I called you Ted?" he asked gently. "I won't if you don't want me to."

"Call me anything you damn please," the boy said roughly.

"All right," Delaney said, still speaking slowly, softly, calmly. "Ted it is. Just let me run through, very briefly, your movements on the day your father was killed, and let's see if I've got it straight. Okay, Ted?"

Maitland made a sound, neither assent nor objection, uncrossed his legs, crossed them in the other direction. He turned in his armchair so one shoulder was presented to Delaney.

"You left here about nine-thirty that Friday morning," the Chief said. "Took the downtown IRT at Fifty-ninth Street. A local. Got off at Astor Place. Had classes at Cooper Union from ten to twelve. At noon you talked awhile with classmates out on the steps, then bought a couple of sandwiches and a can of beer and went over to eat your lunch in Washington Square Park. You were there until about one-thirty. Then you returned to Cooper Union in time for lectures from two o'clock to four. Then you returned directly home. Here. Is that correct?"

"Yes."

"You ate lunch in the park alone?"

"I said I did."

"Meet anyone you know, Ted?"

Maitland whirled to glare at him.

"No, I didn't meet anyone I know," he almost shouted. "I ate lunch alone. Is that a crime?"

Chief Delaney held up both hands, palms out.

"Whoa," he said. "No crime. No one's accusing you of anything. I'm just trying to get your movements straight. Yours and everyone else's who knew your father. That makes sense, doesn't it? No, it's no crime to eat alone in the park. And I don't even question that you didn't meet anyone you knew. I just walked down here from Seventy-ninth Street, and I didn't meet anyone I knew. It's natural and normal. Usually eat lunch alone, Ted?"

"Sometimes. When I feel like it."

"Frequently?"

"Two or three times a week. Why?" he demanded. "Is it important?"

"Oh Ted," Delaney said lightly, "in an investigation like this, everything is important. What are you studying at Cooper Union?"

"Graphic design," Maitland muttered.

"Decoration and printing?" Delaney asked. "Things like that?"

"Yeah," the boy grinned sourly. "Things like that."

"Proportion?" Delaney asked. "Visual composition? The history and theory of art? Layout and design?"

Ted Maitland met his eyes for the first time.

"Yes," he said grudgingly. "All that. How come a cop knows that?"

"I'm an amateur," Delaney shrugged. "I don't know a lot about art, but—"

"But you know what you like," the boy hooted.

"That's right," Delaney said mildly. "For instance, I like your father's work. What do you think of it, Ted?"

"Ridiculous," Maitland said. Scornful laugh. "Old-fashioned. Square. Dull. Out-of-date. Antique. Bloated. Emotional. Juvenile. Melodramatic. Reactionary. Is that enough for you?"

"Saul Geltman says your father was a great draftsman, a great anatomist, a great—"

"Saul Geltman!" Maitland interrupted angrily, almost choking. "I know *his* type!"

"What type is that?" Delaney asked.

"You don't know a thing about art in modern society," the boy said disdainfully. "You're stupid!"

"Tell me," Delaney said. "I want to learn."

Theodore Maitland turned to face him squarely. Leaned forward, arms on knees. Dark eyes aflame. Face wretched with his intensity. Quivering to get it out. Shaking with his fury.

"An upside-down pyramid. You understand? Balanced on its point. And above, all the shits like Saul Geltman. The dealers. Curators. Critics. Rich collectors. Hangers-on like Belle Sarazen. Trendy sellouts like Jake Dukker. Publishers of art books and reproductions. Rip-off pirates. Smart-asses who go to the previews and charity shows. The whole stinking bunch of them. The art lovers! Sweating to get in on the ground floor. Find a new style, a new talent, and ride it. Then sell out, take your profit, and go on to the next ten-day wonder. Leeches! All of them! And you know what that upside-down pyramid is balanced on? Supported by? Way down there? The creative artist. Oh yes! At the bottom of the heap. But the point of the whole thing. The guy who spends his talent because that's all he's got. He's the one who provides the champagne parties, the good life for the leeches. Yes! The poor miserable slob trying to get it down on paper or canvas, or in wood or metal. And they laugh at him. They do! They do! Laugh at him! Well, my father gave it to them. He gave it to them good! He saw them for the filth they are. Parasites! They were afraid of him. I mean literally afraid! But he was so good they couldn't ignore him, couldn't put him down. He could shit on them, and they had to take it. Because they knew what he had. What they'd never have. What they wanted and would never have. My father was a genius. A genius!"

Chief Delaney looked at him in astonishment. There was no mistaking the boy's fervor. It burned in his eyes. Showed in his clenched fists, trembling knees.

"But you told me you didn't like your father's work," Delaney said.

Ted Maitland jerked backward into his chair, collapsed, spread arms and legs wide. He looked at Delaney disgustedly.

"Ahh, Jesus!" he said, shaking his head. "You haven't understood a word I've said. Not a word. Dumb cop!"

"Let me try," Delaney said. "You might not like your father's work, his style, the paintings he did, but that has nothing to do with his talent. *That* you recognize and admire. What he did with his talent isn't what you like at all. Not your style. But no one can deny his genius. Certainly not you. Is that about right?"

"Yes," Maitland said. A voice so low Delaney could barely hear him. "That's about right . . . about right . . ."

"And you?" Delaney asked gently. "Do you have your father's talent?"

"No."

"Will you? Could you? I mean if you study, work . . ."

"No," the boy said. "Never. I know. And it's killing me. I want . . . Ahh, fuck it!"

He jumped to his feet, turned away, almost ran from the room. Delaney watched him go, made no effort to stop him. He sat on the couch a few moments, staring at the empty doorway. Everyone wanting. Either what they could not have, or more of what they had. The poor, greedy lot of them. Talent, money, fame, possessions, integrity—the prizes hung glittering just above their grasping fingers as they leapt, strained, grabbed air and fell back, sobbing . . .

The Chief stood and was moving toward the door when Alma Maitland came sweeping into the room, head up, fists balled: an avenging amazon. He had a moment to admire the mass of coppery hair piled high, the fitted suit of russet wool, the luxuriousness of her body and the glazed perfection of her skin.

Then she confronted him, stood close, directly in his path. For a second he thought she meant to strike him.

"Mrs. Maitland . . ." he murmured.

"What did you do to Ted?" she demanded loudly. "What did you *do* to him?"

"I did nothing to him," Delaney said sternly. "We discussed his movements on the day his father was killed. We talked about art and Ted's feelings about his father's work. If that was enough to upset him, I assure you it was none of my doing, madam."

She shrunk suddenly, shoulders drooping, head bowed. She held a small handkerchief in her fingers, twisting it, pulling it. Delaney looked at her coldly.

"Is the boy getting professional help?" he asked. "Psychologist? Psychiatrist?"

"No. Yes. He goes—"

"Psychiatrist?"

"He really doesn't—"

"How often?"

"Three afternoons a week. But he's showing—"

"How long has this been going on?"

"Almost three years. But his analyst said—"

"Has he ever become violent?"

"No. Well, he does—"

"To his father? Did he ever attack his father or fight with him?"

"You're not giving me time to answer," she cried frantically.

"The truth takes no time," he snapped at her. "Do you want me to ask the maid? The doorman? Neighbors? Did your son ever attack his father?"

"Yes," she whispered.

"How often?"

"Twice."

"During the past year?"

"Yes."

"Violently? Was one or both injured?"

"No, it was just—"

"Mrs. Maitland!" he thundered.

She was a step away from an armchair, and collapsed into it, huddling, shaking and distraught. But he observed that it had been a graceful fall, and even in the chair her posture of distress was pleasingly composed, knees together and turned sideways, ankles neatly crossed. The bent head with its gleaming plait revealed a graceful line of neck and shoulder. Victor Maitland, he reflected, wasn't the only artist in the family.

"Well?" he said.

"Once they fought," she said dully. "Victor knocked him down. It was horrible."

"And once . . . ?" he insisted.

"Once," she said, her voice raddled, "once Ted attacked him. Unexpectedly. For no reason."

"Attacked him? With his fists? A weapon?"

She couldn't answer. Or wouldn't.

"A knife," Delaney said. Declaration, not question.

She nodded dumbly, not showing him her face.

"What kind of a knife? A hunting knife? A carving knife?"

"A paring knife," she muttered. "A little thing. From the kitchen."

"Was your husband wounded?"

"A small cut," she said. "In his upper arm. Not deep. Nothing really."

"Was a doctor called?"

"Oh no. No. It was just a small cut. Nothing. Victor wouldn't see a doctor. I—I put on disinfectant and—and put a bandage on. With tape. Really, it was nothing."

"What is your doctor's name? Your family physician. And where is his office?"

She told him, and he made a careful note of it.

"Does your son own a knife? Hunting knife, a switchblade, pocket knife? Anything?"

"No," she said, shaking her head. "He had a—like a folding knife. Swiss. Red handle. But after he became—became—disturbed, I took it away from him."

"Took it away from him?"

"I mean I took it out of his dresser drawer."

"Where is it now?"

"I threw it away. Down the incinerator."

He stood, feet firmly planted, staring unblinking at the top of her head. He drew a deep breath and exhaled in a sigh.

"All right," he said. "I believe you."

She raised her head then, looked at him. He saw no sign of tears.

"He didn't," she said. "I swear to you, Ted didn't. He worshipped his father."

"Yes," Delaney said stonily, "so he told me."

He turned away and moved to the door. Then paused and turned back.

"One more thing, Mrs. Maitland," he said. "Did you know any of the models your husband used?"

She looked at him, bewildered.

"The girls or women your husband used in his paintings," Delaney said patiently. "Did you know any of them personally? By name?"

She shook her head. "Years ago I did. But not recently. Not in the past five years or so."

"A young girl? Very young. Puerto Rican perhaps, or Italian. Latin-type."

"No, I know no one like that. Why do you ask?"

He explained about the three charcoal sketches of the young model found in Victor Maitland's studio.

"They belong to you, of course," he said. "Or rather to your husband's estate. I wanted you to know they are presently in my possession and will be returned to the estate when our investigation is completed."

She nodded, apparently not caring. He made a small bow to her, and left.

He lumbered over to Third Avenue and turned uptown. In this busy shopping district—big department stores, smart shops, fast-food joints jammed with noonday crowds—he pondered proper Latin. Was it *qui bono* or *cui bono?* He decided on the latter.

Cui bono? The first question of any homicide dick: Who benefits? He had a disturbed son envious of his father's talent. A sexless wife furious at her husband's cheating. An art dealer scorned and humiliated in public. An artist friend jealous of the victim's integrity. A quondam mistress hating his contempt. A mother and sister deserted and left to flounder.

Some very highfalutin motives for murder—but *cui bono?*

Edward X. Delaney ambled northward, considering the possibility of failure by limiting his investigation to these seven suspects. But the Department's investigators had checked out all Maitland's known drinking companions, models, neighbors, prostitutes, even distant relatives and old army buddies. Zilch. So Delaney was left with the seven. *Cui bono?*

He picked up the photostats, paid, and asked for a receipt. He was keeping a careful list of all his expenses, to be submitted to the Department. He didn't expect salary, but he'd be damned if he'd pay for the pleasure of assisting the NYPD.

The house was empty when he returned. But there was a little note from Monica attached to the refrigerator door with a magnetic disk: "Gone supermarketing. You need new shirts. Buy some."

He smiled. It was true the collars on some of his shirts were frazzled. He remembered when men had their collars turned when they got in that condition. Their wives did it, or the shirts were taken to local tailors who had signs posted: WE TURN COLLARS. Put up a sign like that today, and no one would know what the hell you were talking about.

He took a can of cold ale to his study. He took off his jacket and draped it across the back of his swivel chair. But he didn't loosen his tie or roll up his cuffs. He repinned Maitland's charcoal sketches to the map board and slid the photostats in a lower desk drawer. He planned to show them to Jake Dukker and Belle Sarazen, hoping for a make.

He took a swallow of ale, then dialed the office of Deputy Commissioner Ivar Thorsen. He wasn't in, but Delaney spoke to his assistant, Sergeant Ed Galey, and explained what he wanted: an opinion from the Department's legal staff on how Victor Maitland's estate would be divided under the laws of inheritance and succession of New York State.

"The man left no will," Delaney told Galey. "But there's a wife and eighteen-year-old son. Also a mother and sister. I want to know who gets what. Understand?"

"Got it, Chief," Galey said. "I'm making notes. Wife and son, eighteen years old. Mother and sister. How do they split?"

"Right," Delaney said. "That's it."

"The sister a minor?"

"No," Delaney said, thankful he was talking to a sharp cop, "she's in her thirties. How soon do you think I can get it?"

"It'll be a couple of days, at least. But we'll try to light a fire under them."

"Good. Thank you. One more thing, sergeant—is that Art Theft and Forgery Squad still in existence?"

"Far as I know. It's a little outfit. Two or three guys. They work out of Headquarters. Want the extension?"

"Yes, please."

"Hold on."

In a minute, Sergeant Galey was back with the phone number and the name of the commanding officer, Lieutenant Bernard Wolfe.

Delaney made a note, thanked him, and hung up. Two more swallows of ale. Then he called the Art Theft and Forgery Squad. The line was busy. More ale. Busy signal again. More ale. He finally got through, but the lieutenant wasn't there. He left his name and number and asked that Wolfe call him as soon as possible.

He drained off the ale and began writing out a report of his conversations with Theodore and Alma Maitland. He had almost finished when the phone rang, and he continued writing as he picked it up.

"Chief Edward X. Delaney here."

"Chief, this is Lieutenant Bernard Wolfe. Art Squad. I understand you called me?"

"Yes, lieutenant, I did. I'm working on the Victor Maitland homicide in a semi-official capacity."

"So I heard."

"Department grapevine?"

"Not so much the Department as the art-business grapevine. It's a small world, Chief; the word gets around."

"I imagine it does," Delaney said. "And I figure you know a lot about that small world. I think you could be a big help to me, lieutenant, and I was hoping we could get together."

"Be glad to," Wolfe said. "You say when and where."

Delaney started to make a date, then remembered that Sergeant Boone was arranging a meeting with J. Julian Simon.

"Suppose I call you Monday morning and we'll set a definite time and place," he said. "I'll call about ten. Will that be all right?"

Wolfe said that would be fine, and they hung up.

10

On Monday morning, Boone arrived, as usual, at nine A.M. Delaney went out in his shirtsleeves to invite the sergeant into the house.

"I thought we'd spend the day getting caught up," he told Boone. "Paperwork and so forth. And plan where we go from here."

"Fine with me, Chief," Boone nodded. "I brought along my notes on what happened on Friday."

They went into Delaney's study, and in a few minutes Monica brought in cups and a thermos of coffee, and a plate of miniature cinnamon doughnuts. She chatted a few minutes with Sergeant Boone, then left the two men together.

The first thing Delaney wanted to know was about the appointment with J. Julian Simon. Boone said it was set for ten o'clock the following morning, and the Chief made a careful note of it.

Then, both drinking black coffee and munching on their doughnuts, Boone told about his two time trials from Dukker's place to Victor Maitland's Mott Street studio. Delaney made notes as Boone reported. Neither man felt it necessary to comment on the significance of the trials.

At ten, Chief Delaney called Lieutenant Bernard Wolfe of the Art Theft and Forgery Squad and made a luncheon appointment for noon on Tuesday, at Keen's English Chop House on West 36th Street.

"Ever been there?" he asked Boone, after he had hung up.

"Never have, sir."

"Great mutton chops, if you can eat mutton at noon."

"What do you figure on getting from Wolfe?"

"Nothing specific. Maybe some useful background on the New York art scene. And maybe he can mooch around for us and pick up something on Maitland. At this stage I'll take anything—rumors, tips, gossip, whatever. All right, you go first; how did you make out with the Hemley woman?"

Boone had good recall and, consulting his notes only a few times, delivered an accurate report on his lunch and conversation with Susan Hemley. After he had finished, the two men sat in silence a few moments, staring holes in the air.

"Interesting," Delaney said finally. "She told you that Mrs. Maitland thought, quote, There was more to it than that, unquote. And when you pressed her on it, she suddenly had to get back to the office. What was your impression? Did she know and was scamming? Or did she really not know, and had to get back? Which?"

"I don't know," Boone said, troubled. "I've thought about it since, and I can't make a hard assessment."

"Guess."

"I'd guess she didn't know what Alma Maitland was talking about."

"All right. Let's accept that for now. How about Geltman's alibi? She saw him go in around ten, but she didn't see him come out at one-thirty?"

"That's right, Chief. She was at lunch with Alma Maitland, or on her way to lunch."

"And no one else in the office saw Geltman come out?"

"Right again. The office was empty. Everyone was out. So Geltman really has a one-man alibi: J. Julian Simon."

"How's this . . ." Delaney said. "It's not far from Simon's office to Le Provençal, where Hemley lunched with Alma Maitland. So let's say she leaves the office about one-fifteen. The moment she's gone, the coast is clear and Geltman ducks out, goes downtown and knocks Maitland. No, no, no. Scratch that. It doesn't listen. The Geltman staff and customers saw him back in the galleries at one-thirty, so he couldn't have done that."

"Son of a bitch!" Boone said bitterly, and when Delaney stared at him, the sergeant blushed.

"Sorry, sir," he said. "The Simon and Brewster offices are halfway down a long corridor from the elevator. A wood-paneled door leading to the outer office. That's where Susan Hemley has her desk. She said she talked a few minutes with Geltman that Friday morning, then he went into Simon's inner office. That's where she went to set up our appointment. But like a fool, I didn't check."

Delaney blinked twice, then smiled.

"A private entrance," he said. "From Simon's inner office out to the corridor. It isn't unusual to have a setup like that. So lawyers can duck out if there's someone in the outer office they don't want to see. Like a process server or a cop with a warrant."

"Right!" Boone said. "If Simon has a corridor door from his private office, Geltman could arrive at ten, and lam right out again. That would give him all the time in the world to get down to Mott Street, fix Maitland, and either return to Simon's office or go directly back to his Galleries. Sorry I missed that door, Chief."

"No harm done. We can check on it tomorrow. And Hemley said Simon and Geltman are old friends?"

"Yep. Play handball together."

"Cute. Playing ball together. Well . . . we'll see. What kind of a woman is this Hemley? Pretty?"

"Attractive enough. Not beautiful. Very thin. Not too young. Short, blonde, curly hair. No tits or ass. Good legs. Good voice. Not too much in the brains department."

"Sexy?"

Boone thought a moment.

"I'd say yes. Something there. Like if she let herself go, she'd be hell on wheels."

"If Geltman was right about maybe Alma Maitland being a lez, would there be that between them?"

Boone considered again, then sighed.

"Might be," he said. "A possibility. I just can't say. What man could?"

"Certainly not me," Delaney rumbled. "But did she come on with you? You know, man-woman stuff? Make a play? Angling for another date?"

"Nooo," Boone said slowly. "Not really. Polite and friendly, but nothing heavy. Maybe I didn't turn her on. All I can do is tell you my feeling, that if I had invited her to an orgy, she'd have giggled and said, 'Sure!' "

"Well, I'll meet her tomorrow morning and see how my take compares with yours. Now let me tell you about my little soiree with Ted and Alma Maitland."

He reported to Boone everything that had happened during the interrogations of the two. The sergeant listened intently, making occasional notes but not interrupting. When Delaney finished, Boone looked up from his notebook, excited.

"Wow," he said. "That's something. And all new. The business of Ted's violence wasn't in the tub, was it, sir?"

"No. Not a word."

"Can we get the psychiatrist to talk?"

"No way. He'll clam. And legally."

"So Ted boy was having his lunch alone in Washington Square Park. He says. You realize what that means, Chief? Alma says she was shopping alone. Sarazen and Dukker claim they were with each other, but they could have pulled it. Even the mother and sister could have driven down from Rockland in plenty of time for the fun. And Saul Geltman's half-ass alibi depends on J. Julian Simon, his old handball buddy. Beautiful. They're all guilty. What do we do now?"

"What we do now," Edward X. Delaney said, "is construct a time chart. Names listed in a vertical column. Times in a horizontal line. So we can see at a glance where each of the seven was at any fifteen-minute period between nine o'clock that Friday morning and, say, five that afternoon. Or where they say they were. I have some graph paper around here somewhere; that'll get us started."

They had hardly begun their time chart when Monica called them to lunch. She had set it out in the dining room, but it was a do-it-yourself sandwich luncheon. Sour rye, dark pumpernickel, fluffy challeh. Salami, bologna, braunschweiger, turkey. Tomatoes, radishes, cukes, slices of Spanish onion. Herring in sour cream. Olives. Kosher dills. German potato salad and cold baked beans. Dark beer for Delaney and iced tea for Boone. Monica sat with them, picked, and wouldn't let them talk business. So they could do nothing but eat and eat.

After, they helped her clear the table, wash up, get the leftovers put away.

"Just right," Delaney said, kissing her cheek. "Hit the spot."

"Great, Mrs. Delaney," Sergeant Boone said. "I don't have food like that very often."

He thought she murmured, "You could," but he wasn't certain.

Then the two men went back into the study and got to work on the time chart. When they had finished, they had a handsome graph that showed the movements of the suspects almost minute by minute during the day of the murder. And, in colored pencil, it revealed whether the suspect's whereabouts were merely claimed or confirmed by one or more witnesses.

It proved nothing, of course; they didn't expect it would. But it did give them a visual image of all the action, and after it was pinned to the map board, alongside Maitland's charcoal sketches, they gazed at it with approval. It seemed to bring everything into focus.

The Chief went into the kitchen, and brought back a can of beer for himself and a bottle of tonic water for Boone. Then they sat staring at the time chart again and began blowing smoke, trying out scenarios on each other.

"I worked a case—" they both said at the same time. Then both stopped, and both laughed.

"You first," Chief Delaney said.

"It wasn't much, sir," Boone said. "This was just after I made dick three. The precincts had their own detective squads then, and I was working the Two-oh. There was this fancy jewelry shop on Broadway, mostly good antique stuff, and the guy was losing stock. Regularly. Maybe one or two pieces a week. There was just him and his wife in the store, so we figured it had to be boosting. There was no cleaning guy, no signs of forced entry. We put on an inside stakeout, a man in the backroom looking through a peephole while customers were in the store. But no one was lifting. A real mindblower. One day this jeweler is on the Fifth Avenue bus, going downtown, and he sees this beautiful young twist sitting across from him. And she's wearing one of his missing pieces. He said it had to be; it was a brooch of rubies shaped like a rose. He said it was Victorian, and he didn't think there was another in the world like it. Anyway, he played it smart and didn't say anything to the young twist, but he followed her home, and then he called us. Well, to make a long story short, we found out the ruby brooch had been a gift to the young twist from her boyfriend. And where did he get it? From the jeweler's wife. Can you believe it? The boyfriend was a real nogood-nik, a gigolo-type, and was playing the old lady along for what he could get from her. I had to tell the jeweler; not the easiest thing I've ever done. But the point I'm trying to make is this: if it hadn't been for the chance meeting of the jeweler and the young twist on that Fifth Avenue bus, I doubt if we'd ever have broken it, until that jeweler was picked clean, down to the bare walls. It was an accident, a one-in-a-million break."

Delaney nodded. "My story is something like that, but the break was due more to the bad guy's stupidity than to accident. This was an extortion thing. The guy wasn't asking for much: five hundred in small bills. Peanuts considering the rap he was risking. He'd write these letters demanding the five hundred bucks or he'd throw acid on the mark's wife or kids. Nice. God knows how many paid up before one of the victims had the sense and balls to call us. And would you believe it, the extortion letter had been sent by metered mail. I guess the nut figured to save postage by mailing the letter from the office where he worked. We went to the postal inspectors, and it took one day to locate the meter from the number on the postmark, and a four-day stakeout to nab the guy who put the letter through the meter. He was trying it again. I remember he said he needed the money because he was studying at Delehanty—this was when they had civil-service courses—on how to get into the Police Academy. I don't think he ever made it. Well, you're figuring we'll get a break by chance, and I'm hoping for the same thing, but maybe from the stupidity of the killer."

Abner Boone grinned at him.

"Chief, that's figuring we're smarter than the bad guys."

"Any time you start doubting that, sergeant," Edward X. Delaney said seriously, "you better get into another line of work."

11

On Tuesday morning, the Chief sat in Boone's car outside the Delaney brownstone, listening to the sergeant report on his unsuccessful efforts to jog the memories of detectives who worked the original Maitland investigation.

"A cipher," Boone said gloomily. "They all say everything they saw, heard, or learned was in their reports. I'm afraid we draw zilch on this, Chief."

"I still think it was a good idea," Delaney said stubbornly. "Anyone left to contact?"

"Two," the sergeant said. "I'll try them tonight. One's just back from vacation, and the other's on a stakeout, and his loot won't tell me where. Down to Simon's office now?"

"Sure," Delaney said. "First we'll check to see if a corridor door—" He stopped suddenly, and said, "Wait a minute."

He got out of the car and went back into the house, into the kitchen. Monica was sitting on a high stool near the counter, sipping a third cup of morning coffee, making out her day's shopping list, and listening to WQXR on the kitchen transistor. She looked up when he came in.

"Forget something, dear?" she asked.

"Masking tape," he said. "I know we've got some of it somewhere."

"The end drawer," she said. "With the fuses, batteries, flashlight, hammer, screwdriver, pliers, Scotch tape, rubber bands, Elmer's glue, candles, Band-Aids, old corks, paint brushes, a can of—"

"All right, all right," he laughed. "I promised to straighten it out, and I will."

He found the roll of masking tape and tore off a piece about an inch long. Then he took a sheet from Monica's small scratchpad and pressed the tape onto it lightly.

"What are you doing?" she asked curiously.

"Tricks of the trade," he advised loftily. "I don't tell you everything." He kissed her quickly and left again.

"I couldn't care less," she yelled after him.

Back in the car, he showed Sergeant Boone his little sheet of paper with the square of masking tape lightly affixed.

"An old B-and-E artist taught me this trick," he explained. "Suppose you have a lot of panes of frosted glass. You want to identify one of them. In his case, it was the one he wanted to cut. When the light comes through, they all look alike. So if you can get inside, you put a little square of masking tape down in one corner. No one notices it. But when you're outside, with the light coming through, you can easily pick out the pane you want. If J. Julian Simon has a corridor door from his private office, we'll pull the gimmick in reverse. I'll show you how it works."

Boone took his word for it and drove downtown to the offices of Simon & Brewster. They finally found a metered space, three blocks away, parked, and walked back.

The attorneys' offices were on the sixth floor of a modern, ten-story office building. Clean lobby, no doorman, self-service elevator. Chief Delaney looked around, then inspected the register on the wall.

"Lawyers, art dealers, three foundations," he noted. "A trade magazine. A guy who repairs violins. Odds and ends. Not much traffic, I'd guess."

The elevator was small, but efficient enough. Silent. They stepped out at the sixth floor. They still hadn't seen anyone. Boone motioned down the corridor. He paused outside the walnut-paneled door bearing the golden legend: SIMON & BREWSTER, ATTORNEYS-AT-LAW. He looked at Delaney questioningly. The Chief waved him farther along the tiled hallway, then halted. He put his lips close to Boone's ear.

"When Susan Hemley went into Simon's inner office," he whispered, "which direction did she go?"

Boone thought a moment, turning, trying to orient himself. He pointed on down the corridor. They moved that way, to a frosted glass doorway with nothing on it but a number in gilt figures. They walked beyond it and found another door exactly like it, but with a higher number. Delaney looked at Boone, but the sergeant shrugged helplessly.

The Chief went back to the first frosted glass door and, standing to one side so his shadow would not be seen from inside, he unpeeled the little square of masking tape from its paper carrier. He stuck it lightly and deftly to the glass, at eye-height, next to the frame.

"Bright light out here," he said to Boone. "If that's the door to Simon's private office, we should be able to see the tape from inside. For identification. So we don't get it mixed up with a door to a john or a storeroom. Let's go . . ."

He led the way and took off his straw skimmer when he entered the office. It was June 1st.

"Here we are, Miss Hemley," Boone smiled. "Right on time."

"You certainly are," she said. "A little early, in fact. Mr. Simon's on the phone. I'll tell him you're here as soon as he gets off."

"Miss Hemley, I'd like you to meet Chief Delaney. Chief, Miss Susan Hemley."

She held out her hand, and Delaney took it and bent over it in a bow that was almost courtly.

"Miss Hemley," he said. "Happy to meet you. Now I can understand the sergeant's enthusiasm."

"Oh Chief!" she said. "This is such a—a *thing* for me. I've read all about you. Your cases. You're famous!"

"Oh," he said, making a gesture. "The papers . . . You understand, I'm sure. They exaggerate. How long have you worked for Mr. Simon?"

"Almost six years," she said. "He's such a pleasure."

"So I understand," he said. "Well, our business shouldn't take long. We'll be out of your lovely hair before you know it."

Her hand rose mechanically, fingers poked at the tight blonde curls. Eyes glittered behind the black horn-rims.

"It's the Maitland case, isn't it?" she said breathlessly.

He nodded gravely, put a forefinger solemnly to his closed lips.

"I understand," she whispered. "I won't say a word."

A light went out on her six-button telephone. She caught it at once. "He's off," she said. "I'll tell him you're here."

She rose and moved lithely to the door of Simon's inner office. Her full skirt whipped about her good legs. She knocked once, opened the door, entered, closed the door behind her. A ballet.

"You were right," Delaney murmured to Boone. "It's there."

She came back to them in a moment.

"Mr. Simon will see you now, gentlemen," she said brightly.

She ushered them in and closed the door gently, regretfully. The man behind the desk rose and came forward smiling, hand outstretched.

"Chief," he said. "Sergeant. I'm J. Julian Simon."

They shook hands, and Delaney remembered what Lincoln had said about men who "part their name in the middle."

Simon, moving smoothly and confidently, got them seated on a tufted, green leather chesterfield. Then he pulled over a castered armchair in the same leather and sat down facing them. He offered cigarettes in a silver case. When they declined, he returned the case to his inside jacket pocket without lighting a cigarette for himself. He leaned back, crossed his knees casually.

"Gentlemen," he said, "how may I help you?"

He was a shining man, so polished that a steely glow seemed to surround him. Silvery hair brushed to a mirror gleam. A white mustache exquisitely trimmed and waxed. A pink-and-white complexion massaged to health. Teeth too good to be true. Eyes like disks of sky. Fingernails alight with clear polish. Gold wristwatch, tie clasp, and rings, one set with a square diamond, a tiny ice cube.

And the clothes! A suit of hard grey sharkskin with soaring lapels. Shirt of water blue. A tie that appeared to have been clipped from a sheet of chromium. Black moccasins with tassels as bushy as a shaving brush, the leather so glossy it seemed to have been oiled.

And his manner as artfully finished as his appearance. A resonant voice that flowed, deeply burbling. A laugh that boomed. Gestures as smooth, slow, and ornate as those of a deepsea diver. Earnestness in his gaze. Sincerity in his brilliant smile. Elegance in the lift of a white eyebrow or the casual droop of a crossed foot. Altogether, a marvelous product.

"Sorry to bother you again with questions on the Maitland case, counselor," the Chief said, "but we just can't walk away from it."

"Of course not," the lawyer trumpeted. "We all want the crime solved and justice meted out."

"A beautiful office you have here," the Chief said, looking around. A glass door was set into an embrasure beyond the couch. It could not be seen clearly from where they sat.

"Thank you, Chief Delaney," Simon said complacently. He looked with satisfaction at his paneled walls, open bookcases, and framed Spy prints. "Nothing like oak and leather to impress the clients—what?"

The laugh boomed out, and they smiled dutifully.

"I suppose you want to know about Saul Geltman," the lawyer said, "since it's my only connection with the case. As I have heretofore stated, he entered my office, here, at approximately ten o'clock on the morning I've been told Victor Maitland was killed. Saul and I are both busy men, and we had postponed our conference too many times."

"You handle all his legal affairs, sir?" Sergeant Boone asked. "The Galleries too?"

"I do indeed," Simon nodded. "Also, his tax situation and estate planning. And I occasionally offer advice on his investment program, although I admit he sometimes doesn't take it!" Mouth snapped open, china teeth shone. "So we had a lot to discuss when we finally did get together that Friday morning. To reiterate, he arrived at approximately ten A.M. We discussed various matters, and around noon I called out for sandwiches and soft drinks. Which reminds me: I am derelict in my duties as host. I have a small but well-equipped bar here. May I offer you gentlemen anything?"

"Thank you, no," Delaney said. "But we appreciate the thought. Then after lunch you returned to your discussions?"

"Well, actually we talked as we ate, of course. The conference continued until about one-thirty when Saul left and, I understand, returned to the Geltman Galleries. And that's all I can tell you, gentlemen."

"He left at exactly one-thirty, counselor?" Delaney asked.

"Oh, not precisely." Simon waved such exactitude away: a matter of no importance. "Five minutes either way. To the best of my remembrance."

"Counselor, was Mr. Geltman out of your sight at any time on that Friday between ten and one-thirty?"

"Approximately," the lawyer admonished him.

"Approximately," Delaney agreed.

"No, he was not out of my sight between the approximate hours of ten and one-thirty that Friday. Oh, wait!" He snapped his fingers crisply. "He did go into the john. Back there." He jerked a thumb over his shoulder, gesturing at a solid wooden door set into the wall between oak bookcases. "But he was only gone two or three minutes."

"Other than that, he was in your sight every minute during the period specified?"

"He was."

"Thank you very much," Chief Delaney said suddenly, clapped his notebook shut, rose abruptly. "You've been very cooperative, and we appreciate it."

Sergeant Boone stood up, and so did J. Julian Simon. The lawyer seemed surprised at the unexpected end of the questioning, pleasantly surprised. He beamed, grew more expansive, did everything but throw his arms about the cops' shoulders.

"Always happy to help out New York's Finest," he caroled.

"When the lunch came, did Miss Hemley bring it in?" Delaney demanded sharply.

"What?" Simon said, shaken. "I don't understand."

"You ordered sandwiches for you and Geltman. When your order was delivered, did Susan Hemley bring it into your office?"

"Why—ah—no, she didn't."

"Then the delivery man from the deli brought it in?"

"No, that's not the way it happened at all," Simon said, regaining his poise. "Miss Hemley called me on the intercom and said the delivery boy was outside with the lunch. So I went out, paid him, and brought the lunch back in here. But I fail to see—"

"It's nothing," Delaney assured him. "I'm an old woman; I admit it. I like to have every little detail straight, exactly how everything happened. Now I know. It certainly is a handsome office you have here, counselor."

He wandered about a moment, Sergeant Boone following him. The Chief inspected the caricatures on the walls, stroked the oak bookcases, touched the marble top of a small sideboard. And glanced toward the glass door. As did Sergeant Boone. They both saw the little square of masking tape clearly, outlined against the lighted corridor.

There were thanks and handshakes all around. More handshakes and farewells when they left Susan Hemley in the outer office. In the empty corridor, Delaney motioned Boone to stay where he was. Then he moved back to the frosted glass door and, standing to one side again, peeled the tape away. He came back to Boone, rolling the tape into a little ball between his fingers. He dropped it into his side pocket.

"Destroying the evidence," he said. "A felony."

There was a passenger in the elevator when it came down, so they didn't speak. Out on the street, walking toward their parked car, Delaney said, "I don't think he was lying about how the lunch got into the inner office, but just to make sure, check the delicatessen where it came from. Find out if the delivery boy saw Geltman. Also Susan Hemley. Did she take the sandwiches into the inner office, or did it happen as Simon told us? And if it did, did she see Geltman while the door was open? Maybe you better have another lunch with her."

"Can't I do it on the phone, Chief?" Boone asked.

Delaney looked sideways at him, surprised.

"Don't you like her?" he asked.

"She scares me," the sergeant confessed.

"Go on, have lunch with her," Delaney smiled. "She's not going to bite you."

"I'm not so sure," Boone said mournfully.

They sat awhile in the parked car, windows down, waiting for the car to cool. They were silent, going over the permutations and combinations.

"He could have made it out to the corridor," Boone offered finally. "Without Hemley seeing him."

"Could have," Delaney agreed. "Risky but possible. So we scratch another alibi. Now none of them is home free."

Boone nodded gloomily.

"Sergeant," Delaney said, almost dreamily, "I'm a bigot."

Boone turned to look at him.

"What, sir?"

"I am," the Chief insisted. "I have two great unreasoning prejudices. First, I hate Brussels sprouts. And second—" he paused dramatically "—I don't trust men who wear pinkie rings."

"Oh, that," Boone grinned.

"Yes," Delaney said. "That. Run him through Records, will you? Maybe he's got a sheet."

"J. Julian Simon?" Boone said incredulously. "A sheet?"

"Oh yes," Delaney nodded. "Maybe."

"Wow," Abner Boone said, looking at the overhead racks of customers' clay pipes. "This place must be a thousand years old."

"Not quite," Delaney said. "But it didn't open yesterday either."

They were in Keen's English Chop House, waiting for Lieutenant Bernard Wolfe to arrive. The Chief had rated a booth in the main dining room. When the ancient waiter had asked, "A little something, gentlemen?" the Chief had ordered a dry Gibson up, and looked to Boone.

"Just tomato juice for me," the sergeant said stolidly.

"A Virgin Mary," the waiter nodded wisely. "Also known as a Bloody Shame."

Boone grinned at him.

"You're so right," he said.

"If this place ever closes," Delaney said, looking around, "I'm dead. I mean, I'm not talking about the Pavillon and Chauveron and places like that. All gone. But I was never in them. I'm talking about places like Steuben's Tavern and the Blue Ribbon and Connollys on Twenty-third Street. Good, solid eating establishments. All gone. Beveled glass, Tiffany lamps, a mahogany bar. Enrico and Paglieri down in the Village. Moscowitz and Lupowitz over on Second Avenue. The food! You wouldn't believe. Real cops' restaurants when you wanted to spread. Things like boiled beef and horseradish sauce, a nice corn beef and cabbage, venison in season. Once I had wild-boar chops at Steuben's. Can you imagine? Honest drinks. Waiters who knew what it was all about. It's going, sergeant," he ended sorrowfully. "This place is one of the best and the last. If it disappears, where the hell are you going to get mutton in Manhattan?"

"Beats me, sir," Boone said solemnly, and Delaney laughed.

"Yes," he said, "I do get carried away. But it's hard to see the old places die. Although I suppose some good new places are coming along. The blessing of this city. It keeps rejuvenating itself. Well . . . here's our drinks. Now, where's Wolfe?"

And there he was, standing by their booth—but they couldn't believe it.

Tall, slender as a whip, with a devil's black beard and mustache. A suit of bottle-green velvet with nipped waist and flaring tails. A puce shirt, open collar, knotted scarf of paisley silk about a muscled throat. A dark, flashing man, lean, with hard eyes and a soft smile. All of him sharp as a blade, coldly handsome, a menace to every woman on earth and half the men. He took their startled looks, threw his head back, flashing the California whites.

"Don't let the threads fool you," he said. "My working uniform. At home in Brooklyn I wear dirty chinos and basketball sneakers. You must be Chief Delaney. I'm Loot Bernie Wolfe. Don't get up."

They shook hands all around, and he slid in next to Boone. The waiter appeared at his elbow, and he ordered a kir. He seemed to live with that raffish smile.

"Great," he said, looking around at the smoky walls and faded memorabilia. "I'll have a suckling pig on toast. Would you believe the last time I was in here was when I proposed?"

"How long have you been married?" Delaney asked.

"Who's married?" Wolfe asked. "But we're still intimate. On and off."

He kept it up through lunch—rare steak sandwiches for all, with pewter tankards of musty ale for Delaney and Wolfe—and they enjoyed his fresh, bouncy talk. He told them a cute one he had just closed.

"This East Side goniff with a penthouse, apparently plenty of dineros—well, he's into this and that. You know, import-export, plays the commodities market, etcetera. Suddenly, he's got the shorts. Who knows? Maybe he invested in a buggy-whip company or something. Anyway, he can't come up with the scratch, and he's hurting. The banks won't touch him, and he's leery of the sharks. Now this guy has got a nice collection of Matisse and Picasso drawings. Absolutely legit. Authenticated. Loaned out to at least three museum shows. No doubt about them; they're kosher. And insured for a hundred big ones. But that's not enough for him; he needs more to tide him over. Now you've got to know that modern drawings, simple black lines on white paper, are the easiest things in the world to fake. Photograph them. Trace them. Any which way. I mean a good forgery of a Rembrandt, say, that's something. A forgery of a Picasso scrawl, a plumber could do it. All right, so our bad guy hires himself a crew of flatnoses to rip off his own collection. The whole thing is snatched. The heist takes place while the guy is having a dinner party. Four people eating by candlelight, and these nasty pascudyniks bust in, show their heaters, strip the walls and take off. Witnesses—right? He figures that's a hundred G's for him on the insurance. And he knows the drawings will never be recovered because he's told the slobs in the ski masks to burn the shit. And it is shit, because what they took were fakes he had made. The real stuff is being peddled in Geneva—that's in Switzerland. So the guy plans to make it on the insurance plus what he makes on the sale of the real stuff in Europe. Coppish? All right, class, how did teacher break it?"

He grinned at them, back and forth, and both Delaney and Boone pondered.

Finally, the sergeant said, "You got a flash from Geneva that the real drawings were being pushed over there?"

"Nah," Lieutenant Bernard Wolfe said. "International cooperation isn't that good yet. But we're working on it. Maybe if a da Vinci had been glommed, they'd have been alerted. But not on a portfolio of modern drawings. How about you, Chief?"

"The guys in the ski masks tried to unload the fakes over here instead of burning them?"

"Right!" Wolfe said. "They got paid five thou for the ripoff. But then they got to thinking—which was a mistake because they were shmucks. They figured, why settle for the five G's? They could contact the insurance company and collect maybe another ten or twenty. The insurer would be happy to pay that for recovery. So that's what they did. A meet was arranged, and the insurance guy showed up with an art expert to make sure he was buying the true-blue stuff. The expert took one look and laughed. So the insurance company walked and tipped me. One thing led to another, and we busted all their asses. So how can I help you on the Maitland thing?"

They were having coffee and dessert by then. American coffee and fresh strawberries for Delaney and Boone, espresso and a kirsch for Wolfe.

"This art scene," the Chief said fretfully. "We don't know enough about it. It's a whole new world. Saul Geltman, Maitland's dealer—by the way, do you know him?"

"Sure do," Wolfe said cheerfully. "Nice little guy. Take off your rings before you shake hands with him."

"Oh-ho," Delaney said. "Like that, is it? Well, anyway, Geltman told us something of how dealers work with artists. Something about the art-gallery business. What I was hoping to get from you was more about the business of painting from the artist's point of view. How the money angle works."

"The money," Wolfe nodded. "What makes the world go 'round. From an artist's point of view? Okay. An unsuccessful artist, he's going to starve. You're not interested in that. A successful artist, his troubles are just beginning. Let's take a guy like Maitland, who makes it. Ten, fifteen years ago he's selling for peanuts. Today his stuff is pulling maybe two hundred thou. Fine, but what happens to the early stuff he was selling for walking-around money when no one knew who he was? I'll tell you what happens to it: the smart-asses who bought it for kreplach, *they* made the lekach. Buy for a hundred, sell for a thousand. Profits like you wouldn't believe. And the artist gets nothing of that. Not a cent. Is that right? Of course it isn't right. Profiting like that on another man's work. It sucks."

"I agree," Delaney nodded. "Don't the artists scream?"

"Sure they do," Wolfe said. "For all the good it does them. Buy low, sell high. There's no law against it. It's the Eleventh Commandment. Now they're beginning to really *do* something about it. They say when you buy a guy's painting, you should sign an agreement that if you sell for profit in the future, the artist shares. Like ten or twenty percent of the profit. And the guy who buys the painting from the original buyer, if he also eventually sells, he's also got to share his profit with the artist. And so on."

"Makes sense to me," Boone said.

"Of course it makes sense," Wolfe said indignantly. "The present system is ridiculous. The artist sweats out the work; he should get at least a *share* of the bonanza if he hits. But the dealers and galleries and museums are fighting it. The old story: money, moola, mazuma. It'll cut into their take if the artists share. A crock of shit, I tell you. An artist who sold a painting for five hundred bucks ten years ago reads in the paper that it just went for half a mil—how do you think that makes him feel?"

"Is that what happened to Maitland?" Delaney asked.

"Sure," Wolfe said. "Exactly what happened to Maitland. I met him once. He was a six-ply bastard, but he was right on this thing. It drove him up the wall. Could I have another shot, Chief? All this talking is drying me out."

"Of course," Delaney said. "The Department's treat. Another kirsch?"

"No," Wolfe said. "I think I'll go back to the musty ale again. It goes down good. You're not drinking, sergeant?"

"Not today," Boone smiled.

"Good man," Wolfe said. "I spend half my time at exhibition previews and cocktail parties. They booze up a storm. Rots the liver. But it's all for the Department—right?"

Fresh ales were brought for Delaney and Wolfe. The lieutenant took a deep draft, then bent over the table toward the Chief. His black mustache had an icing of white foam.

"Okay," he said. "A successful artist like Victor Maitland gets fucked that way: the early paintings he sold for nothing end up getting traded for zillions, and he doesn't share. But there's another way he gets screwed. Let's take a young artist just starting out. He works his ass off. He's got so much drive and so many hot ideas, he hates to sleep. If he's lucky, he's selling maybe one out of every ten paintings. The others pile up—right? In his studio, the basement, the attic, homes of friends—wherever. Maybe he gives them away just to get rid of them. And a lot of these young artists barter paintings for meals and a place to work. So the years pass, the artist gets a wife and kids, and his stuff begins to sell. The prices go up, up, up. Meanwhile, he's still got the old things that no one wanted. But he keeps them around because that's all he's got to leave to his family. In case he drops dead, it's their inheritance. So one day he does drop dead, and he leaves his wife a few bucks and a studio full of his old paintings. Now this is where the screwing comes in: the U.S. Government, wearing its IRS hat, steps in to evaluate the dead artist's estate. They say all his old paintings have to be appraised at current market value, regardless of when they were painted. In other words, a very early Maitland is worth a hundred G's if the last few Maitlands sold on the open market for a hundred G's. So that's how they figure the estate tax. And New York State figures *their* bite on what the IRS estimates. Sometimes the poor widow goes broke trying to pay those estate taxes, and sometimes she has to sell off the entire collection to make good. Just another sweet example of how society shits on the artist. Well . . . any of this any use to you?"

"Very useful, lieutenant," Delaney said. "You've given us a lot to think about. But tell me this . . . you say when the artist becomes famous and starts to sell at higher prices, he still has a lot of his early, unsold stuff around. So why doesn't he sell that, too, as prices go up? Why not get the cash instead of leaving the stuff to his estate?"

"A lot of reasons," Wolfe said. "Maybe his style has changed completely, and the old stuff looks like crap to him, and he's ashamed of it. Maybe his dealer tells him to keep it off the market. Listen, scarcity is one factor in the price a dealer can ask. If there's a warehouse of the guy's work available, the price drops. If only a few pieces are up for sale, the price goes up and stays up. Why do you think Picasso had so many unsold paintings when he died? Also, a lot of artists know from nothing about estate taxes; they're lousy businessmen. The poor schlemiel thinks he's leaving a tidy nest egg for the wife and kiddies, not knowing how it's going to be reduced by taxes. And also, maybe the artist does a painting that comes out so right, that he likes so much, that he doesn't ever want to sell it. He puts it on his wall and looks at it. Maybe he'll even make little changes in it as the years go by. Lighten a tint here, heavy a shadow there. But he'll keep it for years, maybe never put it up for sale at all. Look, Chief, when you're talking about artists, you're dealing with a bunch of nuts. Don't expect logical behavior from them, or even common sense. They ain't got it. If they had sense, they'd be truck drivers or shoe salesmen. It's a tough racket, and most of them fall by the wayside."

"The reason I asked you why the successful artist didn't sell his old stuff," Delaney explained, "is because there were no paintings in Victor Maitland's studio when the body was found."

Lieutenant Bernard Wolfe was shocked. He jerked back from the table, looking in astonishment from Delaney to Boone.

"No paintings?" he repeated. "Nothing started? No canvases half-done? Nothing on his easel? No stacks of finished paintings? Nothing hung up for the varnish to dry? None of his own stuff on the walls?"

"No paintings," Delaney said patiently. "Not a one."

"Jesus Christ," Wolfe said. "I can't believe it. I've been in a million artists' studios, and every one was jammed with paintings in all stages. The only thing I can figure is that someone cleaned Maitland out. Maybe the guy who whacked him. He should have had at least *one* painting there. He had the reputation of being a fast worker. But *nothing?* That smells."

"We did find three charcoal sketches," Sergeant Boone said. "Geltman claims they were probably preliminary drawings of a new model Maitland was trying out."

"Could be," Wolfe nodded. "They do that sometimes: knock off a few quick sketches of a fresh girl to see if she's simpatico."

"That's another thing," the Chief said. "Do you know many models?"

"My share," Wolfe grinned. "Want me to look at the drawings to see if I can make her?"

"Would you? We'd appreciate it."

"Be glad to. Just tell me where and when. I'm in and out of the office all the time, but you can always leave a message."

Delaney nodded, and called for the bill. He paid, and they all rose and moved to the door. Out on the sidewalk, they shook hands with the lieutenant and thanked him for his help. He waved it away, and thanked them for the lunch.

"And look into that business of no paintings in the studio," he said.

The evening was still young, not yet midnight, and perhaps they thought to talk lazily awhile, or maybe even go downstairs again for a late snack. In any event, the room was still lighted, and they lay awake, temporarily sated, when the bedside phone shrilled.

He cleared his throat and answered.

"Edward X. Delaney here."

It was Rebecca Hirsch, her words tumbling in a torrent, voice screechy, stretched, almost breaking. He tried to interrupt, to slow her down, but she was too distraught to pause. Began weeping, didn't answer his questions. Finally he just let her rattle, until sobs stopped her. He could reckon then what had happened, was happening.

Abner Boone had called her almost an hour previously, obviously drunk. It was a farewell call; he said he was going to blow his brains out with his service revolver. Rebecca had been in bed, had dressed hastily, hurried over in a cab. Boone was falling-down drunk, bouncing off the walls drunk. He had an almost full bottle, and was drinking from that. Gibbering. When she tried to grab the whiskey from him, he had rushed into the bathroom and locked the door. He was still in there, wouldn't come out, wouldn't answer her.

"All right," Delaney said stonily. "Stay there. If he comes out, don't try to take the bottle. Speak quietly to him. And keep out of his way. I'll be right over. Meanwhile, look around. Everywhere. For another bottle. And for a gun. I'll be there as soon as I can."

He hung up and got out of bed. He told Monica what had happened as he dressed. Her face grew bleak.

"You were right," she said.

"I'll send Rebecca back here," he said. "In a cab. Watch for her. I may spend the night there. I'll call you and tell you what's happening."

"Edward, be careful," she said.

He nodded, and unlocked his equipment drawer in the bedside table. His guns were in there, with cartridges and cleaning tools. A gun belt. Two holsters. Handcuffs. A steel-linked "come-along." A set of lock picks. But the only thing he took was a leather-covered sap, about eight inches long. It stuck out of his hip pocket, but the tail of his jacket covered it. He relocked the drawer carefully.

"Come down with me and put the chain on when I leave," he told Monica. "Open it only for Rebecca. Get some hot coffee into her, and maybe a shot of brandy."

"Be careful, Edward," she repeated.

Outside, he paused until he heard the chain clink into place. Then he debated how he could make the best time, cab or walking. He decided on a cab, strode over to First Avenue as quickly as he could. He waited for almost five minutes, then stepped into the path of an on-coming hack showing Off-duty lights. It squealed to a halt, the bumper a foot away. The furious driver leaned out.

"Cancha—" he began bellowing.

"Five to East Eighty-fifth Street," Delaney said, waving the bill.

"Get in," the driver said.

At Boone's apartment house, there was a night doorman on duty, sitting behind a high counter. He looked up as Delaney stalked in.

"Yes?" he said.

"Abner Boone's apartment."

"I need your name," the doorman said. "I gotta ring up first. Rules."

"Delaney."

The doorman picked up his phone, dialed a three-digit number.

"A Mr. Delaney to see Mr. Boone," he said.

He hung up and looked at the Chief.

"A woman answered," he said suspiciously.

"My daughter," Delaney said coldly.

"I don't want no trouble," the doorman said.

"Neither do I," Delaney said. "I'll waltz her out of here nice and quiet, and you never saw a thing."

The doorman's hand folded around the proffered sawbuck.

"Right," he said.

When he got off the elevator, Rebecca was waiting in the corridor, hands wrestling. She didn't look good to him: greenish-white, hair dank and scraggly, pupils dilated, lips bitten. He knew the signs.

"Yes, yes," he said softly. He slid an arm gently about her shoulders. "All right now. All right."

"I didn't," she stammered. "He wouldn't. I couldn't."

"Yes, yes," he repeated in a monotone, drew her into the apartment, closed the door behind him. "He's still in there?"

She nodded dumbly. She began to shake, her entire soft body trembling. He stood apart from her, but touched her with his hands: patted her shoulders, stroked her arms, pressed her hands lightly.

"Yes, yes," he intoned. "All right. All right now. It's going to be all right. Deep breath. Come on, take a deep breath. Another. That's it. That's fine."

"He can't—" she choked.

"Yes," he said. "Yes. Of course. Now come on over here and sit down. Just for a minute. Lean on me. That's right. That's it. Now just breathe deeply. Catch your breath. Good. Good."

He sat beside her a few moments until breathing eased, trembling stopped. He brought her a glass of water from the kitchen. She gulped frantically, water spilling down her chin. He went through the bedroom to the bathroom door. He pressed his ear against the thin wooden paneling. He heard mumbling, a few incoherent words. He tried the knob gently; the door was still locked.

He went back, sat down beside her. He took her hands again.

"Rebecca?" he said. "Better?"

She nodded.

"Good," he said quietly. "That's good. You're looking better, too. Did you find another bottle?"

She shook her head violently, hair flying.

"A gun?"

The headshake again.

"All right. Now I'm going to do something, but I need your help. Do you think you can help me?"

"What?" she said. "Will he—"

"We've got to get the whiskey away from him," he explained patiently, looking into her eyes. "And his gun. You understand?"

She nodded.

"I'm going to break in. As suddenly and quickly as I can. I'll try to get the bottle first. He may resist. You know that, don't you, Rebecca?"

Again she nodded.

"If I get hold of the bottle, I'll hand it to you or toss it to you. Then I'll take care of the gun. But your responsibility is the bottle. Grab it any way you can and run. Take it to the kitchen sink and empty it. Don't worry if it falls. Just make sure it's emptied, in the sink, on the floor, out the window—I don't care. Just get rid of the booze. Can you do that, Rebecca?"

"I—I think I can. You won't—won't hurt him, will you?"

"I don't want to," he said. "But you just worry about dumping the whiskey. All right?"

"All right," she whispered. "Please don't hurt him, Edward. He's sick."

"I know," he said grimly. "And he's going to be sicker. Think you can handle it now? Good. Let's go."

He led her to the bathroom door, a hand under her elbow. He positioned her behind him, to his right. He managed to transfer the leather-covered sap to his righthand jacket pocket. He didn't think she saw it.

He glanced at her, hoped she'd do. He stood directly in front of the bathroom door.

"This is Chief Edward X. Delaney," he called in a loud, harsh voice. "Come out of there, Boone."

There was mumbling. Then a slurred, "G'fuck y'self."

"This is Chief Edward—" Delaney began again, then raised his right knee high, almost to his chin, and drove his right foot against the door, just above the lock and knob. There was a splintering crack, the door sprung wide, smacked the tiled wall, began to bounce back. But by then Delaney was inside, moving fast.

Abner Boone, sitting hunched over on the closed toilet seat, bottle close to his mouth, couldn't react fast enough. Delaney grabbed the bottle away with a wide swipe, tossed it behind him, heard it thump to the bedroom rug, heard Rebecca's gasp. He didn't glance back.

Boone was raising his head in a drunk's delayed response, features changing comically to surprise, outrage. Delaney, swinging an arm from the shoulder, hit the sergeant across the face with an open palm. It smacked the man's head around, left him quivering, face reddening.

"Cocksucker," Delaney said, without expression.

He stepped quickly back through the doorway into the bedroom. Waited tensely. Knees slightly bent. Sap held in his right hand, behind him. He heard water running in the kitchen. Heard Rebecca's loud sobs.

Boone came out with a rush, a roar of fury. Hands reaching. Delaney leaned to one side. Feet firmly planted. As Boone fell past, the Chief put the sap alongside his skull. Not a blow, but a tap. Just laying it on. Almost nestling it on. The street cop's gentling stroke: not enough to split the skin, concuss, or break the bone. A matter of experience. It made the knees melt, the eyes turn up. Boone dropped face down onto the bedroom rug.

The Chief stooped swiftly, found the sergeant's gun. He yanked it from the short holster, slid it into his own jacket pocket. Then he put his sap away. Hip pocket, out of sight. Rebecca came from the kitchen, carrying an empty whiskey bottle foolishly. She saw Boone stretched out, face down. She wailed.

"Is he—" she coughed.

"Passed out," Delaney said crisply. He took the empty bottle from her limp hand, tossed it onto the couch. "You did fine. Just fine. Do you have any money?"

"What?" she said.

"Money," he repeated patiently. "Where's your purse?"

They found her purse on the floor, alongside the couch. She had some singles and a five.

"Take a cab back to Monica," Delaney instructed her. "Wait downstairs in the lobby until the doorman gets you a cab. Give him a dollar. Got that? Take the cab to Monica. She's waiting for you. All clear?"

"Is he—? Will he—?"

"Understand what I just said? Take a cab. Monica is waiting for you."

She nodded, dazed again. He hung the purse on her arm, pushed her gently toward the door. When she was gone, he locked up behind her, put on the chain. Came back and searched for another bottle, another gun. Found nothing. Boone was beginning to stir. Mutter. Make thick, gulping sounds.

Delaney called Monica, gave her a brief report. He told her to watch for Rebecca and to call him if she didn't arrive within twenty minutes. Then he let down all the venetian blinds, closed them. He stripped to his shorts. Boone was heaving in deep retches. He took him by the neck: collar of shirt and collar of jacket. He dragged him across the bedroom floor back into the bathroom, the sergeant's toes making rough furrows in the rug. He lifted and dumped him face down into the tub. Boone's head, arms, shoulders, upper torso were inside the tub. Balanced on the rim on his waist. Hips and legs outside the tub.

Immediately he began to vomit. Food, liquid, bile. It came out of him in a thick flood. Bits of spaghetti. Meatballs. Slime. The stench was something, but Delaney was a cop; he had smelled worse.

He turned on the shower, adjusted it to a hard, cool spray. He let it splay over Boone's head and shoulders. It washed the vomit down to the drain, which almost immediately clogged. The slurry began to back up.

Delaney took hold of Boone's right wrist. The hand hung limply. Using the nerveless fingers as a soft claw, he brushed at the clogged drain until the liquid ran out. It didn't sicken him.

He turned off the shower, dragged Boone back to the bedroom rug. Let him drain a minute, then turned him over. Now the sergeant was hacking and coughing. But his tracheal passage seemed reasonably clear; he was breathing in harsh, grating sobs.

Delaney kneeled beside him and wrestled him out of his sodden clothes. It took a long time, and the Chief was grunting and sweating by the time he got Boone down to his stained briefs. He levered him onto the bed, atop a crumpled sheet and light wool blanket. It seemed to him Boone was breathing okay, but muttering occasionally, twisting, head whipping side to side.

Delaney went into the kitchen, found some paper napkins. He cleaned up the solid vomitus in the bathroom tub as best he could, and flushed the mess down the toilet. He looked in at Boone. No change. So Delaney took a hot shower in his underwear, soaping everything. He wrung out his underwear, hung it on a towel rack. He rubbed himself dry with one of Boone's towels, then knotted it about his thick waist and padded barefoot back into the bedroom. Boone was snoring, mouth open, fretful line between his eyebrows.

Delaney called Monica again, and they talked awhile. She had Rebecca calmed and lying down in the spare bedroom. He told her everything was under control, and he'd be home in the morning. They spoke briefly, sadly, and both said, "I love you" before they hung up. It was necessary.

Still wearing the knotted towel, he checked the apartment again. Everywhere. He could find no more whiskey nor another gun. There were small containers of after-shave lotion and rubbing alcohol. He poured both down the sink, and dropped the empty bottles into the kitchen garbage can. He also looked for money, but found only Boone's wallet in the hip pocket of his damp trousers. It held eighteen dollars in fives and singles. Delaney slid the wallet under a cushion of the living-room couch.

Boone was still sleeping restlessly in the bedroom. Snoring, twitching, turning. Delaney left him there, found a linen cupboard with a scant supply of unpressed sheets and pillowcases. He put a sheet over the living-room couch, an empty pillowcase over the couch arm. He covered himself with another sheet. Before he settled down, he slid his leather-covered sap and Boone's revolver under the couch, within easy reach. Then he put his head on the hard couch arm. He could hear Boone in the bedroom. Stertorous breathing, gasps, moans. An occasional cough. A sob.

Delaney dozed. Light sleep. Awake. Light sleep. Alert. Then, much later, he heard Boone moving, groaning. Delaney reached for the sap, swung his feet onto the floor. He padded gently over to the bedroom door, peeked in. In dim nightlight he could see Boone sitting on the edge of the bed. He was fumbling with pencil and pad on the bedside table, muttering to himself. He wrote something with the exaggerated attention, the tongue-out care of a drunk. Still muttering. Then fell back into bed, began to snore again.

Delaney went in silently, lifted Boone's lower legs and feet onto the wrinkled sheet, covered him with the wool blanket. The man stank stalely. Delaney took the scratchpad back to the bathroom, switched on the light. He read what Boone had scrawled. As far as he could make out, it read: "Mon two clean." Delaney put it aside, turned off the light. He stumbled back to the lumpy couch. He went through the motions of settling down to sleep.

He woke early the next morning, stared wrathfully about at strange surroundings. He remembered the operatic night with disgust, and was thankful things had not been worse. He rose groggily and looked in on Boone. The sergeant was sleeping in the center of the bed, head bowed, spine curved, knees drawn up in the fetal position.

Delaney went into the bathroom. He rubbed cold water on his face, felt the bristle. He looked in the mirror. White. An old man's beard. Boone's shaving gear was in the medicine cabinet, but the Chief didn't use it. He squeezed some toothpaste onto his forefinger and scrubbed his teeth. And he used Boone's comb and brush.

He went into the kitchen. The spareness of supplies and equipment dismayed him. What a way for a man to live! An expensive apartment with sticks of furniture, and nothing in the refrigerator but a hunk of store cheese, an opened package of dried bologna, and two bruised tomatoes.

Delaney found a jar of instant coffee in the cupboard above the sink. He made himself a cup, not bothering to boil water but using hot water right out of the tap.

He was sitting there, sipping slowly, brooding grumpily, when Boone came in. The sergeant was wearing a threadbare robe. His feet were bare.

Neither man said anything nor looked at the other. Boone did what Delaney had done: made a cup of coffee with water from the tap. He also took a little bottle from the cupboard over the sink and popped two aspirin, dry. Then he sat down at the rickety table, facing Delaney.

Boone couldn't lift the full cup. He leaned forward and slurped up a few mouthfuls of the hot brew. Then, the level of coffee well below the rim, he picked up the cup slowly, using both trembling hands. He moved it cautiously to his lips, his head bending far down to meet it.

"You prick," Chief Delaney said tonelessly. "You shit-eating son of a bitch. Bastardly piss-hole. You rotten, no-good motherfucker. You can crawl into a bottle and pull the cork in after you for all I care. But when you hurt a good woman who believed in you, a woman I like and admire, then it becomes my business. And what you've done to my wife. We invited you to our home. You ate at our table. And Ivar Thorsen, who stuck his neck out for you. Not once, but a dozen times. And you shit on all of us, you filthy cocksucker."

Then Boone looked up at him. Eyes dulled and swollen. Bits of white matter in the corners. Smutty shadows below.

"Forget it," he said. Voice thready, he almost coughed. "You're just blowing off. You don't understand."

"Tell me then."

"If I don't count, then no one counts."

"Oh?" Delaney said. "Like that, is it?"

"Yes."

"Why don't you count?"

"I just don't. I'm nothing."

"*You* say," Delaney said furiously. And, not knowing how to refute this without praising a man he had just damned, said nothing more.

They both sat in silence. After a while Delaney made himself another cup of coffee. When he was seated again, Boone rose and did the same thing. This time he was able to get the cup to his lips.

"Am I out?" he asked hoarsely.

"It's up to Thorsen."

"You going to tell him?"

"Of course. I'm not going to cover for you. I'll tell him just how it was."

"He'll take your recommendation," Boone said hopefully. "In or out."

Delaney didn't reply.

"If I told you it won't happen again," the sergeant said, "would you believe me?"

"No."

"I don't blame you," Boone said miserably. "I'd be lying. I can't make a promise like that."

Delaney looked at him pityingly.

"What in Christ's name set you off?"

"I called one of the dicks who worked the Maitland thing. He had just come off a long stakeout, and he and two of his buddies were unwinding in a Yorkville joint. Not too far from here. I figured it was a good chance to talk to him, so I walked over. They were drinking boiler-makers, but no one was juiced. Yet. So I sat in a booth with them. It's been a long time; I had forgotten how good that can be; four cops sitting around drinking, blowing smoke, and kidding. After a while they noticed I wasn't drinking and said I was spoiling the party. I'm not blaming them. No one twisted my balls. So I had a beer. The best I've ever tasted. Ice-cold. Moisture running down the bottle. Creamy head on the glass. That tart, malty taste. After a while I was drinking boiler-makers with them. Then we were all zonked. I don't remember getting home. I remember Rebecca being here."

"You called her," Delaney said.

"I suppose I did," Boone said sadly. "And I remember, vaguely, your being here. Did I call you?"

"No. Becky did."

"Most of it's a blackout," Boone confessed. "Jesus!" he said, and touched his head tenderly behind his ear. "I got a lump. Sore as hell. I must have fallen."

"No," Delaney said, "you didn't fall. I sapped you."

"Sapped me?" the sergeant said. "Well, I guess I needed it."

"You did," Delaney said grimly.

He rose, stalked into the living room, came back with the scrap of paper. He thrust it at Boone.

"What the hell's this?" he demanded. "You wrote it last night. After I got you into bed. You passed out, then got up, scribbled this thing and went back to sleep. 'Mon two clean.' What does that mean?"

Abner Boone stared at the piece of paper. Then he covered his eyes with his hand.

" 'Mon two clean,' " he repeated, then looked up. "Yes. Right. I remember now. When I first got there, before we were all gibbering like

apes, I asked the dick who worked the Maitland case if there was anything not in his reports. Anything he heard, saw or found. Or guessed.
He said no, nothing, Then, almost five minutes later, he snapped his
fingers and said there was something. A little thing. The clunk was discovered on Sunday—right? So naturally they put up sawhorses and
sealed off the house. The local precinct sent over a couple of street cops
to keep the rubbernecks away. Then, on Monday, they were letting tenants in and out, but Maitland's studio was still off-limits. Some of the
lab guys were working in there, and there was a precinct cop on the
landing to guard the door."

Sergeant Boone got up, went to the sink, drank off two glasses of
water as fast as he could gulp them. He brought a third glassful over to
the table and sat down again.

"A couple of days later—the dick who told me the story says maybe it
was Wednesday or Thursday; he can't remember—the precinct cop who
had been guarding the door of Maitland's studio on Monday came to
him and said that on Monday morning two women started up the last
flight of stairs to Maitland's studio. He asked them what they wanted.
The older woman said they were looking for cleaning work to do—you
know, dusting, vacuuming, washing windows, and so forth. The cop told
them they couldn't come up; the guy who lived there was dead. So they
split."

" 'The older woman'?" Delaney said. "Then there was a younger one.
How young? What were the ages, approximately?"

"The dick didn't know," Boone said. "He just said the cop had mentioned two dames, and the older one did the talking."

"Accent?"

"He didn't know."

"White? Black? Spanish? What?"

"The dick didn't know. The cop didn't say."

"Why did the cop wait two or three days before he told the detective
about this?"

"He said he thought at first it was nothing. That the two women really were looking for cleaning work. Then, when he heard the investigation was getting nowhere, he thought it might possibly be something."

"Smart cop."

"Sure, Chief," Boone nodded. "And also, the cop probably figured if
he told a detective, then he was off the hook. Then it was the dick's
problem, not his."

"Right. Did the dick remember the cop's name?"

"No. Never saw him before or after. Says he was a black. That's all he remembers."

"Did he try to check it out? Find the women?"

"No. He thought it was nothing. Just what the older woman said: they were looking for cleaning work to do."

"All right," Delaney said, "now here's what you do: Go down to the Mott Street precinct and check their rosters. Get the name, home address, and badge number of the cop who was on guard duty at Maitland's studio that Monday morning. Don't try to brace him. I want to be there. Just identify him. Then go back to Maitland's Mott Street address. Go during the day, and also in the evening, when most of the tenants will be home from work. Ask them if anyone came around looking for cleaning work to do. During the week Maitland was burned, or any other time before or after. Call me at home tonight. Got all that?"

"Yes, sir," Sergeant Boone said. "Chief, does this mean I'm still in?"

"For today," Delaney said. "Until I have a chance to report to Deputy Commissioner Thorsen. You shithead!"

By the time he had showered, shaved, donned blessedly fresh linen and his favorite flannel slacks (double pleats at the waist), Monica was just putting the finishing touches to his late breakfast: scrambled eggs, onions and lox, toasted bagels with cream cheese, and coffee that didn't taste as if it came out of the tap.

She sat at the oak kitchen table with him, nibbling on half his bagel, sipping coffee. She told him of her problems with Rebecca the previous night.

"She wanted to call every five minutes," Monica said. "She was afraid you'd hurt him. You didn't, did you, Edward?"

"Not enough," he growled.

"Well, she's over there now. She went as soon as I told her you were coming back—to see if he's all right."

"He's all right," Delaney assured her. "And she's a fool. There's no guarantee he won't do it again. He admitted that himself."

"Did you give him back his gun?"

"Yes. He's a cop on active duty and needs it. It makes no difference; if he's intent on suicide, he'll find a way, gun or no gun. Rebecca should stay away from him. Just drop him. He's bad news."

"What are you going to do about him?"

"I don't know. If I bounce him and ask Thorsen to get me another man, he'll flush Boone down the drain."

"Everyone deserves a second chance, Edward."

His head snapped up; he stared at her.

"Is that so?" he said. "Do you really believe that? Ax-murderers and multiple rapists? Guys who blow up airliners and kill infants? They all deserve a second chance?"

"Will you stop that?" she said angrily. "Abner isn't in that class, and you know it."

"I'm just trying to point out that 'Everyone deserves a second chance' is not valid in all cases. It sounds nice and Christian, but I wouldn't care to see it become the law of the land. Besides, Boone has had a second chance, and a third, and a fourth, and so on. Thorsen has given him his second chance, and then some!"

"You haven't," Monica said softly. "Was what he did really so bad? It didn't interfere with his job, did it?"

"No," he said shortly, "but if he does it again, it might."

"You're disappointed in him," she said. And when she saw his expression, she added hastily, "And I am, too. But can't you keep him on, Edward? I know—I think—I feel that if you dump him now, it would be the end of him. Really the end. No hope left."

"I'll think about it," he said grudgingly.

He moved his chair back a bit so he could cross his legs. He lighted a cigar to enjoy with his final cup of coffee. He blew a plume of smoke into the air, then looked at Monica. She was staring moodily into her cup.

Morning sunshine glinted from her shiny hair. He saw the sweet curve of throat and cheek. Solid body planted. Her flesh alive and firm. All of her assertively womanly. The strength!

Then he looked about the warm, fragrant kitchen. Worn things gleaming. Crumbs on the counter. A full larder. All the dear, familiar sights of the best room in the house. The hearth. The drawbridge up, moat flooded.

She saw something in his face and asked, "What are you thinking about?"

"An empty refrigerator," he said, and rose to kiss her.

Abner Boone had showered and shaved, scowling at his hollowed eyes and caved-in cheeks. He dressed, checked his ID and revolver, and started from the apartment. When he opened the outside door, there was Rebecca Hirsch, her hand raised to knock. They stared at each other, her hand falling slowly to her side.

"I just—" she said huskily, then caught her breath. "I just want to see if you're all right."

"I'm all right," he nodded. "Come in."

He held the door wide for her. She came in hesitantly, sat at one end of the couch. He sat across the room.

"You're going out?" she said. "Maybe I better go."

"It can wait," he said. "I want to talk to you. I'm sorry about last night. 'Sorry.' Whatever that means. Rebecca, I don't think we should see each other any more."

"You don't want to see me?"

"I didn't say that. But it's not going to work. Last night proved it."

"Why do you do it, Ab?"

"Lots of reasons. I told the Chief it was because of the filth I see as a cop. That's one reason. It's true. Losing my wife is another reason. That's true, too. Want to hear another reason? I like whiskey. And beer and wine. I like the taste. I like what alcohol does for me."

"What does it do for you?"

"Dulls anxieties. Makes everything seem a little better. Two ways: either there's hope, or it doesn't make any difference if there isn't any hope. Either way, it helps. Can you understand that?"

"No," she said. "I don't understand."

"I know you don't," he said. "I don't expect you to or blame you. It's my fault; I know that."

"What about AA?" she said. "Medicine? Counseling? Therapy?"

"Had 'em all," he said stonily. "I just can't hack it. You better walk."

"There's a way," she said.

He shook his head. "I don't think so. I'm one short step away from a pint of muscatel in a brown paper bag. Shuffling along."

"Jesus!" she gasped. "Don't say that!"

"It's true. Get out while you can."

They sat staring at each other, two species, so different. She with the gloss of unwounded health, he with the pallor of defeat.

"If you could love me . . ." she tried.

"Redeemed by the love of a good woman?" He smiled sadly. "You're something, you are."

"I didn't say that," she said angrily. "You already have my love. You must know that. And it didn't keep you from . . . No, what I meant was your loving me. And knowing you'll lose me if—if it happens again. That might work—if you could love me."

"It wouldn't be hard," he said gallantly.

"You say," she scoffed. "But I think it might be. For you. It wouldn't come easily. You'd have to work at it."

He looked at her curiously.

She flung back her hair, smoothed it from her temples with both palms.

"Oh yes," she said. "My motives are purely selfish. But then, if it kept you from drinking, if it saved your job, your motives would be selfish too, wouldn't they?"

"You're a Jewish Jesuit," he said.

"Am I?" she said. "Not really. Just a woman who knows what she wants and is trying to get it. I lay awake last night thinking about it. It's worth a try. Don't you think it's worth a try?"

He was silent.

She said: "Unless the idea of absolute doom is so attractive to you?"

He shook his head wildly. "I don't like it. I swear I don't. It frightens me."

"Well then?"

"All right," he nodded. "With the understanding that you walk whenever you want to. Okay?"

"Okay," she said.

"One more thing," he said. "Don't, please don't, plead with the Chief for me. If he cans me, he cans me, and that's it."

"I understand," she said gravely.

"You see," he said with a flimsy grin, "I don't want the woman I love begging."

She smiled for the first time, eyes glistening.

"See?" she said. "It's working already."

They went down in the elevator together, making plans. When they separated on the street, he kissed her fingers and she touched his cheek.

12

When Delaney climbed into Boone's car on the following morning, carrying the Maitland charcoal sketches rolled up, the two men carefully avoided looking at each other.

"Morning, sir," the sergeant said.

"Morning," the Chief said. "Feels like rain."

"The radio says partly cloudy," Boone offered.

"My bunion says rain," Delaney stated, and that was that. "Let's get caught up . . ."

Both men opened their notebooks.

"Two items," Delaney said. "About Maitland dying without a will, the Department legal eagles gave me the usual bullshit: maybe this, maybe that. But under New York State law, the widow gets two thousand in cash or property and one-half of what's left. The balance of the estate, after taxes, goes to the surviving child—in this case, Ted Maitland."

"So Alma Maitland is the big winner?" Boone asked.

"Apparently," Delaney nodded. "But the bank accounts and a few piddling investments and the apartment on East Fifty-eighth—that's a co-op—all together don't add up to much over a hundred grand. The big asset in the estate are those unsold paintings in Saul Geltman's show. By the way, here's your invitation. They came yesterday afternoon. Each ticket admits two."

Boone took the card and ran fingertips over the printing.

"Nice," he said. "Geltman's laying out the loot."

"You're taking Rebecca?" Delaney asked.

Boone nodded.

"Monica will call her," the Chief said. "We'll all go somewhere for dinner, and then go over to the Galleries together. All right with you?"

"Sure. How much do you figure those paintings will add to the estate?"

"Didn't Geltman say one would go for a quarter of a mil? Even if he was hyping us, the lot of them should got for a mil, minimum."

"That's a better motive than a hundred grand," Boone observed.

"Oh yes," Delaney agreed. "Maybe that's what the killer figured on: the paintings would automatically increase in value once Maitland had conked. Of course, the IRS will take a nice slice of the pie, and so will the State, but there should be enough left over to keep Alma Maitland off welfare."

"You figure her?" the sergeant asked.

"Capable," Delaney rumbled. "Eminently capable. So is Ted Maitland. As of now, they're the ones with the money motive. I also called Thorsen's office about getting to see Dora Maitland's bank records up in Nyack. Thorsen wants to avoid a court order, if possible. All it'll do is get J. Barnes Chapin sore, and keeping him happy is the point of this whole shmear. So Thorsen is going to work through some local Nyack pols he knows. Maybe they can get the bank to cooperate. I'll be in and out of there, make a few notes, and no one will be the wiser."

The sergeant was silent. The Chief knew what he was thinking: Had Delaney talked to Thorsen? Had he blown the whistle on Boone? Delaney said nothing about it. Let him sweat awhile. Do him good.

"All right," the Chief said finally, "what did you get?"

"A lot," Boone said, flipping the notebook pages. "Some of it interesting. I checked the deli that sent up those sandwiches when Saul Geltman was having his conference with J. Julian Simon. The guy who made the delivery said it happened just like Simon told us: The lawyer came out of the inner office, paid, and took the lunch back inside. The delivery guy didn't see anyone in the office but Simon and Susan Hemley. I called her and made a date for lunch. To find out if she saw Geltman in the inner office when Simon came out to get the sandwiches."

"Or at any other time from ten to one-thirty," Delaney added.

"Right," Boone nodded, making a note.

"Anything else?"

"Yes, sir. Something else. The interesting part. Your prejudice against pinkie rings paid off. J. Julian Simon has a sheet."

"Knew it," Delaney said with satisfaction. "What was he doing—fronting a baby farm?"

"Not quite; no, sir. It goes back twenty years. Twenty-four to be exact. The bus companies in Manhattan and the Bronx were getting hit on a lot of accident claims. More than normal. All of a sudden it seemed like their drivers were a bunch of rumdums, knocking pedestrians down right and left."

"Fallaways," Delaney said.

"Correct," Boone said. "The insurance companies handling the liability got together and ran a joint computer tape. About twenty-five percent of the claims were coming through J. Julian Simon and two doctors he had on the string. Plus a crew of repeat tumblers, of course. The guys with trick knees and backs who can show the right X-rays. So they closed Simon down, and he almost got disbarred. Reading the old reports I got the feeling that a shmear changed hands somewhere along the way. Anyway, he kept his license. And lo and behold, there he is in his oak-and-leather office off Madison Avenue, sporting ten big ones in dental work, and probably wearing silk undershorts with 'The Home of the Whopper' printed on them."

"Well, well," Delaney said, smiling coldly. "A shyst. Who'd have thunk it?"

"You did, sir," Boone said. "You figure he's still playing games?"

"The percentages say yes," the Chief said. "Some bad guys reform and walk the arrow. But don't take it to the bank. Most of them develop a taste for the nasty. All right, one bad mark for Lawyer Simon. How did you make out downtown?"

"I talked to every tenant in that Mott Street building. Not one of them had a cleaning woman. Not one knew of anyone coming around looking for cleaning work. Before, during or after the time Maitland was hit. They all looked at me like I was some kind of a nut. That's a poor neighborhood, Chief. Who can afford cleaning women?"

"That's what I figured," Delaney nodded. "The older woman was thinking fast on that Monday morning and scammed the cop. Did you make him?"

"I got him," Boone said, looking at his notebook. "Here he is . . . Jason T. Jason. His buddies called him Jason Two because there's another Jason, Robert Jason, in the precinct. Jason Two is a black, a big guy, three years in the Department, two citations, some solid arrests and good assists. This week he's on foot. Today he's got the eight to four."

"Good," Delaney said. "Let's buy him lunch."

"This place used to be called Ye Old Canal Inn," the Chief said, looking around the bustling restaurant. "And before that, I don't know what it was called. But there's been a tavern or restaurant on this spot since the early days of New York, when Canal Street was uptown. By the way, there really is a canal here. Underground now. A cheeseburger for me, with home fries and slaw. Black coffee."

He had told the others to order what they liked; the Department was picking up the tab. But they followed his lead. Jason T. Jason was sitting across the booth table from Delaney and Boone. The black cop was big enough to fill half the booth.

"You look like you could handle two burgers," Sergeant Boone told him. "Or three."

"Or four," Jason grinned. "But I'm trying to cut down. You see the latest memo on overweight cops? My sergeant gives me a month to drop twenty pounds. I'm trying, but it ain't easy."

He was almost six-four, Delaney figured, and was pushing 250 at least. His skin was a deep cordovan with a soft, powdery finish. A precisely trimmed mustache ran squarely across his face, cheek to cheek. Dark, dancing eyes. Full lips that turned outward. Hands like smoked hams, and the feet, the Chief noted, had to be bigger than his own size thirteens.

The bulk of the man was awesome. Revolver, walkie-talkie, and equipment dangled from him like tiny baubles on a Christmas tree. If he's got the will to go with the weight, Boone mused, the best thing a bad guy braced by that man-mountain could do would be to throw up his hands and scream, "I surrender! I surrender!"

"Football?" Delaney asked.

"Nah," Jason T. Jason said. "I was big enough but not fast enough. I tried out, but the coach said, 'Jase, you run too long in the same place.' Chief, is my ass in a sling on the Maitland thing?"

"Just the opposite," Delaney assured him. "You did exactly right to tell the homicide dick. If anyone screwed up, he did—for not following up on it. But you can't really blame him either; he probably had a hundred other leads to follow, and figured it was nothing."

"It may still be nothing, Jason," Boone put in. "We just don't know. But we'd like to prove it out one way or another."

"Here's our food," Delaney said. "Want to wait until we finish?"

"I better eat and talk," Jason said. "I get itchy when I'm not on the street."

"I know the feeling," Delaney nodded. "Listen, if you want the rest of your tour off, I can square it with your lieutenant."

"No, no," Jason said. "This won't take long. There's not that much to tell. All right, let's see now . . . That Monday morning they pulled me off patrol and put me to guarding the door to Maitland's studio. Eight to four."

"The sawhorses were down around the house?" Boone asked.

"Right," Jason Two said. "Down and gone. I was posted on the top landing, right outside the door. The lab guys were inside taking up the drains, vacuuming dust samples, and stuff like that. Man it was something! They were even taking scrapings from inside the toilet. Anyway, a little before eleven I was out on the landing."

"Sure of the time?" Delaney said.

"Absolutely. Had just looked at my watch to see how close noon was. Two guys in a squad had promised to bring me sandwiches and a coffee at noon. So at about eleven, these two women came up the stairs. They got halfway up to the landing, where the stairs turn, when they see me standing on top, and they stop."

"Surprised to see you there?" the Chief asked.

"Yeah, surprised."

"Frightened?"

Jason T. Jason took an enormous bite of his cheeseburger and chewed a moment, thinking about it.

"Frightened, yeah," he said. "But I don't think that counts. I'm a big black guy, Chief, wearing a cop's suit and swinging a stick. I scare a lot of people. It helps," he smiled.

"I'll bet it does," Boone said. "What were they? White? Black? Spanish?"

"Spanish," Jason Two said promptly. "Take it to the bank. But whether they were Puerto Rican, Cuban, Dominican Republic, or whatever, I couldn't say. But definitely Spanish. Bright clothes—red and pink and orange. Like that."

Only he was eating now; both Delaney and Boone were taking notes. Jason T. Jason seemed to enjoy his importance.

"Descriptions?" the Chief asked.

"The older woman, say about fifty, fifty-five, she's a butterball. Maybe a hundred-forty. Short. Say five-two or three. I'm looking down at them, you know, it's hard to figure from above. Also, this was like two months ago."

"You're doing fine," Delaney assured him.

"She does the talking, and then I'm positive she's Spanish. Also, she has like a whorey look. But she's so old and fat, maybe she hustles the Bowery. Stringy hair dyed a bright red. The other one is a kid. I figure her from twelve to fifteen. In that range. Maybe five-seven or five-eight. One-twenty. Good body from what I could see. Long black hair hanging loose down her back."

"Pretty?" Boone asked.

"Yeah, pretty," the cop said. "Get her cleaned up, the hair fixed, some decent clothes and makeup, and she'd be fucking beautiful. Sorry, Chief."

"I've heard the word before," Delaney said, writing busily. "How did the talk go?"

"You want me to hold a minute so you can eat?" Jason Two asked.

"No, no," Delaney said. "Don't worry about us. You just keep rolling. What did you say and what did they say?"

"Only the older woman talked. The kid didn't open her mouth. I asked them what the hell they were doing there. The woman said they were going through the house, all the houses in the neighborhood, knocking on doors, looking for cleaning work to do."

"Did she say that immediately after you asked her what she was doing?"

The question came from Chief Delaney. Jason T. Jason stopped eating, frowned, trying to remember.

"I can't rightly recall," he said.

"Guess," Boone said.

"I'd guess maybe she hesitated for a beat or two before she answered."

"You didn't figure she was scamming you?"

"Not then I didn't. Later, when I got to thinking about it, I figured she might have been lying. You know, I been a cop for three years now, and I'm just beginning to realize that everyone lies to cops. I mean ev-

eryone! Even when they don't have to, when there's no point in it. It's automatic. Is it like that in plainclothes, too?"

"If they know you're a cop, it's exactly like that," Delaney nodded. "So they said they were looking for cleaning work. What did you say then?"

"I said there was no work for them on the top floor and to get their ass out of there. The woman said she was told a guy lived on the top floor, and she wanted to ask him. I told her he was fucking dead, and unless she wanted to mop up a puddle of old blood, she better disappear. Maybe I shouldn't have told her that, but I didn't want to stand there arguing with her. Anyway, it worked. She didn't say another word. The two of them turned around and went back downstairs."

"Ever see them again?" Boone asked.

"No," Jason Two said. "Never."

"Anything else you can tell us about them?" Delaney asked. "Their appearance? Any little thing?"

"Let's see . . ." Jason T. Jason said, finishing his cole slaw. "The old woman had a gold tooth. In front. That any help?"

"Could be," Delaney said. "Anything else?"

"The young girl," the cop said. "Something about her. Something funny . . ."

"Funny?" Boone said.

"Not funny ha-ha," Jason said, "but funny-strange. She had like a vacant expression. Kept staring up into the air like she was spaced out."

"Drugs?" Boone asked.

"I don't think so. More like she was maybe retarded or a little flaky. Like something wasn't right there. I mean, she didn't say word one so it was hard to tell. But I got the feeling she was out of it. Off somewhere."

"Recognize them if you see them again?" Delaney asked.

"Is the pope Catholic?" Jason T. Jason said.

"Good," the Chief said. He tore a blank page from his notebook, scribbled down his telephone number and Boone's. "Here are our phone numbers. Keep an eye out on the street. If you make them, call one of us. Or leave a message."

"You want me to hold them?"

"No, no, don't do that. But tail them until they hole up in a restaurant or store or movie or their home. Whatever. Then call us. Don't worry if it takes you off your beat. I'll square it at the precinct."

"Will do," the cop nodded. He took the page, folded it into his wallet. "I better hit the pavement. Nice talking to you gents. I hope something comes of it."

"So do we," Boone said. He and Delaney half rose to shake hands with Jason Two. "Many thanks. You've been a big help."

"Anything else I can do, give me a shout."

They watched him move away. He had to go through the outer door sideways.

"Good cop," Delaney said. "Observant. And he remembers."

"How would you like to be a mugger or purse-snatcher?" Boone said. "You make your hit, you've got the loot, you're running hell-for-leather, you come scrambling around a corner, and there's Jason T. Jason."

"I wouldn't like that," Chief Delaney said. "My God, they're growing them big these days! Well, let's eat. Want a hot coffee?"

They ordered fresh coffee, but ate their cold cheeseburgers and home fries without protest.

"Think the young girl was the model in those Maitland sketches?" Boone asked.

"It fits," Delaney nodded. "How's this: Our first scenario was correct; Maitland picks up a young, fresh twist on Friday. But she's not alone. The woman sounds too old to be her mother, but maybe she's a relative or friend."

"Or madam," the sergeant offered. "Jason said she looked like a hooker. Maybe she's peddling the young kid's ass."

"Could be," the Chief said. "So they go up to the studio on Friday. The girl strips down, and Maitland makes his drawings."

"While the older woman has a drink and leaves her partials on the glass and bottle."

"Right. Maitland likes what he draws, and makes a date to use the girl at eleven on Monday morning. That listens, doesn't it?"

"Does to me," Boone said. "The older woman wouldn't have shivved him on Friday, would she? Because he tried to screw the girl?"

"No way," Delaney said, shaking his head. "They'd never have come back on Monday if that had happened. No, I think when the two of them left the studio on Friday, Maitland was breathing. They were probably the last ones to see him alive."

"Except for the killer," Boone said.

"Except for the killer," Delaney nodded. "I'd like to find those two women. Maybe they saw something. Maybe the guy we're looking for was coming up the stairs on that Friday while they were going down."

"Not much chance of finding them, Chief," Boone sighed. "Unless Jason T. Jason hits it lucky and spots them on the street."

"Stranger things have happened," Chief Delaney said. "You finished? Let's get uptown. We'll brace Alma Maitland first."

Once again they were ushered into that cheerless family room, which, today, smelled faintly of oiled machinery. They hadn't yet seated themselves when Alma Maitland came sweeping in, hatted, tugging on white gloves.

"Really, Chief Delaney," she said angrily. "I was just going out. This is very inconvenient."

He stared at her coldly.

"Inconvenient, ma'am?"

She caught the implication; her face whitened, lips pressed.

"Of course I want to help," she said. "As much as I can. But you might have called."

Both the cops looked at her without expression. A proved technique: say nothing and let them yammer on and on. Sometimes they dug themselves deep simply because they could not endure the silence.

"Besides, I told you everything I know," she said, lifting her chin.

"Did you?" Delaney said, and was silent again.

Finally, with a pinching of features, a small sound of exasperation, she asked them to be seated. They took the couch, sitting almost shoulder to shoulder, a bulwark. She sat in an armchair, in her ladylike position: spine frozen, ankles crossed, knees turned, gloved hands folded demurely in her lap.

"You don't get along with your mother-in-law and sister-in-law, do you?" Delaney said suddenly. It came out more flat statement than question.

"Did they say that?" she demanded.

"I'm asking you," Delaney said.

"We're not close," she admitted. A tinselly laugh. "We both prefer it that way."

"And your late husband? How close was he to his mother and sister?"

"Very close," she said stiffly.

"Oh?" the Chief said. "He only saw them once or twice a year."

"Nonsense," she said sharply. "He saw them at least once a month.

Sometimes once a week. They were always coming down to have lunch or dinner with him."

Neither Delaney nor Boone showed surprise.

"And you didn't attend these lunches and dinners, Mrs. Maitland?" the sergeant asked.

"I did not."

"Did they ever visit his Mott Street studio?"

"I have no idea."

"He never told you they did?"

"No, never. What's all this about?"

Delaney asked: "Did your husband ever contribute to the living expenses of his mother and sister? To your knowledge?"

She laughed scornfully. "I doubt that very much. My husband rarely spent any money that did not contribute to his own pleasure."

"Belle Sarazen considered him a very generous man."

"I'm sure she would," Alma Maitland said furiously. "While I scrimped and saved to make ends meet."

Delaney looked around the room.

"Hardly poverty," he said mildly enough. "Mrs. Maitland, are you aware that unless other claims are filed, you and your son will probably be the sole beneficiaries of your husband's estate?"

"Estate!" she cried. "What estate? This apartment that can't even be sold in today's market for what we paid for it? Bank accounts that will barely cover outstanding bills?"

"The unsold paintings . . ." Boone murmured.

"Oh yes!" she said, with something close to despair in her voice. "And how much of that will be left after Saul Geltman takes his share, and all the tax departments take theirs? I assure you, my husband did not leave me a wealthy woman. Far from it!"

Delaney looked at her closely.

"You have an independent income?" he guessed.

"Some," she said grudgingly. "It's no business of yours, but I suppose you could find out—if you haven't already. My father left me some municipal bonds. He, at least, knew a man's responsibility."

"What does that income amount to?" Delaney asked. "As you said, we can always find out."

"About twenty thousand a year," she said.

"Did your husband know of this income?"

"Of course he did." She paused, then sighed. "Twenty years ago it seemed a fortune. Today it's nothing."

"Somewhat more than nothing," Delaney said dryly, "but I won't argue the point. Mrs. Maitland, I have here the three sketches found in your husband's studio. I know you told me you knew none of his recent models, but I'd like you to take a look at these in case you may be able to identify the girl. I admit the face is just suggested, but there may be enough there."

He rose and, with Sergeant Boone's help, unrolled the drawings and held up each of the three for Alma Maitland's inspection.

"They're very good," she said softly.

"Aren't they?" Delaney said. "Recognize the girl?"

"No. Never saw her or anyone like her before. When will you be finished with these? They're part of the estate, you know."

"I'm well aware of that, madam. They'll be returned when our investigation is completed."

"And when will that be?" she demanded.

He didn't answer, but rolled up the drawings again and secured them with a rubber band. He signaled Boone, and the two moved toward the door. Then the Chief paused and turned back.

"Mrs. Maitland," he said, "one more thing . . . Don't you think it odd that the only work of your husband we found in his studio were these three drawings?"

"Odd?" she said, puzzled. "Why odd?"

"You told us you were a model; you must have been in many artists' studios. We've been told that most painters usually have many works on hand. Unsold paintings. Half-finished works. Old things they don't want to sell. And so forth. Yet all we found in your husband's studio were these three sketches. Don't you think that odd?"

"No, I don't," she said. "My husband was a very successful artist. After he became famous, he sold off all his old work. He was not a sentimentalist; he kept nothing around to remind him of the old days. And his style changed very little; his early work was as good as his most recent paintings. As soon as he finished a new canvas, it was brought to Saul Geltman for sale. Whether I was told of it or not," she added bitterly.

"I see," Delaney said thoughtfully. "Thank you for your time. Do you plan to attend the preview of your husband's memorial show at the Geltman Galleries?"

"Of course," she said, surprised.

"Your son, also?"

"Yes, we'll both be there. Why?"

"We hope to see you then," Delaney said politely. "Good day, Mrs. Maitland."

They drove over to Jake Dukker's studio, and the Chief said to Boone:

"What Jason T. Jason said about everyone lying to the cops—that's true. But there's something else he's going to learn: no one ever volunteers any information either. I'm talking about Dora and Emily Maitland up in Nyack. They said Victor visited them a couple of times a year. They answered my question. But you see the inadequacy of interrogation? If you don't ask the right questions, you find yourself farting around in leftfield. I came away with the impression that Victor was a cold-hearted bastard of a son who wanted as little as possible to do with his mother and sister. Didn't you get that feeling?"

"Absolutely," Boone said.

"Because I didn't ask how often did you *see* Victor. Instead I asked how often did he visit Nyack. Now Alma claims they came down frequently for lunches and dinners with son Victor, and it was one big happy family. Son of a bitch! It's my fault."

"No harm done, Chief," the sergeant said.

"Yes, harm done," Delaney said wrathfully. "Not just because Dora and Emily scammed us, but because now they'll think us pointy-heads and try it again on something else. Well, we shall see. We shall certainly, fucking-ay-right, see!"

They drove on a few minutes in silence, and then Abner Boone asked, somewhat timidly, "What she said about her independent income —twenty thousand a year. You think that's important?"

"No," Delaney said, still fuming. "All it proves is that Victor Maitland was as greedy as the whole slick, avaricious, grasping lot of them. Now we know why he married the Ice Maiden."

In the old elevator, rising with wheezing stubbornness to Jake Dukker's studio, Delaney said: "The second round. Bust in on them without warning. Keep them off balance. Alma reacted fast. You really think she was going out?"

"Wasn't she?" Boone said.

"I'd bet no," the Chief said. "Heard we were there, grabbed up a hat and gloves, and sallied forth. Not an intelligent woman, but shrewd. Let's see how Jake baby reacts."

He reacted as if a visit from police officers investigating a homicide was an everyday occurrence. Came out into the reception area to greet them friendlily, said he was finishing up a photography session and would be with them in a few minutes, offered them coffee, and disappeared. He was wearing a black leather jumpsuit decorated with gleaming metal studs. The pitted cheeks glistened with sweat, and his handshake slid.

True to his word, he welcomed them into the studio ten minutes later. The assistants were dismantling a set that apparently was designed to reproduce a middle-class, suburban living room. No models were present, but they heard dogs barking from somewhere.

"Flea spray," Dukker explained. "A print campaign. Don't get Fido's fleas in your upholstery. Use Fidoff. The hounds were easier to work with than the models. Let's go upstairs and relax."

He led the way up the spiral staircase, and offered them the lip-shaped couch again. They settled for more conventional chairs. Once again Dukker collapsed into the overstuffed baseball mitt.

"How are you coming?" he asked cheerily. "Anything new?"

They looked at him. He sat slumped far down, fingers laced across his bowling-ball belly. The black leather jumpsuit glistened, and so did his face and bare forearms. He smiled at them genially, showing his stained teeth.

"We timed it from here to Maitland's Mott Street studio," Delaney told him. "You could have made it."

The smile held, but all the mirth went out of it. Then it was just stretched mouth and wet teeth, framed by the droopy Stalin mustache.

"I told you I was up here with Belle Sarazen," Dukker said hoarsely.

"So you say," Boone shrugged. "So she says. Means nothing."

"What do you mean it means nothing?" Dukker said indignantly. "Do you really think—"

"She says you like to be spanked," Delaney said. "Is that also the truth?"

"And that you envied him," Boone said. "Hated him because he did his own thing, and you chased the buck."

"The bitch!" Jake Dukker shouted, jerking forward to the edge of his chair. "Are you going to listen— Let me tell you that she— I can't believe that you actually think I— Well, she sold him drugs—did she tell

you that? I know it for a fact. Snappers. Poppers. She kept him supplied. Oh yes! For a fact. And she's got the goddamned nerve to—"

He stopped suddenly, fell back suddenly into the baseball mitt, put
his knuckles to his mouth.

"I didn't," he mumbled. "I swear to God I didn't. I couldn't have
killed him. *Couldn't* have."

"Why not?" Boone said.

"Well, because," Jake Dukker said. "I'm just not like that."

The two cops looked at each other. A unique alibi.

"We figure maybe you were in on it together," Chief Delaney said in
a gentle, musing voice. "You both had reasons. Crazy reasons, but neither of you has what I'd call your normal, run-of-the-mill personality.
You both come up here for lunch on that Friday. The models and assistants are downstairs. You duck out that doorway, take the elevator
down, either drive or take the subway downtown, put Maitland's lights
out, and come back. You could have managed it."

"Easy," Boone said. "I timed it. Myself."

"I don't believe this," Jake Dukker said, shaking his head from side
to side. "I-do-not-believe-this. Jesus."

"It's possible," Edward X. Delaney smiled. "Isn't it? Come on, admit
it; it's possible."

"You're going to arrest me?" Dukker said.

"Not today," Delaney said. "You asked us what's new. We're telling
you—that we discovered you could have done it. Possibly. That's what's
new."

They regarded him gravely as he gradually calmed, quieted, stopped
gnawing his knuckles. He tried a smile. It came out flimsy.

"I get it," he said. "Just throwing a scare—right?"

They didn't answer.

"Nothing to it—right?"

"You ever go down to Maitland's studio?" Sergeant Boone asked.
"Ever?"

"Well, sure," Dukker said nervously. "Once or twice. But not for
months. Maybe not in a year."

"He have any paintings there?" Delaney demanded. "In the studio?"

"What?" Dukker said. "I don't understand."

They were coming at him so fast, from so many angles, he couldn't
get set.

"In Maitland's studio," Delaney repeated. "Did he have paintings stacked against the walls? Like you have. Unsold stuff. Things he was working on. Old paintings."

"No," Dukker said. "Not much. He sold everything he did. He didn't keep things around. Geltman moved his stuff fast."

"And you said he was fast," Boone said. "A fast worker. He sold everything?"

"Sure he did. He could—"

"You on anything?" Delaney asked. "Pot? Pills? Or stronger? From Belle Sarazen?"

"What? Hell, no! A little grass now and then. Not from her."

"But she deals?" Boone said.

"I don't know. For sure. I swear I don't. But I hear things."

"You seemed sure enough about the poppers," Delaney said. "Why to Maitland? Was he hooked?"

"Jesus Christ, no! Just to give him a lift. You start a painting, you've got to be up."

"Not for sex?"

"Vic? No way! He was a goddamned stud. A stud!"

"You have a sheet?" Boone asked. "A criminal record?"

"Are you kidding?"

"We can find out. We're asking politely."

"Traffic tickets. Like that. And . . ."

"And?" Delaney said.

"A party. A drug bust. They let us all go. I don't even know if they kept our names. But I'm telling you. See, I'm telling you."

"Fingerprinted?"

"No. I swear I wasn't."

"You pay Belle Sarazen for the illicit fornication?" Boone asked. "For the spanking? Whipping, maybe?"

"Never! Never!"

"But you had a working relationship," Delaney said. "Right? She'd take a look at your models. Maybe for dates with her important friends. And maybe she'd provide models for you. For dirty playing cards. It worked both ways. And she posed for you. That aluminum-foil painting. A friend of hers bought it. You split the take—right? Real friends. Real cozy. Girls. Drugs on demand. Maybe even boys—who knows? All kinds of swell stuff. Orgies, maybe? Skin shows? The whole bit. Rich, freaky people. Plenty of cash. Something like that. Right?"

"I swear . . ." the artist whispered. "I swear . . ."

"Mr. Dukker," Chief Delaney said formally, "I wonder if you'd do us a favor?"

"What? What? Well . . . sure."

"Take a look at these drawings. The ones we found in Maitland's studio. See if you recognize the girl."

He and Boone held the sketches up before the dazed and shattered Dukker. He looked at them with dulled eyes.

"The son of a bitch," he muttered. "He was so good. He didn't have to think. From the eye to the hand. Nothing in between. Instantaneous."

"You recognize the girl?"

"No. Never saw her before."

"Let's go downstairs," Delaney said. "Okay?"

On the lower level, the Chief went over to the corner drawing table. He spread out the sketches, weighted down the corners so they lay flat.

"You said you were as good as Maitland," he told Dukker. "You said you could imitate his style. You got a Maitland drawing on your wall. So good that he got sore when he saw it. But then he signed it. Now what I want you to do is look at these three drawings and complete the girl. As Victor Maitland would. Just the face. He suggested the shape and features. You fill in the details."

"Jesus Christ," Jake Dukker said, "you don't want much, do you? There's hardly anything to go by."

"Do what you can," Delaney said. "We know you'll be happy to cooperate."

The artist found an 11x14 sketchpad, searched around and picked up a soft carpenter's pencil. He glanced at the three drawings and began to sketch. Hesitantly at first, then with more confidence. They watched him, fascinated. He limned the girl's face with bold outline strokes, then began to fill it in. Hollows. Shadows. Fullness. Glint of eye. Angle of chin and bulge of brow.

"Son of a bitch!" he said enthusiastically. "A beauty! This is how Vic would have done her. Young. Maybe like fourteen. Around there. Innocent. And dumb. Nothing but beauty. That's it. That's her. There you are."

Less than three minutes, Delaney estimated. And he had the portrait of a young, beautiful, empty-eyed girl. A flood of dark hair spilling down. Sensual mouth. Lips parted to show glistening teeth. High cheekbones. All of her bursting with youth, but vacant. Untouched.

He took the three Maitland sketches and Dukker's drawing, and rolled them carefully together.

"Thank you very much," he said. "We'll be seeing you again."

"Soon," Sergeant Boone added.

They left Jake Dukker slack-jawed and shaken. In the elevator, going down, Delaney said, "We're beginning to work pretty good together."

"Just what I was thinking, Chief," Boone grinned. "He's going to call Belle Sarazen now, and scream at her."

"Oh yes," Delaney nodded. "The animals are nipping and clawing at each other. I think we have most of what we need right now."

Boone looked at him, astounded.

"You mean you've . . . ?"

"Got it figured?" Delaney said, amused. "No way. I'm just saying I think we've got the main pieces. Putting them together is something else again. Sarazen will be on her guard. I'll play the heavy; you play the friend. We'll dazzle her with our footwork."

"I like this," Abner Boone said.

"It has its moments," Edward X. Delaney said. "Filthy people! Messy lives!"

The Filipino houseboy showed no surprise when he opened the door and saw them planted there. "Thith way, gentlemens," he said.

He led the way to a small room, almost a corridor between the blood-red bedroom and a bathroom that seemed to be all varicose marble and gold fixtures. The passageway held a massage table and, on a track just below the ceiling, a battery of lighted ultraviolet lamps. They cast a cold blue-white glow that filled the chamber and made it look like a fish tank.

The massage table was covered with a flowered sheet. Belle Sarazen lay face down, her cheek resting on her forearms. She was apparently naked; a pink towel was spread over her rump. She wore black goggles: two disks of semi-opaque glass the size of half-dollars, held together by an elastic.

A similar pair of protective goggles was worn by the muscular young man bending over the table, kneading the muscles of her upper arms and shoulders with long, powerful strokes. He was dressed in white sneakers, white duck trousers, a white T-shirt that had obviously been altered to display his brawny torso. He had the bulging biceps and del-toids of a weightlifter. His flaxen hair was artfully arranged in a cap of Greek curls, with divine bangs that dangled over his forehead.

"Halloo, darlings!" Belle Sarazen sang cheerily, not raising her head. "Don't come into the room or you're liable to go blind or become impotent or something. This gorgeous hunk of meat is Bobbie. Bobbie, say hello to these nice gentlemen, members of New York's Finest."

Bobbie turned his blank goggles toward them and showed a mouthful of teeth as square and white as sugar cubes.

"Take a walk, Bobbie," Chief Delaney said gruffly. "Do your nails or something."

A tambourine laugh came from Belle Sarazen.

"Run along, Bobbie," she advised. "Go play games with Ramon. But don't leave. This won't take long. Will it, Edward X. Delaney?"

He didn't answer.

The goggled Bobbie departed, not forgetting to inflate his massive chest and ripple his triceps as he pushed by the two officers. They stood at the bedroom entrance, outside the glow of the suntan lamps. Belle Sarazen's head was toward them, but they couldn't see her face. Just the long, oiled back. Roped muscles of thighs and calves. Within her reach was a small table and a tall glass of something orange with chunks of fresh fruit floating in bubbles.

"Poor Jake," she murmured. "He called me, you know. I'm afraid you upset him dreadfully."

"You were selling poppers to Maitland," Delaney said wrathfully.

"Selling?" she said. "Nonsense. He was up here frequently. He might have taken a few from my medicine cabinet."

"You have a prescription for those?" Delaney demanded.

"Of course, dear," Belle Sarazen said lazily. "I can give you the name of my doctor. If you care to check."

"Goddamned right I'll check," Delaney thundered.

"Hey, Chief," Boone said nervously. "Take it easy."

"Oh, let him bellow, Scarecrow," she said. "He'll huff and he'll puff, but he won't blow my house down."

"You could have made it to Maitland's studio from Jake Dukker's place," Delaney told her. "We timed it. You and Dukker could have skinned out to the elevator, gone down to Mott Street and zonked Maitland. You come back the same way, and no one downstairs in the studio is any the wiser."

"Now why would I do a silly thing like that, Edward X. Delaney?"

"Because you hated his guts," he yelled at her. "He called you a whore in public. You've got the kind of ego that couldn't take that. And maybe he—"

"Chief," Sergeant Boone said urgently, "for God's sake, cool it. We don't—"

"No, by God!" Delaney said. "I'm going to pin her. Maybe Maitland was ready to blow the whistle on her sweet little rackets. The call girls, the drugs, the sex shows, the whole bit. That would be motive enough."

"Listen here," Belle Sarazen said, raising her head, beginning to lose her flippancy. "What right have you—"

"Oh yes," Delaney nodded. "Dukker told us plenty. Things he didn't tell you he told us. We know all about the models and your important friends. And Bobbie? That muscle-bound butterfly! Is he in on it, too? I'll bet he is! We've got—"

"Guessing," she said sharply. "You and your dirty little mind. You're just guessing."

"How often did Maitland come up here?" Delaney demanded. "Once a week? Three times? Every day? We can check the doorman, so don't lie about it."

"I have no reason to lie," she said, her voice getting colder and thinner. "Victor Maitland was a personal friend of mine. A very special friend. Is it a crime to have friends visit?"

"He gave you money?"

"He gave me gifts, yes. I've already told you that."

"Gifts!" Delaney said. "That's good, that is! Maybe you raised the rates. Maybe he wanted to end it. Maybe he—"

"Chief, Chief," Boone groaned. "Take it easy. Please! We've got no evidence. You're just spit-balling. There's no way we can—"

"I don't care," Delaney shouted. "She killed once and walked. She's not going to do it in my city. She's guilty as hell. If not murder, then procuring and the drug thing. I'm going to rack her up. I swear, I'm going to hang her ass!"

Now Belle Sarazen had raised the upper part of her torso to stare at her tormentor with blank, goggled eyes. She propped herself on her forearms. They could see her small, muscled breasts, like hard shields with shiny pink bosses.

"You just try!" she spat at him. "Just try! I'll make you the laughing stock of New York. I'll sue, and believe me I can afford the best lawyers in the country. By the time I've finished with you, you'll be lucky to have your pension left. I'll drain you dry!"

"You're finished," he screamed at her. "Can't you get that through your scrambled brain? It's all over for you, kiddo. You're finished and down the drain."

He thrust the roll of Maitland drawings into Boone's hands, spun around, stalked off. They heard his thumping footsteps and, far off, the slam of the outside door. Belle Sarazen stared at Abner Boone through her black goggles.

"Wow!" he said. "I've never seen him like that before."

She grunted, got off the table, wrapping the big towel around her, covering herself from breasts to upper thighs. She switched off the sunlamps. She ripped away her goggles.

"The son of a bitch!" she said. "That fucking cocksucker! I'll have his balls!"

"I want to apologize, Miss Sarazen," Boone said earnestly. "He's not going to do those things he said. He's been under so much pressure lately . . . Please, I wish you'd forget what happened."

"Forget?" She laughed—or tried to. It caught in her throat. "No way, baby! Mister Chief Edward X. Delaney has no idea how much clout I can swing in Fun City. He's dead and doesn't know it."

She pushed by him, went into the bedroom. She fell into a blood-red armchair, hooked a knee over one of the arms, foot swinging crazily. She began sucking frantically on a thumb, a maniacal baby with a long-nailed pacifier.

"Look, Miss Sarazen," Sergeant Boone pleaded. "He's retired. You know that. You can't touch him. But I'm on active duty. You go to your important friends, and I'm the one they'll come down on. I'll be walking a beat in Richmond. You know that. I think he was way out of line. Is it right my career should be ruined because he blew his cork? Look, I'm on your side. We've got nothing on you. Not a thing. He was just shooting off at the mouth."

Finally, the hooked leg stopped its mad jerking, the thumb came from her lips with a *plop!* sound. She smiled at him.

"Scarecrow," she said, "I like you. Get me that glass from the other room."

Obediently, he brought her the glass of fruit chunks floating in bubbles. She sipped it slowly, reflectively. He sat down cautiously, bent forward, hands clasped in supplication.

"Is that the truth?" she asked. "You've got nothing on me?"

"The truth," Boone vowed. "All gossip and hearsay. Even what Jake

Dukker told us about you. I mean the drugs and girls and all. How can we use that? He's in on it, too, isn't he?"

"Is he ever!" she said.

"Well, there you are," the sergeant said, sitting back. "Now you know he's not going to make any kind of a signed statement or testify if it means his own ass, too. Right?"

"Right," she said, nodding. "Jake's a weak sister; I've known that all along. If push comes to shove, he'll clam up. I have ways of making sure he does."

"Of course," Boone said encouragingly. "And what Delaney said about Maitland paying you for the sex—hell, that's your personal business. No one's going to court with that."

"Vic paid me for sex?" Belle Sarazen said. She moved her head back and laughed. A genuine, deep laugh that made the towel about her middle billow in and out. "That'd be the day when Victor Maitland paid for a fuck. No way, Scarecrow! No, Vic and I had a little business deal going. You might say we were partners. It was all strictly business."

"Well, I'm certainly glad to hear that," Boone said, smiling. "I didn't think you were that kind of a woman, Belle. In spite of what Delaney said."

"That bastard," she growled.

"As long as it was just business," the sergeant said, with a deep sigh of relief. "What kind of a business were you two in?"

"I helped him out on a few deals," she shrugged. "I have some rich friends. All over the country. Everywhere. Here and in Europe."

"Oh, I see," Boone nodded, still smiling. "You mean you helped his career? His reputation? Helped him sell his paintings?"

"Something like that," she said.

"Nothing wrong with that," Boone said. "Perfectly legit. I imagine you must know a lot of people in the art world."

"Everyone, baby. *Everyone.*"

"I mean, like rich collectors?"

"You better believe it. Top-dollar collectors."

"Well, you could certainly be a big help to any artist," Boone said enthusiastically. "But I thought Saul Geltman handled all of Maitland's stuff?"

"Well, he did and he didn't," Belle Sarazen said vaguely. "There's more than one way to skin a cat. Listen, Scarecrow, are you sure what Delaney said—all that bullshit about procuring and drugs and all—that *was* bullshit, wasn't it? He hasn't got anything to take to the DA, does he?"

"Don't worry," the sergeant assured her. "It's all smoke. It's just that he wants to break this thing so bad he can taste it. Listen, just between you, me and the lamp post, were you really with Jake Dukker every minute from, say, noon till two o'clock on the Friday Maitland was killed? The reason I ask is because right now, Jake's our Number One suspect."

She stared at him a long moment, clinking the rim of the glass against her gleaming teeth. She stared at him, but he could see she wasn't looking at him. Her gaze was unfocussed, going through him, off into the distance.

Finally, she sighed, drained her glass. She picked out a piece of fresh pineapple and began to chew on it. He waited patiently.

"I couldn't swear to it in a court of law," she said dreamily. "I might have fallen asleep up there. I really don't know what he did while I was asleep. I really couldn't say."

"Thank you, Belle," he said humbly. "Thank you very much. Now just one more thing . . . I've got the three sketches we found in Maitland's studio. Would you take a look at them and see if you recognize the model?"

"Sure," she said, straightening up. "Let's have a look."

He slid off the rubber band and handed the drawings to her. She went through them slowly.

"Nice," she said. "I could sell these with one phone call."

"I'm afraid not," he said. "They belong to the estate."

"What a body. Yum-yum. What's this one—the finished head?"

"Jake Dukker did that one. What he thought the girl looked like, done the way he thought Maitland would have done it. Recognize the girl?"

"No. Never saw her before. Wish I could help you—you've been sweet—but I can't. Sorry."

"Just a long shot," he shrugged, rolling up the drawings again. "Well, I'll be on my way."

"Send Bobbie in on your way out," she commanded him. "You bastards interrupted my massage. Bobbie finishes me off with a mink glove. Ever get rubbed down with mink, Scarecrow?"

"No," he said, getting to his feet, "I never have."

"Well . . ." she said speculatively, looking at him, "you keep on being sweet to me and telling me what's going on, and you never know . . ."

Chief Delaney was waiting patiently in the car, slumped down. He was smoking a cigar, his straw hat tilted down over his eyes. He pushed it back when Boone got behind the wheel.

"How did you make out?" he asked.

"Not bad, Chief," Boone said. "You got her so sore, I could play the Father Confessor."

"What did you get?"

"First of all, she doesn't recognize the girl in the sketches. Says she never saw her before. On the drug and prostitution things, she and Dukker are in on it together. Like we figured. But they've probably knocked off while we're sniffing around."

"Only temporarily," Delaney said.

"Sure," Boone agreed. "Also, she's ready to throw Dukker to the wolves. Says now she might have fallen asleep up in his place and couldn't testify that he was there all the time."

"Oh-ho," the Chief said. "Isn't she a nice lady? That's what Dukker gets for telling us about the poppers."

"But the big thing is this: Maitland wasn't paying for her tush. She says. She claims they were in business together. I couldn't get her to spell it out, but it sounded like maybe she was getting her rich friends to buy Maitland's paintings, and she was taking a slice."

Delaney thought about that a moment.

"Fucking Saul Geltman?" he asked.

"That's how it adds up to me, Chief. She said she knows well-heeled collectors all over the country and in Europe. Maybe they were cutting out Geltman."

"Could be," Delaney nodded. "We'll have to check to see if Maitland and Geltman had any kind of an exclusive contract or signed agreement. Look, sergeant, we know Maitland was selling paintings he wasn't telling his wife about. It's very possible he was also selling paintings he didn't tell Geltman about."

"That would give Saul baby motive enough," Boone noted. "Or . . ."

"Or what?" Delaney said.

"This is a wild one, Chief."

"Go ahead, try it."

"Well, this is just a scenario . . . We know Jake Dukker can forge Maitland's style. My God, he proved it to us. Now suppose—"

"I got it," Delaney interrupted. "Maybe Dukker was producing fake Maitlands. Sarazen was peddling them to her rich collector friends, and Maitland found out. So they clipped his wick."

"Right," Boone said.

"It's all jazz," the Chief said. "But I'll ask Lieutenant Wolfe to see if he can find someone, somewhere, who owns a Maitland painting that wasn't sold through Saul Geltman. That would confirm that either Maitland was selling his own stuff on the sly, or Dukker was pushing fakes. Good work, sergeant."

"Thank you, sir."

"And now," Delaney said, sighing, "I suppose I can expect a call from Deputy Commissioner Thorsen expressing the displeasure of all her important friends at the rude way I treated Belle Sarazen."

"No, I don't think so," Abner Boone said. "I told her you had nothing on her, and if she screamed, I'd be the only one who'd get the shaft. I don't think she'll yelp."

"I owe you one," Delaney said.

Boone wanted to say, "We're even," but said nothing.

On the evening following the interrogations of Jake Dukker and Belle Sarazen, Monica and the Chief relaxed in the study with after-dinner rye highballs while he delivered a précis of his day's activities. She sat slouched in the worn leather club chair, her shoeless feet parked up on his desk. He sat in his swivel chair behind the desk, occasionally consulting his notebook and reports as he told her what had been learned.

He followed up the account of Jason T. Jason's encounter with the two Spanish women by showing Monica the drawing Jake Dukker had made of the young model's face, based on the Maitland sketches. Monica guessed the girl's age as fifteen or sixteen. She asked the Chief if he intended to circulate copies of the drawing to the city's precincts, in hopes of locating the girl.

Delaney rose to pin the drawing to his map board alongside the Maitland sketches. He told her that he and Boone had discussed that possibility, but decided against it for the time being, since they had nothing more than a wild hope that the two women might be helpful in identifying the killer. If other, more promising leads fizzled, then Jason T. Jason would be set to work with a police artist, and drawings of both women would be circulated in hopes of locating them.

The Chief described the Mutt and Jeff technique he and Boone had used with Belle Sarazen. He thought the results had justified what they had done, although he admitted it probably meant Boone would have to handle Sarazen by himself in the future. Monica said Sarazen sounded like a dreadful woman, and Delaney told her she'd probably get a chance to meet the lady herself at Saul Geltman's pre-show party. In fact, the Chief said, he hoped Monica would try to meet all the principals in the case at that party; he wanted her take on them.

Monica asked if he really thought Belle Sarazen had sufficient motive for killing Victor Maitland. Would a jury, for instance, believe that a woman had knifed a man to death because he insulted her in public? Monica didn't think so.

Delaney said there might be an additional motive in those "business dealings" Belle Sarazen claimed she had with Maitland. But even if no further motive was uncovered, he still believed Sarazen was capable of killing to revenge a real or even fancied slight to her amour propre. He said Monica's doubts were based on the fact that she assumed Sarazen was a rational human being who acted in a reasonable manner. The truth was, he said, she was an unstable personality who had lived an incoherent life, with a history of irrational acts.

He said, almost as much to himself as to Monica, that one of the hardest things for a cop to learn was that people frequently acted in ways that not only contravened the laws of society, but of intelligence and good, gutter common sense. Cops sometimes failed, Delaney said, because they looked for reason and logic in what was too often an unreasonable and illogical world. They could not grasp the essential *nuttiness* of the human situation. The Chief told Monica of a homicide he had worked in Greenwich Village when he was a lieutenant . . .

This kid had come out of the midwest. A college kid, good family, money. He wanted to get into the theatre, and his parents agreed to bankroll him for two years. So he came to New York, signed up for courses in an acting school, began to make the rounds.

The freedom in the Village in the 1960s almost literally exploded his mind. Drugs. Sex. Whatever he wanted. He couldn't handle it. Trying to reconstruct it later, the cops could nail some of it and guess the rest. The kid never did get hooked on the hard stuff, but he was dropping acid and bombed out of his gourd most of the time on pills and booze. He moved into a loft with five or six others, men and women. Different cast every night, but the play never changed. He was fucking everything that moved and being used the same way himself. He had to experience everything: that was the road to revelation and great art. After a while, he couldn't even judge the quality of pleasures.

One night he strangled the young girl he was sodomizing. It could have been another man or a child; that night it happened to be a woman. After they got him dried out and off the pills, they asked him why he had done it. He looked at them, puzzled. He didn't know. He actually didn't know. The victim was almost a stranger to him. It had just occurred to him to kill her, to experience that, and so he had done it.

It was the freedom, Delaney said somberly to Monica. It was partly the drugs, he agreed, but mostly it was the freedom. Complete, without any restraint. There were no rules, no laws, no prohibitions. Moral anarchy. The kid was really surprised, Delaney said, when he finally realized he was going to be punished for what he had done. He couldn't understand it. It didn't seem to him all that big a deal.

The Chief told Monica that it frequently happened that way with people who couldn't handle freedom. They didn't know self-discipline. They acted only on whim, impulse. They couldn't sacrifice the pleasure of today for the satisfaction of tomorrow.

He thought that might be what was happening to Belle Sarazen. She lived in a world of easy money, easy thrills. No rules, no laws, no prohibitions. Total liberty, and a greed for kicks. It was, Delaney acknowledged, a difficult motive to present to a jury. They looked for neater reasons: vengeance, hate, lust, jealousy. It was hard to convince reasonable people that someone could kill casually, without motive. But it did happen. It was happening more and more often.

So motive was important, he told Monica, but not so important as to make an experienced cop rule out motiveless crime. Sarazen sold drugs and bodies; that was evident. Was it such a quantum leap from that to pushing a knife into someone who annoyed you? Especially when you believe nothing is wrong, everything is right?

Monica shivered, and hugged herself. She asked her husband if that meant Belle Sarazen was the leading suspect. He said no, that what he said about her could also be said about Jake Dukker. And Alma Maitland, Ted Maitland, and Saul Geltman had firmer, more conventional motives.

And the mother and sister? Monica wanted to know. Did they also have motives?

Delaney said that none were presently apparent, but that didn't mean none existed.

Monica sighed, and after a while she asked if his working lifetime as a cop, in dealing with things like the Maitland homicide—which, he had to admit, had a depressing sordidness about it—if dealing with the baseness of people had not soured him on the human race.

He thought a long time, and finally said he didn't think it had. He had learned, he told her, not to expect too much from people, and thus avoided being constantly disappointed. Abner Boone, on the other hand, Delaney said, was a closet romantic. And this was probably the cause of his drinking. Boone said it was the "filth" of police work, but he really meant the evil of human beings. He expected so much good and found so little.

Edward X. Delaney said he expected little, and sometimes was pleasantly surprised. And so he kept his sanity. And it was also important, he added stoutly, that his own life, his personal life, be ordered and coherent. That was a cop's salvation.

Monica said she hoped Rebecca Hirsch could help Abner Boone achieve that. The Chief said he hoped so, too. Then they each had another rye highball, talked about summer camp for the girls, and argued drowsily about whether or not onions should be grated into potato pancakes.

13

They ordered coffee and dessert, then Chief Delaney rose and excused himself. Sergeant Boone followed immediately. Monica and Rebecca Hirsch watched their men troop away, the Chief lumbering, Boone bouncing after him.

"Has he been behaving?" Monica asked.

"So far," Rebecca said.

"You can never trust him," Monica said severely. Then she smiled sadly. "I'm beginning to talk like Edward."

Rebecca covered Monica's hand with hers. "That's all right. We know it. We take it a day at a time."

Monica freed her hand, glanced at her watch.

"Worried about the girls?" Rebecca asked.

"It's the first time they've been alone at night. They've got to learn sometime. But I think I'll give them a call to say good night. When the men come back."

In the lavatory, Delaney and Boone relieved themselves at adjoining urinals.

"I had lunch with the Hemley woman," Boone said in a low voice. "She never saw Geltman after he entered the office about ten o'clock. When Simon came out to pay for the sandwiches, he closed the door to his private office behind him."

"Tricky business," Delaney said.

"You think the two of them have the balls for something like that?"

"Sure," the Chief said equably. "The risk wasn't all that big."

"And I got a call from Jason T. Jason," Boone went on as they zipped up and began washing their hands. "He's been spending a few hours a day of his own time, in plainclothes, wandering around looking for the Spanish woman and the girl."

"Good for him."

"He thinks they might have come from east of the Bowery. Maybe around Orchard Street. A lot of Puerto Ricans around there, he says. I think he was hinting maybe we could get him detached from patrol to spend all his time looking for the women."

"Well . . . not yet," Delaney said. "He's ambitious, isn't he? Nothing wrong with that. I'll get a list of Maitland's hangouts from the file, and we'll have Jason Two check them out. Maybe Maitland met the woman in a bar, or near one. Will Susan Hemley be at the party tonight?"

"She said yes."

"Does Rebecca know you had lunch with her?"

"Yes, sir. I told her."

"That's good," Delaney said. Faint smile. "I wouldn't want her to misunderstand if Hemley says something. If Emily Maitland shows up, and you get a chance to talk to her, mention casually that we know about all the times she and her mother came down from Nyack for lunches and dinners with Victor."

Boone stared at him a moment before they went out to rejoin the ladies.

"I get it," he said finally. "You want to know if they took the bus or train or if they drove down in that big, old Mercedes."

"Right," Delaney said. "You're beginning to think like me."

When the Chief saw the crush of people inside the Geltman Galleries, with more arriving every minute, he turned to the others and said: "If we get separated in the crowd, suppose we all meet right here on the sidewalk at midnight. That'll give us more than two hours. Should be long enough to see everything."

They all agreed, and plunged into the mob.

Delaney saw the Mephistophelian features of Lieutenant Bernard Wolfe. The detective was wearing a collarless suit of black velvet, ruffled mauve shirt, glittering studs, and cufflinks that looked like glass eyes. He bent low over Monica's hand.

"Watch this guy," Chief Delaney advised his wife with heavy good humor. "He's dangerous."

"I can believe it," she said, staring at the lieutenant with admiration. "And I thought all cops bought their clothes at Robert Hall."

"The costume's a scam," Wolfe grinned at her. "Actually, I'm a brown shoes and white socks guy."

"I'll bet," she scoffed.

"You know all these people?" Delaney asked, maneuvering to keep from being jostled away.

"Most of them," Wolfe nodded. "Want to meet anyone?"

"Not at the moment," Delaney said. "If you can get Geltman alone for a minute, will you ask him if Belle Sarazen ever helped him find buyers for Maitland's paintings? Keep it casual. And keep me out of it."

"Consider it done," Wolfe said. "Mrs. Delaney, there's food and a bar in the back. Bring you something?"

"I'll come with you," she said. "I'm supposed to circulate. Orders."

"Your husband trusts you?" the lieutenant said, turning his raffish smile on Delaney.

"Yes, he does," Monica said. "Damn it."

"Edward X. Delaney!" came the gurgling laugh, and the Chief turned slowly to face Belle Sarazen. She was sleek as a steel rod, silvery hair flat and gleaming, whippy body molded in a metallic sheath that could have been sprayed on.

"What's the X. stand for?" she demanded.

"Marks the spot," he said, the "joke" he had repeated all his life without humor or even lightness.

"You two boys whipsawed me, didn't you?" she said, showing her Chiclet teeth.

He inclined his head.

"Clever," she said, looking at him curiously now. "And I fell for it. I thought I was smarter than that."

"So did I," he said.

She laughed and clutched his arm to her hard breasts.

"Want to meet anyone?" she asked.

"No, thanks," he said. "But I'd like to see the paintings."

"The paintings?" A burlesque leer of cynical disbelief. "Who comes to these things to look at paintings?"

"Mrs. Maitland," Sergeant Boone said. "Nice to see you again. May I present Rebecca Hirsch?"

The women looked at each other.

"My son, Ted," Alma Maitland said. "Miss Hirsch. Sergeant Boone of the New York Police Department."

Ted Maitland stared at them, not speaking.

"We're trying to see the paintings," Boone said. "But the crowd . . ."

"What do you think of them?" Rebecca asked Ted Maitland.

He glared at her with something close to hatred.

"You wouldn't understand," he said.

Chief Delaney bulled his way toward the wall. Finally, the mob thrust him close. He was pressed into one of the small, three-sided alcoves. Three paintings. Each, he noted, signed carefully at the bottom right-hand corner: VICTOR MAITLAND, 1978. The signature surprised him. Not the flamboyant script he expected, but neat, bookkeeper's handwriting in black print. Name and date. Almost legalistic in its precision and legibility.

Three views of what was obviously the same model: front, back and profile. Exhibited together, the effect was of seeing her in the round, of grasping all. A heavily fleshed, auburn-haired woman. Sulky eyes. Sullen mouth. Tension of fury in clenched fists, muscled thighs. She jutted from the canvas, challenging.

"Look at the impasto," someone said. "A hundred bucks' worth of paint there."

"It'll be crackled in a year," someone said. "He never would let it dry properly. Take the money and run."

"Dynamic dysphoria," someone said. "The furious Earth Mother. The son of a bitch could draw. But strictly exogenous. I can resist it— and her."

"You better, dearie," a woman said. Brittle laugh. "They'd have to peel you off the ceiling."

Delaney half-listened. He stared at the defiant nude. He heard the mumbles of smart talk. He saw only life caught and held in vibrant colors that jangled the eye and forced him to see what he had never seen before.

"You like?" Jake Dukker asked, thrusting his head around to peer into Delaney's face. "I know the model. Bull dyke."

"Is she?" Delaney said. "She's beautiful. He caught the anger."

"And the box," Dukker laughed. "Look at that castrating box. You find the girl yet? The young girl in the drawings?"

"No," Delaney said. "Not yet."

"I saw you come in with Delaney," Belle Sarazen said. "You his wife?"

"Yes. Monica Delaney. You must be Belle Sarazen."

"Oh, you know?"

"My husband described you. He said you were very beautiful."

"Well, aren't you nice, sweetie. And did he tell you all about me?"

"Very little, I'm afraid. My husband never discusses his cases with me."

"Too bad. I imagine it could be exciting being in bed with a cop. Listening to him talk."

"It's exciting even if he doesn't talk."

"See you around, kiddo."

"Nice to see you again, Miss Maitland," Abner Boone said. "Is your mother here, too?"

"Around somewhere," Emily Maitland said breathlessly. "My land, isn't this just fascinating? I love it!"

"Love the paintings?"

"Those, too. Vic was such a naughty boy! But this crowd! The famous people! Have you ever seen such beautiful people?"

"Men or women?" he asked.

"All of them," she sighed. "So grand and skinny."

"Did you drive down?" the sergeant asked, wishing she had not worn that shattering flowered muumuu.

"Oh yes," she said, looking about with wide, shining eyes. "We always drive down."

"When you had lunch and dinner with your brother?" he pressed. "You drove?"

"Oh look!" she breathed. "That gorgeous man in the velvet suit and ruffled shirt. The devil!"

"Would you like to meet him?" Boone asked. "I know him. I'll introduce you."

"Would you?" she gasped. "Maybe he'll let me take him home to Nyack and keep him under a belljar."

Abner Boone looked at her.

"Having a good time, dear?" Edward X. Delaney asked. "Did you get a drink? Some caviar?"

"I'm doing fine," Monica assured him. "I know what you mean about his paintings, Edward. They're very strong, aren't they? They're sort of . . ."

"Of what?" he asked.

"A little crazy?" she said cautiously.

"Yes," he agreed. "A little crazy. He wanted to know it all, have it all, and show it. That way he could own it."

She wasn't sure what he meant.

"I met Belle Sarazen," she said.

"And . . . ?"

"Very sexy. Very hard. Bitchy."

"Could she kill?"

Monica looked at him queerly.

"I think so," she said slowly. "She's very unhappy."

"No," he said. "Just greedy. Will you do me a favor?"

"Of course. What?"

"See that young fellow over there? Under the spiral staircase? Alone? That's Ted Maitland. Victor's son. Go talk to him. Tell me what you think."

"Could he . . . ?"

"You tell me."

"Talked to Saul," Lieutenant Wolfe said, grinning. The crowd shoved him tightly against Delaney.

"Oh?" Delaney said, smiling broadly in return. Two friends laughing, enjoying a joke.

"He says he works with Sarazen, like half the dealers on Madison Avenue. She finds buyers. Here and in Europe. Takes ten percent."

"From the dealer or the artist?"

"You kidding? The artist, of course. No dealer's going to reduce his take."

"So they worked together on Maitland's stuff?"

"Occasionally. He says."

"Mooch around, will you, lieutenant? Maybe she and Maitland were cutting him out."

"Oh-ho. Like that, was it?"

"Could be."

"I'll see what I can dig. By the way, I may run away with your wife."

"I'd mind," Delaney said. "Great cook. Come up for dinner?"

"You say when."

Boone put his back against the wall. He held his glass of gingerale chest-high, stared with a vacant smile. Guests pushed by, stepped on his toes, slopped his drink. He paid no attention; he was watching Saul Geltman and the Maitlands, mother and daughter. The agent had the two women crowded into a corner. He was speaking rapidly, gesturing. Emily was listening intently, head lowered. Dora seemed out of it, leaning back, swaying, eyes closed.

To the sergeant, it looked as if Geltman were trying to sell them something. He was almost spluttering in his eagerness to convince. He took hold of Dora's shoulder, shook it gently. Her eyes opened. Geltman moved closer and spoke directly into her face. Her hand, clenched into a fist, rose slowly. For a moment, Boone thought she was going to hit the agent: punch him in the mouth or club him on the head. But Emily Maitland grabbed her mother's arm, soothed her, took hold of the menacing hand. She pried the fist open, straightening the fingers, smiling, smiling, smiling . . .

"Chief!" a harried Saul Geltman said. "Glad you could make it. You've met Mrs. Dora Maitland? Victor's mother?"

"I've had that pleasure," the Chief said, bowing. "A pleasure again, ma'am. A beautiful show. Your son's paintings are magnificent."

" 'Nificent," she nodded solemnly.

Zonked, Delaney thought. Boone was right: she's on the sauce.

"Pardon me a moment," Saul Geltman said. "The critics. Photographers. It's going well, don't you think?"

He turned away. Delaney grabbed his arm, pulled him back.

"One quick question," he said. "Did you have a contract with Maitland?"

Geltman looked at him, puzzled. Then his face cleared, and he laughed.

"No contract," he said. "Not even a handshake. He could have walked away any time he wanted to. If he thought I wasn't doing a good job. Sometimes artists jump from dealer to dealer. The second-raters looking for instant success. Gotta run . . ."

He disappeared. Delaney steadied Mrs. Maitland with a firm hand under her elbow. He steered her skillfully, got her against a wall. A waiter passed, and Delaney lifted a glass of something from his tray. He folded Dora Maitland's fingers around it. She stared at it blearily.

"Scotch?" she said.

"Whatever," he said. "How I enjoyed my visit to your lovely home."

She raised those dark, brimming eyes and tried to focus. Lurched closer. The oiled ringlets swung around his face. He caught the musky scent.

"You'll see," she said in a curdled voice. "Like it was. When I get the money . . ."

"Oh?" he said lightly. "Well, I can imagine all the improvements you'll make. When you get the money. But won't it be very costly to restore the house and grounds?"

"Don' you worry," she said, patting his arm with floating fingers. "Plenty of—"

"There you are, Mother!" Emily Maitland said brightly. "I was wondering where you'd got to. Chief Delaney, how nice to see you again. Land, but isn't it hot? How I'd like a glass of that nice fruit punch. Chief? Please?"

"My pleasure," Chief Delaney said, and moved toward the bar. But when he returned with the glass of punch, the Maitland women were gone. He looked about, searching for them.

"If you can't find a customer, I'll take that," Susan Hemley said. She plucked the glass from Delaney's fingers. "Remember me? Susan Hemley? You liked my hair."

"How could I ever forget?" he said gallantly. "Enjoying yourself?"

"A lot of fags," she said. "You and the sergeant are the only straight men in the place."

"You're very kind," he said, without irony. "And the paintings? What do you think of them?"

"Alma says . . ." she giggled, then tried again. "Alma thinks they're vulgar and dirty. All that skin. Alma thinks they're like, you know, porn."

"Does she?" he smiled. "So that's what Alma thinks. What do you think?"

"Live and let live," she shrugged.

"My sentiments exactly," he told her. "I'm sorry to hear Mrs. Maitland doesn't approve of her husband's work. She modeled for him, didn't she?"

"A long time ago," Susan Hemley said. "She's changed."

"Now she doesn't like the nudes?"

"Well, she does and she doesn't," Susan Hemley said vaguely. "Doesn't like all the bare ass. But still, they do sell, don't they? And who can argue with money?"

"Not me," he assured her.

"You were kidding, weren't you?" Jake Dukker asked Sergeant Abner Boone.

"Kidding? About what?"

"What you and the Chief said. Me a suspect."

"Oh, that," Boone said. "No, we weren't kidding. Sarazen claims she went upstairs with you at noon all right. On that Friday. But then she fell asleep. She says. So she can't swear you were there until one-thirty or two. She doesn't know what you were up to."

Dukker's face blanched. The pits of his cheeks became black pimples. His mouth opened and closed.

"She . . ." he tried.

"Oh yes," Boone said, nodding. "She can't remember a thing."

He smiled and moved away.

"I talked to Ted Maitland," Monica said. "At least I tried to."

"And?" the Chief asked.

"Nothing. All he did was grunt. Did you notice the bandage?"

"What bandage?"

"Ah-ha," Monica said triumphantly. "I'm a better detective than you are."

"Did I ever deny it?" he said. "What bandage?"

"On Ted's wrist."

"Which wrist? Or both?"

"On his left wrist. Under his cuff."

"So," Delaney said, with a bleak smile. "The boy's got a thing for sharp edges."

"Maybe it was an accident," Monica said.

"Maybe it was guilt," the Chief said. "I'll ask Ted and Alma about it, but I know what I'll get from them. Zilch."

The pot didn't disturb him; he had smelled marijuana before. And the swirls of perfume and whiffs of deodorant-masked sweat he could identify and accept. It was something else: a smell that was not a scent, but in the air, permeating the hard chatter he heard, the gargled laughter.

Perhaps it was the way they disregarded Victor Maitland's paintings, or debated their cash value with cold eyes. He glimpsed the lorn figure of Theodore Maitland standing near a keen J. Julian Simon, and he remembered what the boy had said: the upside-down pyramid of the art world. All this glitter and the clang of coin sprouting from the lonely talent of a doomed creative artist who was, at the bottom, secretly derided. If they could, if it was possible, they would prefer that art could be produced by means other than individual pain. A factory perhaps. A computer. Anything they could understand and control. But wild genius daunted them; to accept it demeaned their own brutal lives. They lived off another man's talent and travail, and despised him for it to hide their own empty envy and want.

That was what he smelled: the greed of the contemptuous leeches. Their scorn hung in the air, and they turned their backs to those tortured, blazing paintings on the walls. They knew everything, but they knew nothing. This loud, brazen, laughing crowd reminded him so much of the drunken throng that gathered beneath the hotel ledge and turned white faces and wet lips upward, screaming, "Jump! Jump!"

Delaney and Boone, standing apart, exchanged what they had learned.

"We've got to get back to Nyack," the Chief said. "Dora's counting on money. 'Plenty of money,' she said. Where? From whom? She doesn't inherit."

"They drove down," Boone said. "For those lunches and dinners. Emily didn't say so, but I know. God, what a mess."

"No," Delaney said, "not a mess. Just a disorder. No pattern at all. What we've—"

But then a woman screamed. Commotion. The crowd surged toward the bar. More screams. Shouts. Then laughter. Cries.

"What the hell," Delaney said. "Let's take a look."

The press of heated bodies was thick, jammed. They pushed, shoved, slid by, working their way to the bar. Voices were high, everyone gabbling, excited, eyes shining.

"He hit her," a man said happily. "Slammed her in the chops. She fell into the punch bowl. I saw it. Beautiful."

Boone grabbed his shoulder.

"Who?" he said harshly. "Who hit who?"

"Whom," the man said. "Jake Dukker hit Belle Sarazen. Right in the chops. I saw it. Knocked her ass over tea kettle. Loverly! Great party!"

Delaney put a hand on Boone's arm.

"Let's stay out of it," he said, his lips close to the sergeant's ear.

"My doing," Boone grinned. "I told him she had thrown him to the wolves."

"Good," Delaney nodded. "Maybe we'll visit them both again. Just to listen. Let's find our women and go home. I've had enough."

"See the paintings, Chief?" Boone asked.

"Some. I'll come back in a few days when I can really look. Alone."

They sat awhile in Boone's car, discussing the evening's events, reporting on what they had seen and what they had heard. Chief Delaney and the sergeant listened intently as Monica and Rebecca Hirsch exchanged opinions on people they had met, subjective reactions to appearance, manner, dress, and style.

"What about Alma Maitland?" Delaney asked. "The widow?"

"What about her?" Monica said.

The Chief tried to phrase it delicately.

"Is she—ah—interested in—ah—well . . . women?"

The two women looked at each other and burst out laughing.

Monica took her husband's hands in hers.

"What an old foof you are," she said. "Sometimes. Is she a lesbian? Is that what you want to know?"

"Yes," he said gratefully.

Monica thought a moment.

"Could be," she said. "Becky, did you get any reaction?"

"I'd say she is," Rebecca nodded. "She may not know it, but she is. And Saul Geltman is gay; that's obvious. Belle Sarazen is a cruel bitch. I'm glad she got slugged. Jake Dukker is a complete nut. But it's Ted Maitland who really scares me."

"Why is that?" Boone asked.

"Repressed violence," Rebecca said promptly. "He's right on the edge. Did you notice his fingernails? Bitten down to the quick."

"Did either of you get to meet the mother and daughter?"

"I didn't," Rebecca said.

"I met the daughter," Monica said. "A lonely girl. But underneath all that flab there's drive and ambition."

"Dreams?" Delaney asked.

"Definitely," his wife said. "Big expectations. She kept looking at the way other women were dressed and said, 'I like that. I'm going to get that.' And I asked her when, and she said, 'Soon.' She knows what she wants."

"Interesting evening," the Chief said. "Let's go home. How about you folks coming in with us for coffee-and?"

"And what?" Rebecca asked. "I fell off my diet too far tonight."

"And nothing," Monica said. "No, wait, I have a pound cake in the freezer."

"Good enough," Delaney said. "Toasted pound cake; I can endure that. We'll take our shoes off, and the postmortems will continue."

They had to park almost a block away. They strolled back to the Delaney brownstone, the two men together in front, the women following, all of them chatting.

The men trudged up the stone steps of the stoop, still talking, Chief Delaney taking out his keys. He stopped suddenly. Two steps from the top. Boone, not watching, bumped into him. He began to murmur an apology, then stopped. He saw it, too.

The front door, the fine old oak door, was open a few inches. The light that had been left on in the hallway streamed through. Around the lock and knob, the door was scarred, crushed, splintered. A piece had been broken away and lay on the landing.

"Stay here," Delaney said to Boone.

The Chief went back down to the sidewalk. The two women were just coming up. Delaney stopped them. He stood directly in front of Monica, took hold of her upper arms.

"Listen to me," he said in a cold, dead voice. "Do exactly what I tell you."

"Edward, what—"

"Just listen. The house has been broken into. The door is smashed open."

"The girls!" she wailed. He gripped her tighter.

"I want you and Rebecca to walk slowly next door to the precinct house. Don't run. Don't scream or yell. Go into the station. Identify yourself to the desk sergeant. Tell him what's happened. Tell him to send some men, anyone he can spare. Got that?"

She nodded dumbly.

"Tell the sergeant that Boone and I will be inside. That's very important. We'll both be inside. Be sure the desk sergeant and the men he sends know that. I don't want them to come in blasting. You understand, Monica?"

Again she nodded. Rebecca stepped closer to her. Delaney stood back. The two women linked arms. The Chief gave his wife a tight smile.

"All right," he said. "Now go."

She hesitated a moment.

"It's all right," he assured her. "Now go get help."

The women turned. Delaney watched them walk steadily, with measured step, back toward the precinct house. Then he rejoined Abner Boone. They moved up slowly, silently to the top landing. They stood at the hinged side of the jimmied door.

"You carrying?" Boone whispered.

Delaney shook his head.

The sergeant slid his revolver from the hip holster beneath his suit jacket.

"Back way out?" he asked in a low voice.

"Dead end," Delaney said. "Courtyard. No way."

Boone nodded, pushed the safety off, crouched.

"You stay here," he commanded. "I'll go in fast and low. Keep away from the open door, sir."

Delaney didn't answer. Boone set himself. Bent lower. Pushed off with a thrust of his thighs. Hit the door with a shoulder. It flung wide, banged the opposite wall, began to bounce back.

By then the sergeant was in. Down. On the floor. Rolling. Ending up against the entrance-hall wall. Gun held in both hands. Propped up. Pointing.

Nothing. No sound. No movement.

"I'm coming," Delaney called. "Upstairs. Along the hall. Second door on the right. My gun's there. You lead. I'll follow. Ready? Let's go!"

They went with a rush, Boone scrambling to his feet. Dashing up the staircase. Delaney pounding after him. Down the hall. To the half-open bedroom door.

Boone rolled in again. Ready. In a few seconds Delaney reached around from the hallway. Snapped on the light. Took a quick glance around. Nothing. He had his keys out. Unlocked his equipment drawer in the bedside table. Took his loaded S&W .38 Chief's Special. A belly gun. Two-inch barrel. Flicked off the safety.

"You," he said to Boone, "take downstairs and the basement. Put all the lights on and leave them on. I want everything—closets, behind drapes, under couches . . . the works. Be careful of the men coming in from the precinct."

The sergeant nodded and was gone.

Delaney stalked down the hallway to the girls' bedroom, following his gun. He was stiffly erect, making an enormous target. He didn't care. His stomach was sour with fury and sick fear. He tasted copper.

The light was on in their bedroom. He stepped through the doorway, gun first, without crouching. Then, that moment, he would kill, and he knew it.

The room was vacant. The bed was mussed, blankets and sheets scattered. The Chief turned slowly. He went down on one knee to peer under the bed. He swept the drapes aside. He went into the bathroom. Empty.

He came back into the bedroom. There was a sound from the closet. A small, mewing cry. He stood to one side. He gripped the knob, flung the door wide. He shoved his gun forward.

They were down on the floor. Mary and Sylvia. Cowering behind hanging clothes. They were hugging each other, weeping. They looked up at him, eyes wide and blinking.

He groaned, dropped to his knees. He gathered them into his arms, weeping with them. Hugging them. Kissing them. They all, the three of them, wept together, rubbing wet cheeks, all talking at once, sobbing. Holding each other. Patting. Stroking.

He heard the sound of feet pounding up the staircase, along the hall. And Monica's despairing scream, "Edward! Edward!"

"Here!" he yelled, laughing and holding the girls to him. "We're here. It's all right. It's all right."

An hour later, the entire house had been twice searched thoroughly. No evidence of the intruder had been found. The precinct men departed, shaking their heads dolefully at the chutzpah of a B&E artist who selected a home next door to a station house.

Chief Delaney had insisted on making his own individual search, into every corner of every room, the attic, the basement, the back courtyard. As fear waned, cold fury grew. Worst of all was the disgust, knowing your home, your sanctuary, your private and secret place had been invaded, pillaged. It was a stranger putting his hands upon your body, feeling you, prying you out. And, hard to understand, there was shame there. As if, somehow, you had connived in your own despoiling.

The girls, once they had been calmed, petted, and clucked over, told a strange story. They were in bed, asleep, had heard nothing. But then the light in their bedroom had been switched on; a man stood in the doorway. He was wearing a mask, a knitted ski mask. Mary thought he was tall. Sylvia thought he was short. They agreed he was wearing a raincoat and carrying something. An iron bar. But it was flattened on one end.

The intruder ordered them into the closet. He said he would remain in their room, and if they came out of the closet or made any noise, he would kill them. Then he slammed the closet door. They huddled, terrified and weeping, not daring to move.

Monica and Rebecca, outraged, got the girls back into bed. They sat with them in the lighted bedroom. Chief Delaney and Sergeant Boone went back to the kitchen, nerves twanging. It was then almost two A.M. They had their delayed coffee and cake, lifting cups with trembling hands. They discussed the *Why?* For apparently nothing had been stolen. The things in plain view—transistor radio, portable TV set, silver service—had not been disturbed. Nothing touched, nothing taken.

Rebecca Hirsch, white-faced, came into the kitchen and heard the last part of their discussion.

"Maybe he got scared away," she suggested nervously. "He broke in, and put the girls in the closet. Then some cops came out of the station house, or he saw a squad car pull up, or he heard a siren. So he just walked away."

"It could have happened that way," Sergeant Boone said slowly, looking at Delaney. "An addict with an itch and no sense."

"That's probably what it was," the Chief said, with more confidence than he felt. "A hophead trying to make the price of a fix. He just picked the first place he came to. Our bad luck. He springs the door. Then he gets spooked and takes off. Without hurting the girls. Our good luck. Then he moves on to some other place. I'll check tomorrow. Maybe some other house on the block got hit."

None of them believed it.

Rebecca was silent. She sat huddled, shrunk in on herself, tight hands clasped between her knees. Delaney didn't like her color.

"I think a brandy would go good," he said heartily. "A wee bit of the old nasty."

Rebecca lifted her head. "I'll take some up to Monica. And warm milk for the girls."

The Chief rose, went into the study. Then he saw it. The third time he had been in this room in the last hour, and he saw it for the first time. He went back into the kitchen and got the others. Insisted on shepherding them into the study. Pointed toward his empty map board.

"That's what it was," he said. "The three Maitland sketches we found in his studio. The Jake Dukker drawing of the young model. That's what he came for. That's what he got."

"Jesus Christ," Abner Boone said.

14

Chief Delaney sat reading the *Times* in his study on Saturday morning, waiting patiently for nine o'clock, when, he figured, he could decently call Deputy Commissioner Ivar Thorsen at home. But his own phone rang fifteen minutes before the hour.

"Edward X. Delaney here."

"Edward, this is Ivar. I just heard what happened. My God, right next door to a police station! Are you all right? Monica? The girls?"

"Everyone's all right, Ivar. Thank you. No one was hurt."

"Thank God for that. What did they get?"

Delaney told him. There was a silence for a moment. Then . . .

"How do you figure that, Edward?"

"It could have been just for the intrinsic value of Maitland's last drawings. But I doubt that; they took Dukker's sketch, too. I think it was the killer, or someone hired by the killer. Has Boone been reporting to you, Ivar?"

A brief silence again, then: "Yes, he has, Edward. I didn't want to bother—"

"That's all right. At least I don't have to fill you in. The break-in happened during the preview of Maitland's last show at the Geltman Galleries. They were all there—everyone connected with the case. But it was a mob scene, Ivar. Any one of them could have skinned out, cabbed up here, grabbed the drawings, and returned within half an hour. Or hired someone to do it."

"Risky, Edward. Next door to a precinct house?"

"Sure, risky. So it must have been important. I think what we were hoping for happened: that Spanish woman and the young girl saw the killer on Friday. Either near the studio or actually in the house, maybe on the stairs. The killer sees the sketches, remembers the women, and figures maybe they can finger him. So he grabs the drawings, thinking that'll end any chance we have of finding the witnesses. But he doesn't know about the photostats I had made, or Officer Jason, who saw the women on Monday."

"Who knew about the sketches?" Thorsen asked.

"All of them did," Delaney said. "Except Dora and Emily Maitland, and they could have been told about them."

"Talking about Dora and Emily . . ." Thorsen said. "I've got something for you. It *could* be something. It could be nothing. Our contact with J. Barnes Chapin called. Dora's in the hospital. Emily found her this morning lying at the bottom of a cliff. In the back of their house."

"I know the place. A steep slope down to the river."

"Fell or pushed, the deponent knoweth not. Anyway, the lady's got a busted arm, a torn ligament in her knee, and sundry cuts and bruises."

"She had a snootful when I saw her at Geltman's bash."

"Edward, that must have been a very wet party."

"It was."

"So she fell?"

"Not necessarily," Delaney said, remembering the scene Boone had reported witnessing between Saul Geltman, Dora and Emily Maitland. "Maybe someone gave her a gentle nudge."

Thorsen sighed. "I'll ask the Nyack blues to look into it. So where do we go from here?"

"I was going to call you," Delaney said. "Here's what we need . . ."

He spoke steadily for almost five minutes, carefully explaining the reasons for his requests. When he finished, Thorsen agreed to everything.

Jason T. Jason would be detached from patrol duty and assigned to the Maitland investigation. His first task would be to work with a police artist in creating likenesses of the Spanish woman and the young girl he had seen. Reproductions of the drawings would be circulated to all Manhattan precincts with a "Hold for questioning" request.

"And to the newspapers and TV stations?" Thorsen asked. "It would help, Edward. Prove to J. Barnes Chapin that we're working on the case and getting close."

Delaney thought a moment.

"Yes," he said finally. "The danger is that the killer will get to the women before we do. Goodbye witnesses. But I'm willing to risk that for spooking the killer and maybe panicking him into doing something stupid. He hasn't made any mistakes yet, as far as I can see. Let's give him, or her, a chance. What's happening with the Nyack banks?"

"I've been working on it, Edward, I really have. But these things take time; you know that. I hope to have some word on Monday."

"Good enough. If they won't cooperate, we'll have to get a court order, and screw J. Barnes Chapin."

"It's that important?"

"Yes," Chief Delaney said stonily, "it's that important."

"All right, Iron Balls," Thorsen sighed. "It's not the first time I've crawled out on a limb for you."

"Never sawed it off, have I?"

"No," Thorsen laughed. "Not yet you haven't. How's Boone getting along?"

"Fine."

"Staying sober?"

There was the briefest of pauses before Delaney said, "Far as I know."

The moment Thorsen got off the phone, the Chief called Abner Boone and briefed him on what was happening.

"You handle Jason Two," he told the sergeant. "Get him to a police artist first thing Monday morning. Take along that set of photostats I gave you. If the artist can't come up with good likenesses, take the stats to Jake Dukker and have him do another drawing."

"He should be willing to cooperate," Boone said.

"I'd say so," Delaney said dryly. "Even if he was the guy who grabbed the original Maitland sketches. He doesn't know we have photostats. If you go to him, watch his face when you show him the copies; I'll be interested in his reactions."

"Will do," Boone said. "Anything else?"

"Better make sure Jason Two knows how to operate. By Monday morning, I'll have a list of Maitland's hangouts. You can stop by and pick it up on your way downtown. I think that's about all."

"Chief, should Jason Two flash his tin or work undercover?"

"I'll leave that to you," Delaney said. "And to him. Whichever you feel will get the best results. And try to figure how we're going to get the home address of Martha, the Maitlands' housekeeper up in Nyack. If all goes well, we'll be heading that way next Friday."

All that being accomplished, Edward X. Delaney carefully clipped from the morning *New York Times* the news story on the preview of the Victor Maitland Memorial Show. The headline read: SLAIN ARTIST REMEMBERED AT GALA. There was a small photo of Saul Geltman and a large photo of Belle Sarazen. She had been photographed standing next to a Maitland oil. The contrast between her hard, silvery slimness and the lush nude made an eye-catching picture. The caption referred to "Belle Sarazen, well-known patroness of the arts . . ." Chief Delaney grunted.

Monica and the girls were out, shopping at Bloomingdale's for last-minute items before Mary and Sylvia departed for summer camp on Monday. The windows were open wide; a warm breeze billowed through. It promised a shining day in early June, one of those rare marvels: big sky, washed clouds, a smoky sun, air smelling green and eager.

Savoring his quiet solitude, wondering if it was too early for a chilled beer and deciding it was, Edward X. Delaney carried the original file folders of the official Maitland investigation to his desk, sat down, prepared to draw up a list of the bars, restaurants, cabarets, and other public places known to have been frequented by the victim. Then Jason T. Jason could . . .

But, as had happened to him before on other cases, he found himself reading once again every document in the file. Not that he had any great hope of happening upon a revelation he had previously missed; it was just that official paper fascinated him. The most laconic police document was an onion, Chief Delaney decided, a goddamned onion. The layers peeled away, and the thing got smaller and smaller until you were left with a little white kernel you could hold between thumb and forefinger. And what was that? The truth? Don't count on it. Don't take it to the bank.

His eyes skimmed the autopsy report for the third time. And in the "Incidental Notes"—a heading that invited inattention—he read about an enlarged liver; evidence of a broken arm, healed normally; some old lung lesions, healed normally; perhaps a heart murmur in Victor Maitland's youth, healed normally. And, almost as an afterthought, the PM noted casually: "Possible polymyositis."

Delaney blinked, reading that and set the report aside.

He had filled six personal pocket notebooks since he began the Maitland investigation (and he assumed Sergeant Boone had done the same). In his methodical way, Delaney had Scotch-taped a précis of each notebook to the inside of the front cover so he wouldn't have to paw through the lot to find a particular fact or statement he wanted. So it didn't take him long to find the notebook that contained his second interrogation of Alma Maitland, and the name of the Maitlands' family physician.

Dr. Aaron Horowitz, Delaney had written, followed by "dwn blk," which in Delaney shortland meant that the doctor's office was down the block from the Maitland apartment on East 58th Street.

He looked up Dr. Aaron Horowitz's number in the Manhattan telephone directory, using a magnifying glass to read it. He dialed and, as he expected, this being a Saturday, was connected with an answering service. When the operator asked him if he cared to leave a message, Delaney had no qualms at all in telling her it was an emergency, a matter of life-or-death, a police matter, and please have Dr. Horowitz call him at once.

He just had time to settle back, peel the cellophane wrapper from his first cigar of the day, and pierce it, when his phone shrilled. He thought even the ring was angry, but perhaps that was an after-the-fact reaction —after he heard the voice of Dr. Aaron Horowitz.

"What the hell is this?" the doctor screamed, after Delaney identified himself. "What's this 'emergency' shit? This 'life-or-death' shit? What the hell you pulling here?"

"Doctor, doctor," Delaney said, as soothingly as he could. "It *is* an emergency, a matter of life-or-death, a police matter. It concerns a patient of yours. His name is—"

"You got your brains in your ass?" Dr. Horowitz demanded. "The doctor-patient relationship is privileged. You didn't know that? I won't tell you a word about any patient of mine."

Chief Delaney took a deep breath. "This is a *dead* patient," he yelled at Dr. Horowitz. "You got no fucking privilege, no fucking right to deny information to the police about a deceased patient."

"Who says so?" the doctor shouted.

"The courts say so," Delaney thundered, and then launched into a brilliant flight of fantasy. "In case after case—the most recent being Johnson versus the State of New York—the courts have held that a medical practitioner has no right, by statute or by precedent, to withhold vital information regarding a deceased patient from police officers discharging their legal duty."

It was amazing how easily educated men could be conned.

"What patient you talking about?" Dr. Aaron Horowitz said grudgingly. He was no longer yelling.

"Victor Maitland."

"Oh . . . him."

"Yes, him," Delaney said sternly. "All I want is five minutes of your time. Can't you spare five minutes from your golf game?"

"Golf game!" Dr. Horowitz said bitterly. "Very funny. I'm laughing all over. For your information, my dear Chief Delaney, I am at Roosevelt Hospital, and I got a kid who's going. From what? Nobody knows from what. Meningitis maybe. Some golf game!"

"If I come over now," Delaney said, "can you spare me five minutes?"

"Can't it wait till Monday?"

"No," Delaney said, "it can't. Five minutes is all I need. I'll be there in half an hour."

"If you're coming, how can I stop you?" Horowitz said.

Delaney took that for acquiescence. He slammed down the phone, grabbed up reading glasses and notebook, and was on his way.

In addition to a normal dislike of all hospitals, Edward X. Delaney had special reason for aversion to Roosevelt: it was the hospital where his first wife, Barbara, had languished and died. It was, he admitted, irrational to hold a building accountable for that, but it was the way he felt. He knew that if, God forbid, he was ever stricken on the steps of Roosevelt Hospital, his first words to those who ran to aid him would be, "Take me to Mount Sinai, goddammit!"

He finally located Dr. Aaron Horowitz in the surgeons' lounge, a small cheerless room with a television set, a couch and two armchairs covered with orange plastic, a card table and four folding chairs, and not much else.

Dr. Horowitz turned out to be a small man, about a head shorter than Delaney, but as old, if not older. He had a pinched, disillusioned face. He wore steel-rimmed spectacles. There was a horseshoe of white hair around his scalp, but it was mostly bare skin, tan and freckled. He was wearing a white surgical gown. A mask hung loosely around his neck. He didn't offer to shake hands, and Delaney stood well away from him, across the room.

"You got some fucking nerve," the doctor said wrathfully. "What the hell's so important about Victor Maitland it couldn't wait for Monday?"

"You ever treat him for a knife wound?" Delaney asked. "In the arm?"

"No. Is that the emergency, the matter of life-or-death?"

"There's more," Delaney said. "The autopsy report said 'Possible polymyositis.'"

"'Possible,'" Horowitz sneered. "That's good. I like that."

"You knew about it?" Delaney asked.

"Knew about it? Of course I knew about it. The man was my patient, wasn't he?"

"What is it—polymyositis?" Delaney asked. "Like bursitis or arthritis?"

"Oh sure," Horowitz said. "Just like it. Like death is like fainting."

Delaney stared at him a moment, not comprehending.

"Death?" he said. "You mean it's fatal?"

"In Victor Maitland it was terminal. Or would have been if someone hadn't killed him first."

Delaney took a small step backward.

"Terminal?" he repeated hoarsely. "You're sure?"

Dr. Aaron Horowitz threw up his hands in disgust.

"Why don't you have the Board investigate me?" he jeered. "Am I sure? What kind of a shit-ass question is that? You want to see Maitland's file? You want to read the tests? How the corticosteroid therapy failed? You want the opinions of two other—"

"All right, all right," Delaney said hastily. "I believe you. How long did he have it?"

Horowitz thought a moment.

"About five years maybe," he said. "I'd have to check his file to be sure."

"How long would he have to live?"

"He should have been dead a year ago. The man had the constitution of an ox."

"How long would he have lived if he hadn't been killed? Just a guess, Doctor. You won't be asked to testify. I'm not taking any of this down."

"A guess? Maybe another year. Two, three at the most. This isn't an exact science, you know. Everyone's different."

"Did he know it? Did you tell him?"

"That he was dying? Sure, I told him."

"How did he react?"

"He laughed."

Delaney stared at the doctor.

"He laughed?"

"That's right. What's so unusual? Some people cry, some break down, some don't do anything. Everyone's different. Maitland laughed."

"Did he ever tell anyone else he was dying?"

"Now how in hell would I know that?"

"But you never told anyone else? His wife, for instance?"

"I told no one. Just Maitland. Your five minutes are up."

"All right, Doctor," Chief Delaney said. "Thank you for your time." He turned to go, had the corridor door opened when he paused, turned back. "How's that kid you mentioned?" he asked.

"Died about twenty minutes ago."

"I'm sorry," Delaney said.

"Zol dich chapen beim boych!"

"Zol vaksen tsibelis fun pipik!" Edward X. Delaney said to an amazed Dr. Aaron Horowitz.

The Chief went directly to a lobby phone booth and looked up the phone number of Saul Geltman. The art dealer was home and, Delaney could tell, wasn't overjoyed to hear from a cop on a bright, sunshiny June afternoon. But he agreed to see him, asked him to come up. It turned out Geltman lived way over east, in one of the new high-rise apartment buildings overlooking the East River and Brooklyn beyond. Delaney took a cab and finally got to smoke the cigar he had prepared an hour ago. The cab interior was plastered with signs that read: PLEASE DO NOT SMOKE. DRIVER ALLERGIC. But Delaney lighted up anyway, and the driver didn't say anything. Which was wise, considering the Chief's mood.

Delaney had told Sergeant Boone he wanted to see Saul Geltman's apartment, believing there was no better way to judge a man's character than to get a look at his home. It was a secret place where a man, if he wished, could take off the mask he presented to the world. It revealed his tastes, idiosyncrasies, needs and wants, strengths and weaknesses. If a man had a lot of books, that told you something about him. The titles of the books he owned told you more. And *no* books told you even more.

But the presence or absence of a private library was an obvious clue to a man's personality. Chief Delaney sincerely believed you could better judge by the pictures on his walls, the carpets on the floor, ashtrays on the desk. And if all these things had been selected by his wife or an interior decorator—well, that too revealed something, didn't it?

But more than rugs, paintings, ashtrays, or books, Delaney was interested in the ambience of a man's home. Was it cold and contrived, or warm and cheery? Was it as cluttered as the man's own mind or as serene as his soul? The Chief never ceased marveling at how many criminals lived in hotels, furnished rooms, and motels, their rootless lives mirrored by their transient surroundings. And like most cops, Delaney had seen old cons who lived in square chambers with a cot, dresser, chair. Not because they couldn't afford better, but because they were attempting to reproduce the institutional life for which they subconsciously yearned and to which they inevitably returned.

The home of art dealer Saul Geltman was on the east side of the seventeenth floor of the high-rise apartment house. The building itself was constructed of glazed brick tinted a light green, with horizontal bands of picture windows. The lobby was small, spare, tiled, with a single piece of abstract stainless-steel sculpture as the sole decoration.

The living room of Geltman's apartment, Delaney estimated, had to be forty by twenty. It was all windows on the east side, with glass doors at each end opening onto a terrace as long as the room itself, but only half as deep. There were two bedrooms, two bathrooms, a combined kitchen and dining area separated by a serving counter with a butcher's-block top. All the rooms were well proportioned, airy, smiling. The ceilings were higher than Delaney had expected; the floors were parquet.

But it was the manner in which this joyous apartment had been furnished that delighted the Chief. There was an eclectic selection of antiques, leaning heavily to light-wood French provincial. A plenitude of gleaming copper, brass, and pewter ornaments. A zinc-covered dining table set on a cast-iron base. Polished carved oak caryatids supporting a black marble sideboard. Worn Persian and Turkish rugs on the parquetry. Chair fabrics and drapes in a pleasantly clashing rainbow of plaids, candy stripes, and rich, nubbly wools.

And all spotless, glittering, almost overwhelming in its comfortable perfection. It stopped just short of being a department-store model apartment. Delaney did not miss the "careless elegance" of tossed art magazines on the pitted teak cocktail table, the carefully arranged informality of the bookcase, with a few art books tilted, a few lying on their sides, but the entire display ordered in such a manner that it pleased the eye, and the Chief wondered if there could be any art without artifice.

"Beautiful," he said to Saul Geltman, who had shown him through with great enthusiasm, giving the age (and frequently the cost) of each antique, pointing out amusing bric-a-brac, calling Delaney's attention to a seventeenth-century desk reputed to have six secret drawers—although Geltman had found only five—and a set of eighteenth-century carved walnut bookends which, joined together, proved to be an old man buggering a goat.

"Not bad for a poor kid from Essex Street, huh?" Geltman laughed. "Now all I got to do is pay for it!"

"You decorated the place yourself?" Delaney asked.

"Every stick I personally selected," the little art dealer said proudly. "Every fabric, every rug, ashtrays—the lot. I'm still working on it. I see something I got to have, I buy it, bring it up, get rid of something. Otherwise this place would be a warehouse."

"Well, you've done wonders," the Chief told him. "There isn't a single thing here I wouldn't like to have in my home."

"Really?" Geltman said, glowing. "You really mean that?"

"Absolutely," Delaney said, wondering at the other man's need for reassurance. "Excellent taste."

"Taste!" Geltman cried, looking about with shining eyes. "Yes! Well, I couldn't play the fiddle, and I can't paint, so I suppose whatever creative talent I have came out here." He looked down, let his fingertips drift softly across the top of a charming pine commode, the drawers and doors fitted with hammered brass hardware. "I love this piece," Geltman murmured. "Love it. Sounds silly, I know, but—" He stopped suddenly, straightened up, smiled at Delaney. "Well," he said briskly, rubbing his palms together, "what can I get you to drink? Wine? Whiskey? What?"

"Do you have any beer?" the Chief asked.

"Beer. Of course I have beer. Heineken. How's that?"

"Just fine, thank you."

"Sit anywhere. I'll be right back."

Delaney selected a high-backed wing chair at the rear of the room, facing the expanse of glass. He settled himself and, for the first time, saw there were two men on the terrace, seated in chairs of white wire at a white cast-iron table. The Chief was startled. He had not seen them before, nor had Geltman mentioned that he had guests.

The two men, youths actually, were almost identically clad in short-sleeved knitted white shirts, trousers of white duck, white sneakers. They lounged indolently in their chairs, not facing each other but turned so they could watch the river traffic below.

There was a bottle of rosé wine on the white table, sparkling in the sunlight. As Delaney watched, both youths raised crystal glasses slowly to their lips and sipped. Viewed through sheer ecru curtains, the scene had the feel of an Edwardian garden party, peaceful and haunting, frozen in an old sepia photograph, faded, emulsion cracking, corners bent or missing, but the moment in time and place caught like a remembered dream: languid youth, sunshine over all, a breeze that would kiss forever and a day that would never die.

"I'm sorry," he said when Geltman came back, "I didn't know you had company."

"Oh, just two local boys," Geltman said lightly. "Stopped by to raid my wine cellar."

He had brought the opened bottle of beer on a silver salver, along with a glass of a tulip design. The glass had been chilled; frost coated the sides.

"You do it with an electric gadget," Geltman laughed. "Instant frosting. Silly, but it looks nice."

"Tastes better too," Delaney said, pouring his beer. "Nothing for you?"

"Not at the moment. Well, what can I do for you, Chief? More questions?"

The little man sat on the arm of a club chair, facing Delaney at an angle. Geltman's back was to the windows, his face in shadow. He was wearing bags of light grey flannel, a turtleneck sweater of white wool. His cordovan moccasins gleamed wickedly. The bracelet of heavy gold links was much in evidence, catching the light, but Delaney saw none of the nervous vigor the dealer had displayed in his gallery. No slumping, straightening, twisting, gesturing. No drumming of fingers or smoothing the thin, brown-grey hair across his skull. Saul Geltman seemed composed, at peace. Because, Delaney supposed, he was in his own home.

"More questions, yes," the Chief said. "But first I'd like to thank you for having us to your party. We enjoyed it."

"I'm glad you did." Geltman grinned. "See the *Times* story this morning? Wonderful! Of course Belle and Jake Dukker misbehaved, but an art show isn't counted a success without at least one fight. Did you get to see the paintings? In that mob?"

"Not as much as I wanted to. I'd like to come back."

"Of course. Any time. They'll be there for a month, at least. We're charging admission. For a charity. But ask for me at the door."

Delaney waved the suggestion away.

"Are the paintings selling?" he asked.

"Marvelously," Geltman nodded. "Most of them are sold. Only a few left, and they'll go soon enough."

Delaney looked around the elegant room.

"You don't have any Maitlands?" he observed, half-question, half-statement.

"Can't afford him," the dealer laughed. "Besides, it's bad business to have artists you represent in your own home. Buyers suspect you'd save the best for yourself. Which is true, of course."

Delaney held his frosted glass to the light, admiring the dark, glowing amber of the beer. He took a deep, satisfying swallow. Then he held the stemmed glass in both hands, tinked the edge of the glass gently against his teeth.

"You knew he was dying?" he asked.

Then he heard, for the first time, soft laughter from the terrace. The two youths, wine glasses in hand, were standing at the railing, looking down at something on the East River.

When he looked back, he saw Geltman had slid from his perch on the chair arm. Now he was in the chair, sitting sideways, his legs hooked over the opposite arm.

"Yes," he told Delaney, "I knew."

"You didn't tell us," the Chief said flatly.

"Well . . ." Geltman sighed, "it's not the kind of thing you like to talk about. Also, I couldn't see how it could possibly help you find the guy who did it. I mean, how could it help?"

Delaney took another sip of beer. From now on, he decided, he would frost his glasses.

"It might help," he said. "It just might. I'm not saying it would help explain other people's actions, but it might help explain Maitland's."

Geltman stared at him a moment, then shook his head. "I'm afraid I don't understand."

"The doctor says that when he told Maitland he had a fatal illness, Maitland laughed. I believe that. It's in character with what we've learned about the man. But I don't care how hard he was, how cynical, what a lush. Hearing a thing like that would change his life. The life he had left. It *had* to. He'd do things he wouldn't otherwise do. Make plans maybe. Or try to jam as much into his remaining days as he could. *Something*. It would result in something. The man was human. Just ask yourself how you'd react if you got heavy news like that. Wouldn't it affect the way you'd live out your days?"

"I suppose so," Geltman said in a low voice. "But I knew about it, and I didn't see any change in him. He was still the same crude, mean son of a bitch he had always been."

"When did you learn about the illness?"

"About five years ago, I think it was. Yes, about then."

"He told you himself?"

"Yes."

"Did he tell anyone else, to your knowledge? His wife, for instance? His son?"

"No," Geltman said. "He told me I was the only one he was telling. He swore me to secrecy. Said if I told anyone, and he learned about it, he'd cut my balls off. And he'd have done it, too."

"Did you tell anyone?" Delaney asked.

"Jesus, no!"

"His mother? His sister? Anyone?"

"I swear I didn't, Chief. It's just not the sort of thing you go around blabbing about."

"No," Delaney said, "I suppose not. You say you saw no change in his conduct? His personality?"

"That's right. No change."

"He didn't, to your knowledge, make any special plans? Men sentenced to death usually tidy up, put their affairs in order."

"He didn't do anything special. Not to my knowledge."

"Well," Delaney sighed, finishing his beer, "he certainly didn't seem to make any effort to leave his wife and son well provided for. They inherit, but not much."

"They'll do all right," Geltman said shortly. "With the sale of the last paintings. Even after taxes, they'll come out with half a million. At least. I'm not shedding any tears for them. Another beer, Chief?"

"No, thank you. That just hit the spot."

He looked out onto the terrace again. The languid youths were draped again in their white wire chairs, lounging comfortably. As Delaney watched, one of them, a golden-haired boy, tilted his head back and, holding the wine glass high above him, let the last few drops of wine spill into his mouth and onto his face. The other youth laughed.

"It was some muscle disorder," Delaney said. "As I understand it."

"Yes," Geltman said.

"It didn't affect his painting? For five years?"

"Not noticeably," the art dealer said.

"What does that mean?"

"The buyers didn't notice," Geltman said. "The critics didn't. But Maitland did. And I did."

"How? How did it affect his painting?"

"He said there was a—well, not pain, but a stiffness. That's how he described it—a stiffness. In his hands, arms, shoulders. So he took something that seemed to help."

"Poppers? Snappers?"

"Yes."

"From Belle Sarazen?"

"I don't know where he got them."

"But they helped?"

"That's what Vic told me. He said they loosened him up. You can see it in his last paintings. The stuff he did in, oh, the last year or two. They were looser, the line not as sharp, the colors harsher, brighter. It's a subtle thing. I think only Vic and I could see it. No one else saw any change. They were still the same old Maitlands. Still as wonderful, still as evocative, as stirring."

"Yes," Edward X. Delaney said. "Stirring."

He heaved himself to his feet, cleared his throat.

"I thank you, Mr. Geltman," he said. "For seeing me. The hospitality."

"My pleasure," the little man said. He thrust himself up from the chair, slid over the arm to land agilely on the balls of his feet. "Hope it helped. Getting anywhere, are you?"

"Oh yes," Chief Delaney said. "Definitely."

"Good," Geltman said. "Glad to hear it."

They moved to the entrance hall. Delaney turned back to look around that fabulous room one more time.

"A kind of dream," he said.

"Yes," Saul Geltman said wonderingly, looking at Delaney. "That's exactly what it is—a kind of dream."

Then the Chief glanced out to the terrace. The two youths were standing again, at the railing. Their long, fine hair whipped in the breeze like flame. One had his arm around the other's waist.

Again, Delaney had the impression of a remembered photograph. White-clad youths against a china-blue sky. A tomorrow that would never come. No future at all. But an endless now, caught and held.

"Beautiful, isn't it?" Saul Geltman said softly.

Edward X. Delaney turned to him, smiling faintly. He quoted: "'Golden lads and girls all must, as chimney-sweepers, come to dust.'"

He left then, as Saul Geltman was trying to compose some kind of response, his face slack and struggling.

15

By Wednesday of the following week, copies of a police artist's sketches of the Spanish woman and the young model had gone out to all Manhattan precincts. They had also been distributed to newspapers and TV stations. The *Daily News* had given them a nice display on page 4, under a two-column head: NEW LEAD IN MAITLAND SLAYING. And the drawings had been shown on the evening news programs of channels 2 and 7, with a phone number that any citizen with information could call.

In addition, Jason T. Jason had been taken off patrol and assigned full-time to the Maitland investigation. He was enthusiastic about his new job and, according to Sergeant Boone, was spending about eighteen hours a day checking out the list of Maitland's known hangouts and just wandering the streets of the Lower East Side, showing pocket-size reproductions of the police sketches to pushcart vendors, bartenders, beauty-parlor operators, shop owners, street peddlers, pimps, prosties, hustlers, bums—anyone who might have seen one or both of the women.

Also during this week, Abner Boone ran another time check and proved to his satisfaction, and that of Chief Delaney, that it would have been no problem for Ted Maitland to get from Cooper Union to the Mott Street studio, zap his father, and return to Cooper Union in time for his two o'clock lecture.

Boone was also able to determine the last name of Martha, the housekeeper of Dora and Emily Maitland up in Nyack. Her last name was Beasely. The sergeant discovered this by calling the Maitland home. The first time he called, Emily Maitland answered and Boone hung up. The second time, a harsh, twangy voice said, "Maitland residence."

Boone said, "I'm trying to locate Martha Jones. Is this Martha?"

"Well, it's Martha," the housekeeper said, "but my name ain't Jones; it's Beasely."

"Sorry to bother you," Abner Boone said, and hung up. He then checked the Nyack telephone directory and got Martha Beasely's home address.

On Thursday, Deputy Commissioner Thorsen phoned Delaney and told him that Mrs. Dora Maitland's Nyack bank had agreed to cooperate; the Chief could examine her account. But it was all on the qt, and Delaney was to speak only to an assistant vice-president who would be present during his examination to make certain Delaney did not alter or remove the records. The Chief readily agreed to that.

So, all in all, it was a busy, productive week—lots of phone calls, meetings, writing of reports and new time charts—and as they drove up to Nyack on Friday morning, Chief Delaney and Sergeant Boone sourly agreed they were not one step closer to finding the killer of Victor Maitland. Though neither would admit discouragement, they weren't exactly bubbling over with optimism either.

"Still," Delaney said, "you never know when a break's going to come, or from what direction. I had a partner once in the One-eight Precinct. He had worked the homicide of a young woman raped and strangled in her apartment. All the leads petered out. They chewed on it for weeks and months, and then the file got pushed to the back of the tub. You know how it is: there's so much new stuff coming along, you just can't give any time to the old. So more than a year later, the NYPD gets a letter from a woman out in Ohio, Michigan, Indiana—some place like that. She had signed up for the Peace Corps, got sent to Africa, caught some kind of a fever, and was sent home. Now this Peace Corps girl had her mail forwarded to her in Africa—right? And she was a good girlfriend of this girl who got knocked off in New York. And while she's in Africa, a letter is forwarded to her from this girl who got zonked. This letter is all little jokes about a new guy she's met, he's got a red beard, his name is David and how nice he is, and all that, and she's got to close this letter and mail it fast because this David is coming over for dinner. This letter, which the Peace Corps woman had saved and sent to the New York cops, was dated the day the girl got snuffed. The Peace Corps woman didn't know her friend had been killed till she got back to this country. So the dicks go to the old file and find a married guy named David—he's got a red beard, too—who worked in the dead girl's office. They broke him, and that was that. But that's how a break came along that no one counted on."

"We should be so lucky," Boone said mournfully.

"We will be," Edward X. Delaney said confidently. "Our cause is just."

And Sergeant Boone didn't know if he was kidding or not; one of these days he was going to ask the Chief for a blueprint of his sense of humor.

On the drive up, they talked a lot about Victor Maitland's fatal illness. The sergeant couldn't get over it.

"Everyone talks about what a stud he was and how he was pronging everything in sight," Boone said. "And now we find he was dying, and knew it. Chief, you think that's why he was so busy in the sack? Trying to cram in as much as he could before he passed?"

"No," Delaney said, "I don't think so. His reputation as a stallion goes way back. Remember what Saul Geltman said about him in Greenwich Village twenty years ago? He was getting more than his share even then. No, I don't think getting the death sentence from Doc Horowitz turned him on. But I'll bet my bottom dollar that it set him off some other way. Sergeant, it's impossible to hear news like that and not have it affect your life style *some* way."

"But Geltman told you no," Boone reminded him. "Said Maitland didn't change at all."

"Geltman," Delaney said broodingly. "I like that little guy. I really do. But there's something about him . . ." The Chief held his open hand a few inches from his temple, palm cupped, fingers spread. He turned the whole hand a short way, as if he were turning a big dial. "Something just a little off up there. Something too much."

"The young boys on the balcony?"

"No. Well . . . that's part of it maybe. But his apartment. The beautiful things he owns. The *things!* He loves them. You should have seen him touch them. Did everything but kiss the tables. I've never seen such a passion for things. They were magnificent, I admit it. But still, they were just things. When he's as old as I am, he'll realize you spend the first half of your life accumulating things, and the second half getting rid of them. I think if I had broken his crystal tulip glass, he'd have cried."

"Things never turned me on," the sergeant said.

"No?" Delaney said. "I never would have guessed it from the luxury of your apartment."

Boone grinned, but resolved to visit his local Woolworth's and buy some decent glasses.

The sergeant dropped Delaney off in front of the bank. The Chief told him to take his time finding and talking to Martha Beasely. When he was finished, he could pick Delaney up at the bank or, if he wasn't there, to try the tavern across the street. The bar had a big sign in the window reading: YES, WE HAVE COORS!

The assistant vice-president of the bank turned out to be young, wistful, with a blonde mustache that didn't quite make it. He ensconced Delaney in one of the small, private rooms in the safe-deposit vault. On the desk was a stack of folded computer printouts, two small reels of microfilm in labeled boxes, and a microfilm-reading device.

"Know how to work this thing?" he asked the Chief.

"Sure," Delaney said. "Start. Stop. Advance. Rewind. I can handle it."

"Right," the banker said. "Well . . . uh . . ."

Then he asked a few eager questions about police work. ("Must be a fascinating life. Tell me, do you . . . ?") But when he realized this New York City cop was going to answer only in grunts, or not at all, he finally gave up, disregarded the agreement, and said, "Just tell the man outside when you're finished." Then he departed, leaving behind the faint scent of Canoe.

Chief Delaney closed the door and locked it. He put on his reading glasses, took off his jacket, and settled down in a tubular steel chair with a meagerly padded seat cushion. He laid out notebook and pen. He started on the stack of computer printouts, and had worked barely fifteen minutes when he knew he wasn't going to need notebook or pen. Zilch.

The printout was a record of Mrs. Dora Maitland's checking and savings accounts for the previous six months. The microfilm carried similar information for the past seven years. When Chief Delaney realized he was going to find no startling revelations, he began going faster and faster, flipping microfilm through the electric viewer almost as fast as he could press the Advance button. He finished everything in a little more than an hour.

Dora Maitland had a savings account that began with a total of slightly more than six thousand dollars and was gradually reduced by small withdrawals (usually fifty or a hundred dollars) to a current total of slightly less than four thousand dollars. The withdrawals showed no periodic pattern. During the period covered by the records, no deposits other than accumulated interest had been made.

The records of the checking account did show patterns but they seemed entirely innocent to Delaney. For instance, there were quarterly deposits of precisely the same sum: $117.50. That was probably a stock dividend. And regular semi-annual deposits of $375 were probably municipal-bond coupons.

There were weekly checks written in the amount of $125, which, the Chief guessed, could be Martha Beasely's salary. And there were odd-cents sums for electricity, telephone and, he assumed, living expenses.

There was a check written annually for more than two thousand dollars, and Delaney thought that was the property tax. He could find no monthly schedule of disbursements large enough to be mortgage payments, so he assumed the Maitland home was free and clear.

When he had finished, he sat there a few moments, shoulders drooping, staring balefully at the unmarked page of his notebook. What he had been hoping for, of course, were large deposits or withdrawals. A single big withdrawal, for instance, might indicate payment to a hired killer. Hefty checks drawn at regular intervals sometimes signaled payments to a blackmailer. But what Delaney was particularly looking for was a record of big deposits. It would then be a reasonable assumption that Victor Maitland, a very successful artist, was contributing handsomely to the support of his mother and sister, with whom he was on friendly terms. But apparently Dora and Emily had been telling the truth: Victor gave them nothing. At least the bank accounts revealed nothing.

From all indications, Dora and Emily Maitland were getting by—but just. They owned their home and grounds, but their total net worth—their cash worth—rarely ran over five thousand dollars, according to these records. It just didn't make sense when the loving son was selling paintings at 100 G's, and Edward X. Delaney didn't believe it for a minute. Something smelled—and it wasn't Canoe.

The Chief told the vault attendant he was leaving, and tramped across the sun-baked street to the tavern. It was a hot, steamy afternoon, and he carried his jacket and straw skimmer. The bar was just as desolate as Delaney's mood—a big, empty barn of a place, reeking of stale beer and a creosote disinfectant, with sawdust on the floor and a piebald cat yawning around. There were two silent customers at the bar, slumped over their beers, and a bartender just as silent. He was sucking on a toothpick, staring out the flyblown window and waiting patiently for the end of the world.

The Chief ordered a Budweiser. He paid for it and took bottle and glass to a back booth. The place was dim enough, and cool, and quiet. He drank the beer slowly, taking little sips, sitting stolidly and avoiding unnecessary movement.

What angered him, he knew, was that he felt he was being tricked and made a fool of. Someone of intellect was toying with him. Whichever way he turned, that path had been anticipated and blocked. All his training, experience, all his crafts and instincts brought to nothing by a guy who had probably killed *for the first time!* That's what hurt most: a beginner, a goddamned amateur, and he had Edward X. Delaney snookered. In such a smoldering mood, he could understand why cops used their fists and saps. The frustration curdled the stomach and rubbed nerve ends raw.

He was on his second beer when Abner Boone came lounging in. He took off his sunglasses, glanced around, spotted Delaney and nodded. He stopped at the bar for a Coke, gulped it down, ordered another. He brought that one to the Chief's booth and slid in opposite him.

"Jesus," he said, "feels like ninety. And high humidity. Been waiting long?"

"Not so long," Delaney said. "I was thinking about food, but I'm not really hungry. You?"

"I can skip," the sergeant said. "Right now I just want to cool off. My shirt's sticking."

"Take off your jacket," Delaney suggested.

"Ahh, I'm carrying," Boone said. "Someone will spot the heat and call the locals. I'll be all right." He dug his notebook from his inside pocket. "I hope you did better than I did, Chief."

"I did, shit!" Delaney said, so vehemently that Boone looked up in surprise.

Delaney told the sergeant what he had discovered—or what he had not discovered.

"All negative," he said. "The only thing it proves, or apparently proves, is that Maitland was making no contributions to his mother and sister. And they already told us that."

"Could Dora have an account in another bank? Or Emily? Or maybe safe-deposit boxes loaded with cash?"

Delaney shook his head. "Thorsen checked all that out first thing. This was the only bank. How did you make out with Martha Beasely?"

"More questions than answers," Boone said, flipping through his notebook. "That's what snows me about this thing: every time we do something we get more problems. For instance, Martha Beasely claims she's been working for the Maitlands for almost four years. And in all that time she never even saw Victor Maitland or Saul Geltman. Knew they existed and visited occasionally because Dora and Emily talked about them. But Martha Beasely never laid eyes on them. Now how do you figure that?"

"Easy," Delaney said, straightening up, leaning forward, interested now. "Maitland and Geltman made sure they only came up on Martha's day off, or maybe at night, when she wasn't there."

"But *why?*"

"That's something else again. I don't know that, sergeant. But I'll bet they timed their visits so the housekeeper wouldn't see them. What else?"

"A lot of nothing. Dora hits the bottle, just like we figured. She takes a lot of naps, but some afternoons she can't stand up. Emily never goes out by herself as far as the Beasely woman knows. No dates. No boyfriends coming around. No phone calls except from old family friends."

"Well . . ." Delaney sighed, "that's that."

"No, sir," Sergeant Boone said. "Not quite. Something else. Another question. This Beasely woman was very tight at first. Suspicious. Wouldn't open up. But then I told her it had to do with Victor Maitland's tax troubles, that he claimed he was supporting his mother and sister, and we didn't think he did. Then she opened up and started complaining about how much money she made at the Maitlands—or how little. Says she makes a bill and a quarter for five and a half days. Does the cleaning and laundry, and usually cooks lunch for all of them. She says they've got less money than she has, so Victor couldn't have been supporting them. Then I said that was a big house with lots of grounds to take care of—you know, laying it on thick with the good-old-boy accent—and she said Emily and Dora had to take care of the grounds themselves because they can't afford a man to come in once a month to do it. Anyway, just talking away—this Martha Beasely is a widow and a gabber when she gets going—she said Emily is pretty good at mowing that big lawn, cutting down dead branches, odd repair jobs around the house, and stuff like that. I said something about that was a fair piece of lawn to keep mowed, and she said about two years ago they bought a second-hand power mower, which Emily learned how to use. And she mentioned that Emily keeps the power mower and a lot of other garden stuff, rakes and tools and junk, in that old barn."

"Oh-ho," Delaney said.

"Right," Boone nodded. "My ears perked up, I asked her how come? I said they had told us the doors of that barn had been nailed shut years ago because their old man had hanged himself in there, and I had *seen* them nailed shut. This Beasely woman said yes, the wide front doors were nailed shut and even locked with a rusty old padlock. But there was another door, a narrow back door, and inside was like a little shed where they kept the power mower and garden tools. Sorry I missed that other door, Chief."

"That's all right," Delaney said. "Maybe Emily wanted you to miss it."

"Well, why the hell would they make a big sentimental thing about nailing shut the doors of a place where the old man did the Dutch, and then have a back door that's open? Doesn't make any sense, does it, sir?"

"Nooo," the Chief said slowly. "Not much. Is that back door unlocked?"

"Beasely says yes. Says she's been in there once or twice. Nothing in there but the power mower, rakes and so forth, a can of gasoline, some old buckets, a tarp, and so forth. Old, rusty shit like that. But still . . ."

"Yes . . . still," Delaney nodded. "I wouldn't give it a second thought except that they made sure we knew about the nailed doors. They didn't even have to mention it. Who cares? Not us, because it didn't have anything to do with our investigation. Did it?" He thought a few moments, then finished his beer. "You're sure you're not hungry?" he asked Boone.

"I can wait till we get back to the city."

"Where are you parked?"

"Right around the corner."

"Well, let's do this . . . I'll drive, and we'll go out to the Maitland place. I'll drop you off just before we get to their driveway. You stay in those trees for a few minutes. I'll drive up to the house. I want to see Dora and Emily anyway, to ask them if they knew Victor was dying from polymyositis. Geltman said they didn't know. But maybe he was lying, or maybe he didn't know they knew. Anyway, I'll keep the two of them busy inside the house for, oh say fifteen minutes. That long enough for you?"

"Sure," Abner Boone said. "I can make it. I'll keep the barn between me and house, so in case they glance out the windows or from the porch they won't spot me. You'll pick me up on the road?"

"Right," Delaney said. "The same place I drop you. The housekeeper didn't say how big that storage place was, did she?"

"No. She just called it a tool shed. Like it was, at most, maybe ten feet by ten feet. Probably smaller."

Delaney thought a moment, eyes squinched, trying to remember.

"That barn's got to be at least fifty by thirty," he said.

"At least," Boone nodded.

"So there's a lot of space inside there left over," Delaney said. "Now I'm curious."

"Me, too," Sergeant Boone said.

On their way out to the Maitland place, Delaney driving, Boone said, "You don't happen to have a set of lock picks, do you, sir?"

"I own a set, but I haven't got them with me," the Chief said.

"I didn't bring mine either," the sergeant said. "A fine couple of dicks we are. Well, I've got a screwdriver, pliers, and a short jimmy in the trunk. I'll have to make do."

Delaney pulled off the road just before they got to the turnoff to the Maitland place. Trees screened them from the house. Abner Boone got out, and borrowed the keys long enough to open the trunk and take out his tools. Then the two cops compared watches.

"Let's make it about fifteen to twenty minutes," Delaney said. "About that. But take all the time you need; I'll wait for you."

"I should be able to do it in that," Boone agreed. "If I'm not out in half an hour tops, send in the Marines."

Delaney nodded, started up the car, drove slowly ahead. He glanced in the rearview mirror. The sergeant had disappeared. The Chief turned into the Maitland driveway.

He felt sure they were home—the big, black Mercedes was parked in the driveway—but he banged that tarnished brass knocker again with no result. He was beginning to wonder if they had strolled away somewhere when the door was opened a crack, a bright eye surveyed him, then the door was opened wide.

"My land!" Emily Maitland said. "It's Chief Delaney. Now this *is* a pleasant surprise!"

She stood in the open doorway, bare feet spread and firmly planted on the warm floor boards. She was wearing a caftan of tissue-thin Indian cotton. He was aware that she was naked beneath the semi-transparent cloth. Glimpsed dark shadows of oval aureoles and triangular pubic hair. But most of all, he saw the obese, randy body, thighs bursting, quivering melon breasts, all of her seemingly exploding outward, straining the seams of the flimsy garment she wore. And balanced on everything, the puffy throat, chin rolls, a bland, innocent face scarred by shrewd, glittering eyes.

"Miss Maitland," Delaney said, smiling genially, "it's good to see you again. Forgive me for not calling you first, but something important came up, and I decided to drive up at once in hopes of catching you at home."

"Of course," she said vaguely, looking over his shoulder. "And where is Sergeant Boone?"

"Oh, he's taking a day off," the Chief said. "Even cops need a rest now and then. May I come in?"

"Land!" she said. "Here we are tattling on the stoop! Of course, you come right in, Chief Delaney. Mama's a bit indisposed today, but I'm sure she'll be happy to see you. Mama, look who's here!"

She led him into a dim, musty parlor, where Dora Maitland reclined on a Victorian loveseat, the upholstery a faded maroon velvet, worn and shiny. Delaney could hardly make her out in the gloom: just another rococo whatnot and knickknack, fitting in perfectly with the antimacassars, belljars and dried flowers, china figurines, feather fronds and ornate paperweights, mahogany paneling and stained wallpaper, dust and murk—an archeological dig, an age lost, a culture gone.

She was wearing a peignoir of satin, the weave showing its age. One arm, in a soiled plaster cast, was cradled in a canvas sling. A knee was heavily bandaged, the surrounding flesh puffed and discolored. The pulpy body lay flaccid, spread. But resting on a suede pillow was that incredible cigar-box head: the flood of glossy black ringlets, skin of dusty ivory, flashing eyes and carmined lips half-pursed in a promised kiss.

"How nice," she murmured drowsily, holding out a limp hand. "How nice."

Chief Delaney touched those soft, hot fingers, then, without waiting for an invitation, sat in a sprung armchair from which he could see, dimly, Dora on the couch and Emily standing nearby. The daughter had picked up a sphere of glass in which a simulated snowfall floated. She bounced it back and forth in her plump hands, almost caressing the hard globe, feeling it, stroking it, her eyes on Delaney.

"Forgive me this intrusion," he said solemnly, his own voice sounding to him like a recording. "Sorry about your accident, Mrs. Maitland. At least that's what the Nyack cops called it—an accident. But I'm not here to talk about that. Did you—either of you or both of you—know your son and brother was dying of a fatal illness?"

There were a few seconds of breathy silence. Then:

"My land!" said Emily Maitland.

"What?" said Dora Maitland.

"Whatever do you mean, Chief Delaney?" Emily asked. "A fatal illness?"

"Oh yes," he nodded. "Polymyositis. A muscle disorder. I have spoken to his doctor. I don't like being the one to tell you this, but Victor Maitland was dying. Should have been dead a few years ago. In any event, he hadn't long to live. A year or two at the most."

He was staring at Dora Maitland and saw, through the dusk, her face gradually tighten, slowly congeal. Tears welled and ran from her eyes, leaving smudged tracks down her cheeks.

"Victor," she choked. "My baby."

"I'm sorry," Delaney said humbly. "But it's true. Did either of you know?"

They shook their heads, two porcelain dolls, the round heads wagging back and forth.

"He never told you? Never mentioned it?"

Again the wagging.

"Oh Mama," Emily said. She set aside the crystal paperweight, put her hands lightly on her mother's shoulders. "Isn't that just awful? Land, I don't know what to say. Do you, Mama?"

"Emily, my medicine," Dora Maitland said with great dignity. "Sir, would you care for . . . ?"

"Oh no," Delaney said hastily. "Nothing for me. Thank you."

He was watching Dora and didn't see where the glass came from, the full glass that appeared like magic in Emily's hand. Probably on the floor, tucked under the loveseat when I came in, Delaney thought. He watched Emily hand the drink to Dora, pressing her mother's fingers around the glass. A colorless liquid. Gin or vodka. No ice. She could be sipping water.

"You think it has something to do with my son's murder?" Dora Maitland asked, the voice low-pitched, husky, not quite raspy but as furred as the worn velvet couch.

"It might," Chief Delaney said, wanting to stretch this charade to fifteen to twenty minutes. "It might not. Victor's wife never mentioned his illness?"

"We saw her so seldom," Emily said. "She never said a word, no."

"And Saul Geltman? Never told you about it?"

"Saul? Saul knew about it?"

"Yes, he knew."

"No, Saul didn't tell us about it."

Delaney nodded. He looked around the cluttered room. "I'm surprised you don't have any of your son's paintings, Mrs. Maitland. He never gave you any?"

"He gave us two," Emily Maitland said. "Portraits. Of Mama and me. They're hanging in our bedrooms." She giggled. "The one of me's a nude," she said.

"Ah," Delaney said. "And when did he do those?"

"My land, it must have been years ago," Emily said. "Twenty years ago. At least. He was just starting."

"To paint?" Delaney asked.

"To sell," Emily said. "Vic drew things and painted since he was seven years old. But he just started to sell twenty years ago."

"Well," Delaney said, "they're worth a lot more now."

"I should think so," Dora Maitland nodded, and couldn't stop nodding. "A lot more now."

Delaney glanced at his watch, rose to his feet.

"Thank you, ladies. Sorry to have troubled you."

"Land," Emily Maitland said. "No trouble at all."

"Maybe it's all for the best," Dora Maitland muttered.

The Chief didn't know what she meant, and didn't ask. Emily saw him to the door.

"Say hello to Sergeant Boone for me." She smiled mischievously.

"I'll surely do that, Miss Maitland," Chief Delaney said seriously.

He walked down the steps, heard the door close behind him. He stood at Boone's car while he slowly lighted a cigar. Then he took off his jacket, got in, started up. The car was an oven: no air stirring at all. He drove out to the main road, stopping across from the point where he had dropped Boone. But there was no sign of the sergeant. Delaney cut the engine, puffed calmly, waited.

About five minutes later, Abner Boone appeared among the trees on the other side of the road. He lifted a hand to Delaney, then came slouching across the pavement. He opened the back door, tossed the tools onto the floor. He stripped off his jacket. His shirt was soaked through. Sweat sheened on his face and glistened in the gingery hair on the backs of his hands.

"Like a sauna in there," he said to Delaney. "I'm demolished."

He got in and Delaney started up. Boone found a rag in the glove compartment, and tried to wipe some of the grime from his palms.

"They knew about Maitland's illness," the Chief said. "Claimed they didn't, but they were lying. How did you do?"

"About like Martha Beasely described it," the sergeant said. "There's a path from the gravel driveway to this back door. The path's been used a lot: grass beaten down, practically bare earth. The door itself is unlocked. Made of vertical planks with an inside Z-shaped frame. Looks as old as the barn itself. Original issue. Inside is this shed, like Martha Beasely said. About six by four. I paced it off. Goes up to the eaves. A lot of junk in there. The power mower, garden tools, a five-gallon can of gas, a box of hand tools, most of them rusty. Pieces of pipe, an old, cracked sink. Stuff like that. Mostly junk."

"Earth floor?"

"No, it's planked. But earth right below. No cellar or foundation. The floor's just a few inches above the ground. I got the screwdriver down in a crack between two of the planks and poked around. Just dirt."

"And that's all?" Delaney asked. "Just that tool shed?"

"No," Sergeant Boone said, turning sideways to look at the Chief. "There's more. There's an old tarp hanging on the back wall. A greasy piece of canvas just hooked over a couple of nails. Like it was hung up to dry. There's a door behind the tarp."

"A door," Delaney nodded, with some satisfaction. "Behind the tarp. Hidden."

"Right," Boone said. "A modern door. A flush door. Solid, I'd say; not hollow. Hinged from the other side."

"Locked?"

"Oh yes. A good tumbler lock. Maybe a Medeco. But no door knob.

No handle at all. Just that lock. You spring that and push the door open."

"You couldn't spring it?"

"No way. Not with a screwdriver and pliers. I figured you didn't want me to jimmy the door."

"You figured right. Got any idea what's behind the locked door?"

"No, sir. No cracks. No tracks. Nothing. So I put the tarp back the way it was, came out, and closed the outside door. Now get this . . . I'm around the back of the barn, looking around. High up, right under the peak of the roof, there's a small window that's been boarded up. It's like fifteen, maybe eighteen feet from the ground. No way to get to it. And even if I had had a ladder, it was really sealed tight. Heavy planks nailed across it every which way. So while I'm staring at it, I hear a click, and then there's a low hum."

Delaney took his eyes off the road long enough to glance at Boone. "What the hell?" he said.

"Right," the sergeant nodded. "Just what I thought. So then I went back into the shed, pulled the tarp aside again, and put my ear on the door. I could hear it better: a low, steady hum. A drone. Like machinery."

"I can't believe it," the Chief said wonderingly.

"How do you think I felt?" Abner Boone said. "At first I thought I was hearing things. But then there was a click again, and the humming stopped. Just like that. Then I knew. An air conditioner."

"Jesus Christ," Delaney said.

"Had to be," the sergeant said. "Working on a thermostat. The temperature inside gets too high, and it kicks on automatically. So then I went outside again to see if I could find where the damned thing vents. That's what took me so long. I finally found it. There's a half-moon hole in the ground for runoff from the roof gutter. It's lined with rocks. Old, old, old. Anyway, the vent grille has been set into that. Below ground level but open to the air. Neat. If it drips, who's to notice? In fact, you'd never see the vent at all unless you went looking for it."

"An air conditioner," Delaney said, shaking his head. "What the hell they got in there—a meat market? The walls lined with hams and sides of beef?"

"Who the hell knows?" Boone said wearily.

"We'll never get a warrant," Delaney said.

"No way, sir," the sergeant agreed.

"Think you could pick that lock?"

"I could give it the old college try. I guess we'll have to, won't we?"

"I guess we will," Chief Delaney nodded. "We've got no choice."

They stopped at a gas station on the way back to New York, and Abner Boone washed up and tried to scrub a grease stain from the knee of his slacks, with no success. Then he took the wheel, and they drove into Manhattan without exchanging half a dozen words, both frowning because of what they were thinking. Once Delaney said, "He had to do something," but Boone didn't reply, and the Chief said nothing more.

Monica was out when they arrived at the Delaney brownstone. The Chief poked around in the refrigerator, and brought out bread, mustard, cold cuts, cheese, a jar of kosher dills, and an onion. He and Boone made their own sandwiches, two for each, and carried them into the study balanced on squares of paper toweling; no plates, nothing to wash up but a couple of forks and knives. The Chief took a can of Ballantine ale, and Boone had a bottle of tonic water. No glasses.

They ate slowly, in silence, still ruminating, their eyes turned downward and blinking.

"Look," Chief Delaney said, beginning to work on his second sandwich—salami and onion on pumpernickel—"let's do this . . ." He tore a sheet from his yellow legal pad and pushed it across the desk to Abner Boone. He put a pencil alongside it. "You write what you think are the three biggest question marks in this mess. I mean besides who wasted Maitland. The three things that bug you the most. I'll do the same. Then we'll read each other's list and see if we're thinking along the same lines."

"Only three questions?" Boone said. "I can think of a hundred."

"Just three," Delaney said. "The three you think are most important. Most significant."

"I'm game," the sergeant said, picking up the pencil as Delaney took out his pen.

The Chief's list of the three most puzzling aspects of the case read as follows:

1. Why were no paintings found in Mott Street studio?
2. Where's the big money coming from that Dora and Emily Maitland are counting on?
3. Why didn't Victor Maitland, knowing he was dying, change his life style or make special plans?

Delaney looked up, but Boone was staring into space, pondering. So the Chief worked on his sandwich while the sergeant began writing again. Finally he nodded he was finished. They exchanged lists, and Delaney read what Boone had written:

1. What's in the Maitlands' barn?
2. Why didn't Maitland contribute to support of mother and sister?
3. Why did Victor Maitland and Saul Geltman arrange Nyack visits so Martha Beasely wouldn't see them?

"Jesus Christ," Abner Boone said disgustedly, "we're not even worrying along the same lines."

Chief Delaney raised his eyes slowly, stared at the sergeant a moment. Then he took his own list back, placed it alongside Boone's, read them both again. Then he raised his eyes again.

"Sure we are," he said softly. "We're both on the same track. Closer than you think. Look at this . . ."

He took a pair of scissors from his top desk drawer. He trimmed the excess paper from the bottom of his and Boone's lists and dropped the scraps neatly into the wastepaper basket concealed in the well of his desk. Then carefully, slowly, he scissored each list into three parts. Now he had six slips of paper, six individual questions. He placed them in a single column and began to move them around.

Interested, Abner Boone rose, moved behind Delaney, bent over his shoulder. He watched the Chief try the six questions in various sequences. Then Delaney got them in an order that pleased him, sat back staring at them.

"Well?" he asked Boone, not looking at him.

The sergeant shook his head.

"I still don't get it," he said.

"Read them again," the Chief urged.

Now the list read:

1. Why didn't Maitland contribute to support of mother and sister?
2. Why didn't Victor Maitland, knowing he was dying, change his life style or make special plans?
3. Why were no paintings found in Mott Street studio?
4. Why did Victor Maitland and Saul Geltman arrange Nyack visits so Martha Beasely wouldn't see them?

5. Where's the big money coming from that Dora and Emily Maitland are counting on?

6. What's in the Maitlands' barn?

Boone straightened up. He put his hands on his hips, bent backward until his spine cracked, stretched, took a deep breath.

"Chief," he said, "are you thinking what I'm thinking?"

"I sure am," Delaney said, trying not to sound excited. "I've got to make some phone calls . . . You sit down. Or make yourself another sandwich. Or open another—no, wait. There's a job you've got to do while I phone."

He went to his bookcase, got the oversized art volume of the works of Victor Maitland, the book Boone had loaned him. He showed the sergeant the section listing the artist's *oeuvre*.

"This book was published six months ago," Delaney said, "and probably written at least six months before that. So the list won't be right up to the minute. But it should tell us if we're thinking straight."

"What you want is the number of known paintings Maitland did every year—right?" Boone asked.

"Right!" Delaney said. He wanted to clap the sergeant on the shoulder, but didn't. "The list starts twenty years ago, when he began to sell. You get on the numbers, and I'll call Jake Dukker."

He had no trouble getting Dukker's studio, but the receptionist told him the artist was busy in a shooting session and couldn't come to the phone.

"What's he doing—photographing pornographic confirmation cards?" Delaney said. "You tell Jake baby this is Chief Edward X. Delaney, New York Police Department, and if he doesn't get his tuchas to the phone, there'll be a man in blue up there in— Oh hello, Mr. Dukker. Forgive me for bothering you, but I know how anxious you are to cooperate. Just one short question this time: How long did it take Victor Maitland to do a painting?"

Abner Boone raised his head from his counting to listen to Delaney's conversation.

"I know, I know . . . Look, you told us he was a fast worker, Belle Sarazen told us he was a fast worker, Saul Geltman told us he was a fast worker. All right—how fast? . . . Uh-huh . . . I understand . . . And if he was pushing it? . . . Yes . . . I get it . . . But on an average, what

would you say? . . . Yes . . . So that could be at least fifty a year? . . .
Yes . . . No, I'm not going to make you swear to it; it's just for my own
information . . . And you're faster?" Delaney winked at the listening
Abner Boone. "I understand completely, Mr. Dukker. Thank you very
much for your kind cooperation."

He hung up and made some quick notes on his pad while talking to
the sergeant.

"Says it depends on the artist," he said rapidly. "Some can spend a
year on a single canvas. Maitland worked fast, like everyone told us.
Twenty or thirty a year. Easily. One a week if he pushed it. Maybe even
more, Dukker says. Didn't even let the layers of paint dry properly. Jake
baby says Maitland could do a painting overnight on a bet, but let's
figure an average of one a week to be on the conservative side. How you
doing?"

"Give me a couple of more minutes," Boone said. "It looks good."

Delaney waited patiently while the sergeant counted the number of
known paintings Maitland produced each year. Finally, Boone pushed
the book away and studied his list.

"All right," he said, "here's how it stands: Beginning when the list
starts, he did about twenty a year, then thirty, then more, and more,
until he's doing like fifty paintings a year. This is on the average. Then,
five years ago—"

"When he learns he's dying," Delaney put in.

"Right. About five years ago, suddenly it goes to twelve, ten, fourteen, eleven paintings a year. His annual production fell way off."

"The hell it did," the Chief said. "If anything, he began working
harder and faster. If he turned out fifty paintings a year, say, for the
past five years, and you subtract the number of known paintings listed
in that book, how many paintings are unaccounted for?"

"About two hundred," Boone said, staring at his list. "Jesus, two
hundred missing paintings!"

"Missing, my ass," Delaney said. "They're in the Maitlands' barn.
That explains the air conditioner, doesn't it?"

"I'll buy that," Boone nodded. "Now give me the why."

Delaney grabbed for his Manhattan telephone directory.

"I'm going to call Internal Revenue Service information," he told the
sergeant. "You get on the phone in the hallway and listen in. I don't
want to have to repeat the conversation; it'll probably be a long one."

Boone took his second sandwich and what was left of his bottle of tonic into the hallway. Delaney dialed IRS information and was answered by a recorded message telling him all the information lines were busy, and would he please wait. He hung up, dialed again, and got the same message. Went through it again, and on the third try decided to wait. He held the phone almost five minutes, and then a growly voice came on, saying, "Information. Can I help you?"

"I'd like some information on gift taxes," the Chief said.

"What do you want to know?" the voice growled.

"How much can I give to relatives—or to anyone—without paying taxes on it?"

"An individual can give three thousand a year to as many donees as he wants."

"And the donor doesn't have to pay any tax on that, and the donee receiving the gift doesn't?"

"Right," the growler said.

"Look," Delaney said, "that's for money. Cash. What about things—like, oh say sterling silver, antiques, stamps, coins, paintings—stuff like that?"

"The same holds true. The value of the annual gifts cannot exceed three thousand if they're to be tax-free."

Delaney was getting interested. Like most cops, he was intrigued by how the system could be fiddled.

"Suppose I sell something to a relative or friend," he suggested, "for, say, a hundred dollars, and it's really worth five thousand. Then what?"

"Then you're in the soup," the voice growled. "If we find out about it. Gifts of *anything*—antiques, stamps, coins, paintings, whatever—are evaluated at current market value at the time of the gift. We hire expert appraisers. If the sale price is obviously out of line, then the person who fakes the purchase has to pay tax on the value over three thousand."

"If you find out about it," Delaney reminded him.

"If we find out—right," the growler said. "You want to take a chance of being racked up on tax fraud, go right ahead; be my guest."

"Let me ask you another question," Delaney said. "All right?"

"Sure. This is more interesting than most of the stuff I get."

"Let me give you a for-instance. Suppose I own ten acres of land. Now the value of that land is three thousand dollars, and I sign the land over to my son, say. That's okay, right?"

"If the value of the land is legitimate, it's okay. It would mean that surrounding land, similar acres, are going for that price. Then, sure, that would be a legal gift, tax-free."

"All right, let's say it's legal. I've got proof those ten acres are worth three thousand. They're a gift I make to my son. Tax-free. But then, about ten years later, or fifteen, or twenty, oil is discovered on that land, and suddenly those acres are worth a million dollars. What then? Was it still a legal gift?"

There was silence on the other end of the phone. Then:

"That's a good one. First time I've had that thrown at me. Look, I got to admit the tax laws about gifts are murky. We know a lot of people get away with murder, and there's nothing we can do about it. Mostly because we never hear about it, never learn about it. But to get back to your question . . . you give land to your son legitimately worth three thousand. Right?"

"Right."

"Then, years later, oil is discovered on that land, and it greatly appreciates in value. Have I got it correct?"

"Yes, correct."

"Then it's your son's good luck. That's the way I interpret the regulations. I may be wrong, but I don't think I am. When you gave that land to your son, you didn't know there was oil on it, did you?"

"No, I didn't."

"No hanky-panky? There were no acres around it or near it producing oil?"

"No. None."

"Then, like I said, it's your son's good luck. The gift is legitimate. We'll take our cut from the sale of the oil."

"Thank you very much," Chief Delaney said.

"Thank *you*," the voice growled. "A welcome relief from old dames wanting to know if they can deduct the cost of dogfood for their poodles."

Delaney hung up. Abner Boone came walking in from the hallway. He was frowning.

"It's tax fraud, isn't it?" he asked.

"That's how I see it," Delaney nodded. "Sit down. Relax. Let me give you a scenario. A lot of it's smoke, but I think it makes sense."

Delaney leaned back in his swivel chair. He lighted a cigar, put his hands behind his head, stared at the ceiling. Boone slumped in the cracked club chair, cigarettes and matches in his lap.

"All right," the Chief said, "let's go . . . Interrupt me any time you think I'm flying too high, or you have something to add.

"Let's start about six years ago. Victor Maitland's stuff is beginning to bring really high prices, and he's turning out like fifty paintings a year. Now this is supposition, but maybe Geltman's getting a little itchy. Sure, he's making a lot of money off Maitland, but maybe the dealer's worried that the artist is doing too many paintings too fast. Remember what Geltman said about scarcity being a factor in the price of art? But let's skip that for the moment. Six years ago, everything's coming up roses for Victor Maitland.

"Then, suddenly, Doc Horowitz tells him he's dying. He's got maybe three years. Wham, bang, and pow! Maitland laughed, according to Horowitz, but don't tell me news like that wouldn't shake a man. Maitland's first reaction is that now he's got to work harder and faster in the days he's got left. Because he really is an obsessed creative artist, and he wants to know it all, own it all, and prove it on canvas. But then he starts thinking—working harder and faster for whom? The IRS? He's already paying heavy income taxes, and if he works more and sells more, he pays more. Save up his paintings to leave to his heirs? Then the IRS and New York State take an enormous inheritance tax."

"Lieutenant Wolfe told us how Maitland felt about that," Boone observed.

"Correct. So Maitland goes to Geltman and tells him his problem, and Geltman takes him to see J. Julian Simon. I figure it's got to be a lawyer who figured out this whole cockamamie scheme. It's got shyst written all over it. After all, they're going to risk tax fraud, a Federal rap. But Simon figures out ways to reduce the risk to practically nil."

"Who benefits?" the sergeant asked.

"*Cui bono?*" the Chief smiled. "I asked myself that a long time ago, and didn't have the answer. Maitland wanted his mother and sister to benefit. Maybe he hadn't been giving them anything. Maybe he'd been tossing them nickels. But he knows they're just getting by, and that the old Maitland homestead in Nyack is going to rack and ruin. Now that he's dying, he gets an attack of the guilts. He wants his mother and sister to benefit, and screw the IRS; they're taking plenty on his income taxes. That's how I think Maitland would figure it."

"What about his wife and son?"

"Fuck 'em. That's what Maitland would think, and probably said to Geltman: Fuck 'em. The wife has twenty grand a year of her own, doesn't she? She's not going to starve. And Victor figures he'll leave enough cash and legitimate paintings in the Geltman Galleries to give his son a start. The kid gets about half the estate after taxes, remember. No, Maitland wants his mother and sister to be the big winners."

"Then Dora and Emily were in on it?"

"Had to be; it was their barn being used for storage. I guess they felt sorry about Victor dying and all—maybe that's why Dora's on the sauce —but they were consoled by all those beautiful paintings piling up in the barn. Their inheritance. This is how I figure they worked it:

"Say Maitland did a minimum of fifty paintings a year after he learned he was dying. Ten or fifteen of those would go to the Geltman Galleries to be sold normally. An artificial scarcity, so the price of Maitlands kept climbing. The other twenty-five or more paintings were put in the barn. Brought up there by Maitland or Geltman when Martha Beasely wasn't around to see them unload the station wagon."

"And when Dora and Emily came down for lunch or dinner," Boone said, "they took paintings back with them. In the Mercedes."

"Right," Delaney nodded. "And if the IRS ever found them, Dora and Emily and Saul Geltman would claim those paintings had been done twenty years ago, when Maitlands were selling for a hundred bucks. Listen, the guy's style never changed that anyone could notice. And you heard what the IRS man said on the phone. At a hundred bucks, a fair market value twenty years ago, Maitland could give thirty paintings to his mother and thirty to his sister every year, and still keep within the legal gift limit. How could the Feds prove the paintings had been done in 1978, when Maitlands were selling for a hundred G's and more?"

"They'd have to keep a record," Boone said slowly. "Some kind of a ledger like the one Geltman showed us for the legitimate sales."

Delaney pointed a finger at him.

"That's it," he said. "You've got it. Double-entry bookkeeping. The art dealer's got an illustrated record book proving the painting was done in 1958 and given to Dora or Emily as a gift. All as phony as a three-dollar bill, of course, but the IRS would have a hell of a time fighting it."

"Why didn't Victor let Dora and Emily sell off some of the paintings while he was alive? They'd have to pay taxes on their profit, but they could get started on renovating that old place."

"Because Geltman convinced them that the prices of Maitland paintings were going up, up, up, and the longer they held on, the more they'd eventually make. And when Maitland conked, the price of his paintings would go through the roof. Just the way it happened. Listen, J. Julian Simon and Saul Geltman worked this out very carefully. And, for their reward, I suppose Geltman had an arrangement with Dora and Emily. When Victor Maitland died, the stored paintings would be sold off slowly, ten or twenty a year, to keep the price up. Geltman would handle the sales, perfectly legitimately, and take like fifty percent."

"From which he'd pay J. Julian Simon his share for setting up the scam."

"That's the way I figure it," Delaney nodded.

"That's it," Boone said. "That's got to be it."

"Sure," Edward X. Delaney said. "Except for one thing. Who slammed Victor Maitland?"

16

Jason T. Jason felt like a detective, even if he didn't have the rank. Like most young men and women who join the cops, wherever, this was what he thought police work was all about: prowling around in plainclothes, asking questions, solving homicides. Three years' duty on uniformed patrol had dimmed the vision, but never quite obliterated it. And now it was coming true.

At the suggestion of Sergeant Abner Boone, and with the aid of his wife, Jason Two dressed like your normal denizen of the lower depths for his role as detective. He wore a fuzzy maroon fedora with a brim four inches wide, pinned up on one side with a rhinestone as big as the Ritz and a long feathered plume waving in the air.

His jacket was fringed buckskin over a ruffled purple shirt open to the waist. Around his neck hung an enormous silver medallion on a beaded necklace. His skintight jeans were some kind of black, shiny stuff, like leather, and his yellow boots had platform soles and three-inch heels.

His wife said this costume made Jason T. Jason look like the biggest, raunchiest pimp in New York, and she made him wear a raincoat over it when he got into and out of their car in front of their Hicksville, Long Island, home. His two young sons thought their father's outfit was the most hilarious thing they had ever seen, and he had to crack them a few times before they'd stop yelling, "Hey, Ma, superstud is home!"

Jason T. Jason enjoyed every minute of his assignment. He liked people, and found it easy to gossip with them and relate to their problems. He wasn't self-conscious about his enormous size, and discovered that, perhaps because of it, there were many who liked to be seen talking to him or drinking with him. It made them proud, as if they were in the company of a celebrity.

He found he was putting in a twelve-hour day on the new job, sometimes more, but he talked it over with Juanita, his wife, and they decided he'd push it. The opportunity was one most patrol officers would give their left nut for, and if he helped break the case, he'd get a commendation at least, and an on-the-spot promotion to dick three wasn't unheard of.

He had had the usual basic training at the Academy, and had learned more in the three years on patrol, of course, but nothing in his background had prepared him for this job. He told Juanita he probably would be making a mess of it if it weren't for the counsel and assistance of Abner Boone. The sergeant taught him the tricks of the trade.

For instance, Boone told him, suppose you're tailing a guy for some reason, and you want to find out his name. You see him go up and talk to another guy for a few minutes, then move off. So you go up to this other guy, but you don't flash your tin and demand, "What was the name of the man you were just talking to?" Do that, and the chances are the guy will stiff you, or lie. But if you come up smiling and say, "Hey, man, was that Billy Smith you were just talking to?" then the chances were pretty good the guy might say, "Billy Smith? Hell, no, that was Jack Jones."

Similarly, Boone said, when Jason T. Jason went into a bar on the Lower East Side, he shouldn't march in, flash his potsy at the bartender, show the police artist's sketch of the Spanish woman, and demand, "Have you seen this woman?" Even if the guy had, he was going to clam after that treatment.

The better way, the sergeant told Jason Two, was to amble into the bar, order a beer, sip it slowly, and when the bartender wasn't busy, ask lazily, "Mary been around lately?" And if the bartender said, "Mary? I don't know no Mary," then Jason was to say, "Sure, man, she comes in here all the time. Here, I got this little drawing of her." The bartender might still clam, but he might say, "Oh her. Her name ain't Mary, it's Lucy." Or June, or Sue, or whatever.

"It's all in knowing how to manipulate people," Abner Boone told the black cop. "A good detective's got a thousand tricks to make people tell things they don't want to tell, or do things they don't want to do. You've go to study human nature and what makes people tick. I always figured you can catch more flies with honey than you can with vinegar, but I know a lot of dicks don't feel that way. Just the opposite; they come on strong. You've got to find the way that suits you best and gets the best results for you."

Jason told Juanita he thought Boone's way suited him best; it really made him uncomfortable to lean on people. So he ambled all over the Lower East Side, smiling, chatting up a storm with bartenders and shop-keepers. Some of them guessed he was a cop, but never came right out and asked. His costume and manner must have been convincing because once, on Norfolk Street at high noon, a pretty young hooker, white, sidled up to him and said she wouldn't mind joining his stable. Jason told this story to his wife, thinking she'd be amused. She wasn't.

He made some progress, but not much. Using Boone's system, he had wandered into a Forsythe Street greasy spoon and casually asked the Puerto Rican waitress, "Mary been around lately?" It worked just as the sergeant said it might, and the waitress identified the drawing of the woman as "Mama Perez," first name unknown, who came in occa-sionally with the young girl in the second sketch. This girl, introduced as Mama's niece, was named Dolores, last name unknown.

Sergeant Boone ran "Mama Perez" through records, and came up with nothing. There were more than 750 Perezes listed in the Manhat-tan telephone directory, and they weren't about to start on *that* unless absolutely necessary.

So Jason T. Jason continued his daily rounds, becoming a familiar figure around Orchard and Rivington and Delancey streets. But now he could ask casually, "Seen Mama Perez lately?" He went as far west as the Bowery and as far east as Roosevelt Drive. Sometimes he worked nights and the early-morning hours, and he went into hairy places. But perhaps because of his size, he never got mugged. There was one night, under the Williamsburg Bridge, when he thought four young punks were going to try to take him. But he sauntered slowly away whistling, and sweating, and they faded off when he came into a lighted section.

The worst experience he had during this period was not with the shtarkers of the Lower East Side, but with Sergeant Abner Boone.

Boone came down to join Jason occasionally, usually at night, to make the rounds with him for a few hours and teach him more tricks.

Boone wore dirty sneakers and khaki jeans, and a stained nylon Windbreaker. He didn't wear any socks, and some shirt buttons were missing. No one looked at him twice.

Jason noticed that when he and Boone went into a bar together, the sergeant would always order a draft beer, and then let it just sit there, getting flat, the head disappearing.

The first time this happened, Jason Two said, "Not drinking?" And Boone smiled tightly and said, "Not tonight." It happened two or three more times; Boone never touched his beer. Finally, Jason, who had a huge thirst and a huge capacity, took to saying, "Mind if I finish that?" When Boone nodded, Jason would drain his glass, too, before they departed.

When Jason T. Jason had his worst experience, he and Boone had been covering Bowery booze joints where you could get a double shot for fifty-five cents, but most of the customers wisely stuck to bottled beer. Jason Two and the sergeant came off the Bowery at Grand Street and started meandering eastward. They turned the corner onto Eldridge Street, where Jason's car was parked, and there was a squad car pulled into the curb at an angle, the roof lights still flashing. Both cops were out of it and working, although there wasn't much for them to do except try to keep the gathering crowd moving.

It looked like two old winos had gone at each other with broken bottles. This was surprising; old winos rarely had enough strength to twist the cap from a pint of muscatel. But maybe it was a grudge or a vendetta. In any event, they had sliced up each other thoroughly—there was an eyeball lying on the sidewalk—and it was obvious one of the winos was dead and the other, a flag of slashes, was breathing in thick, wheezy gasps in a diminishing rhythm.

The young cops who had caught the squeal didn't know what to do. They had radioed for help, but there was no way to stop the dying man's bleeding or to bandage him, unless they could swaddle him up like a mummy. Blood ran across the sidewalk, over the curb, into the gutter. A gush, a river, a flood of blood. The smell was thick on the hot night air. Boone hadn't caught one of these in a long time; he had almost forgotten that blood smelled.

He started walking away, fast, and Jason Two had to hurry to catch up to him. Boone wheeled into the first open bar he came to and ordered a boilermaker. He put the shot down with a flick of his wrist and a single gulp, swilled the beer, and ordered another before Jason even had time to swing his bulk aboard a bar stool.

Oh-oh, the black cop thought. I got trouble.

He did, too. Within an hour, Sergeant Abner Boone was falling-down drunk and talking stupidly. Following one of Boone's own tips—"Never argue with a drunk, a nut, an armed guy, or a woman"—Jason agreed with everything the sergeant said, and tried to get him out of there. But Boone wouldn't go, insisted on ordering another drink. Suddenly he stopped babbling, became silent and morose. He staggered off to the can.

While he was gone, Jason debated what he should do. He had never faced a situation like this before. He had gotten pissy-assed drunk with fellow cops, and usually helped one or more of them home, all of them boisterous and roaring. But Boone was Jason's superior officer, and he didn't even know where the sergeant lived. He wondered if he should call Chief Edward X. Delaney and explain the situation, but decided that wouldn't be right. He didn't know what to do.

Boone seemed to be staying in the can a long time, and Jason Two thought he might have passed out in there. But when Jason went in, he saw Boone hadn't passed out; the sergeant was sitting in a pool of urine and vomit, his back against the filthy tiled wall, and he was trying to eat his gun. His forefinger stroked slowly at the trigger. Jason T. Jason almost fainted.

He got the revolver away from Boone and began slapping his face to bring him around. After a while, the sergeant started weeping, and covered his face with his hands—whether to hide his tears or so he couldn't be slapped anymore, Jason didn't know. But he got Boone up on his feet, propped in a corner, and he wiped the sergeant off with wet paper towels as best he could.

Then Jason bent down from the waist and pulled Boone forward over his shoulder. He straightened up easily, holding the sergeant with one arm, and carried him out of the can, out of the bar, down Eldridge Street to Jason's car. He had a copy of that afternoon's *Post* in the car, and he had the foresight to cover the back seat with newspaper before he dumped Boone in there. The sergeant was completely out now. He was a mess, dirty and stinking.

Jason Two searched his sticky pockets with the tips of his fingers and found out where Boone lived. But he didn't know if the sergeant was married. If he was, Jason didn't want to deliver him to his wife in that condition. Sighing, Jason T. Jason realized the only thing he could do was to deliver Abner Boone in that condition to *his* wife. Juanita wasn't going to like it, but Jason didn't see where he had any choice. So he drove Sergeant Boone home to Hicksville, Long Island.

His wife wasn't happy about receiving an unexpected, smelly, and unconscious guest at that hour. But after Jason Two told her what had happened, she nodded grimly and helped him get Boone undressed, showered off, and under a blanket on the couch in the half-basement that Jason was still hoping to finish one of these days. The only time his wife *really* got sore was when she was washing out Boone's filthy clothes, and Jason said, "That's really white of you, hon."

Because the sergeant had tried to eat his gun, Officer Jason T. Jason decided to sit up with him till morning, fearing Boone might wake up and try to hurt himself again. But the sergeant slept right through, groaning and grinding his teeth. He awoke sick and sober, looked around, saw Jason sitting nearby.

"Thanks," Abner Boone said huskily, holding his head.

Jason didn't say anything. A week later Sergeant Boone sent Mrs. Juanita Jason about fifty bucks' worth of roses with a timid note of apology and thanks. And he sent Jason's two boys authentic-looking plastic Colt .44 revolvers that shot soap bubbles.

"That's what he should have," Juanita said.

Sergeant Boone never came down to the Lower East Side again to make the rounds with Jason T. Jason. But he spoke to Jason every day on the phone, listened to his reports, offered advice and encouragement. Neither of them ever mentioned that night again.

So Jason Two continued his rounds alone, paying particular attention to the places on the list Boone had given him: the known hangouts of Victor Maitland. During his prowling, the black cop broke up one knife fight, collared one purse-snatcher, and reassured one old lady who was convinced her neighbor was beaming cancer rays at her through their adjoining wall. Other than that, his assignment was uneventful—just the way he wanted it. He was confident that, given time, he would find Mama Perez and Dolores. But he feared Chief Delaney would get impatient with his lack of progress and ship him back to uniformed patrol.

He tried to change his routes and hours every day, and on the Friday night of his third week of searching, he planned to cover the section between Canal and Delancey, from the Bowery to Essex. Around midnight, he was ambling north on Ludlow Street, past a dark brick building that looked like a garage or warehouse. There was a gloomy alley alongside it, shadowed where the street light failed to penetrate.

Movement in the alley caught his eye. He slowed, stopped, then moved a few steps closer. He glimpsed a swirl of light-colored fabric, a woman's dress, and his heart stopped its frantic pounding.

"Hey there, baby!" he called cheerily.

She came out a little farther into the light.

" 'Allo, beeg boy," she said. "Wanna have fon?"

Then she smiled, and he saw the gleam of a gold tooth.

17

They spent a lot of time planning it, and even more debating its necessity. On the same Friday night Jason T. Jason was jiving Mama Perez in a Ludlow Street alley, Chief Edward X. Delaney and Sergeant Abner Boone were driving up to Nyack, still discussing the advisability of what they were about to do.

"We could have slipped Martha Beasely a finiff," Boone said. "To tip us off when Dora and Emily are out."

"Look," Delaney said, "if Dora and Emily are involved in icing Maitland, and it comes out that we pulled an illegal search, then they take a walk and we're left with bubkes. It's risky enough as it is, but we'd be stupidos to bring the Beasely woman into it."

"I'm still not sure it's worth it, Chief," Boone fretted.

"It's worth it if we find something that ties in with the kill. Right now, I admit, all we got is presumption of tax fraud. I couldn't care less. It's a matter for the Feds, and we'll tip them when the time is right. But a homicide takes precedence, and I don't think this tax scam exists in a vacuum. I think it's got something to do with why Maitland got the shiv. Also, to tell you the truth, it's just curiosity; I want to make sure we're guessing right. Besides, look at it this way, if Dora and Emily catch us breaking and entering, they're not going to squeal; it would just point the IRS to the treasure trove that much sooner."

"But what if the local blues show up?" Boone said mournfully. "Or the State cops?"

"We'll handle that when we have to," Delaney said. He glanced at Boone, puzzled by the sergeant's uncertainty. Boone had shown up for work a week previously with a spoiled complexion, shadowed eyes, and a breath smelling so strongly of mint that it had to be a coverup. The Chief was convinced Boone had fallen off the wagon again. He seemed sober enough now, but twitchy. "Want to drop me off at the Maitland place?" the Chief asked him. "I'll go in alone, and you stand lookout."

"Nah," the sergeant said. "I'll come along. If only to see how well I learned my lessons."

Boone was referring to a three-hour crash course he had taken under the tutelage of Detective first grade Sammy ("The Pick") Delgado. Sammy, who worked mostly safe and loft heists, was reputed to be the best cracksman in the New York Police Department. He had initiated Sergeant Boone into the arcane skill of the two-handed pick, a delicate operation in which two needle-thin picks are operated simultaneously to spring a good tumbler lock. Sammy just loved watching TV shows in which the dick or private eye opened a solid lock with a plastic credit card.

In the back of Boone's car was the equipment they thought they'd need: a big battery lantern, two penlights, a Polaroid camera with flash, several squares of black cloth about napkin-size, two jimmies, a few other tools, and a first-aid kit they hoped wouldn't be needed. Both cops were armed; both carried their kits of lock picks, plus a small can of oil and a nozzled tube of liquid graphite.

"All we need are ski masks," Boone observed.

They had timed their arrival for 1:00 A.M. Drove slowly past the Maitland home and saw no lights in the house itself, though low-wattage bulbs burned in converted carriage lamps on both sides of the outside door. They U-turned on the road, drove past again, and pulled up so far off the verge that branches scraped the car roof and windows. Boone switched off the engine and lights. They sat silently for almost ten minutes, until their eyes became accustomed to the darkness. During that period only one car passed on the river road.

Finally, Delaney said quietly, "You wait here. I want to check the Mercedes. Fifteen minutes."

He slid out of the car cautiously. Boone was surprised at how lightly and quietly the big man moved. There was a three-quarter moon, but clouds were heavy enough to dim the light. Delaney disappeared into black shadows. Boone sat stolidly, aching for a cigarette.

The Chief was back in ten minutes, appearing with startling suddenness at Boone's window.

"It's parked," he whispered. "They're in. Let's go."

Both men were wearing dark slacks, shirts, sweaters, shoes. They carried tools and equipment in two burlap bags, swaddled in the squares of black cloth to prevent clinking. Boone went first, one of the penlights switched on and held low; a small circle of dim light jerked along at his feet.

They were city cops, not woodsmen; they could not avoid snapping dried twigs on the ground and blundering into branches. But they moved slowly, stopping frequently to snap off the light, stand and listen. They made a wide circle to keep the barn between themselves and the house. It was a humid night, but a cool river breeze helped. The smells were unfamiliar: rank earth, a brief stench of some live animal, the odor of sappy things, an occasional thick, sweet smell of flowers. Once they heard the rush and scamper of a small beast running. It spooked them.

They came up alongside the barn. Boone turned the penlight aside briefly to show Delaney the rock-lined drain pit and the air-conditioner vent. Neither man spoke. They waited for clouds to obscure the moon completely before they slipped around the corner. The sergeant led the way into the shed, the Chief following close behind, one hand on Boone's shoulder.

They closed the outside door softly behind them, made a quick sweep of the shed with the watery penlight beam, then set to work. They took the canvas tarp from the wall and hung it across the ill-fitting outside door so light would not escape through the chinks. Then they moved close to the hidden door and went into the drill they had planned.

Chief Delaney held a square of black cloth between the lock and the house, to provide additional masking. He held the penlight in his mouth, gripping it lightly in his teeth, more firmly with his lips. Boone found the tube of liquid graphite, gave the key opening a little squirt, and selected two picks from the kit in his hip pocket. They were long needles, one pointed, one with a tiny paddle head.

He inserted the pointed lock pick into the keyhole, began to probe gently, staring up into the darkness. ("No use staring at the lock," Sammy Delgado had said. "Your eyesight will fuzz. It's all in the touch, all in the feel.") But Boone touched nothing, felt nothing. He swabbed around gently, trying to catch a tumbler. But the pick kept slipping in his sweaty hands. He left it there, sticking from the lock, stooped and rubbed fingers and palms on the dusty floorboards. Then he went back to his probing, blinking nervously. Finally, he shook his head in the gloom. Delaney dropped one corner of the masking cloth, took the pen-light from his mouth, switched it off. He moved his head closer to Boone's.

"Want me to try?" he whispered.

"Not yet. Let me rest a minute and get rid of the shakes. Then I'll try a hook."

They stood there in the blackness, both trying to breathe deeply. The shed held the day's heat and the must of years. It stuffed their nostrils, clotted their eyes. They smelled themselves, and each other.

"All right," Boone said in a low voice. "I need the light down here for a second."

Delaney held the penlight to illuminate the sergeant's dusty hands fumbling at his pick kit. He replaced the pointed pick, withdrew one with a tiny hook at the end. They went back to their original positions, Boone probing now with the hooked pick, frowning thoughtfully up into the darkness. He felt the pick catch.

"Got one," he breathed.

He slid the paddle-tipped pick into the keyhole alongside the hook. Now he was working with both hands, the paddle searching for clearance as the hook turned a tumbler.

It took almost half an hour, and they stopped to rest and listen three times. But finally the paddle pick slid firmly in; they both heard the satisfying click. Boone slowly turned his wrists until both elbows were pointing upward as Delaney pressed a knee softly but firmly against the door. The final click was louder as the tang pulled back. They stopped, sweating, listened again. Then Delaney nudged the door open.

The light was switched off. Both sat on the floor for a few minutes. Delaney kept his hand carefully on the sill of the opened door, to prevent it from swinging shut. They felt a waft of cool air pouring from the interior.

"Let's go," Boone said.

They got to their feet, picked up their burlap bags. The sergeant pushed the door open slowly.

"Wait," Delaney said.

He wedged a wrapped screwdriver and pliers into place across the lower inside hinge so the door was immobilized. They moved cautiously: a slow-motion film.

The first thing they did was to check the inside of the door. There was a knob, and when Boone satisfied himself that it worked the long tang, he withdrew his picks and slid them back into his kit. Delaney removed the hinge obstruction, and closed the door softly behind them. They were in.

"A felony," the Chief said.

"The door fits tightly," Boone said. "Okay for the lantern?"

"Sure," Delaney said. "Here, I've got it."

He unwrapped the black cloth, stuffed it back into the burlap bag. He straightened up, held the lantern waist-high, snapped it on. A powerful beam probed straight ahead, so bright that their eyes squinted. Then widened. They saw it all.

The interior of the old barn had been insulated, and rough wooden racks built almost to the roof. A sturdy ladder leaned against a wall. A heavy air conditioner was emplaced in a corner. There was a wooden kitchen table, a single wooden chair. And nothing more. Except the paintings.

They were everywhere. On the racks. On the floor. Leaning against the walls. Not in stacks, canvas against canvas, but singly, apart, to dry and gleam. In the glare of the lantern, burning faces stared at them, eyes blazed, mouths mocked.

Delaney and Boone stood frozen, awed by the liquid fire of color that poured over them. They had a sense of shame, of having invaded a church, violated a holy place. There were a few still lifes, landscapes, portraits. But most of the paintings were nudes, bursting Victor Maitland nudes, strangling with their ripeness, gorgeous tints of cream and crimson. Shadows of violet. Hidden parts, secret nooks. Arms reaching, eager legs grasping.

"Jesus Christ," Boone whispered.

They stood and stared, stared, stared. The Chief moved the lantern beam slowly about. In the shifting illumination, now bright, now gloom, they saw swollen limbs quiver, move languorously. They choked in a sea of flesh, drowning. Bodies came writhing off canvas to embrace, entwine, suffocate with breath of steam and hair of flame.

Delaney flicked off the lantern, and they heard themselves breathing heavily.

"Too much," the Chief said in the darkness. "All together like this. Too strong. Too much to take."

"What do you figure?" Abner Boone said hoarsely. "About two hundred of them?"

"Say two hundred," Delaney said. "Say a minimum of a hundred grand a painting."

"Say twenty million," Boone said. "In a wooden barn. I can't believe it. Let's lift ten or so, Chief, and take off for Rio."

"Don't think I haven't thought of that," Delaney said. "Except I know I could never bring myself to fence them. Let's take another look. Use the penlight this time."

The weak light was a relief; they were no longer dazzled, befuddled. They moved to the nearest painting, a dark, rope-bodied nude, torso twisted, hip sprung, legs and arms like serpents, and a wicked smile that challenged. Boone moved the circle of light to the lower righthand corner. They saw that neat bookkeeper's signature, Victor Maitland, followed by the date: 1958.

"Son of a bitch," Delaney said. "Try another."

They went from painting to painting. All were dated 1957, 1958, 1959, a few 1960. None more recent.

"Beautiful," Boone said. "Not only a fake record in Geltman's safe, but a fake date right there on the painting. The IRS will have a sweet job proving they were done a year ago."

"They thought of everything," Delaney marveled. "It had to be J. Julian Simon. *Had* to be. It smells of the legal mind at work. Let's get some shots. Just to prove this harem exists."

Boone held the lantern, turned on for added illumination while Delaney shot a pack of color Polaroid with flash. The colors of the prints weren't as rich as the oils of the paintings, but the overall shots were impressive: a crowded mint of art.

They gathered up all their equipment, stowed it into the burlap bags. They inspected the floor carefully to make certain they were leaving no track of their presence.

They went out slowly, cautiously, guided by the beam of a penlight, now weak and flickering. Boone wiped the inside knob before he stepped through to the shed. He closed the door by inserting a hooked pick into the keyhole, then pulling the door to him until the tang snicked into place. They quickly hung the greasy tarp back in its original position. They waited a few moments in darkness, listening. Then they moved silently outside.

They both glanced toward the Maitland house. Even as they did, a light came on in an upstairs window. They didn't rush, but they didn't dawdle either. Around the corner, down the side, into the trees. Twenty minutes later they were headed back to New York, both of them smoking furiously.

"What do we do now?" Boone asked. "Brace Geltman?"

"What for?" Delaney asked. "It's just a tax rap. He won't scare. J. Julian Simon maybe. He's the key to Geltman's alibi. But why should he talk? Shit, shit, and shit. Maybe Belle Sarazen."

"Why her?"

"Possible motive. Oh God, I don't know, sergeant. Just fishing."

"Maybe the wife found out about the tax scam and got sore. Because those paintings wouldn't be included in the estate, in her inheritance."

"Another possibility," Delaney sighed. "We've got plenty of those. Want me to drive awhile?"

"No. Thank you, sir. I'm fine. Steadying down now. How the B-and-E guys get the balls to do that, I'll never know."

"I suppose it gets easier with experience."

"I don't want to find out," Boone said. "Stop for coffee-and, if we can find a place that's open?"

"Let's go straight in. You stop by; Monica left a fresh pot and some cinnamon buns for us in the kitchen."

"Sounds good," the sergeant said, and began driving faster.

It was past three A.M.; the Chief expected Monica had been asleep for hours. But when they pulled up in front of the Delaney brownstone, the living-room lights were on; he saw the figure of his wife standing at the curtains, peering out.

"Now what the hell?" he growled.

They went up the stairs with some trepidation, hands hovering near gun butts. But Monica unlocked the door for them, safe, eager to tell her story.

Jason T. Jason had called several times. He had also tried calling Abner Boone's apartment. He told Mrs. Delaney he would call every fifteen minutes, on the quarter-hour, until the Chief returned home, and Jason could talk to him.

"Did he say what it was?"

"No, he just said it was important, and he had to report to you or Abner as soon as possible. He's very polite."

The two cops looked at each other.

"In trouble?" Delaney suggested.

"Or he's found Mama Perez," Boone said. "One or the other."

"Well . . ." Delaney looked at his watch. "About ten minutes before he calls again."

"The coffee's warm," Monica said. "I'll just turn up the light. The two of you wash up. You look like you've been digging."

They sat around the kitchen table, sipping their coffee, munching their cinnamon buns. Monica refused to go to bed; she wanted to hear what had happened.

Delaney was telling her about that incredible cache of paintings when the phone rang. He picked up the kitchen extension. He had already set out paper and pencil, ready to take notes.

"Edward X. Delaney here," he said. "Yes, Jason . . . So I understand . . . We've both been out . . . Yes . . . Good. Excellent. Where? . . . Right . . . Between what streets? . . . You're sure she's in for the night? . . . All right, hang on a moment . . ."

He covered the receiver with his palm, turned to the others, smiling coldly.

"Got her," he said. "Orchard Street, just south of Grand. Top floor of a tenement. Apparently she's a hooker, but Jason says she's in for the night. If not, he'll tail her."

"I better get down there," Abner Boone worried. "He won't know what to do."

"Yes," Delaney nodded, "you better go. Send Jason home. If he wants to go. But he sounds excited. I'll join you in the morning, and we'll brace her then. Call here every hour on the hour."

He got back on the phone and asked Jason Two his exact location. He jotted down a few notes.

"Stay right there," he ordered. "Sergeant Boone is on his way. If she leaves the house, you follow and try to keep in touch with me here. Have you eaten tonight? . . . All right, we'll take care of it. Good work, Jason."

He hung up, looked at his notes with grim satisfaction.

"You'll find him on the corner of Orchard and Grand," he told Boone. "He'll be watching for you. For God's sake, don't lose her. If you need more men, call me here."

"We won't lose her, sir," Boone promised.

"Has he eaten?" Monica asked. "Jason?"

"No. Not since yesterday afternoon."

"I'll make some sandwiches," she said.

"Good," the Chief said gratefully. "Big, thick sandwiches. He's a big man. And we have that quart thermos. Sergeant, take that with coffee. You'll never find any place open at this hour."

They equipped Boone with coffee, sandwiches, extra cigarettes, all the dimes they had in the house, for phone calls, and sent him on his way.

"Mrs. Delaney," he muttered, before he left, blushing, head lowered, "could you call Rebecca for me and explain? Why I can't—uh—see her?"

"I'll call, Abner," she promised.

"Call her where?" Delaney asked after Boone had departed.

"His apartment," Monica said shortly. "They're living together now."

"Oh?" the Chief said, and they took their coffee mugs into the study. He showed her the Polaroid color shots he had taken in the Maitland barn.

"I can't believe it," she said, shaking her head.

"I saw it, and I can't believe it," he told her. "Overwhelming. All that color. All those nudes. What a thing. It shook me."

"What will you do now, Edward?"

"Get photographs together of everyone connected with the case. I think I have most of them in the file. J. Julian Simon I don't have. And maybe Ted Maitland. I'm not sure; I'll have to check. Then tomorrow we'll show them to Mama Perez and ask her who she saw at Maitland's studio that Friday morning."

"You think she'll tell you?"

"Oh, she'll tell us," he said. "One way or another."

18

Like most cops, he was superstitious, and so he considered it a good omen that he was able to find photographs of all the principals in the folders of the Maitland file. The photos of J. Julian Simon and Ted Maitland had been taken with a telephoto lens by a police photographer at Victor Maitland's funeral. They were grainy enlargements, but clear enough for identification.

He put all the photos in a manila envelope, and added a set of photostats of the three sketches found in Maitland's studio. At the last minute he also added the clippings of the *New York Times* article describing the Maitland gala at the Geltman Galleries. The article included photos of Belle Sarazen and Saul Geltman.

The Chief had everything prepared by the time Abner Boone called at nine A.M. on Saturday morning. The sergeant and Jason T. Jason had the Perez tenement under surveillance. Mama was still up in her sixth-floor apartment. They had investigated a paved rear courtyard, but the only exit from that was by a narrow walkway alongside the building. It emerged on Orchard Street, so Boone didn't think there was any way for Mama to leave the building without their seeing her.

"Unless she goes across the roofs," the Chief said.

Delaney told the sergeant to stay right where he was, that he'd join them within an hour. He figured he'd take the subway down, then thought the hell with it, and stopped the first empty cab he saw. He was keeping a careful account of his expenses and, even with cabs and gas for Boone's car, they seemed modest enough to the Chief. In any event, the expenses were Thorsen's problem, not his.

He sat in the back of Boone's car, the two active-duty cops in the front seat, while they told him what they had turned up—which wasn't much. Mama's real first name was Rosa, though everyone on the street called her Mama. Apparently she was a hooker—Jason Two confirmed that—but Boone guessed she was drawing some kind of public assistance; even in that neighborhood the successful prosties were younger and flashier.

They had also collected a few facts about Dolores. The young girl wasn't related to Mama Perez. Her full name was Dolores Ruiz, and she was the daughter of Maria Ruiz, who lived on the sixth floor, right next to Rosa Perez. Maria Ruiz apparently didn't have any man. She worked long hours, cleaning office buildings, and Mama Perez befriended Dolores during the day: took her shopping, to the movies, etc. Dolores, the neighbors said, wasn't right in the head.

"Does the Perez woman peddle the girl's ass?" Delaney asked them.

Jason said he didn't think so. During his chat with Mama in the Ludlow Street alley, he had politely rejected her proposition but hinted broadly that he might be interested in a younger girl. She hadn't taken the bait.

The three sat there, aware of the noisy, bustling street but staring at the entrance of Mama Perez' tenement. It was an ugly grey building, the front stones chipped and covered with graffiti, most of it in Spanish. Overflowing garbage cans almost blocked the sidewalk. There was a pack of scrofulous cats darting up and down the stoop, into and out of the narrow alley, and even prowling across the rusty fire escape bolted to the front of the tenement. As they watched, sidewalk vendors began setting up their folding tables and arranging their stocks of plastic sunglasses and sleazy T-shirts.

"Well," the Chief said finally, "let's go have a talk with Mama."

"How do you want us to handle it, sir?" Boone asked. "Come on strong?"

"No," Delaney said. "I don't think we'll have to do that. Nothing physical anyway. Jason, did she make you as a cop?"

"No way, Chief."

"Well . . . come up with us just the same. It'll blow your cover, but she'll realize we've got her on soliciting, at least, and that'll give us an edge."

The three got out, and Boone locked the car carefully.

"I hope I'll still have wheels when we get back," he said mournfully.

The entrance and hallways of the walk-up tenement were about what they expected: scummed tile floors, walls with the rough, puckered look of fifty years' painting, the outside coats chipped away in places to show multicolored pits—green, pink, blue, brown, green, blue—like archeological digs revealing the layers of ages. Electric bulbs were broken, landing windows cracked, the wooden bannisters carved with dozens of initials or just whittled carelessly. And the smell. It hung in the air like a mist, as if someone had sprayed this place and the fog would never disappear or even diminish.

There had been no names in the slots of the broken bells, but the bank of mailboxes—some of them with jimmied lids—showed R. Perez in apartment 6-D. It also showed M. Ruiz in 6-C. On the second floor, Delaney checked the tin letters nailed to apartment doors and found that D was the farthest to the rear. They continued their slow climb upward, stepping aside to let children clatter down, laughing and screaming, and once to allow the slow descent of a painfully pregnant woman dragging along two smeary-faced tots.

They paused in the sixth-floor hallway to catch their breath, then moved back to stand alongside the door marked D. The tin letter was missing; the D had been scrawled on the green paint with a black Magic Marker. Boone put his ear close, listened a moment, then looked at the others and nodded. Delaney motioned them clear, so no one was standing directly in front of the door. Then he reached out and rapped sharply.

No answer. He knocked again, louder. They heard movement, the scuff of dragged steps.

"Who?" a woman's voice called.

"Board of Education," Delaney said loudly. "About Dolores Ruiz."

They heard the sound of locks being opened, a chain unhooked. The door opened. Jason T. Jason immediately planted one of his enormous feet on the sill.

The woman looked down at that protruding foot, then up to the face of Jason Two. Then she looked slowly at Delaney and Boone.

"Sonnenbitch," she said bitterly. "You got badges?"

Boone and Jason flashed their ID. She didn't seem to notice that Delaney showed her nothing.

"Can we come in, Mama?" the Chief asked pleasantly.

"You got a warrant?" she demanded.

"A warrant?" Delaney said. He looked at the other two men, then back to Rosa Perez. "Why should we have a warrant? This isn't a bust, Mama. We don't want to toss your place. Just talk, that's all. A few questions."

"About what?" she said suspiciously.

Delaney dug the photostats of the Maitland sketches from his envelope. He held them up for the woman to see.

"About these," he said.

She stared, and her punished face softened. She almost smiled.

"Beautiful," she said. "No?"

"Very beautiful," Delaney nodded. "May we come in and talk about them?"

Grudgingly, she stepped aside, swinging the door open wider. The three men filed in. The Chief took a quick look around. A one-room apartment. A box. About thirteen by thirteen, he guessed. A narrow closet with a cloth curtain pulled aside. A kitchenette hardly larger than the closet: sink, cabinet, two-burner gas stove, a small, yellowed refrigerator. There was one window in the room, a closed door opposite. Delaney glanced at the door, looked at Jason, motioned with his head. The cop took three steps, stood to one side, opened the door slowly, peered inside cautiously. Then he closed the door.

"Small bathroom," he said. "Sink, tub, toilet, cabinet. And another door on the other side."

"Another door?" Delaney said thoughtfully. He turned to Mama Perez. "You share the bathroom with Maria and Dolores Ruiz?"

She nodded.

"Sure," he said. "Originally this was all one apartment, but the landlord broke it up into two for more money—right?"

Again she nodded.

"Mama, can we sit down?" he asked her. "We want to talk—just a friendly talk—but it may take a few minutes."

She told the story without hesitation, speaking fluently. They listened gravely and never interrupted her.

On that Friday morning, she had taken Dolores Ruiz out to Orchard Street to buy the girl a pair of summer sandals. This crazy man had rushed up to them on the street and grabbed Mama's arm. He said he was an artist and wanted to paint pictures of Dolores. He would pay if Dolores posed for him. In the nude. Mama could be there while he worked, to protect Dolores' honor. But he wanted to see Dolores' body, to see if it was as good as he thought it was.

So they all piled into a cab, and he took them to the Mott Street studio. Dolores undressed, and the crazy man did three drawings and said he wanted Dolores to pose for him. He said he'd pay five dollars an hour, so they agreed to come back on Monday morning. Then they went away. They came back Monday morning at eleven, and found out the man was dead. Later she learned he had been murdered. She read it in the newspapers and saw it on TV. And that's all that happened.

There was a short silence after she finished. They believed every word she had said. Then . . .

"Did you have a drink?" Sergeant Boone asked. "In the studio?"

"Yes. Wan."

"Did Maitland have a drink?" Delaney asked.

"He drank," she nodded. "From the boatal. Crazy man."

"When Dolores undressed," the Chief said, "did she have a safety pin somewhere on her clothes? Did she drop it?"

Rosa Perez shrugged. "Maybe. I don't know."

"Maitland was alive when you left the studio?" Boone asked.

She turned her head slowly, looked at him shrewdly.

"You tink I keel heem?"

"Was he alive?" Boone repeated.

"He was alive," Mama Perez nodded. "Why should I keel heem?"

"Is Dolores here?" Chief Delaney said. "Now? In her apartment?"

The woman straightened slowly. The stone eyes focussed on him.

"What you want weeth Dolores?"

"Just to see her, ask her a few questions."

Mama Perez shook her head.

"Dolores she don' onnerstan'."

"Get her," Delaney said.

She sighed, rose to her feet. She was wearing a cheap cotton wrapper, a thin, flowered shift. She smoothed the cloth down over her bulging hips in a gesture that was coquettish, almost girlish.

"You hurt Dolores," she said casually, "I keel you."

"No one's going to hurt Dolores," the Chief told her. "Jason, go with her."

Rosa Perez went to the bathroom door, Jason right on her heels. She went through the bathroom, knocked on the far door. Delaney and Boone heard a chatter of Spanish.

They sat waiting. The summer sun streamed through the big window. The little apartment, right under the roof, was suddenly a hotbox, steaming. Chief Delaney rose, stalked to the window, pulled it open. He had to struggle with it; the heavily painted frame was swollen. But he finally got it open wide. He leaned far out, hands propped on the low sill. He looked down. Then he came back into the room, closed the window halfway.

"Six stories straight down to the cement courtyard," he reported to Boone. "You'd think she'd have a window guard—one of those iron grilles you screw on. If this kid—"

"Dolores," Mama Perez said. "Beautiful, no?"

They looked at the vacant-faced girl standing near the doorway to the bathroom. Her arms hung straight down at her sides. She was barefoot. She was wearing a pink rayon slip. They saw what Victor Maitland had seen. The youth. Ripe youth. Ready. And long, glistening black hair. Empty perfection in that mask-face. Eyes of glass. Erupting flesh.

"Hello, Dolores," Delaney said, smiling. "How are you?"

She didn't answer, didn't even look at him.

Delaney took the photostats of the Maitland sketches to her and held them up.

"You, Dolores," he said, still smiling.

She looked at the drawings but saw nothing. Her face showed nothing. She scratched one arm placidly.

"Ask her to sit down," the Chief said to Mama Perez.

The woman muttered something in Spanish. The girl walked slowly to the unmade bed, sat down gently. She moved like bird flight, as pure and sure. She was complete. She composed space.

"You sit down, too, Mama," Delaney said. "A few more questions."

"More?"

"Just a few."

He and Rosa Perez took their seats again. Boone and Jason T. Jason stood at opposite walls.

"We've been looking for you," Chief Delaney said. "You and Dolores. Drawings of you were in the newspapers and on TV. You saw them?"

For the first time she hesitated. Delaney saw she was calculating how the truth might hurt her.

"I saw," she said finally.

"But you didn't come forward. You didn't come to us to ask why we wanted to find you."

"Why should I?" she asked.

"Right," he said equably. "Why should you? Well, Mama, we wanted to find you to ask you about someone you and Dolores may have seen that Friday morning."

"Someone we seen?" she said. "We seen lots of peoples that morning."

"In the building where Maitland's studio is," Delaney said patiently. "On the stairs maybe. Or coming up the outside steps. Somewhere close."

Rosa Perez shook her head.

"I don' remember," she said. "So long ago. I don' remember."

"Let me help you," Delaney said. He took all the photographs and newspaper clippings from his manila envelope. He arranged them neatly on the Formica-topped table, all facing Mama Perez.

"Take a look," he urged her. "A good long look. Take your time. Did you see any of these men or women near Maitland's studio that Friday morning?"

She glanced quickly at the photos, then shook her head again.

"I don' remember," she said.

"Sure you do," Chief Delaney said quietly. "You're a smart woman. You notice things. You remember things. Take another look at them."

"I don' remember."

Delaney sighed. He stood up, but he left the photographs lying there.

"All right, Mama," he said. "But we weren't the only ones looking for you."

She stared at him blankly.

"The killer is looking for you too," Delaney said. "He must have seen the newspaper stories and the TV, just like you did. He's afraid you saw him and will recognize him. So he's looking for you. He doesn't know we have Officer Jason there, who actually saw you and Dolores on Monday morning. So we found you first. But he'll keep looking. The killer."

"So?" she said, shrugging. "How he's going to find me?"

Delaney looked at her with admiration. She hadn't yet lost her nerve.

308   LAWRENCE SANDERS

"I'm going to tell him," he said.

He watched her face pull tight under the thick makeup. Eyes widened. Lips stretched back to show sharp, cutting teeth. The gold incisor gleamed.

"You?" she gasped.

"Oh, not directly," Delaney said. "But the newspapers have been after us. And the TV stations. They're interested. They want to know: Have you found the woman and girl? We ran the drawings for you; have you found them? So now I'll have to tell them, yes, we found the woman and the girl, thanks to you. And this is their address."

She understood. He didn't have to spell it out for her.

"You do that?" she asked tentatively.

"Oh yes," he said. "I would."

"You are not a nice man," she said.

"No," he agreed. "I'm not."

She flared suddenly into a screamed stream of Spanish that he could only guess was curses, a flood of invective spat at him.

"I don' care!" she yelled in English. "I don' care! Let heem come! Let heem keel me!"

He waited until she was screamed out, until she calmed, sank back in her chair, glaring at him, still muttering. He could afford to wait; he had the key to her.

"Not you," he said. "Not only you. Dolores, too. He'll hurt Dolores."

She stared fiercely at him a moment longer before she crumpled. She never did weep. But the hand that went out was trembling, the finger wavering that pointed to the newspaper photograph of Saul Geltman.

"Thees wan," she said in a low voice. "On the stairs. Me and Dolores, we were coming down. He was going up. We saw heem. He saw us. Thees ees the man."

They were back in Boone's car, watching Orchard Street fill up with street vendors and the Saturday afternoon shopping crowd, streaming down from all over New York for bargains. Delaney sat in the back seat again, an unlighted cigar in his fingers.

"Can I ask you a question, Chief?" Jason T. Jason said, without turning around.

"Ask away," Delaney said expansively. "Any time."

"If she hadn't identified anyone in the photos, would you have given her address to the papers? Like you told her you would?"

"Sure. After putting a twenty-four-hour guard on her. Use her as bait. Smoke him out."

"Wow," Jason Two said. "I learn something new every day. Well, anyway, we got him."

Abner Boone made a sound.

"Something, sarge?" Jason asked innocently.

"We haven't got him."

"Haven't got him?" the black cop said indignantly. "She fingered him as being on the scene of the crime at the right time. I can testify to that."

"Oh sure," Boone said. "That and half a buck gets you on the subway."

"It's no good, Jason," Delaney amplified. "Suppose we take that to the DA's office and ask them to seek an indictment of Saul Geltman for Murder One. Okay, they say, what have you got on him? We say, we got an old Puerto Rican whore who saw him near the scene of the crime about the time it was committed. Okay, they say, what else have you got? That's all, we say. Then they fall on the floor holding their ribs and laughing before they kick our ass out of their office. Jason, we have no *case*. You can't convict a man of homicide because he was in the neighborhood about the time the killing took place. Where's the weapon? What's the motive? Where's the legal proof? The sergeant's right; we've got nothing."

Jason looked back and forth, Delaney to Boone, frowning.

"You mean this dude is going to walk?"

"Oh no," Delaney said. "I didn't say that. He's not going to walk. He probably thinks he is, but he's wrong."

"Still," Abner Boone said, turning sideways in the driver's seat to look at Delaney, "he must be having some wet moments. Here's how I see it:

"Geltman goes down to Mott Street on Friday morning to burn Maitland. On the stairs, going up to the studio, he meets Mama and Dolores. He sees them, they see him. Maybe Mama even hustles him right there; she's got the balls for it. But the important thing is that he's got no way of knowing they just came down from Victor Maitland's studio. Right, Chief?"

"Right."

"Okay. So Saul baby goes up, ices Maitland, and skins out. He goes through his little scam as the anxious agent and then, on Sunday, he returns to the studio, allegedly discovers the body, and calls the cops.

Now it gets cute. When the blues come, they find the three drawings Maitland did of Dolores. Geltman is there and recognizes the girl he met on the stairs on Friday. He wants the drawings, but we won't give them to him. I know; I was there. So he goes home sweating, hoping nothing will come of those damned drawings because he's afraid the girl may identify him, not knowing she's a wet-brain."

"Then you and I come around asking questions about the girl," the Chief said.

"Right!" Boone said. "Now he's really shitting. Those fucking sketches could cook him if we found the girl. So he thinks fast—hand it to him—and invites us to his show. You particularly, Chief."

"Sure," Delaney nodded. "To get me out of the house so he can lift the drawings."

"Which he does," Boone continued. "Hell, he could be missing from that mob scene for an hour, and no one would realize he was gone."

"Or he could have hired a smash-and-grab lad," Delaney suggested.

"Easily," Boone nodded. "Maybe one of his golden boys. Anyway, now he's got the sketches and he figures he's home free and can relax. But then, a couple of days later, he picks up the paper and lo! there's the police drawings of Mama and Dolores. He must have had a cardiac arrest right then. Imagine how he felt! Thought it was a piece of cake, and now he finds out the cops know about Mama and Dolores. And that's the mood he's in right now. Is that about the way you see it, Chief?"

"Just right," Edward X. Delaney approved. "I figure that's about the way it happened. But I don't think he's all that spooked. Listen, this is one cool monkey. When I went up to his apartment unexpectedly, he didn't turn a hair. My God, those Maitland drawings were probably right there, in one of his beautiful cabinets."

"Wouldn't he keep them in the office safe?" Boone asked.

"Oh no," Delaney said. "Too many people in and out of the place. Too dangerous. That marvelous apartment is his secret place, his dream. He'll have them there. And won't destroy them, as he should, any more than Mama Perez would spit on her velvet hanging of Jesus on the Cross. They're beautiful things, holy things."

"Search warrant?" Boone asked.

"Mmm . . . maybe," the Chief said slowly. "But not yet."

Jason T. Jason had listened closely to this exchange, had followed most of it.

"How we going to nail him?" he asked.

"I don't know," Delaney confessed. "He's got an alibi we've got to break. And I'd like to see a motive. You can convict without establishing motive—but it helps. Especially when you've got damned little else."

"Funny," Abner Boone said, shaking his head. "Saul Geltman. You know, I like the little guy."

"I do, too," Chief Delaney said. "So?"

Boone had no answer to that.

"Sergeant," Delaney said, "think you can stay awake for a few more hours?"

"Sure, Chief. No sweat."

"I'm going to call Deputy Commissioner Thorsen and ask for more men. Round-the-clock surveillance of Mama Perez."

"Could we pull her in as a material witness?" Boone asked him.

"Maybe," Delaney said. "But it would tip our hand, and she's no good to us in the slammer. A loose tail should be enough. Just to make sure she doesn't skip."

"What about Geltman, sir? Want him covered, too?"

"No. He's not going to run. Unless he spots a tail, and that might panic him. Surveillance of Mama will be enough for starters. You brief the new men when they show up. I'll try to have the first one down here in an hour or so."

"What do you want me to do, sir?" Jason T. Jason asked anxiously, fearing his brief career as a detective was drawing to a close.

"Go home and get some sleep," Delaney told him. And then when he saw the man's expression, he said, "Report to Sergeant Boone on Monday morning. In plainclothes. That means a business suit, not that Superfly outfit."

Jason T. Jason smiled happily.

19

He had prepared a "Things to do" list, and even a time-sequence chart, but on Monday morning all his carefully plotted plans went awry.

He got through to Bernie Wolfe on the first call, but the lieutenant was unable to help him.

"I'm due in court in an hour, Chief," he explained. "Testimony on a Chagall-forgery case. One of my men is out sick, and my other guy is in Brooklyn, digging into the cutting of some Winslow Homer etchings from a library's file copies of the old *Harper's Weekly*. It's happening more and more."

"Look, lieutenant," Delaney said desperately, "what I need is poop on how the loss of income from Maitland's work will affect the Geltman Galleries. Can Saul continue in business with the other artists he handles, or will he go broke? I figure the best answer to that would come from his competitors on Madison Avenue."

"Or Fifty-seventh Street," Wolfe added.

"Right. Could we do this: if I send Sergeant Boone and another guy to meet you in court, could you give them the names of, oh say a dozen art dealers they could check today and try to get a rundown on Geltman's financial problems?"

"Of course," Wolfe assured him. "That's easy."

"Good. I'll have Boone call you and set up a meet."

"By the way, Chief, I've been mooching around a little. I got nothing hard, but there's some vague talk that you could buy a Maitland painting without going through Geltman Galleries."

"Uh-huh," Delaney said. "Now that's interesting. Many thanks, lieutenant. I'll have Boone call you. And don't forget to call when you can make dinner."

Then he had to wait for the sergeant's hourly report.

"We still got Mama Perez in sight," Boone said cheerfully. "She tumbled to the stakeout and blew her cork. But one of the new men speaks Spanish, and we got her calmed down. Told her the cover was for her protection, and for Dolores'."

"Good," Delaney said promptly. "That could be a plus. How's Jason working out?"

"Fine," Boone said. "Very eager. Chief, he's faster than he said he was. He and I were coming back to his car from breakfast, and there was a punk working on the front window with a bent coat hanger. He saw us and took off, Jason Two pounding along right behind him. Must have chased the kid two blocks, but he caught him. That Jason can run."

"What did he do to the punk?"

"Frisked him, then kicked his ass and turned him loose."

"Sound judgment," Delaney said. "Got good men on Mama Perez today?"

"Oh sure. Old-timers. Not too fast, but they know the job."

"Then here's what I want you and Jason to do . . ."

He instructed Abner Boone to call Lieutenant Wolfe and arrange to meet him in court. To get a list of art dealers and to check them out on the finances of Geltman Galleries.

"Competitors are usually happy to gossip about a rival," he told Boone. "Take Jason with you, and the two of you divide up the list. Cover as many dealers as you can. Brief Jason on the case so he knows what's going on. I'll be out most of the day, but you'll be able to get me here later this afternoon. If I'm not in, Monica probably will be, so you and Jason come over and wait for me."

"Yes, sir," the sergeant said. "You think we'll nail him, Chief?"

"Sure we will," Delaney said, with more confidence than he felt.

Then, going down his list, he called the office of J. Julian Simon. Susan Hemley answered, and he forced himself to chat casually with her for a few minutes. Finally . . .

"Think I could see the big man this morning, Susan?" he asked.

"Oh no, Chief," she said. "He didn't come in. He's due in court this morning."

"My God," he groaned. "Is *everyone* going to court this morning?"

"Beg pardon?"

"No, no. Nothing. Listen, do you think he'll be in at all today?"

She said Simon expected to be back by three or four in the afternoon at the latest. Delaney told her he'd take a chance and show up around that time in hopes the counselor could give him a few minutes. He was very respectful.

Then yielding to circumstances, he resolved to revise his schedule and barge in on Belle Sarazen without notice. But first he made some peculiar preparations.

He went to the odds-and-ends drawer in the kitchen cabinet and rummaged until he found what he sought: a small waxed-paper envelope containing a few faucet washers. It wasn't an authentic glassine envelope, but he thought it would serve the purpose. He dumped the washers into the cluttered drawer, then filled the envelope with a teaspoonful of confectioners' sugar. He folded the tab over twice and secured it with a little square of Scotch tape.

He slid the packet into the side pocket of his seersucker jacket. He wondered if he should carry a gun, but decided against it. He set his sailer squarely atop his head and sallied forth, lumbering over to First Avenue to get a cab, and resisting the desire for a morning cigar.

Either the doorman recognized him from previous visits, or something in the Chief's manner convinced him that stopping this big, vaguely menacing man would be unwise. In any event, Delaney went directly to the elevator bank without being questioned. As usual, the Filipino houseman, Ramon, answered his ring.

"Yeth?"

"Miss Sarazen in?"

"Ith she expecting the gentlemens?"

"Why don't you ask her?" Delaney said.

Ramon hesitated, then finally allowed Delaney to enter.

"Pleath to wait," he said, and disappeared.

But Delaney didn't stay in the hallway. He went immediately into the monochromatic living room, the one decorated in the blue-grey-violet shade he could not identify. He looked about swiftly, took the little envelope of sugar from his pocket, and slipped it under the plump seat cushion of a softly upholstered armchair. Then he took up his position at a caned straight chair facing it. He stood stolidly, hat in hand, and waited.

She came sailing in, barefoot, a white robe billowing out behind her. It was closed from neck to hem with a wide industrial zipper. Suspended from the tab was an English bobby's whistle.

It was evident she had come directly from bath or shower. The fine, silvered hair was wet and plastered flat. The skin of her face shone; her body exuded a damp, sweetly soapy scent. But he had little time to admire her; she was not pleased to see him, and her attack began immediately.

"Now look," she said angrily. "I'm getting sick and tired of this crap. I want—"

"What crap?" he asked.

"This hassling," she said hotly. "I want—"

"What hassling?" he said. "I'm not hassling you."

"Well, what the hell are you doing here, then?"

"Look, Miss Sarazen," he said, as calmly as he could, "I just have a question or two I'd like to ask. Is that hassling?"

"I've been talking to some smart lawyer friends of mine," she told him. "Very important people. And they tell me I don't have to answer another goddamn question. If you want to arrest me, then go ahead, and I'll stand on my rights. But I'm not going to answer any more questions."

"Sure you are," he said gently. "You really are, Miss Sarazen. Because you're an intelligent woman and know what's best for you. Couldn't we sit down—just for a moment? It won't take long, I promise you."

She stared at him. He saw her indecision, and knew she was teetering; it could go either way.

"You help me," he said, "and I'll help you."

"How could you help me?" she scoffed.

"Sit down," he urged. "Let me tell you about it."

She made a sound of disgust, but fell back into the plump armchair where he had hoped she would sit. She hooked one knee over the arm; a bare foot jerked up and down irritably.

He sat on the edge of the caned chair, leaning forward, his straw hat clasped between his knees. His manner was solemn, intent—a solicitor advising a client of the grave consequences of her foolish acts.

"These smart friends of yours . . ." he said. "I suppose they're important men. In business and politics and society. But when they tell you not to cooperate with cops, they're giving you bad advice, Belle. You don't mind if I call you Belle, do you?"

She made an impatient gesture.

"You see, Belle, they know the law all right. And they assume that cops have to follow it. That's true—up to a point. Most cops do follow the law and police regulations. Your smart friends know this and take advantage of it."

"You bet your ass they do," she nodded. "That's why I listen to what they tell me."

He sat back, relaxed, crossed his knees. He held his skimmer on his lap, his hands clasped across it.

"Well, Belle," he said, almost dreamily, "there are laws without end, and police regulations without end. Books and books of them. But now I'm going to let you in on a secret. Most cops—those who have been around for a while—go by another book. Although you can't really call it a book because it's never been written down. What it is is a large collection of tips, tricks, hints, procedures, techniques, and so forth. Stuff that one cop tells another cop. Listen, we're all on the front line, and the only way we can survive is to exchange information, trade secrets, learn from each other. And some of the stuff was bought with blood. Not necessarily how to break the law, but how to get around it. You follow?"

She didn't answer, but he thought he saw interest; he was getting to her.

"Some of the stuff cops talk about when they get together are little things," he continued. "Like how a pusher delivered horse in a metal capsule stuck up his ass. Or how to check inside the boot of a guy you're frisking; some of these dudes carry a blade in there. Or how to puncture the taillight of a car you're following, so the rear end shows one red light and one white and is easier to spot. Or how an undercover cop should wear mirrored sunglasses, so he can stop to polish them and use the glasses like a rearview mirror to make sure no one's on his tail. Little tricks like that. Cop talk. Nothing illegal about that, is there?"

Almost against her will, she was listening to him, fascinated. The bare foot stopped jerking up and down. She straightened in her chair, leaning back comfortably, but watching him and listening.

"And we talk cases, too, of course," he went on. "Unsolved cases, and cases that were broken, and how they were broken. Shop talk.

That's all it is, Belle: shop talk. Whenever cops get together. In a bar, in a restaurant, at law school, in their homes. It always gets around to shop talk. And police conventions? You wouldn't believe! For instance, I remember I went to a police convention once in Atlantic City. After the formal program during the day was finished, we all got together at night and exchanged cases. Ways to beat the bad guys. Well, there was this one fellow there from a town in Texas. Not a small town, I guess, but not so big either. This guy—let's call him Mike—told us about a cute one he was involved in down there. There was this bentnose in their town, a crud with a long drug sheet pushing a lot of shit to school kids. A couple of the kids OD'd, and Mike knew the source was this bad guy. Knew it, but couldn't prove it. So he decided to take him. He got himself a glassine envelope of horse. You know cops can usually lay their hands on some smack, stuff taken in a raid and never turned in."

"And then I suppose he planted it and arrested the pusher for possession," she said, really intrigued now.

"No," Delaney said. "The cop, this Mike, had a better idea. He waited for the pusher to come home. Then he unloaded his revolver and set it loosely in his holster, the strap unsnapped. He had a backup squad of two other cops. They were in the hall and on the stairs, outside. So Mike broke into the pusher's apartment. 'Where's your warrant?' the crud screams. 'Right here,' Mike says, waving a folded sheet of paper at him. You'd be surprised how even these so-called smart guys can be conned. So Mike shoves him around a little and then tosses the place. Naturally he finds the envelope with the shit in it. While all this is going on, Mike keeps walking around in front of the bad guy, the unloaded gun practically falling out of his holster. You should have heard him tell the story; it was hilarious. He said he kept throwing his hip at the pusher, but the guy wouldn't take the bait. Then, when Mike found the horse and laughed and told the pusher he was going to take him in, and the crud would get twenty years at least, *then* he went for Mike's gun, grabbed it from the holster, said Mike wasn't taking him anywhere, and ducked out the door. And of course the backup guys saw him come running out waving a gun, and they blew him away. They reloaded Mike's gun before they called the brass. So it all ended happily."

She looked at him curiously.

"Why are you telling me all this?" she asked.

"Well," the Chief said thoughtfully, "I was trying to convince you that your smart, important friends don't have all the answers. You see,

Belle, if you ever get into trouble, serious trouble, these pals of yours will drop away like the leaves of October. Most of them are married men—right? With responsible jobs and good reputations. You don't really think they're going to put their cocks on the line for you if you get into serious trouble, do you? You'll call, and they'll be in conference, or out of town, or in Mexico on vacation. Believe me, Belle, don't count on them if you get in serious trouble."

"Serious trouble," she repeated. "You keep saying, 'Serious trouble.' What serious trouble could I get in?"

"Oh . . ." he said, gesturing loosely, "like if I said goodbye to you, walked out of here, called the narcotic guys and told them a gabber had informed me that you had a stash of horse up here. The narcs would come galloping and tear this place apart."

"What do I care?" she laughed. "I wouldn't touch heroin. They'd find nothing."

"Sure they would," he said softly. "Under the cushion you're sitting on."

She stared at him, not understanding at first. Then her face whitened; she grew old. She jerked to her feet, flung the seat cushion aside, grabbed up the little envelope. She looked down at it in her hand, raised her head, looked at him.

"You bastard," she breathed. "You bastard!"

"Belle," he laughed. "Oh Belle!"

He stood up, placed his hat carefully on his chair. He walked to her, plucked the envelope from her shaking fingers. He ripped off the top, dumped the white powder into his other palm, licked it clean.

"Powdered sugar," he told her. "Just a demonstration. That you and your important friends don't know all the tricks, Belle. Not all of them. Cops have their little ways, too."

"Powdered sugar?" she said dully.

"That's right," he smiled. "But of course you don't know if I've planted other envelopes of the real stuff in other places, do you?"

He had locked her eyes with his, and she could not look away.

"What do you want to know?" she asked hoarsely.

"That's better," he said. "Now sit down and relax, and let's not have any more crap about your smart lawyer friends."

He replaced her seat cushion. He took her by the elbows and helped her sit down. Then he went back to his caned chair.

"Feeling all right?" he inquired solicitously.

She nodded jerkily.

"Good," he said briskly. "This won't take long now. What kind of business dealings were you having with Victor Maitland?"

She started hesitantly, but he spurred her with sharp, stern questions, and her story didn't take long. About six months before he was killed, Victor Maitland had come to her and asked if she could sell his paintings in the U.S. and abroad. She said sure, and she wanted 35 percent. He said screw that; he was paying Saul Geltman that commission, and if that was her price, what did he need her for? So they finally settled for 20 percent on sales under $100,000, and 15 percent on those over.

"Maitland was to okay the price before the sale?" Delaney asked.

"Of course," Belle Sarazen said.

"So the only one you were shafting was Saul Geltman?"

"Vic said he didn't have a contract with him," she said defensively.

"Apparently he didn't," Delaney nodded. "Go on . . ."

So she had put the word out among her important friends in this country and Europe, and she sold everything Maitland brought her.

"Don't worry," she told the Chief. "I declared my take on my income-tax return."

"I'm sure you did," he said gravely. "How many paintings did you sell?"

"About ten before he was killed," she said. "We were cleaning up."

"Wasn't Maitland worried that Saul Geltman would find out?"

"Worried?" she laughed. "Vic? No way, darling. That guy didn't worry about anything—except getting enough loot to live the way he wanted to. He did say the buyers should agree to keep their purchases secret and not lend the paintings for shows for at least five years."

"And they agreed?"

"Of course. Listen, Vic was selling at bargain-basement rates. Much less than they'd have to pay if they went through Geltman."

"Oh-ho," Delaney said. "I'm beginning to see why your business was so good. You were his discount operation."

"Right," she agreed.

"You said the only thing Maitland worried about was getting the money to live the way he wanted to. Belle, what did he do with his money? Where did it all go?"

"Taxes took like half."

"I know, but still . . ."

"Liquor," she said. "Parties."

He looked at her, not believing.

"How much liquor can you buy?" he said. "How many parties? You said you sold ten paintings. Say the average price was fifty G's. That's half a cool mil. Say your commish was twenty percent. That leaves him four hundred thousand. Say he paid his legitimate tax on that—which I doubt—and it ran as high as fifty percent. That still leaves him two hundred thousand, just through you, not counting his take from Geltman Galleries. Are you trying to tell me he spent two hundred thousand dollars on booze and parties?"

She was silent a few moments. Then the bare foot began jerking nervously again. She started smoothing her damp hair with her palm.

"You won't believe this," she said.

"At this stage," he said, "I'll believe anything."

"Well, he didn't want anyone to know," she said. "About the money, I mean. He was giving most of it away."

"Giving it away? To whom?"

"Young artists. In the Village, SoHo, downtown, Brooklyn. Here, there, everywhere. He wandered all over the city. Going to little galleries. To guys' lofts. Studios. When he found someone he thought had talent, he'd stake them. Put them on salary. That's where all his money was going."

"Jesus Christ," Delaney said. "I don't believe it."

"You better believe it," she nodded. "It's the truth. I know some of the artists he bankrolled. Want to meet them?"

"No," he said slowly, "I'll take your word for it. Did Geltman know about this?"

"I don't know. I doubt it."

"His wife?"

"No way. He didn't tell her *anything*."

"Let's get back to the paintings you were selling for him. Did Geltman find out?"

"Oh sure," she said. "He'd have to—eventually. The art scene's a tight little world. Everyone knows everyone else. People talk. There are no secrets for long."

She said that Saul Geltman had gone to London to attend an art auction at Sotheby's. At a party, he had heard a man bragging about a Maitland he had just bought at a bargain price. Geltman got himself invited to the guy's apartment to see it. He took one look and knew it hadn't come through his gallery. He came back to New York, and he and Maitland had a knock-down-drag-out fight. Geltman said not only was Maitland depriving him of his rightful commission, but he was depressing the price of Maitland paintings all over the world. The artist had told Belle Sarazen of his bitter argument with Saul Geltman.

" 'Fuck him,' " she quoted Maitland as saying. " 'Geltman's taken care of. For the rest of his life. Where does he get off complaining that I'm selling my own work? I don't need him. I don't need anyone!' "

"So you continued selling Maitland's paintings?" the Chief asked her.

"Sure, I did," she said. "It wasn't *illegal,* was it?"

"No," he said, "it wasn't illegal. Tell me this, Belle—did you happen to notice the dates on the paintings Maitland brought to you to sell? When were they done?"

"They were all early stuff," she said. "Painted twenty years ago. In 1957 and '58. Like that. But just as good as his newer things. You couldn't tell the difference."

"There wasn't any," he said.

She looked at him, puzzled. "That's what I said."

He nodded and got up slowly, preparing to leave. He didn't want to hear any more. He had heard enough. But he turned at the door.

"Belle," he said, "why didn't you tell us all this a long time ago? When we first came up here?"

She lifted her chin.

"I didn't want to get involved," she said.

He sighed resignedly, and turned again to leave. This time she stopped him.

"Edward X. Delaney," she said, "you didn't plant any other envelopes around here, did you? With the real junk?"

"Why Belle," he said, with a curdy smile, "you don't think I'd do anything *illegal,* do you?"

He would never get to the end of people—never. He came to this chastening realization during a slow, ruminative walk through Central Park, from Belle Sarazen's apartment to the East Side. He ambled ponderously, leaning forward a bit, his straw hat tipped to shield his eyes from the burning June sun.

What surprised Edward X. Delaney, what shocked him, was the discovery of what the doomed Victor Maitland was doing with his wealth. To hear suddenly that this gross, brawling, vicious man was capable of such anonymous generosity was equivalent, Delaney reflected mournfully, to learning that Attila the Hun had endowed a home for unwed mothers.

He had lunch on the terrace at the Central Park Zoo. Had a hotdog and a beer, then went back in for another frank and beer. He ate and drank slowly, hearing the trumpeting and screeching and howling of caged animals. It seemed a good place to put it all together, give it form and sequence—this story of craving humans.

Victor Maitland had died, Delaney decided, because he lived too long. It was true. If he had lived only three or four years, as Dr. Horowitz had predicted, the tax fraud would have gone like silk, Saul Geltman would be assured of a good annual income from those paintings stored in the barn, Alma and Ted would have been left a comfortable legacy from the final sale, Dora and Emily would have restored the old homestead, and everyone would have lived happily ever after. If Victor Maitland had died . . .

But the son of a bitch didn't die, wouldn't die. Not the way he was supposed to. He lived, and lived, and lived. And there were all those beautiful paintings drying in the Nyack barn. What the hell. Might as well turn a few of them into ready cash and have some fun before he conked. Maitland might think that way, Delaney guessed. There were so many finished paintings; selling off ten or twenty or more wouldn't make all that difference.

Except to Saul Geltman. It made a lot of difference to Saul. He was trying to keep the price high for Maitland's paintings. So he fed them into the market carefully. And the barn paintings were as much his inheritance as Dora's and Emily's. He could live twenty years on his commissions from those. What was it Maitland had told Belle Sarazen? "Fuck him. He's taken care of. For the rest of his life."

Then Geltman learned about the secret sales, and it all began to come apart. No commissions for him on the secret sales. Worse, it was bringing the market price down. How could he depend on scarcity when anyone could go to the Sarazen woman and get a discount Maitland? And the artist *lived!* The bastard *lived!* And was working and grinding out more and more paintings. It was time to turn off the faucet. Yes, Delaney reckoned, Geltman must have figured just that: it was time to turn off the faucet. Victor Maitland's death would solve everything.

The Chief walked into the offices of Simon & Brewster, all beaming geniality. But the lubricious Susan Hemley was absent from her desk. In her place was a stiff, bespectacled young man with a grey complexion. The desk was bare; the young man sat as if nailed to the chair, hands clasped so tightly atop the desk blotter that knuckles showed white.

"Yes?" he asked coldly. "May I help you?"

"Is Miss Hemley in?"

"No."

"Mr. Simon? I called for an appointment. My name is Chief Edward X. Delaney."

"Chief?"

"New York Police Department."

"Oh. Just a moment."

He rose jerkily to his feet, crossed to Simon's door, knocked in a rough manner. He entered without pausing and slammed the door behind him. He was out again in a moment, scowling.

"Mr. Simon will be with you shortly. Take a chair."

They sat in silence, trying not to stare at each other.

"Are you also an attorney?" Delaney asked finally.

"No," the young man said angrily. "I was hired as a paralegal assistant."

It was evident that his conception of paralegal employment did not include serving as a receptionist. Delaney had the feeling that if he offered sympathy, the young man would either start screaming or burst into tears. So the Chief sat without speaking, straw hat balanced on his knees, and endured the long, silent wait, guessing this was J. Julian Simon's little oneupmanship ploy.

Eventually, twenty minutes later, the man himself came bustling from his inner office, hand outstretched, perfect teeth gleaming.

"Sorry to keep you waiting," he smiled, and offered no apology.

"I'm in no hurry," Delaney said equably. "'The mills of the gods . . .' and so forth and so forth."

As usual, Simon looked as though he had been oiled and polished. A day spent in court had not dulled his knife-edge creases, disturbed his elaborately coiffed hair, or tangled his perfectly groomed mustache. Today the shirt was light blue polka dots on white, the tie knitted maroon silk, the suit itself a shiny navy linen with white buttons and lapels like vertical stabilizers.

He ushered the Chief into his private office, sat him down, inquired solicitously as to his health, adjusted the drapes to block more of the late-afternoon sunlight, and offered a drink. When it was politely declined, he mixed himself a Rob Roy at his handsome bar with all the care of a mad scientist distilling the elixir of life. It was not, Delaney judged, Simon's first Rob Roy of the day.

"Five hours in court," the attorney boomed. "Endless delays. Boring, boring, boring. But you know all that, I'm sure."

"Cops know all about waiting," Delaney agreed. "It's part of the job. But eventually, I've noted, things get done. If you have the patience."

"Of course, of course," Simon said. He took a sip of his drink, said, "Aah!" and settled back more comfortably into his leather swivel chair. "Is this an official visit, Chief?"

"Not exactly," Delaney said. "I guess you might say it's a courtesy call."

"Oh?" Simon said, puzzled.

"Counselor, as a member of the bar, you're an officer of the court. That's true, isn't it?"

"Yes, of course."

"And I'm acting in the capacity of an officer of the law. So you might say we're on the same side. Don't you agree?"

Simon nodded, watching the Chief carefully now.

"So I felt it only right," Delaney continued, "that I come to you directly and give you the facts before taking official action."

Simon finished the Rob Roy in a gulp. He rose, stalked to the bar, busied himself stirring another. His back was turned to Delaney. When he spoke, his mellifluous voice had lost its honeyed drip.

"What's this all about, Delaney?" he demanded.

"Are you a friend of Saul Geltman?"

The lawyer brought his drink back to the desk, sat down heavily in the swivel chair. He raised the glass but didn't sip; he stared at Delaney over the rim.

"You know I am," he said.

"Do you *want* to be a friend of his?"

"What the hell is that supposed to mean?"

"I'm trying to discover just how far out on a limb you'll crawl for him. Who ate the sandwiches?"

"What?" Simon said, bewildered. "What are you talking about?"

"The sandwiches you ordered for lunch," Delaney explained patiently. "For you and Geltman. On that Friday. Who ate them? He wasn't here for lunch. Did you eat them all? Throw the extras away? Or did he come back for his later?"

"I have told you again and again that—"

"You've told me shit," Delaney said harshly. "What kind of sandwiches were they, counselor?"

"Delaney, what's this with the sandwiches?"

"What kind were they? Tunafish? Egg salad? Meat? What?"

"Well, if you must know, they were roast beef on whole wheat bread with diet soda."

"What did you have for lunch last Tuesday, counselor?"

"Last Tuesday?" Simon said. "Who can remem—"

He stopped suddenly, too late. Delaney grinned at him.

"Right," he nodded. "Can't remember what you had for lunch last Tuesday. Who can? I can't. But you remember perfectly that more than two months ago you had roast beef on whole wheat bread with diet soda. Geltman volunteered the same information. Unasked, by the way. That's the trouble with amateurs: they talk too much. Now, counselor, as an expert in cross-examination, wouldn't you say that the fact that both you and Saul Geltman remember exactly what you had for lunch two months ago suggests rehearsal, if not collusion?"

J. Julian Simon rose to his feet, somewhat unsteadily.

"This conversation is at an end," he said thickly. "I'll thank you to leave."

Delaney also stood up. He unbuttoned his jacket, raised the tails high. He turned slowly, so Simon could see his shirted torso.

"Look," he said, "I'm not wired. Frisk me if you like. No bugs, no transmitter, no recorder. This talk is just between you and me, counselor."

"No more talk," Simon said.

"For your own good," Delaney urged, rebuttoning his jacket and sitting down again. "In your own interest. Don't you want to hear what I've got?"

Simon suddenly seemed drained. That ruddy complexion, nourished by a thousand facials and hours under the sunlamp, became as soft and puckered as a deflated balloon. He fell rather than sat back in his chair.

"Sure you want to hear," Delaney went on grimly. "So you'll know what you're up against if you decide to be Saul Geltman's friend. He comes in here around ten that Friday morning. You close and lock the door to the outer office. Look, now I'm Saul Geltman . . ."

The Chief rose, strode quickly to the frosted-glass door leading to the outside corridor. He pushed the button release on the lock. He opened the door, stepped halfway through, then turned to wave at J. Julian Simon.

"Bye-bye," he said merrily.

Then he came back inside, relocked the door, took his seat again.

"No one saw Saul Geltman in this office after he arrived at ten o'clock," he went on. "Not Susan Hemley, not even the guy from the deli who brought the lunch. No one. We checked."

"I did," Simon said hoarsely. "He was here all the time."

"Was he? Stick with that story, counselor, and your ass is up for grabs. A subpoena. Testimony before a grand jury. Questions. About your business, taxes, your record. Publicity. Your picture on the six o'clock news holding a copy of the *Wall Street Journal* in front of your face. Is that what you want, counselor? Are you willing to go through all that for the sake of your friendship with Saul Geltman?"

"The man is my client. You have no right to—"

"No right?" Delaney thundered. "No right? Don't give me that crap, you lousy shyster. You think we don't have your sheet? You think we don't know how close you came to disbarment? Don't talk to me about privileged lawyer-client relationships. I'm not talking about your client now, I'm talking about you, about obstruction of justice, perjury, and accessory to homicide. How's that for openers?"

"You're guessing," Simon cried. "Guessing! You've got nothing. You come in here and—"

"I've got an eyewitness," Chief Delaney said triumphantly. "An eyewitness who saw Geltman near Victor Maitland's studio the morning he was killed. At a time you say he was up here eating roast beef on whole wheat and drinking diet soda with you. An eyewitness, counselor! Think of it! A responsible citizen, pillar of the community, who picked Saul Geltman's picture out of a dozen others and will swear he was there at that time. Plus supporting physical evidence. Is your friendship worth it? *Think,* man! Use your goddamned brain! Now's the time. You can work a deal; you know that. Get out of the way of the landslide, Mr. Simon. It's coming. You can't stop it. And if you repeat that stupid statement of yours under oath, you'll be swept away. You and your Spy caricatures and your oak bookcases and all this swell stuff—all gone. Nothing left."

Edward X. Delaney rose abruptly to his feet.

"An eyewitness," he repeated softly. "Who saw him. Think of that! Well, you give the problem a lot of thought, counselor, a lot of careful consideration. If you decide you'd like to amend your statement, that you made a mistake and maybe Saul Geltman did step out of your office for an hour or two, why just give me a call. I'm in the book. Take your time. Think it over carefully. I'm in no hurry. I'm a patient man. I learned how by cooling my heels in lawyers' offices. Take care, counselor. See you around."

He left a shaken, slack-jawed J. Julian Simon slumped behind his leather-topped desk, holding his cocktail glass in trembling fingers. Delaney left the office building quickly, crossed to the north side of East 68th Street. He walked a half-block westward, toward Fifth Avenue, and stood partly concealed by trees and parked cars, but in a position where he could observe the entrance to the building he had just left.

He reckoned it would take at least ten minutes for J. Julian Simon to start his adrenaline flowing with another Rob Roy, to call Saul Geltman at the Galleries on Madison Avenue, and to summon him with the news that the sky was falling. But it was almost twenty minutes before the little art dealer came scurrying around the corner, almost trotting in his haste. He rushed into the building, and Edward X. Delaney, smiling, wended his way slowly homeward, lighting a cigar. He didn't, he acknowledged, know exactly what the hell he was doing; he had no definite plan. Yet. But he wanted Saul Geltman scared witless. It could do no harm.

When he entered his brownstone, he found Monica, Abner Boone, and Jason T. Jason seated around the kitchen table, laughing, and sharing a bowl of potato chips. Monica was drinking a martini, Boone a bottle of club soda, and Jason Two was working on a can of beer. They all looked up as he came clumping in.

"Hullo, dear," Monica said. "What have you been doing all day?"

"Threatening people," he said cheerfully. "Thirsty work. Don't I get a reward?"

"The pitcher's in the icebox," she said. "Lemon peel already cut."

"Perfect," he nodded, and poured himself a martini over ice and added a twist. Then he pulled up a chair to join them, and looked at Boone. "How did it go, sergeant?"

"Good enough, sir. I think. Between us, we hit eleven dealers. Four of them wouldn't say one way or another. Didn't know or wouldn't talk. The other seven said that without Maitland, Saul Geltman is down the drain."

"Two of my guys said he's got no one heavy enough to pay the freight on Madison Avenue, Chief," Jason put in. "High-rent district. They said he might be able to stay in business downtown, but not on Mad. Ave. Unless he comes up with another Maitland."

"Chief," Boone said, "you remember we asked him the same question the first time we talked to him. He said that the death of Maitland would hurt him, but not all that much, that he'd survive."

"Sure he would," Delaney said. "With twenty million dollars' worth of Maitland's stuff in the Nyack barn. Here's what I got . . ."

He gave them brief accounts of his meetings with Belle Sarazen and J. Julian Simon. They listened intently, silent and fascinated. When he finished, Monica got up to pour herself another drink, freshen her husband's glass, and put another can of beer before Jason Two.

"Then he's guilty, Edward?" she asked. "No doubt about it?"

"No doubt about it," he said. "Proving it is something else again."

"Uh, Chief," Jason said. "Sounds to me like we got motive now. And opportunity, if this lawyer guy chickens out on the alibi. No weapon, I admit. But enough to rack him up. No?"

Chief Delaney looked at Boone.

"What do you think, sergeant?"

Abner Boone shook his head angrily.

"No way," he said. "I don't see it. Indictment maybe. Possibly. But I'll bet the DA won't prosecute. Too thin."

"Thin?" Jason T. Jason cried. "My God, it seems to me the man's tied in knots."

"No, Jason," Delaney said. "Sergeant Boone's right. We'd never get a conviction on the basis of what we've got. Look, everyone thinks a Not Guilty verdict means innocence. Not necessarily. Sometimes it just means the prosecutor hasn't proved his case beyond a reasonable doubt. Usually in cases like that, the DA doesn't even go to trial. He wants to show a good conviction rate. Prosecuting an obviously weak case is a waste of time for him, the taxpayers, everyone."

"Look, Jase," Boone said to the disappointed cop, "everything we've got so far is circumstantial. That's not too bad; most homicide prosecutions are based on circumstantial evidence. How often do you get an eyewitness to a killing? But we've got nothing that will stand up in court."

"Right," Delaney nodded. "Belle Sarazen's report of the heavy argument between Maitland and Geltman is hearsay. Not admissible. And if J. Julian Simon decides to repeat his lie under oath, who do you think the jury's going to believe—a slick Madison Avenue lawyer or a been-around hooker ready for Social Security?"

"You mean Saul Geltman is going to get away with this?" Monica said indignantly.

"Ah," Chief Delaney said. "We shall see. Geltman knows now that we have an eyewitness placing him at the murder scene at the right time. Let's figure he saw those police drawings in the newspapers and on TV, so he knows we were looking for her. And he knows what a danger she represents to him because he saw Mama Perez and Dolores near Maitland's studio that Friday morning."

"So?" Monica said.

"So," Edward X. Delaney said dreamily, "let's help him find her."

But Deputy Commissioner Ivar Thorsen wasn't enthusiastic when Delaney spelled it out for him on the phone that evening.

"Sounds like entrapment to me, Edward," he said.

"For God's sake," Delaney said, "entrapment is legal junk. It all depends on whether the judge got laid the night before. We're not luring him into committing a crime; we're giving him a choice. If he's really innocent—which he isn't—he'll laugh at us and walk away. Maybe even report it to the cops. But if he's guilty—which he is—he'll take the bait. Ivar, this guy is sweating; I know he is. He'll bite."

"The cost . . ." Thorsen groaned.

"Not so much," Delaney said. "One or two tech men working a day or so. We'll keep the equipment simple. I've got enough personnel with Boone and Jason and the guys watching Mama Perez. What do you say?"

"A helluva risk to the Perez woman."

"She'll be protected."

"If it goes sour, it's my neck."

"I know that, Ivar," Delaney said patiently. "Want me to go ahead on my own, and we'll pretend this conversation never took place?"

"No," Thorsen said. "Thanks for the offer, but it wouldn't work. You need my okay to draw the equipment. And you need that to nail him—right?"

"Right. Well? Are you in?"

There was silence for a few moments. Delaney waited.

"Look, Edward," Thorsen said finally, "let's do this: make the approach first. If he bites, I'll authorize what you need. If he doesn't go for it, then all bets are off and the bastard walks. Agreed?"

"After what he did to Mary and Sylvia?" Edward X. Delaney said. "Never."

20

They were dawdling over their lunch coffee. Chief Delaney was reading an early edition of the *Post,* smiling over a story about a Chicago cat-burglar who had tried to squeeze through an iron-barred gate and got his head caught. He had to call the cops to pry him free. Monica, chin in hand, was listening to the kitchen radio.

"Piano Sonata Number Two," she said dreamily. "Prokofiev."

"Sam Prokofiev?" Delaney asked, not looking up. "Used to play third base for the Cincinnati Reds?"

"That's the man."

"Fast hands," he murmured. "But he couldn't hit."

Then he looked up. They stared at each other solemnly.

The news came on at 2:00 P.M., and Delaney put his paper aside. The first items dealt with a flood in Ohio, a famine in Pakistan, and the indictment of a California Congressman for malfeasance and misfeasance.

"And mopery," the Chief muttered.

Then the announcer said:

"The body of a middle-aged man was removed from the ruins of a luxury apartment on the upper East Side of Manhattan early this morning following a three-alarm fire that routed almost a hundred tenants of the building and caused extensive fire and water damage. The dead man

has been tentatively identified as J. Julian Simon, a prominent attorney
. . . In Italy, sources close to the—"

Delaney reached across the table, clicked off the radio.

"Did he say . . . ?" Monica faltered.

"That's what he said," Delaney snapped. "J. Julian Simon. Sometimes I'm too fucking smart by half," he added savagely.

He had his hand on the kitchen phone when it shrilled under his
fingers. He jerked it off the hook.

"Edward X. Delaney here," he said furiously.

"Edward," Ivar Thorsen said breathlessly, "did you hear the—"

"I heard," the Chief said angrily. "God damn it to hell! It's my fault,
Ivar."

"Then you think—"

"*Think,* shit! The little bastard knocked off his old handball buddy
when he started to come apart. Now all we got is Simon's original statement, and Geltman's still got his alibi. He thinks! Ivar, you've got to
handle this. I haven't the clout. Where's the body now?"

"I don't know, Edward. On the ME's slab, I suppose."

"Will you call and tell them to carve the roast very, very carefully?
Especially look for knife wounds, particularly in the back."

"All right," Thorsen said faintly.

"Or evidence of drugging or heavy drinking. Then call your contact
at the Fire Department, and put a bee in his ear. Victim was involved in
hanky-panky, foul play suspected, and so forth and so on. Was the fire
deliberately started? Evidence of arson? Tell them to go over that apartment with a comb."

"Will do, Edward."

"Get back to me as soon as you've got anything. Please, Ivar?"

He banged the phone back on the hook. He couldn't look at Monica.

"Edward," she started, "it isn't your—"

"He's gone," he said loudly. "He's just gone."

She thought he meant J. Julian Simon—but he didn't. He stamped
into the study, slammed the door behind him. He threw himself into his
swivel chair. He held out his hands before him, saw them trembling. It
was, he knew, the rage of humiliation. It was his bruised ego that was
suffering. Snookered and made a fool of, again. He wondered just how
much of his successful career had stemmed from an exaggerated sense
of his own talents and shrewdness. Well, he reflected ruefully, little Saul
Geltman was giving him a lesson in humility.

He tried to put the man together. It was a crossword puzzle with too many clues. Geltman was this, he was that. He was cruel, he was tender. He was profound, he was frivolous. Edward X. Delaney, struggling with reports, notes, memories, couldn't get a handle on the man. The "handle" he was looking for was motivation.

He had been a cop long enough to know that only rarely did people act with singleness of purpose. Motives were usually jungles, a complexity of drives and incentives. A son who fed an arsenic sandwich to his aged, ailing father might say, "I did it to ease his pain," and believe it. Dig a little deeper, and you found that the killer was in hock to the shys and needed his legacy to keep his kneecaps from being splintered; that he had the hots for a young twist who demanded he show some green before she said Yes; that his sick father was a whining, incontinent, spiteful invalid. But it was also true that the victim was in extreme and constant pain. So?

Delaney's analysis of Saul Geltman was interrupted by a call from Ivar Thorsen. The Deputy Commissioner was excited.

"Edward? They were way ahead of us. They'd already found them. Multiple stab wounds in the back. Similar to the MO on Maitland. It was definitely a homicide, according to the ME who did the autopsy. He happens to be the guy who did Maitland, and he says it could be the same knife. I've alerted the Fire Department. Their investigators are already there."

"That's fine, Ivar," Delaney said heavily. "But nothing to the press on this. *Nothing!* Let that midget think he's scammed us. Can you send some men around with photos of Geltman? Maybe someone saw him at the scene—doorman, neighbors, anyone. It's a long shot, but we've got to go through the motions."

The Deputy Commissioner said he'd take care of it, but it wouldn't be easy; the manpower cuts were hurting.

"I know," Delaney said consolingly, "but it's only for a few days. A week at the most."

Thorsen was silent for a beat or two.

"Think you can wrap it up by then?" he asked casually.

"One way or another," Delaney said, deliberately enigmatic. "Did Boone tell you about the tax fraud?"

Thorsen said he had, and that he supposed they'd have to tip the IRS eventually. He wondered what effect that would have on the sympathies of J. Barnes Chapin, learning that the NYPD had blown the whistle on his sister.

"It could be a plus if you handle it right," Delaney told him. "Have a meet with Chapin and lay it out for him. Tell him we'll hold off tipping the Feds if he can convince his sister to get religion and spill her guts about the whole con—how it was set up, who was involved, and so forth. Tell Chapin the IRS probably won't even charge Dora and Emily; they'll be so happy to find that treasure house of Maitland paintings. It'll mean that Dora and Emily inherit zilch, and Alma and Ted Maitland become wealthy, but that's the way the cream curdles. At least Chapin's sister and niece won't go to the slammer. In return, he should be happy to cooperate on that bill you want passed."

"Edward, you should have been a politician," Thorsen said.

"God forbid."

"Well, I like it. And I think it'll work."

"Hold off talking to Chapin until I give you the go-ahead."

"Will do. Anything else?"

"Could you come up with, say a few hundred dollars from the discretionary fund? You know, the money put aside for gabbers and dope buys?"

"A couple of hundred? What for?"

"Don't you trust me, Ivar?"

"Sure I do, Edward. For a hundred, tops."

"All right," Delaney laughed. "I'll try to get by on that. It's for Mama Perez. I'll lay it out of my own pocket, and you make good. Agreed?"

"Agreed."

Then Edward X. Delaney went back to his analysis of the character of art dealer Saul Geltman. He made a list of possible motives and, on the basis of what he knew or guessed about the man, gave each motive a value rating of one to ten. Then he eliminated minor or superficial goads that might drive a man to murder. What he was left with was the obvious and simple spur of greed.

The problem with covetousness—for money, physical possessions, power—was that it was an open-ended motive; there was no end to it. A man compelled by a desire for revenge, for example, might kill, and that would finish it. Act committed, need satisfied. But there was no end to greed. It fed upon itself. More never led to satiety; more led to more. In a way, it was an addiction. "Yes," says the multimillionaire, "I have a lot of money. But I don't have *all* of it!"

In Geltman's case, Delaney decided, greed was driving him to acts he had never imagined. Obsessed with a passion for more, with a fear of losing what he had already gained, he had surrendered to his addiction, whirling down into a maelstrom of deceit, treachery, murder. All the while stroking his zinc-covered dining table, sipping fine cognac from a Baccarat snifter, and murmuring, "Mine, mine, mine!"

The Chief was still at his musings when Monica came into the study bearing two rye highballs. She gave her husband his, then perched on the edge of the desk next to him, her good legs dangling.

"God bless you, child," he said, taking an appreciative sip, stroking her bare calf. "I'll remember who offered aid in my hour of need."

"What's the need?" she asked. "What are you doing?"

"Trying to understand why Saul Geltman is Saul Geltman, and not Edward X. Delaney, say, or even Jake Dukker. Here's a philosophical question for you: Which is worse—to want all the good things of life and never get them, or to get them and then lose them?"

She considered a moment, her glass at her lips.

"You understand the question?" he asked.

"Oh, I understand it," she said. "I'm just trying to decide. I guess it would be worse to want things and never get them."

"Why?"

"Because if you had them and then lost them, at least you could console yourself with the thought that, for a while, you had it all and were happy. But not having, *never* having, would just be constant frustration."

"Mmm," he pondered. "That's your personal reaction."

"Of course," she said. "That's what you wanted, wasn't it?"

"Yes. No. Actually, I was wondering how Saul Geltman would answer that question."

"Saul Geltman," she said. "I still can't believe it. That nice little man."

"Oh, everyone speaks very highly of him," Delaney said with heavy sarcasm. "One of the nicest guys I ever met had just murdered his mother, father, two sisters, a brother, and the family dog. With a hammer yet. While they slept. I don't think Geltman would agree with your answer. Just the opposite. I told you once, it's when want turns to need that the trouble starts."

She looked at him.

"I want you," she said.

He looked at her.

"I need you," he said.

"Then let the trouble start," she said, sliding off the desk and taking him by the hand.

"In the middle of the afternoon?" he said.

"Why not?"

"Depraved," he said, shaking his big head.

But he rose immediately to his feet and followed her upstairs.

21

His first intention was to approach Rosa Perez by himself and try to sell her on his scheme. But he finally decided to brace her with Sergeant Boone and Officer Jason in attendance. They were all three big men; while they would not threaten physical harm, their massive presence would have a psychological effect. He had used it before: a suspect surrounded by looming and glowering giants, unconsciously intimidated, imagination creating the fear—and eager cooperation.

But Mama wasn't having any.

"You tink I'm nuts?" she said indignantly.

Patiently, Delaney went through his prepared speech. What they were asking was really a very small thing: a single phone call to Saul Geltman for starters. She was to say she was the eyewitness who had seen him near Maitland's studio the morning of the murder. She was also to tell Geltman she had made a tentative identification to the cops, but maybe she could change her mind. After all, she was a very poor woman. Etc., etc.

Then, if Geltman sounded interested, she was to set up a meet with him in her apartment. Delaney would take it from there. And that's all there was to it.

Mama said no.

Delaney told her that putting Geltman in the slammer was the only way she could guarantee her own safety, since the art dealer was sure to come gunning for her. When that had no effect, the Chief reminded Rosa that Geltman had also seen Dolores, and for the sake of the girl's safety, the phone call should be made.

She waffled a bit on that, but then stoutly decided that she and Dolores and Dolores' mother would move, and Geltman would never find them. So Delaney offered her fifty dollars to make the call. The gold tooth gleamed, but Mama still refused. And she remained adamant even after the ante was raised to a hundred dollars, and Delaney swore she would be in no physical danger.

"We'll be in the next room watching everything during the meet," he assured her. "He makes one cute move, and we smear him. Dolores won't even be here. You're a strong woman; you can hold off one puny little guy for a few seconds, can't you? I'll bet you've handled bigger bums than him and never got hurt. And there's that yard for your trouble. A cool hundred dollars for a few minutes alone with this guy. Mama, he's practically a *midget!* What do you say?"

She was tempted, they could all see that, but she wouldn't commit herself. She was a small, bulky woman with eyes as bright as berries, a wise mouth, tartish voice, a manner that alternated between street twist and saucy virgin.

Chief Delaney, stymied, noted her frequently coquettish manner. Seeing behind that damaged face, he realized she must have been a beauty forty years ago, and she remembered.

"Your picture in all the papers, Mama," he said softly. "If you help us. Television interviews. Rosa Perez Helps Capture Killer. Everyone will see you. Everyone will know who you are. You'll be someone. Someone, Mama. Rosa Perez. Famous."

"On TV?" she asked slowly, and he knew he had her.

It was decided the phone call would be made from the Chief's brownstone. Both Boone and Jason owned small tape recorders. The sergeant's had a suction-cup attachment for telephone use. He'd tape the call from the hallway extension with Jason standing by with his recorder as backup. Delaney and Rosa Perez would place the call from the study.

They spent an entire afternoon on rehearsals. Mama was not an educated woman, but her parents had not raised her to be a fool, and she had added street wit and a shrewd understanding of human foibles. Delaney prepared a script for her to follow, but soon discarded the text and let her speak her own argot. They tossed questions at her—things they thought Saul Geltman might ask—and, after an initial hesitation, she began to answer all their queries with just the right mixture of bravado and cupidity. Delaney thought she'd do very well indeed.

After the rehearsal, on the ride uptown, Jason Two said, "What a bimbo! I think she's really enjoying this."

"She's the center of attention," Delaney said, "and that pleases her. We'll go with the call tomorrow afternoon about three o'clock. He should be back from lunch by then."

"If he goes for it, Chief," Boone asked, "and he makes the meet, what have we got? You figuring on aggravated assault or assault with a deadly weapon?"

"Hopefully," Delaney nodded. "If not that, we'll have another link with the Maitland kill at least. But I'm betting he'll show with his trusty blade, all charged up to off her."

"He won't pay the blackmail?" Jason said.

"He's not that stupid," Delaney said. "He'll guess it's just the first installment, and he's got to silence her permanently. That's how I'd figure if I was him."

"You think he's got the balls to take her?" Boone said.

"He did it twice," Delaney said somberly. "It gets easier."

The call was set for Thursday afternoon. The Chief had planned it that way so Monica would be absent on her weekly stint as a hospital volunteer; he preferred she not be aware of his use of Rosa Perez as bait. Jason T. Jason was assigned the task of chauffering Mama uptown in his car. Boone and Delaney met early in the brownstone to arrange chairs, and set up and test the small tape recorders.

Jason arrived on schedule a little after two o'clock. Delaney was touched to see that Mama Perez had dolled-up for the occasion. She was wearing a shiny purple dress with an embroidered bib of seed pearls, only a few of which were missing. She carried a white plastic handbag with a black poodle painted on one side. Her platform soles gave her an additional three inches of height; the straps wound about fat calves bulging under rose-tinted stockings or pantyhose. The makeup was thick and startling: green eyeshadow, patches of pink rouge, and puckered Cupid's-bow lips.

"You look terrific," Delaney assured her.

"You like?" she said delightedly, then shrugged casually. "Is nothing."

She asked for a drink, and he promptly brought her a double whiskey with water on the side, having no doubts that she could handle it. Sergeant Boone and Jason went into the hall to man their equipment. Delaney had Rosa Perez sit in the swivel chair behind the study desk. He pulled a straight chair close to her where he could listen to the conversation by leaning forward, his ear pressed to the receiver. He was prepared to break the connection if she crossed him.

A few minutes before three o'clock, he dialed the number of Geltman Galleries and handed the phone to Mama Perez. She hitched forward on the padded chair, her back straight, looking very serious and intent.

"Geltman Galleries," a woman's voice said.

"Meester Geltman," Mama Perez said.

"May I ask who's calling?"

"He don' know me. Tell heem eet's about Victor Maitland."

"Victor Maitland? Perhaps I can help you. What is it—"

"Meester Geltman," Rosa repeated sternly. "Is important. You jus' tell heem."

"Just a moment, please."

They waited. Delaney nodded encouragingly at Mama Perez and made an O sign with thumb and forefinger. She flashed her gold tooth in a surprisingly impish smile.

They heard clicks on the phone as the call was switched. Then . . .

"Saul Geltman speaking. Who is this, please?"

"You don' know me," Mama Perez said. "I seen your peecture een the paper. But I seen you before that."

"Oh?" Geltman said easily. "What was that—"

"Sure I seen you," she went on quickly. "On the stairs. Victor Maitland's studio. On Friday morning. The day he was keeled."

"I don't know what you're talking about," Geltman said.

"You know," Mama Perez said. "You know. I seen you there, an' you seen me. Right, Meester Geltman?"

"I haven't the slightest—"

"I tol' the cops I taught it was you," she continued. "I peeked your peecture out. But maybe eet wasn't you. Maybe I make a meestake. Eet was a long time ago. I only seen you a meenute. So I could maybe make a meestake. You onnerstan', Meester Geltman?"

There was silence a moment. They heard his breathing. Then he said, "Wait a minute; I'll be right back." Then they heard the scrape of a chair on the floor, footsteps, the sound of a door being closed, footsteps, the creak of the chair as he sat down again.

"Would you give me your name, please?" he asked pleasantly.

"No," Mama Perez said. "You don' need to know. I'm jus' a poor woman, Meester Geltman. A *poor* woman. You onnerstan'?"

"I think I do," he said, his voice still steady. "Did the cops put you up to this?"

"The cops?" Mama repeated. She laughed scornfully. "Focking cops! I speet on the cops!"

She spoke that rehearsed line with such genuine vehemence that even Delaney was convinced. He figured that either Geltman would believe, or the whole scam would die right there.

"What do you want?" Saul Geltman asked, and the Chief took a deep breath, guessing the art dealer was hooked.

"I wan' five tousan'," she said. "I wanna go back to Puerto Rico. I wanna get out of thees steenking seety an' nevair come back."

"Five thousand dollars?" Saul Geltman said. "That's a lot of money."

"Not so much moaney. Not eef I go away an' nevair come back. You onnerstan', Meester Geltman?"

"I think I do. What about the young girl who was with you?"

"My daughter. She goes back weeth me. We nevair come back. Nevair."

"And what happens if the cops find you in Puerto Rico?"

Mama Perez laughed again. "In Puerto Rico? Nevair, Meester Geltman. But eef they do, then we don' remember. We don' remember who we seen near Victor Maitland's studio that Friday morning he was keeled. We forget. For five tousan' we forget."

"Well . . . uh . . ." Geltman said cautiously, "maybe we could discuss it. Come to some arrangement to our mutual benefit."

"Five tousan'," Rosa Perez said definitely. "Een cash. No check. Cash money. Small beels."

"You've figured this out very carefully, haven't you?"

"Oh sure."

"And have you figured out how the money is to be delivered to you?"

Delaney put a finger to his lips, shook his head. Mama nodded and said nothing on the phone.

"I asked how the money was to be delivered," Geltman repeated. "Have you thought of that?"

"N-n-no," Rosa Perez stammered. "You mail eet to me?"

"Mail five thousand cash?" Geltman said. "I don't think that would be smart, do you?"

"No. Maybe not so smart."

"Of course not," he said smoothly. "I can see you're an intelligent woman. Why don't we meet somewhere, and I'll hand over the package in person?"

"Where we meet?" she said suspiciously.

"Oh, I can think of half a dozen places," he said. "Central Park, Grand Central Station, and so forth. But the problem is privacy. We really want privacy for our little transaction, don't we? You live in Manhattan?"

"Oh sure. Downtown."

"You live alone?"

"Oh sure. Jus' me an' my daughter."

"Not your husband?"

"My hosbon' he don' leeve weeth us. He's gone."

"I see. Well, why don't I deliver the package to you where you live? You give me your name and address, and I'll bring it to you. How's that?"

"Well . . . I don' know . . ."

"It's the best way," he assured her. "Then we'll have privacy—right?"

"I don' like eet," she said. "Maybe I come to where you leeve?"

"No," he said. "Definitely not. It's got to be at your place or the deal is off."

"Well," she said dubiously, "all ri'. But no mahnkey beesness."

"It's the best way," he repeated. "I'll just drop off the package and be on my way. And you'll be on your way to Puerto Rico. How does that sound?"

"All ri', I guess," she said. "Today?"

"Not today," he said. "I can't get the money today. It's after three; the banks are closed. How about tomorrow?"

"Tomorrow I work," she told him. "Saturday?"

"Fine," he said. "I'll have it by then. Noon on Saturday? How's that?"

"Hokay," she said. "Eet sounds hokay. Five tousan' een small beels."

"You'll get it," he said confidently. "Now what's your name and where do you live?"

She gave him the address on Orchard Street, and told him to come to Apartment 6-D. Rosa Perez.

"Fine," he said heartily. "Your daughter will be there?"

"Oh sure."

"Good. Thank you for calling. I'll see you at noon Saturday."

He hung up. Mama Perez replaced the receiver gently. Edward X. Delaney leaned forward and kissed her cheek.

"You're beautiful, Mama," he said.

Sergeant Boone and Jason T. Jason came in beaming from the hallway, carrying their tape recorders.

"Got every blessed word," Boone said happily.

22

Chief Delaney had them all wait around until he got through to Ivar Thorsen. He played the tape over the phone and then, at the Deputy Commissioner's request, ran it through again.

"All right, Edward," Thorsen said, after the second hearing, "you can have what you want. Let's get this over with."

"Sure," Delaney said. "I'll keep you informed on what's happening. I think you better plan to be in your office on Saturday so I—"

"I always am," Thorsen said ruefully.

"—so I can reach you afterward," Delaney went on. "You might be thinking about a press statement."

"You're awfully confident," the Deputy Commissioner said.

"That's right," the Chief acknowledged, "I am. I think it would be best if you kept me out of it. The publicity I mean. Let the Department take the credit. You know—'A cooperative effort of all concerned.' That kind of shit."

"I understand."

"Can we get a search warrant for his home and office? To look for the Maitland sketches and the weapon?"

"I don't see why not—with that tape."

"We won't use it until noon on Saturday. Also—say on Friday night—

you might call J. Barnes Chapin and give him the bad news about his sister's tax scam."

"I'm not looking forward to that."

"Take my word for it, Ivar, he'll thank you for the advance notice and owe you one."

"When are you tipping the IRS?"

"I'm not; you are. Goodwill for the Department. I suggest you hold off until Saturday morning. That'll give Chapin time to find a lawyer for Dora and Emily Maitland. Let's see, what else . . . ? Well, I guess that about covers it. If there's anything more I need, I'll let you know."

"I'm sure you will," Thorsen said. "Congratulations, Edward."

"Jesus!" Delaney cried. "Not so soon! You'll put the whammy on it."

He hung up and turned to the others.

"It's going down," he told them. "Let's get organized . . ."

The first thing he ordered was closer surveillance of Rosa Perez.

"This monkey may get an attack of the smarts," he said, "and decide to show up a few hours or even a day early. I wouldn't like that."

So they moved the plainclothesman inside Mama's building, and sat him on a milk crate in the back of the ground-floor lobby, where he could observe anyone entering from the front or the rear door from the concrete courtyard. And they made certain the trap to the roof in the sixth-floor ceiling was bolted from the inside.

Rosa was a problem; she refused to stay put in her own apartment. So Jason Two was assigned as her personal bodyguard. He accompanied her on shopping trips to drugstore and bodega, and even went drinking beer with her on Thursday night. The other cops started calling him Papa Perez, which he didn't think was so funny.

Arrangements were made for Dolores and Maria Ruiz to stay with relatives on Friday and Saturday, and Maria agreed to let her apartment be used temporarily by the police. She gave her permission after a long, sparkling argument with Mama Perez. Chief Delaney could understand a few words and phrases in Spanish, but he couldn't follow that loud, fiery exchange. It sounded to him mostly like threats and curses, but Jason told him later it was really a friendly business discussion; they were deciding how to divide Mama's hundred-dollar bounty.

The tech man selected by Sergeant Abner Boone arrived early Friday morning, and Delaney told him what was needed. The electronics specialist made a survey of the Perez and Ruiz apartments, took some measurements, and departed. He was back by noon with a van loaded with equipment. Boone helped him upstairs with his gear, and they set to work.

It was decided to leave the cloth curtain of the narrow closet pulled aside. It revealed a rod of hanging dresses and coats, shoes on the floor, a shelf above with odds and ends: a carroty wig on a plastic form, a cigar box of sewing materials, a small overnight bag, three hats, some assorted junk. To this collection they added a small, round vanity mirror held upright on a brass easel. But the mirror was two-way glass, and behind it they concealed a miniature TV camera with wide-angle lens and a sensitive omnidirectional microphone. The tech figured they'd be able to pick up all of the one-room apartment except for the bathroom and the near corner of the kitchenette.

The flat cable was run down the inside of the closet and out a hole drilled through the base close to the floor. The linoleum was then lifted to conceal the cable between floor covering and baseboard. It continued in similar manner across one end of the bathroom and through a hole drilled in the far wall at the floor.

Inside the Ruiz apartment, the cable was connected to both a videotape machine and a small black-and-white TV monitor with an eight-inch screen. A transmitter provided backup protection by sending a simultaneous signal to another monitor and videotape recorder in the electronics van parked across Orchard Street. The van, with antennae on the roof, was painted white with blue signs on both sides: BIG APPLE TELEVISION REPAIR & SERVICE: YOUR SATISFACTION IS OUR REWARD.

It took most of Friday to install the equipment in the Perez and Ruiz apartments, and it was almost midnight before it was working to the satisfaction of the specialist. Men observing the monitors in the Ruiz apartment and in the parked van had a reasonably clear TV picture of activity in Mama Perez' apartment, and the sound was loud and clear. The videotape recorders picked up both.

Chief Delaney treated everyone to coffee-and when the task was completed. They discussed job assignments, and the electronics specialist promised to bring along a buddy on Saturday to handle the equipment in the van while he took care of the hardware in the Ruiz apartment. The Chief said he wanted Boone and Jason upstairs. The plainclothesmen who had been on surveillance would cover the entrance of the tenement from across the street and warn by walkie-talkie when Saul Geltman arrived. Delaney asked everyone to show up by eight A.M. for final tests and run-throughs.

Then Sergeant Boone drove him home. During the ride they discussed how they would handle it:

The door of the bathroom on the Perez side would be left open, so Geltman could glance in there if he was suspicious of being mouse-trapped. The bathroom door on the Ruiz side would be locked. If Geltman asked about it, Mama Perez would explain that it led to the adjoining apartment, but no one was home there. After Geltman was settled in the Perez apartment, the Ruiz door would be quietly unlocked. The turnbolt had already been oiled, and Delaney was satisfied it could be opened slowly and quietly without alerting Geltman.

In case of emergency—and both Delaney and the sergeant knew that "emergency" meant a Geltman assault on Mama Perez—Jason T. Jason would go in first, fast, followed by Boone and Delaney, all armed. In addition, once Saul Geltman was inside the Perez apartment, the surveillance men across the street would move over to take backup positions on the sixth-floor landing and on the stairs.

They went over it two or three times, trying "what ifs" on each other, and planning their response to a variety of possible situations. By the time Boone pulled up in front of the Delaney brownstone, they figured they had done as much plotting as they could. The rest depended on chance and luck.

Before they parted, the Chief offered his hand to a surprised Sergeant Boone. They shook once, a hard up-and-down pump.

He knew Monica would still be awake, and called upstairs to let her know he was home. Then he made his security rounds before he turned off the downstairs lights and tramped up to the bedroom. Monica had been reading in bed, covered only with a sheet, but her glasses were pushed up and her novel was face down when he entered the room. He went over to kiss her cheek.

"You smell like a goat," she smiled.

"Don't I though?" he said. "I'm tired and dusty and grumpy. A hot shower for me."

"Did you eat, dear?"

"Sure I did."

"What did you have?"

"Pizza for lunch and chili for supper."

"My God," she said, "your stomach will be rumbling all night."

"I suppose so," he agreed. "But I really enjoyed it."

"Edward, do you realize that I've hardly *seen* you for the past two days?"

"I realize," he said.

"Well . . . tell me: what's going on? What have you been doing? The Geltman thing?"

"Let me get my shower first."

They kept a bottle of brandy and two small snifters on the shelf of his clothes closet. When he came from the shower, tying the drawstring of his pajama pants, he saw that Monica had left the bed long enough to pour each of them a good snort. She was back under the sheet, but sitting up, her heavy, tight breasts exposed. She was warming her glass between her palms. His drink was on the bedside table.

"Oh my," he said happily. "Oh my, oh my, oh my."

He sat on the edge of the bed and touched the brandy to his lips, taking a sip so small the liquid seemed to evaporate on his tongue. He realized, almost with a shock, that he was content. He put a hand on the sheet covering his wife's hard thigh.

"I love you," he said.

"No romance, buster," she said sternly. "Just talk. What have you been doing?"

He hadn't wanted to tell her, hoped he wouldn't have to, knowing it might diminish him in her eyes. But he could not plead "top secret" or "official business." Not to her. So he sighed and spelled it out, going through it rapidly but making no effort to conceal the fact that he was using Mama Perez as bait, and no matter how detailed and careful their plans, there was still a good possibility the woman would be hurt. Or worse . . .

"If Geltman tries to take her," he said, "Jason will be right there, on top of him. Boone says he's fast. But still . . ."

Monica was silent, thoughtful, her lips on the rim of her glass, but not sipping.

"Was it your idea, Edward?"

"Yes. I suppose you think I'm some kind of a monster."

She smiled. "Some kind."

She never ceased to surprise him.

"Then you think it's worth the risk?"

"Will it put Geltman away?" she asked.

"Oh, it'll put him away all right. Or help to. I can't let him walk, Monica. I'd never forgive myself if I let him off the hook."

"I know," she said, almost sadly. "God's surrogate on earth."

"Oh Jesus," he said, "I don't see myself that way at all. Not anymore. It's a personal thing. Like he slapped my face, or hurt someone I loved."

She looked at him, astonished.

"Edward, you never even *knew* Maitland."

"What difference does that make?"

"What if he hadn't been an artist whose work you admire? What if he had been a shoemaker, say, or a butcher?"

"No difference at all," he said doggedly.

"I believe you," she sighed. "I just wish I could understand you. Completely."

"And I you," he said. "I can never get to the end of you."

"Maybe it's best this way," she said.

"Sure it is. Like Maitland's paintings. I can't understand the attraction. Can't analyze it. But I can feel it. Respond to it. Know it provides something I want. Like you."

"Like you," she said. "Tired?" she asked.

"Oh yes. Beat."

"Maybe we'll finish our drinks, you get into bed, and we'll just hold each other."

He looked at her. She looked at him.

"We can start that way," he said.

23

Delaney was dressing the following morning when the phone rang. It was Boone. He apologized for calling so early. The sergeant wondered if maybe they should put a tail on Saul Geltman, in case he decided to run. The Chief considered it a moment, then decided against it.

"If he spots a tail, all bets are off," he told Boone. "We'll just have to believe he plans to make the meet with Mama Perez at noon, as planned."

The sergeant agreed that was probably best, and confessed he was getting antsy. The Chief said that was understandable, he was too, but last-minute changes of plans had soured many a good setup, and he wanted this scam to go down as rigged. He told Boone that if he wanted to keep busy, and stop fretting about possible fluffs, to check on the search warrant Commissioner Thorsen had promised. If it had been issued, the sergeant was to select two good men to make the toss—but not before noon.

Then the Chief finished dressing, and strapped on his short-barreled belly gun. He slipped the packet of Polaroid shots of the Maitland barn into his jacket pocket. At the last minute he also took his handcuffs, wrapping them in his handkerchief so they wouldn't jangle.

He had only grapefruit juice, a slice of unbuttered toast, and two cups of black coffee for breakfast.

"Very good," Monica approved. "You're getting heavy as a bear. Ask me; I know."

"Let's have no lascivious tittle-tattle at breakfast," he said. "How did you sleep?"

"Fine. How about you?"

"Went out like a light."

"So did I," she said. "Too bad the light didn't. It was still burning this morning."

They both laughed, and then, as they ate, they discussed a trip they were planning for the Fourth of July weekend. They were going to rent a car, leave early, drive up to the girls' camp in New Hampshire, and spend the entire three days with them.

"How about Rebecca and Boone?" Delaney said suddenly. "Should we ask them to come along?"

"That would be fun," Monica said. "But we'll be staying at a motel. It won't embarrass you, will it?"

"My God, Monica," he said grouchily, "you must think I'm an old fuddy-duddy."

"Not at all," she said. "You're the youngest fuddy-duddy I know."

He smiled, humor restored, and put his empty dishes in the sink.

"I better go," he said. "Expect me when you see me."

They embraced briefly, and she kissed his chin.

"Take care," she said lightly.

On Orchard Street, already beginning to fill up with shoppers, he made the rounds of electronics van, surveillance team, and the Perez and Ruiz apartments. He found everyone present except for Abner Boone, who had called and said he'd be there by eleven o'clock.

Delaney then took Mama Perez aside, sat her down, and went over with her once again what she was to say and how she was to act. On his instructions, she was wearing one of her oldest dresses, a shapeless sack of faded rayon. Her feet were thrust into worn mules, and she had removed most of her heavy makeup. To him, she looked old, weary, vulnerable. He hoped that was the way Saul Geltman would see her.

Abner Boone arrived, reported the warrant had been obtained, and two dicks were standing by to toss Geltman's apartment and office at noon.

"They'll get in," the sergeant assured Delaney. "They're good men; they'll con the super."

Then they ran a noise-level test, with Jason T. Jason acting the part of Saul Geltman. The problem was to adjust the volume of sound on the TV monitor in the Ruiz apartment so it was loud enough for them to hear, but not so loud that it would carry through the wall between apartments, and Geltman would hear his own voice booming back at him. They cut it down as low as they could, so they had to put their heads close to the set, but nothing could be heard in the Perez apartment.

They took a final look around to make certain there was no track of their presence. Then they filed into the Ruiz apartment, leaving Mama Perez alone. Delaney was the last to leave.

"When this is over," he told her, "win, lose, or draw, I'm buying you a half-gallon of the best whiskey I can find."

"Ooh," she said, eyes widening. "You stay tonight, help me dreenk eet?"

He laughed and patted her veined cheek. If she was fearful, he could see no sign of it. He went into the Ruiz apartment. The bathroom door was locked. They settled down to wait. They watched Mama on the monitor. She moved slowly about her apartment, made a cup of coffee, sat down to drink it and leaf through a Spanish magazine. When she took her empty cup to the sink, they saw her pause before one of her painted plaster saints. Her lips moved, and she crossed herself. No one smiled. They waited in silence.

They remained silent as their watches showed 11:30, 11:45, 12:00, 12:15. At 12:20, Jason T. Jason muttered, "Come on. Come *on!*"

At 12:26 the walkie-talkie Sergeant Boone was holding crackled into life, and the surveillance man across the street said, "He's coming. North to south. Alone."

They pushed closer to the TV monitor.

"Stopping," the walkie-talkie reported. "Looking around. Looking at the building. Going up the steps. He's in."

Boone put his lips close to the mike, pressed the Send button.

"Give him five minutes," he whispered. "Then move across to backup. Got it?"

"Got it. Will do. Out."

Delaney looked at the others: Boone, Jason, the electronics man.

"No movement," he warned in a low voice. "Strangle before you cough or sneeze."

They all nodded. Eyes on the TV screen. Waiting . . .

They heard the knock on the door of the Perez apartment. Watched Mama start, freeze, then move slowly to the door.

"Who?" she called.

They didn't hear the reply, but Mama turned the lock, slipped the chain, opened the door. Her body blocked their view, but they heard the voice.

"Rosa Perez?"

"Yesss. You Meester Geltman?"

"I am indeed. May I come in?"

"Oh sure. Come in."

She stood aside then. Saul Geltman sauntered into the room. He was carrying a small, paper-wrapped package. He looked around. Mama Perez closed the door but, following Delaney's instructions, didn't lock or chain it.

"Nice place you've got here," Geltman said tonelessly, staring about.

He glanced at the open closet, the kitchenette, peered through the open door of the bathroom.

"You share the bathroom?" he asked lightly.

"Oh sure. But nex' door, they ain't home."

He walked slowly into the bathroom. Now he was off-screen, but they heard him try the bathroom door to the Ruiz apartment.

"Is locked," Mama said.

"So I see," Geltman said.

He came back into the main room, still looking around.

"And where is your daughter?" he asked pleasantly.

"At the bodega," Mama Perez said. "Shopping. She come back soon. Feefteen meenutes maybe. Half an hour."

"Good," he said. "I'd like to meet her. May I sit down?"

"Oh sure. Anywhere."

They watched Geltman look at the furniture. He started to sit in the upholstered armchair, then changed his mind.

"I'll bet that's *your* chair," he smiled winningly.

He selected one of the tubular aluminum chairs. He pulled it free of the table, turned it to face the armchair. He gestured.

"After you, Mrs. Perez," he said gallantly.

He waited until she was seated in the armchair. Then he sat down gracefully in the straight chair. He put the package on the table. He crossed his knees negligently.

In the Ruiz apartment, Chief Delaney touched Officer Jason's arm, pointed toward the bathroom door. The big black nodded, rose slowly to his feet. He moved lightly, cautiously to the door. He put his fingers on the turnbolt, looked back at Delaney. The Chief put up his hand, signaling Jason to wait.

"Do you mind if I smoke?" Saul Geltman asked.

"Hokay," Mama nodded. "Is hokay."

"Will you join me?"

"Oh sure."

Geltman rose to proffer a silver case. While he was going through the business of lighting their cigarettes, Delaney nodded to Jason. He opened the lock easily, slowly. They watched the screen. Apparently Geltman heard nothing. Jason tiptoed back to his original position.

Geltman lounged back casually, smoking his cigarette with an elegance so exaggerated that the watching cops realized, for the first time, how wound-up he was, how tight and anxious. On the black-and-white TV monitor he appeared to be wearing a loosely cut black suit, white shirt, black tie, black shoes. He looked, Delaney thought, like a miniature undertaker, and he wondered where Geltman was carrying a weapon, if he had one.

"Well now," the art dealer said. "We seem to have a problem, don't we?"

"Problem?" Mama said. "*You* got a problem. I got no problem."

"Yes, of course," he said with a clenched smile. "That's very true. Tell me, did you go to the police or did they find you?"

Rosa lowered her head, and they didn't catch her reply in the Ruiz apartment.

"I wonder how they did that?" Geltman said. "Well . . . no matter. I still don't understand how they managed to get drawings of you and your daughter. Do you?"

"He hired my daughter," Mama said. "The artist. To pose for heem. I went back weeth her on Monday. A cop was there. He seen us."

"Oh-ho. I understand. Bad luck. For me, I mean," he added hastily.

Mama jerked her chin toward the package on the table.

"You breeng the moaney?" she asked.

"Of course. As I promised."

"Five tousan'? Small beels?"

"Just as you requested. When will you and your daughter leave for Puerto Rico?"

"Soon. Maybe nex' week."

"And you say you'll never return?"

"Nevair," she vowed.

He nodded. Holding his cigarette butt, one hand cupped underneath, he looked around for an ashtray. Rosa Perez stood up, moved to the kitchenette. For a moment her back was turned to Geltman, and Delaney tensed. But the little art dealer didn't move. Mama came back with a saucer, and they stubbed out their cigarettes. The Chief found he was gripping his own knees tightly. He forced himself to spread his hands limply.

"When did the police ask you to identify my photograph?" Geltman asked.

He's stalling, Delaney decided. What for? Hasn't the blood for it? Waiting for Dolores? What?

"Couple days ago," Mama Perez said. "They show me a lot of peectures. 'Who was the man you seen?' they ask me."

"And you picked out my picture?"

She nodded.

"You're certain it was me you saw, Mrs. Perez?"

Again she nodded. "But I tol' them I ain't sure."

"Very smart of you," he smiled. "Very intelligent. Well, I'm glad you called and we got together. Mutual benefit, you might say."

He reached out, pushed the package slowly across the table toward her.

"Open it," he said harshly. "Count it."

She stood, moved to the table, took up the package. Saul Geltman also stood. He stretched. All his movements easy, nonchalant. He slid his hands into his trouser pockets.

Delaney grabbed Jason's arm, jerked, nodded. Jason glided across the floor, stood at the bathroom door, his hand lightly on the knob. He stared back at Delaney. The Chief pointed at Boone. The sergeant moved up behind Jason. He slid his revolver from the hip holster. He thumbed off the safety. He, too, stared back at Delaney. Both cops had a strained, stretched look, lips drawn back from glistening teeth.

On the screen, Mama Perez was fumbling with the package. It was tightly wrapped with Scotch tape. She struggled to tear it open.

Saul Geltman was now directly behind her, a few feet away. He spread his feet a little wider. He braced himself. His hands came slowly from his pockets. Delaney saw the gleam.

"Go!" he shouted. "Take him!"

Boone had been right: Jason was fast. The black flung back the bathroom door. Went hurtling through. Boone dashed after. Both men roaring. Geltman caught. Stoned by sound. Head pulled. Neck stretched. Face twisted. Mama Perez suddenly bowed. Stooping. Back tensed for the knife held high, twinkling in sunlight.

Jason didn't go for the knife hand. No punch, no blow, no karate chop. He simply ran into Geltman, a full body block. Charged into him and tried to keep running, knees pumping high, feet slipping on the polished linoleum.

Geltman bounced off him. Just smashed away. Hair and knife flying, arms and legs every which way. His limp body, boneless, landed half on the bed, half off. Slowly, slowly, slipped onto the floor, and Jason clamped one big foot on the back of his neck.

"Stay here," Delaney snapped at the tech. "Keep the tape rolling."

He lumbered into the Perez apartment. Jason was jerking a dazed Saul Geltman to his feet. Boone put the muzzle of his revolver to Geltman's teeth. Mama Perez had retreated from the action. She was facing them, back against the wall. Hissing faintly. Delaney pulled out his handkerchief. Handcuffs clattered to the floor. He ignored them, but picked up the knife carefully by the tip, using the wadded handkerchief. He placed the knife on the table, alongside the torn package. One corner was ripped open; he could see the stack of cut newspaper.

Sergeant Boone holstered his revolver. He took a come-along grip on one of Geltman's arms. Jason clamped the other. The art dealer looked about wildly, hair and clothes in disarray. Delaney thought everything was under control when Mama Perez came off the wall.

"Sonnenbitch!" she screamed. "Bestid!"

She came leaping across the room, hands clawed, and jumped on Geltman before they could block her. It looked as if she were trying to shin up his body, one leg crooked around his, one knee slamming at his groin, a hand tearing at his throat, fingers raking at his eyes. While she screamed, screamed, screamed. Spanish and English. Curses, oaths, obscenities, execrations.

Delaney got an arm about her thick waist from behind. Boone and Jason tugged Geltman in the other direction. But they could not peel Rosa Perez away. She clung to Geltman, pounding on his skull with her fist, spitting in his face. Clawing, biting, butting him with her head. The five of them stood swaying, one tight group, pressed tightly together, staggering to keep their balance.

Delaney turned his face toward the door. "Brady!" he yelled desperately.

In a few seconds the backup man came dashing in from the hallway, revolver held out in front of him. The man posted on the stairs was hard on his heels. They holstered their guns and joined in, prying Mama's fingers loose, one by one, bending them back, then twisting her arms behind her as Delaney strained mightily at her waist, and Boone kicked one of her legs loose.

Finally, huffing, sweating, cursing furiously, they got the maddened woman off Geltman and dragged her away.

"Jesus Christ!" Delaney panted. "Take her in the other room and sit on her!"

The backup men hustled Mama Perez, still kicking and spitting, into the Ruiz apartment. The Chief followed them in there.

"Got enough tape?" he asked the tech man.

"Plenty, Chief. All you'll need."

"Good. Keep it rolling till I tell you to disconnect."

He went back into the Perez apartment, closing both bathroom doors behind him. They sat Saul Geltman down in a straight-backed aluminum chair facing the big window. Sergeant Boone took the other tubular chair. Delaney sat in the armchair, and Jason T. Jason stood with his back against the door.

All four of them were breathing heavily, limp and exhausted in that hotbox of a room under the roof. Boone and Jason loosened their ties, unbuttoned their collars. No one spoke for several minutes. Then Saul Geltman attempted to dust himself off.

"I have a comb in my hip pocket," he said. "Can I reach for it?"

The Chief nodded. The art dealer took out a little black comb and straightened his hair. Then he took out his handkerchief, dabbed delicately at the shallow scratches on his face.

"I'm bleeding," he said.

"I'm sorry about that, Mr. Geltman," Delaney said without irony, "but you really can't blame her."

"I want to call a lawyer," Geltman said. "I know my rights."

"I'm afraid you don't," the Chief said gently. "You're not entitled to a phone call until you've been booked. You haven't even been arrested yet. Am I correct, sergeant?"

"That's correct, sir. When we arrest him, we read him his rights."

"That's how it's done," Delaney said, spreading his hands. "I thought we could just sit here a few minutes, relax, get our breath back. Just talk a little. Talk about why you assaulted that poor woman with a knife."

"I didn't assault her," Geltman said indignantly. "I just took the knife out to help her open a package."

"Assault with a deadly weapon," Delaney said tonelessly.

"It's your word against mine," Geltman said.

"Well . . . no," the Chief said. "Not quite. Look at this . . ."

He rose, stepped to the open closet. Geltman turned his head to watch him reach up and push aside the small, round mirror.

"A TV camera," he explained to the little man. "Picks up image and sound. Records it on videotape. It's still running."

"Shit," Saul Geltman said.

"Yes," Delaney said.

"Well, then, you were tapping my phone. That's how you knew I'd be here. And the phone tap was illegal."

The Chief sighed. "Oh, Mr. Geltman, do you really think we'd do that? No, she called from a private phone. We had the owner's permission to tape the call."

"I'd like a glass of water," Geltman said.

"Sure," Delaney said. "Jason?"

Geltman was given not one but two glasses of water. He drained both greedily, wiped his lips with his soiled handkerchief. He looked around. He seemed punished but not defeated. There was a spark in his eye. He tried for a smile and settled for a smirk.

"Miserable place," he said with a theatrical shudder. "How people can live like this . . ."

"I've seen worse," Delaney shrugged. "Didn't you tell me you came from Essex Street? You must have lived in an apartment something like this."

"A long time ago," Geltman said in a low voice. "A long time . . ."

"Uh-huh," Delaney nodded. "Well, that's really what I wanted to talk to you about: how you live now. And how you're going to live. You don't have to admit anything. I'm not asking for a confession. I just want you to take a look at these, please."

He took the Polaroid photos from his jacket pocket, leaned forward, handed them to Geltman. The art dealer looked at the top one, shuffled through the pack hurriedly, then shriveled back into his chair. His face had gone slack. He tossed the photos listlessly onto the table.

"So that's all over," Delaney said briskly. "The IRS was notified this morning, and I imagine they're up there right now, taking inventory. They'll pump Dora and Emily, of course. My guess is that Dora will sing first; she's the weak reed. She'll implicate you and Simon."

Geltman made a gesture, a hopeless flap of his hand.

"I don't mean to suggest you'll go to jail for tax fraud," Delaney said. "You might, but I don't think the Feds will prosecute. They'll be happy enough when they add up the estate. Oh, you might get a fine and probation, and a personal audit, of course. But I doubt if anyone will draw jail time for this. It means the end of Dora's and Emily's dreams, naturally, but then it makes millionaires of Alma and Ted. I don't derive any particular satisfaction from that, do you?"

"No," Geltman said shortly.

"And talking about the end of dreams," the Chief continued, "there goes your guaranteed future, doesn't it? I think you've sold your last Maitland painting, Mr. Geltman."

The art dealer made no reply. For a moment or two no one spoke. Then . . .

"My God, it's hot in here," Edward X. Delaney said. He rose, strode to the big window, struggled with it a moment, then threw it wide open. He leaned far out, hands propped on the sill, drew a deep breath. He looked down. He came back into the room, dusting his hands, leaving the window open. "Six floors straight down to a cement courtyard," he reported. "You'd think they'd have a guard on a window like that. Well, anyway we'll get a breath of air."

He sat in the armchair again, leaned back, laced his fingers across his middle. He looked at Saul Geltman reflectively.

"Now let's talk about the murder of Victor Maitland," he said. "Premeditated murder because the man that killed brought a knife along. He didn't kill in a sudden flash of passion with whatever weapon came to hand; he brought his weapon with him. That's premeditation in any court in the land."

"I didn't kill him," Geltman said tightly.

"Sure you did," Delaney said. "You know it; we know it. I thought, just from simple curiosity, you'd like to know what we've got. Well, for starters, we've got motive. Your discovery that Maitland was sneaking paintings from the barn and peddling them secretly through Belle Sarazen. They were his paintings, and he could do anything he wanted with them. But to your way of thinking, those paintings were as much your inheritance as Dora's and Emily's, and the dying Victor Maitland was robbing you. Crazy. Not only that, but he was depressing the price of Maitlands by shoveling out more and more paintings. Right, Mr. Geltman? So you had a big fight with him about it, and he told you to go fuck yourself. Right, Mr. Geltman?"

"Conjecture," the art dealer said. "Just conjecture."

"'Conjecture,'" Delaney repeated, amused. "A legal term. You played a lot of handball with your late pal J. Julian Simon, didn't you, Mr. Geltman? By the way, do you notice I call you 'Mr. Geltman' and not 'Saul'? That's not going by the book. It's cop psychology to use first names when talking to a suspect. It diminishes them, robs them of dignity. Like stripping a man naked before you question him. But I wouldn't do that to you, Mr. Geltman; I have too much respect for your intelligence."

"Thank you," he said faintly, and sounded sincere.

"All right," Delaney said, slapping his knees. "So much for motive. A few rough spots here and there, but I think a little more digging will fill it out nicely. Now we come to opportunity. I suppose Lawyer Simon told you that we tumbled to your little con of skipping out his back door into the corridor. You must have done that, you see, because Rosa Perez and Dolores saw you near Victor Maitland's studio at a time when Simon said you were in his office."

"It's his statement against what they claim," Geltman said hotly.

"His *statement*," Delaney said. "Too bad he isn't alive to testify in court, isn't it?"

"I was shocked when I heard he was dead."

Delaney stared at him reflectively a few moments, then sighed.

"You weren't thinking too straight, Mr. Geltman," he said softly. "Getting a little frantic, were you? The bloodhounds nipping at your heels, and your dear chum having an attack of the runits about facing a perjury rap. So you had to take him out—right? Wait, wait," Delaney said, holding up a hand. "Just let me finish. It hasn't been announced yet, but we know Simon didn't die in that fire. Surprise! He was a clunk before he fried. Lung analysis proved that. And the Medical Examiner found the multiple stab wounds in his back. And the fire laddies think whiskey was used to make sure the whole place went up in a *poof!* They found the empty bottles. A terrible waste! Oh yes, we know how Simon died, Mr. Geltman. We have men flashing your photograph to tenants in Simon's building, cab drivers, everyone in the neighborhood. Sooner or later we'll find *someone* who saw you at or near the scene. So if I were you, I wouldn't count too much on your late buddy's statement to alibi you for the Maitland kill."

Saul Geltman had sought to interrupt this breezy recital. As it progressed, his eyes widened, mouth opened. He slipped farther down in his chair like a man hammered. He stared at Delaney, stricken.

"Well," the Chief said briskly, "that takes care of opportunity. Now we come to the weapon . . ."

He rose, stepped to the table, bent far over the knife. His nose was almost touching it. Then he put on his glasses and bent over it again.

"Nice," he said. "French. High-carbon steel. Holds a good edge a long time. It might have been used to slice Maitland and Simon; the length and width of the blade fit the description of the wounds in the autopsy reports. I'll tell you, I'd never use a knife like that to murder someone, Mr. Geltman. First of all, the blade is too thin. It might hit a rib on the first jab and snap. Also, no matter how you wash it, you can never get a wood-handled knife clean. Tell him, sergeant."

"The wood handle is riveted to the blade," Boone explained. "But no matter how much you scrub, blood has soaked in between wood handle and steel. The lab guys pop the rivets, take off the wood, and examine the steel tang for blood seepage. Then they take tiny particles from the inside of the wood handles and examine *them* for blood. They can tell if it's animal or human. If it's human, they can usually determine the type. And tell if it matches Simon's or Maitland's."

"That's how it's done," Delaney nodded. "That's how it will be done on this knife."

"I didn't do it," Geltman muttered.

Delaney started back to his chair, replacing his glasses in his breast pocket. Then he returned to examine the knife again.

"You know," he said, "this is what cooks call a boning knife. It looks to me like it's part of a matched cutlery set. Very nice and very expensive. Sergeant, I think we better send those detectives back to Mr. Geltman's apartment again to pick up the other knives in the set and put them all through the lab."

Geltman was bewildered.

"Detectives?" he said. "Back to my apartment again?"

"Oh, I didn't mention that," Delaney said, snapping his fingers lightly. "We got a search warrant. To toss your apartment and office. They're looking for those three sketches we lifted from Maitland's studio—and you lifted from my home. Think they'll find them, Mr. Geltman?"

"I'm not going to say another word," the art dealer said.

"You put my daughters in a closet, you fucker!" Delaney screamed at him.

Geltman closed his mouth firmly, clenched his jaws. He crossed his legs and began to drum slowly with his fingers on the top knee. He refused to meet Delaney's eyes, but stared out the open window, seeing a rooftop, a wide patch of blue sky, a puff of cloud floating lazily.

"Motive, opportunity, weapon," Chief Delaney went on inexorably. "And now, on top of that, we've got you on attempted subornation. Got it on tape. And on top of *that,* assault with a deadly weapon. How does it sound to you, Mr. Geltman?"

No answer. Delaney let the silence build awhile, frowning slightly, looking down at his flexing hands. Jason shifted his weight from foot to foot at the door. Sergeant Boone sat perfectly still, eyes never leaving the art dealer.

"I'll be honest with you, Mr. Geltman," Delaney said finally. "I don't think the DA will go for a Murder One conviction."

Geltman started, uncrossed his knees. Then he did stare at Chief Delaney, leaning forward a little in his eagerness.

"I think you'll get a smart lawyer who'll do some plea bargaining and advise you to plead guilty to a lesser charge. Murder Two, maybe. If he's a *very* smart lawyer, he might even get you a manslaughter rap. The point is, no matter how you slice it, you're going to do time, Mr. Geltman. No way out of that. Jason, you want to make a guess?"

"Fifteen to twenty-five, Chief," Jason boomed.

"Sergeant?"

"Eight to ten," Boone said.

"My guess is somewhere between," Delaney said thoughtfully. "About ten to fifteen before you're up for parole. Fifteen years, Mr. Geltman. Great Meadows, I suppose. Or maybe Attica. A hard place like that."

Saul Geltman made a sound, a small sound deep inside him. His stare slid off Delaney, lifted, moved across the ceiling, stopped at the square of summer sky outside the open window.

"Ten to fifteen," Delaney nodded. "A smart lawyer could get you that. A smart, *expensive* lawyer. Your gallery will go, of course. You couldn't have kept that without Maitland anyway; we know that. And that beautiful apartment of yours. All your lovely things. You know, Mr. Geltman, I think that was the most magnificent home I've ever seen. Truth. I remember so much about it: those soft-toned rugs, that elm's-burl highboy, the polished wood and gleaming brass. The way everything seemed to go together. You were right: it was a dream, a beautiful dream. All gone now, of course. I suppose the IRS will sell the stuff at auction to pay your fine. Or you'll have to sell it to pay for your defense. Other people will own those lovely things. But your beautiful home will be broken up, the dream destroyed."

His voice had taken on a curious singsong quality, an almost musical cadence. Far away he could hear, dimly, street sounds: vendors' chants, traffic, blare of horns, shouts and cries. But the other men in the room heard only the soft drone of Delaney's voice, words that painted pictures and mesmerized them.

"All gone," the Chief repeated. "The beauty, the softness, the rich comfort of it all. Very different from where you're going, Mr. Geltman. For fifteen years. You'll be in a ten-by-ten concrete cell with two other guys and a pisspot. And those guys! Animals, Mr. Geltman. Rough studs who'll have you serving them hand and foot. Literally hand and foot, if you get my meaning. Food you can hardly stomach. A routine so boring that your imagination shrivels as your hope withers. Because every day is exactly like every other day—*exactly,* Mr. Geltman—and those fifteen years might as well be fifty years, or a hundred years, or a thousand, that's how far away the end of them will seem to you. But all that's not the worst part of prison, Mr. Geltman. Not to a man of your intelligence and sensibility and taste. Remember when we talked in your gallery about Maitland's work, and you said you thought his paintings were the idea or conception of sensuality? Well, prison is the conception of ugliness. It is complete greyness, greyness in walls and clothing and even in food. And eventually the greyness in the skin of old cons, and a greyness of the soul. Dismal, gloomy. No bright colors there. No music. No real laughter or song. No beauty anywhere. Just hard, grey ugliness that seeps and presses all around. To a man like you, it means—"

It happened so quickly, so suddenly, that viewing the videotape later, a board of inquiry agreed it could not have been prevented.

Saul Geltman jerked to his feet as if plucked up by the hand of God.

He tilted forward, saved himself from falling by taking three running steps to the open window.

He went out like a man doing a header from the high board, arms extended, head tucked down.

His toes didn't even tick the sill.

He cleared it, and he sailed.

They heard the noise when he hit.

Boone flinched. Jason shuddered. Edward X. Delaney had heard that sound before, and slowly closed his eyes.

"Oh my God!" Boone groaned. He leapt to his feet, rushed to the window. He propped his hands on both sides, leaned out cautiously, looked down. He turned back to the room, face blanched.

"They'll need a blotter," he reported.

Chief Delaney opened his eyes, stared at the ceiling.

"Well," he said to no one, "he didn't walk after all, did he?"

It was late in the afternoon before everything was done that had to be done. Deputy Commissioner Ivar Thorsen took command of the investigation, received signed statements of all involved, impounded the videotapes, issued a report to the newspapers, granted a short interview to TV cameramen.

The three Maitland sketches were found in Geltman's apartment. Rosa Perez was slipped her hundred-dollar baksheesh, and Delaney didn't forget her half-gallon. Mama selected dark rum. The television equipment was removed, and the Perez and Ruiz apartments were restored, as completely as possible, to their original state.

The body of Saul Geltman was removed to the morgue in a blue plastic bodybag. Sawdust was scattered on the stained indentation in the concrete courtyard.

Abner Boone offered to drive Delaney home, and the Chief accepted gratefully. It took them awhile to get free of downtown traffic, but once they got on Third Avenue, they began to make good time, Boone driving at a speed to hit all the greens.

"By the way," Delaney said, "over the Fourth of July weekend, Monica and I are going to rent a car and drive up to New Hampshire to visit the girls. We wondered if you and Rebecca would like to come along."

"Like to very much," Boone said promptly. "Thank you, sir. I'll ask Rebecca; I'm sure she'll go for it. But why rent a car? We can take mine."

"I'll tell you," Delaney said dreamily, "all my life I've wanted to drive a Rolls-Royce, and I never have. I thought I'd surprise Monica and rent a great, big black Rolls. She'll get a kick out of it, the kids will flip and it'll be a treat for me. It's about an eight-hour trip, I figure, so I thought we could pack a hamper and have lunch on the road. You know, cold fried chicken and potato salad. Stuff like that."

"Sounds wonderful," the sergeant laughed. "Count us in. A Rolls-Royce, huh? Would you believe I've never been in one?"

"I haven't either," Delaney smiled. "Now's our chance."

Then they were silent. Past 34th Street, traffic lightened, and Boone relaxed at the wheel.

"Chief . . ." he started.

"Yes?"

"When you were talking to Geltman before he jumped . . . I mean about his beautiful home, and how lousy prison life was . . ."

"Yes?"

"I thought you were . . ."

"You thought I was what?"

"Ahh, hell," Abner Boone said, staring straight ahead. "I guess I was imagining things."

"Sure you were," Edward X. Delaney said genially, lighting a cigar.